PE

Praise for Want to Play?

'Outrageously suspenseful . . . the thriller debut of the year' Harlen Coben

'A powerful thriller and an ingenious plot . . . the gripping narrative and vivid characterisation make an auspicious debut' *Observer Review*

'A thrilling page-turner with a nail-biting finish . . . the story races along, helped by some sparkling dialogue and colourful characters' *Sunday Telegraph*

'A gripping read with quirky characters and just the right level of thrills and devilish twists' *Guardian*

'Edge of your seat drama' *Star Magazine*

'Scary, with dialogue straight out of the Sopranos and a plot to rival *Se7en*' *Radio Times*

'A gripping and inventive novel with plenty of nail-biting moments right to the last page. A terrifying read' *Daily Express*

'Some of the best new blood work in the genre . . . Scary, funny, witty, and genuinely perplexing right to the end' *Glasgow Herald*

'An absolute cracker, heavy on atmosphere, lively characterisation and snappy dialogue'
Glasgow Evening Times

'Think *Birdman*, think *The Straw Men* . . . with crackling dialogue and an up-to-the-minute, leave-the-light-on plot, this electrifying debut will match them both'
Mystery and Thriller Club

'Written with such skill and polish you would think it could be Tracy's tenth . . . a strong new voice in the thriller genre'. *USA Today*

'A soundly plotted thriller that fires on all cylinders'
Publisher's Weekly

'Tracy gets her writing career off to a fiendish start . . . a thoroughly enjoyable, unputdownable book' *This Day*

'It's been a long time since I picked up a mystery as riveting and engaging as this one . . . Harlen Coben called it "the thriller debut of the year". He could have dropped the word "debut" – it's going to be tough for anyone to top it' *Grand Rapids Press*

'Look out thriller world, here's P. J. Tracy . . . one of the most amazing, imaginative, compelling off-the-wall debut novels in many moons' *Denton Record-Chronicle*

'An impressive debut thriller which kept me awake long enough to appreciate the dawn chorus . . . a compulsively readable tale that kept me guessing all the way to the end' *South Africa Sunday Independent*

Praise for Live Bait

'A slick enjoyable thriller . . . PJ Tracy is about to become a household name' *Daily Mirror*

'Tracy's second offering doesn't disappoint . . . Put it with your passport and your money so you don't forget to take it on holiday' *Time Out*

'A tense edge-of-your-seat thriller' *OK!*

'PJ Tracy's *Live Bait* proves one thing conclusively: that the phenomenal *Want to Play?* was no fluke, and that in Tracy we have an American suspense writer with all the credentials to sit firmly in the upper echelons of top crime novelists' Barry Forshaw

'Rich with humour and occasionally moving, this one's a winner . . . her second novel, will be as acclaimed as her first' *Irish Examiner*

'With generous doses of humour and suspense, this sharp, satisfying thriller will rivet readers from the start' *Publisher's Weekly*

'A truly brilliant crime thriller, fast-paced and edgy, full of deception and retribution with the essential incredible twist!' *Newmarket Journal*

'For those who mourn that Patricia Cornwell ain't what she used to be, Tracy's a wondrous discovery' *Entertainment Weekly*

'Eclectic characters and zingy dialogue . . . exhilarating' *People*

'A fun rush of a read . . . the combination of humour and an excellent mystery is addictive'
Rendezvous Magazine

'This is a series well worth shelving with the rest of the aristocrats of mystery writing. Move over, Sue Grafton'
Washington Times

ABOUT THE AUTHOR

P. J. Tracy is the pseudonym for the mother-and-daughter writing team of P. J. and Traci Lambrecht. They are the authors of the award-winning and bestselling thrillers *Live Bait*, *Dead Run*, *Snow Blind*, *Play to Kill*, *Two Evils* and the Richard and Judy Book Club pick *Want to Play?* All six books feature detectives Gino and Magozzi and maverick computer-hacker Grace MacBride. P. J. and Traci both live near Minneapolis, Minnesota.

Live Bait

P. J. TRACY

PENGUIN BOOKS

PENGUIN BOOKS

Published by the Penguin Group
Penguin Books Ltd, 80 Strand, London WC2R 0RL, England
Penguin Group (USA) Inc., 375 Hudson Street, New York, New York 10014, USA
Penguin Group (Canada), 90 Eglinton Avenue East, Suite 700, Toronto, Ontario, Canada M4P 2Y3
(a division of Pearson Penguin Canada Inc.)
Penguin Ireland, 25 St Stephen's Green, Dublin 2, Ireland (a division of Penguin Books Ltd)
Penguin Group (Australia), 707 Collins Street, Melbourne, Victoria 3008, Australia
(a division of Pearson Australia Group Pty Ltd)
Penguin Books India Pvt Ltd, 11 Community Centre, Panchsheel Park, New Delhi – 110 017, India
Penguin Group (NZ), 67 Apollo Drive, Rosedale, Auckland 0632, New Zealand
(a division of Pearson New Zealand Ltd)
Penguin Books (South Africa) (Pty) Ltd, Block D, Rosebank Office Park,
181 Jan Smuts Avenue, Parktown North, Gauteng 2193, South Africa

Penguin Books Ltd, Registered Offices: 80 Strand, London WC2R 0RL, England

www.penguin.com

First published in the United States of America by G. P. Putnam's Sons,
a member of Penguin Group (USA) Inc. 2004
First published in Great Britain by Michael Joseph 2004
Published in Penguin Books 2005
This edition published 2013
001

Set in Monotype Garamond
Typeset by Rowland Phototypesetting Ltd, Bury St Edmunds, Suffolk
Printed in Great Britain by Clays Ltd, St Ives plc

ISBN: 978–1–405–92647–8

I

It was just after sunrise and still raining when Lily found her husband's body. He was lying faceup on the asphalt apron in front of the greenhouse, eyes and mouth open, collecting rainwater.

Even dead, he looked quite handsome in this position, gravity pulling back the loose, wrinkled skin of his face, smoothing away eighty-four years of pain and smiles and worries.

Lily stood over him for a moment, wincing when the raindrops plopped noisily onto his eyes.

I hate eyedrops.

Morey, hold still. Stop blinking.

Stop blinking, she says, while she pours chemicals into my eyes.

Hush. It's not chemicals. Natural tears, see? It says so right on the bottle.

You expect a blind man to read?

A little grain of sand in your eye and suddenly you're blind. Big tough guy.

And they're not natural tears. What do they do? Go to funerals and hold little bottles under crying people? No, they mix chemicals together and call it natural tears. It's false advertising, is what it is. These are unnatural tears. A little bottle of lies.

Shut up, old man.

This is the thing, Lily. Nothing should pretend to be what it's not. Everything should have a big label that says what it is so there's no confusion. Like the fertilizer we used on the bedding plants that year that killed all our ladybugs, what was it called?

Plant So Green.

Right. So it should have been called Plant So Green Ladybug So Dead. Forget the tiny print on the back you can't read. Real truth in labeling, that's what we need. This is a good rule. God should follow such a rule.

Morey!

What can I say? He made a big mistake there. Would it have been such a problem for Him to make things look like what they are? I mean, He's God, right? This is something He could do. Think about it. You've got a guy at the door with this great smile and nice face and you let him in and he kills your whole family. This is God's mistake. Evil should look evil. Then you don't let it in.

You, of all people, should know it's not that simple.

It's exactly that simple.

Lily took a breath, then sat on her heels – a young posture for such an old woman, but her knees were still good, still strong and flexible. She couldn't get Morey's eyes to close all the way, and with them open only a slit, he looked sinister. It was the first thing that had frightened Lily in a very long time. She wouldn't look at them as she pushed back the darkened silver hair the rain had plastered to his skull.

One of her fingers slipped into a hole on the side of his head and she froze. 'Oh, no,' she whispered, then rose quickly, wiping her fingers on her overalls.

'I told you so, Morey,' she scolded her husband one last time. 'I told you so.'

2

April in Minnesota was always unpredictable, but once every decade or so, it got downright sadistic, fluctuating wildly between tantalizing promises of spring and the last, angry death throes of a stubborn winter that had no intention of going quietly.

It had been just such a year. Last week, a freak snowstorm had blustered in on what *had* been the warmest April on record, scaring the hell out of the budding trees and launching statewide discussions of a mass migration to Florida.

But spring had eventually prevailed, and right now she was busy playing kiss-and-make-up, and doing a damn fine job of it. The mercury was pushing seventy-five, the snow-stunned flora had rallied with a shameless explosion of neon green, and best of all, the mother lode of mosquito larvae was still percolating in the lakes and swamps. Giddy, sun-starved Minnesotans were out in force, cherishing the temporary delusion that the state was actually habitable.

Detective Leo Magozzi was stretched out on a decrepit chaise on his front porch, Sunday paper in one hand, a mug of coffee in the other. He hadn't forgotten about last week's snowstorm and he was pragmatic enough to know that it wasn't too late for another, but there was no point in letting cynicism ruin a perfectly beautiful day. Besides, it was a rare thing when he could practice the sloth he'd always aspired to – homicide detectives' vacations were always contingent on murderers' vacations, and murderers seemed to be the hardest-working citizens in the country. But for some inexplicable reason, Minneapolis was enjoying the longest murder-free spell in years. As his partner, Gino Rolseth, had put it so eloquently: Homicide was dead. For the past few months they'd had nothing to do but work cold cases, and if they ever solved all of them, they'd be back on the beat, frisking transvestites and wishing they'd been dentists instead of cops.

Magozzi sipped his coffee and watched as the neighborhood masochists engaged in all manner of personal torture, huffing and puffing and sweating as they raced furiously against a climatic clock that would have them locked indoors again in a few months' time. They jogged, they Rollerbladed, they ran with their dogs, and celebrated every degree that rose on the thermometer by shedding another article of clothing.

It was one of the things Magozzi loved most about Minnesotans. Fat, thin, muscled, or flabby, there were no self-conscious people in this state when the weather got warm, and by the time you got a nice day like this one, most of them were half naked. Of course this was not always a good thing, certainly not in the case of Jim, his extremely hirsute next-door neighbor. You could never be really sure if Jim were wearing a shirt or not. He was out there now, possibly shirtless, possibly not, hard at work preparing the flower beds that would put him in pole position for next month's Beautiful Gardens of the Twin Cities Tour. If Jim was trying to shame Magozzi into being a better homeowner, it wasn't going to work.

He looked out at his own sorry excuse for a yard – a couple of mud puddles from last night's rain, some brave dandelions, and a few blue spruce in various stages of demise. Occasionally he had a fleeting memory of what the place had looked like before the divorce. Flowers everywhere, Kentucky bluegrass standing at attention, and Heather out there each day with sharp instruments and a stern expression, frightening plants into submission. She'd been good at frightening things into submission – it had certainly worked on him, and he'd been armed.

He was on his second cup of coffee and almost to the sports section when a Volvo station wagon pulled into the driveway. Gino Rolseth hopped out, lugging an enormous cooler and a bag of Kingsford. His belly tested the generous limits of a Tommy Bahama shirt, and beefy legs poked out from a terrible pair of plaid Bermuda shorts.

'Hey, Leo!' He lumbered up onto the porch and dropped the cooler. 'I come bearing gifts of animal flesh and fermented grain.'

Magozzi lifted a dark brow. 'At eight o'clock in the morning? Tell me this means Angela finally kicked your sorry ass out, so I can call her and propose.'

'You should be so lucky. This is charity. Angela's folks took her and the kids to some craft thing at Maplewood Mall, so I had a free Sunday, thought I'd liven up your so-called life.'

Magozzi got up and looked into the cooler. 'What's a craft thing?'

'You know, those places with all the booths where people knit houses out of old grocery bags and stuff like that.'

Magozzi rummaged in the cooler and pulled out a package of sickly looking, plump, gray-white sausages. 'What are these things that look like your legs?'

'Those are uncooked brats, imported all the way from Milwaukee, you food pygmy. Where's your grill?'

Magozzi gestured toward a rusty old Weber in the corner of the porch.

Gino nudged it with his foot and it collapsed. 'We're going to need duct tape.'

Magozzi hefted a suspicious-looking, dark orange brick of cheese. 'Twelve-year cheddar? Is that legal?'

Gino grinned. 'That stuff'll make you weep with joy, I promise. Got it at a great little cheese house in Door County. Somebody forgot about a wheel in the cellar and found it twelve years later, covered in about a foot of mold. Nirvana, my friend. Pure nirvana. It's amazing what a cow and some bacteria can do.'

Magozzi sniffed it and cringed. 'Oh yeah. Every time I see a cow I think, Hey, wouldn't it be great to get some bacteria and really do something with this thing. Why do you have a file folder in the cooler?'

'It's a cold case.'

'Very funny.'

Gino lifted the grill and another leg fell off in a shower of rust. 'This one's from ninety-four. Thought we could take a look at it later. You know, just to keep our hand in, in case anyone ever kills somebody in this town again. You remember hearing anything about the Valensky case?'

Magozzi sat down on the chaise and opened the folder. 'Sort of. The plumber, right?'

'That's the one. Shot seven times, three of them in places I don't even want to think about.'

'Plumbers charge too much.'

'Tell me about it. But other than that, this guy was damn near a candidate for sainthood. Some Polack who actually made it out of the war alive, emigrated to the good old US of A, started a business, married, had three kids, deacon at his church, scout leader, the whole American dream, then bled to death on his own bathroom floor after someone used him for target practice.'

'Suspects?'

'Hell no. According to the reports in there, everybody loved him. Case dried up in about two seconds.'

Magozzi grunted and tossed the folder on the floor. 'Most guys with a free Sunday would probably find something else to do, like sit on a bench at Lake Calhoun and count bikinis.'

'Yeah, well, I'm a crime fighter, I have a higher purpose.' Gino ran a hand through his hedge of closely cropped blond hair, reconsidering. 'Besides, it's probably too early for bikinis.'

They got the call before Magozzi had finished duct-taping the legs back on his grill. Gino had gone inside to unload the cooler, and when he came back out to the porch he was beaming.

'Hey, want to go see a body?'

Magozzi sat back on his heels and frowned. 'You found a body in my kitchen?'

'Nah. Phone rang while I was in there, so I picked up. Dispatch got an honest-to-God homicide call. Uptown Nursery. The owner's wife found him this morning by one of the greenhouses and figured it was a heart attack, because the guy is pushing eighty-five and what else would drop a man that age? So she called the funeral director. He finds a bullet hole in the guy's head and calls nine-one-one.'

Magozzi looked wistfully at the grill and sighed. 'So what happened to the on-duty guys who are supposed to be taking this?'

'Tinker and Peterson. Just what I wanted to know. They just took a call at the train yard over in North-east. Found some poor bastard tied to the tracks.'

Magozzi winced.

'Nah, don't worry. Train never hit him.'

'So he's okay?'

'Nope, he's dead.'

Magozzi looked at him expectantly.

'Don't look at me. That's all I got.' He jumped when his shirt pocket spit out an irritating, tinny version of Beethoven's Fifth.

'What *is* that?'

Gino pulled his cell phone out of his pocket and stabbed viciously at buttons half the size of his chubby fingers. 'Goddamnit. Helen keeps programming in all these weird rings 'cause she knows I got no clue how to change it.'

Magozzi grinned. 'That's funny.'

Beethoven spoke again.

'Fourteen-year-olds are only funny when they belong to somebody else . . . shit. I'm gonna invent one of these things with big fat buttons and make a jillion dollars . . . Hello, this is Rolseth.'

Magozzi stood and brushed the rust off his hands, listened to Gino grunt into the phone for a few seconds, then went inside to lock up. By the time he got back out to the porch, Gino had retrieved his gun from the car and was hooking it to the belt that almost held up his Bermuda shorts. He looked like an armed and dangerous tourist.

'I don't suppose you've got a pair of pants that would fit me.'

Magozzi just smiled at him.

'Aw, shut up. That was Langer on the phone. He

and McLaren just got called in for a suspected homicide – "suspected" meaning someone did a little interior design with a few gallons of blood, but there's no body. And guess what?'

'He wants us to take it?'

'Nah, Dispatch told him we were on the nursery thing, that's why he called. The bloody house is just a few blocks over.'

Magozzi frowned. 'That's a pretty decent neighborhood.'

'Right. Not exactly a killing field, and all of a sudden we've got two possibles in one day. And there's another thing. The guy who lives in that house is – or was – also in his eighties, just like our guy.'

Magozzi thought about that for a minute. 'He's thinking cluster? What, that some psycho's running around killing old people?'

Gino shrugged. 'He was just giving us a heads-up. Thought we should keep in touch in case something clicks.'

Magozzi sighed, looked longingly at the Weber. 'So we're back in business.'

'Big-time.' Gino paused for a moment. 'You ever think there's something wrong with a job where you only have something to do if someone gets murdered?'

'Every day, buddy.'

3

Marty Pullman was sitting on the closed toilet lid in his downstairs bathroom, staring down the muzzle of a .357 Magnum. The round black hole looked very large, which worried him. Worse yet, the toilet faced the big mirror on the sliding doors that enclosed the bathtub, and he wasn't too keen on watching his own snuff film. He thought about it for a minute, then got into the bathtub and slid the doors closed behind him.

He smiled a little as he aimed the shower nozzle toward the back of the tub and turned the spray on full blast. He may have made a mess of his life, but he sure as hell wasn't going to make a mess of his death.

Finally satisfied, he sat down in the tub and put the muzzle in his mouth. Water poured over his head, his clothes, his shoes.

He hesitated for just a few seconds, wondering again what, if anything, he'd done last night. Not that it would matter now, he thought, slipping his thumb through the trigger guard.

'Mr Pullman?'

Marty froze, his thumb quivering on the trigger. Goddamn it, he was hallucinating. He had to be. No one ever came to this house, and certainly no one would just let himself in – except maybe a Jehovah's Witness, which made him glad he had the gun.

'Mr Pullman?' The male voice was louder now, closer, and he sounded young. 'Are you in there, sir?' A forceful knock rattled the bathroom door in its frame.

The gun tasted terrible as he pulled it from his mouth, and he spat into the water swirling toward the drain. 'Who is it?' he shouted, trying his best to sound scary and aggressive.

'Sorry to disturb you, Mr Pullman, but Mrs Gilbert told me to break the door down if I had to . . .'

'Who the hell are you and how do you know Lily?' Marty shouted.

'Jeff Montgomery, sir? I work at the nursery?'

The kid spoke only in questions. God, that was irritating. Marty looked down at the gun and sighed. He was never going to get this done. 'Stay right where you are. I'll be out in a minute.'

He scrambled out of the tub, stripped out of his drenched clothes, then stuffed gun, clothes, and shoes into the hamper. He wrapped a towel around his waist, then opened the bathroom door.

A tall, good-looking kid – eighteen or nineteen at most – was standing awkwardly in the hallway, hands stuffed into his jeans pockets.

'Okay. Here I am. Now tell me why Lily wanted you to break my door down.'

Jeff Montgomery had big blue eyes that grew comically wide when he noticed the thick scar that slashed a diagonal across Marty's bare chest. He looked away quickly.

'Uh . . . I didn't actually break down your door? It was open? And Mrs Gilbert has been trying to call you forever, but no one answered your phone? And jeez, Mr Pullman, I'm really sorry, but Mr Gilbert passed away.'

Marty didn't move for a minute; didn't even blink; then he rubbed the heel of his hand hard against his forehead, as if it would help him absorb the information. 'What?' he whispered. 'Morey's dead?'

The kid pressed his lips together and scowled down at the floor, trying not to cry, and Marty's opinion of him shot up a few degrees, even if he did end every sentence with a question mark. Anyone who liked Morey enough to cry for him couldn't be all bad.

'He was shot, Mr Pullman. Someone shot Mr Gilbert.'

Marty didn't say anything, but he felt the blood drain from his face as if someone had just pulled a plug. He sagged sideways against the bathroom door frame, glad it was there to hold him up.

Jesus Christ, he hated this world.

4

'Come on, Leo. Stop at Target or someplace so I can buy a pair of pants,' Gino grumbled from the passenger seat.

Magozzi shook his head. 'Can't. Crime scene's getting older by the minute.'

Gino plucked unhappily at the legs of his shorts. 'This is totally unprofessional.' He blew out a noisy sigh and looked out the window.

He'd always liked this part of Minneapolis. They were on Calhoun Parkway now, circling Lake Calhoun only a little slower than the bikers who decorated the asphalt trail in their brightly colored costumes. There were even a few windsurfers out today, dancing across the water with their triangle sails.

'Damn, I hate this part.'

'At least we don't have to tell her,' Magozzi said. 'That's something.'

'Yeah, I suppose. But we still have to ask her questions, like did she shoot her husband in the head.'

'That's why we get the big bucks.'

There was a squad on the street and another one blocking the driveway of the Uptown Nursery when Magozzi and Gino arrived. A couple of uniforms were standing around with rolls of yellow crime-scene tape, looking lost. Magozzi showed his badge when one of them approached the window. 'You got a grid staked out? You want us to park on the street?'

The uniform took off his hat and wiped his shiny forehead with a sleeve. It was already hot in the sun, especially on asphalt. 'Hell, I don't know, Detective. We got no clue where to string the tape.'

'Gee, how about around the body?' Gino suggested.

The cop bristled a little. 'Yeah, well the wife moved the body.'

'*What?*'

'That's right. She found him outside and moved him into the greenhouse. Said she didn't want to leave him out in the rain.'

Magozzi groaned. 'Oh, man . . .'

'Lock her up,' Gino muttered. 'Tampering with evidence, destroying a crime scene. Lock her up and throw away the key. She probably killed him anyway.'

'She's about a million years old, Detective.'

'Yeah, well that's the thing about guns. Old people, kids, anybody can use 'em. They're equal-opportunity murder weapons.' He got out of the car and slammed the door and started walking slowly toward the big greenhouse in front, eyes down in case the rain had missed a bloody footprint or something.

The uniform watched him go, shaking his head. 'That is not a happy man.'

'Normally he is,' Magozzi replied. 'He's just pissed because I wouldn't let him stop and change into some long pants before we came here.'

'You gotta give him points, then. Those are some bad legs.'

'Who belongs to the other squad?'

'Viegs and Berman. They're walking the block, hitting the neighbors. Couple of bike patrols are baby-sitting the body inside, but I wouldn't be surprised if the old lady has them watering plants or something.'

'Yeah?'

The uniform wiped his brow with his sleeve again. 'She's a piece of work, that one.'

'You got a feeling about her?'

'Yeah. I got a feeling her husband's getting the first rest he's had in years.'

Magozzi caught up to Gino in the middle of the lot, staring at the hearse angled in front of the greenhouse.

'We got no crime scene,' Gino grumbled. 'Rain trashed it first, then the funeral director drove his tank all over it, and . . . oh, man. Are you seeing what I'm seeing?'

Behind and almost hidden by the hearse was a white '66 Chevy Malibu convertible, red leather interior, positively cherry. Gino had lusted after it from the first time he'd seen it.

'Huh,' Magozzi grunted. 'What do you think?'

Gino clucked his tongue, the envy as ripe as ever.

'Gotta be his. There isn't another one like it in the Cities.'

'So what's he doing here?'

'Beats me. Buying flowers?'

Neither one of them had seen Marty Pullman since he'd left the force a year ago, a few months after his wife had died. Not that they'd known him that well even when they were all carrying the same badge. In Minneapolis, Homicide and Narcotics didn't mix nearly as often as they did on TV. It was just that once you saw Marty, you weren't likely to forget him. He still had the wrestler's physique that had taken him to State in high school. Short bowlegs, massive chest and arms, and dark eyes that had looked haunted even before they were. They'd called him Gorilla back when he'd still had a sense of humor, but those days were long gone.

The big glass door of the greenhouse opened, and Pullman walked out to meet them.

'Man,' Gino said under his breath. 'Looks like he lost about fifty pounds.'

'Hell of a year for him,' Magozzi said, and then Marty was there, shaking their hands, his expression as sober as ever.

'Magozzi, Gino, good to see you.'

'What the hell, Pullman?' Gino pumped his hand. 'You take up gardening, or did you join up again and nobody told me?'

Marty blew a long, shaky breath out through puffed cheeks. He looked like he was teetering on the edge of something. 'The man who was shot was my father-in-law, Gino.'

'Oh shit.' Gino's face fell. 'He was Hannah's dad? Oh man, I'm sorry. Shit.'

'Forget it. You had no way of knowing. Listen, you don't have much of a scene here.'

Magozzi heard the quaver in his voice, and decided to hold off on the sympathy until the man was strong enough to accept it. 'So we heard,' he said, pulling out a pocket notebook and a pen. 'Anybody else here this morning besides you and the funeral director?'

'A couple of the employees – I sent them home, but told them to stay put, that you'd be checking in with them before the day was out. I blocked off where Lily said she found Morey with my car, but that's about the best I could do.'

'We appreciate it, Marty,' Magozzi said, wishing he could walk away from this one. Lily Gilbert had lost her daughter one year, her husband the next. Magozzi didn't know how you survived that kind of double tragedy, and asking her the questions he had to ask suddenly seemed like an appalling act of cruelty. 'You think your mother-in-law will be able to talk to us?'

Marty managed a half smile. 'She's not falling apart, if that's what you mean. Lily doesn't do that.' He glanced toward the main greenhouse. 'She's in there. I tried to get her to go to the house – it's on the back of the lot, behind all the greenhouses – but that's not about to happen until they take Morey away. ME's on the way, right?'

Magozzi nodded. 'He'll do a little on-site before they move him. I don't think you want her around for that.'

'Hell, no, I don't. But Lily will be wherever she wants to be. That's just the way she is.' He sucked air in through his teeth. 'There's something else.'

Magozzi and Gino waited quietly.

'After she got him inside, she washed him. Shaved him. Changed his clothes. He's lying in there on one of the plant tables all decked out in his funeral suit.'

Gino closed his eyes briefly, trying to hold his temper in check. 'That's not good, Marty.'

'Tell me about it.'

'I mean, her son-in-law was a cop. She had to know she was destroying evidence.'

'She's damn near blind, Gino. Can't even get a driver's license anymore. Says she never saw any blood. I'm guessing the rain washed it away before she got out here. He caught it in the head, small caliber right behind the left temple, and he's got this great head of thick white hair . . . hell, even I had to look for it and I knew it was there.'

'Okay.' Gino nodded, letting it go for the moment.

Magozzi made a note to have the crime-scene techs collect the clothes the dead man had been wearing when he was shot. 'Anything you can think of that might help us out here?' he asked.

Marty's laugh was short and bitter. 'You mean like

who'd want to kill him? Sure. Look for somebody who'd pop Mother Teresa. He was a good man, Magozzi. Maybe even a great one.'

The air in the greenhouse was hot and swampy, laden with the scent of wet earth and vegetation. Long tables filled with plants were lined up in two rows, leaving a narrow central aisle – it looked like every other greenhouse Magozzi'd ever been in, except for the front table, which held a corpse in a black suit instead of potted flowers.

Even dead and laid out for viewing, Morey Gilbert was still a formidable presence. Very tall, very well-muscled, and better dressed than Magozzi had ever been in his life.

Two young bike cops fidgeted near the body, trying to pretend it wasn't there.

'Where are they?' Marty asked them.

'Your mother-in-law took the old gentleman back there, sir.' One of the bike patrols tipped his head toward a door in the back wall.

'What's back there, Marty?' Magozzi asked.

'The potting shed, a couple more greenhouses. Lily probably wanted Sol out of here for a while. He was pretty shook up.'

'Sol?'

'He's the funeral director who called it in, but he was also Morey's best friend. This is a tough one for him. Hang on, I'll get them.'

Gino waited until Marty was out of earshot before whispering to Magozzi. 'Her husband is dead, and she's consoling the funeral director? That's a little ass-backwards, isn't it?'

Magozzi shrugged. 'Maybe that's how she holds it together, by taking care of other people.'

'Maybe. Or maybe she didn't like her husband very much.'

They walked over to the front table to take a closer look at the dead man before the family came back. Gino used a pen to lift the white hair, exposing the bullet hole. 'Tiny. I suppose you could miss it if you were half blind, but I don't know.' He looked up at the bike patrols. 'You guys can take off now if you want. We got it covered. Send copies of your reports up to Homicide.'

'Yes sir, thank you.'

Magozzi was looking at Morey Gilbert's face, seeing a person instead of a corpse, starting to form the kind of bond that always linked him to victims. 'He's got a nice face, Gino. And he was eighty-four, still running his own business, taking care of his family . . . Who'd want to kill an old man like this?'

Gino shrugged. 'Maybe an old woman.'

'You're just pissed because she moved the body.'

'I'm *suspicious* because she moved the body. I'm pissed because you made me come here in short pants.'

They both took a step away from the table when the back door opened and Marty came through with his little geriatric entourage, led by a tiny, wiry old woman with silver hair cropped close to her head.

She wore a long-sleeved white blouse under child-sized bib overalls, and thick glasses magnified her dark eyes, making her look a little like Yoda.

A tough Yoda, Magozzi decided as she drew closer. There was no sign that she'd been crying, no surrender to despair, or to age, for that matter, in the straight backbone or squared shoulders. She was barely five feet and probably never saw ninety on a bathroom scale, but she looked like she could roll over Cleveland.

The elderly man who followed in her wake was a different story. Grief was weighing him down, pulling at his puffy, red eyes and a mouth that trembled.

Magozzi thought it was interesting that Marty reached out as if to touch the old woman's arm, but pulled back at the last minute. Apparently not a touchy-feely relationship. 'Detectives Magozzi and Rolseth, this is my mother-in-law, Lily Gilbert, and this is Sol Biederman.'

Lily Gilbert stepped up to the table and laid a hand on her dead husband's chest. 'And this is Morey,' she said, frowning at Marty as if he'd been rude to exclude his father-in-law from the introductions, simply because he was dead.

'Marty tells us your huband was a wonderful man, Mrs Gilbert,' Magozzi said. 'I can't imagine what a terrible loss this must be for your family. And for you, too, Mr Biederman,' he added, because tears were running freely down the old man's face now.

Lily was staring at Magozzi intently. 'I know you.

You were all over the news last fall for that Monkeewrench thing. I saw more of you than I did of my own family.' She gave Marty a pointed look, which he studiously ignored. 'So, you have questions, am I right?'

'If you think you're up to it, yes.'

Apparently she was not only up to it; she decided to skip the questions and go straight to the answers. 'All right. So this is what happened. I got up at six-thirty, just like I always do, made some coffee, came out to the greenhouse, and there was Morey, lying in the rain. Marty thinks I should have left his father-in-law outside with the rain falling in his eyes; left him there so strangers could come and see his mouth filling with water . . .'

'Jesus, Lily . . .'

'But this is not how families take care of each other. So I brought him inside, made him presentable, called Sol, and then I called Marty, who hasn't answered his phone in six months.'

'Lily, it was a crime scene,' Marty said tiredly.

'And I should know this? Am I a policeman? I called a policeman, but he didn't answer his phone.'

Marty closed his eyes, and Magozzi had the feeling he'd been closing his eyes to this woman for a long time. 'I'm not a policeman anymore, Lily.'

Magozzi had an immediate flashback to a day almost a year gone, when he'd passed Detective Martin Pullman as he went out the front doors of City Hall, carrying his career in a cardboard box, looking like he'd been run over by a truck. 'You'll be back, Detective,' Magozzi had said, because he didn't know what else to say to a man who had lost so much, and worse yet, he didn't understand a man who could walk away so easily from a job he loved. Marty had smiled, just a little. 'I'm not a detective anymore, Magozzi.'

Magozzi shifted back to the present in time to hear Gino asking the usual litany: Was anything missing? Any sign of a break-in? Did Morey Gilbert have any enemies, any unusual business dealings? . . .

'"Unusual business dealings?"' Lily snapped. 'What's that supposed to mean? You think we're growing marijuana in the back greenhouse or something? Running a white slavery ring? What?'

Gino had never responded very well to sarcasm, and his face started to turn red. They'd dealt with their share of grieving relatives over the years, and Gino did okay with the ones who fell apart. They tore him up, and he suffered for a long time afterwards, but at least he knew how to respond to them. People were supposed to fall apart when a relative died. That fit in with Gino's image of life and death and love and family, and made it easy for him to be soft-spoken, gentle, as comforting as a cop could be in such a situation. But the angry ones who lashed out, or the stoic ones who kept their feelings close to the vest, always threw him into a tailspin, and Lily Gilbert seemed to be a combination of the two.

'Excuse me, Mrs Gilbert,' Magozzi interrupted

gently, eliciting an eye roll from Gino. 'Would it be too difficult for you to take me outside and show me where you found your husband? Maybe walk me through it, step-by-step, while Gino talks to your friend Sol? We can get through this faster, then.'

The reminder of finding her husband's body brought the first sign of weakness to her eyes. Just a flicker, but it was there.

'I'm really sorry to have to ask you to do this. If it's too hard, we don't have to do it right now.'

Her gaze sharpened immediately. 'Of course we have to do it now, Detective. Now is all we have.' She marched toward the door, a little old soldier focusing on the mission, so she didn't have to think of anything else. Magozzi hurried to open it for her.

'Wait just a minute.' Marty frowned. 'Where's Jack, Lily? Why isn't he here yet?'

'Jack who?'

'Damnit, Lily, don't tell me you didn't call him . . .'

She was out the door before he finished.

'Shit.'

'Who's Jack?' Magozzi asked, still holding the door.

'Jack Gilbert. Her son. They haven't talked in a long time, but Jesus, his father just died . . . I gotta call him.'

While Marty went to the checkout counter and started punching numbers into the phone, Gino walked over to Magozzi and said under his breath, 'Listen, while you're out there talking to the old lady, why don't you ask her how a ninety-pound peanut managed to drag over two hundred pounds of dead weight all the way in here, then heft it onto that table.'

'Gee, Mr Detective, thanks for the tip.'

'Glad to help.'

'You don't like her much, do you?'

'Hey, I like her fine, except for the fact that she's got a personality like ground glass.'

'Huh. She never mentioned your outfit. I'd say that was a kindness.'

'This is the deal. I'm thinking, How the hell did she move him? So I answer myself: Gee, maybe she didn't. Maybe she shot him in here, and just said he was killed outside so we'd think we didn't have a crime scene.'

Magozzi thought about that for a minute. 'Interesting. Devious. I like the way you think.'

'Thank you.'

Magozzi opened the door to go outside. 'But she didn't do it.'

'Damnit, Leo, you don't know that . . .'

'Yeah. I do.'

5

Detective Aaron Langer had reached that point in life when you stopped hoping the next year would be better than the last, and just hoped that it wouldn't be as bad.

That's what happened when you hit middle age. Old people you loved got sick and died, young people you hated got promoted over you, the market crashed and took your retirement funds with it, and your body started to look like your father's did when you used to think you would never, ever let yourself go like that. If anyone ever told five-year-olds the truth about life, he thought, there'd be a rash of kindergarten suicides.

So far the job had gotten him through the worst of it. Even when his mother had been dying of Alzheimer's, even when his 401(k) had run off to Brazil with his financial planner, the job had been his refuge, the one part of his life where the line between good and evil was clean and sharp, where he knew exactly what to do. Murder was evil. Catching murderers was good. Simple.

Or at least it had been, before the secret. Now the line he had walked for his whole life was horribly blurred, and he barely knew where to step. What he needed most was a good, clear-cut case of senseless homicide that would perversely make sense of the world again, and at last, it looked like he had one.

'Langer, would you quit smiling? You're giving me the creeps.'

He looked at his partner, horrified. 'I was smiling?'

Johnny McLaren grinned at him. 'Sort of. Not really. I mean, your teeth weren't showing or anything. Besides, I know how you feel. After four months of nothing to do I almost went out and killed somebody myself.'

Langer closed his eyes, desperate to justify almost smiling in a bloody room where some poor soul had certainly died. 'It isn't that, McLaren,' he said sadly, and then he looked away, because he couldn't say anything more.

Most of the carnage in Arlen Fischer's house was in an otherwise pristine living room – specifically, on a once-ivory sofa that looked like it had spent a good deal of time on a slaughterhouse floor. Jimmy Grimm, star crime-scene tech of the Bureau of Criminal Apprehension, walked in, took one look at the blood patterns on the sofa, and said, 'That's an artery hit, guys. It should have dropped him. He was what? Eighty-nine?'

'Unless the old guy was the shooter,' McLaren suggested. 'Maybe it's somebody else's blood, and Fischer's out there right now burying him in the woods.'

'God, I love a mystery.' Grimm put his hands on

his hips and looked around, a rotund man in white disposable coveralls and slippers. Langer thought he looked a lot like the Michelin Man. 'Wow. This is really interesting.'

'What is?' asked McLaren, but Jimmy didn't hear him. He was bent over the sofa, already in another world – *his* world – where the only things he listened to were the stories blood splatter and minutiae told him.

Frankie Wedell, one of the patrolmen who'd secured the scene, approached the living room entrance and stopped. 'You guys remember how to do this, or do you need a little refresher course from the boys in the trenches?'

McLaren looked over at him and grinned. Frankie was the oldest officer on the force, a patrol by choice, and had trained more recruits than he could count, McLaren and Langer among them. 'This *is* our refresher course, old man,' he cracked. 'Homicide Light – no body. How the hell are you, Frankie?'

'I was a whole lot better before the radio caught fire this morning. Damn near broke my heart to hear about Morey Gilbert over at Uptown Nursery.'

McLaren's grin faded. 'That one's going to break a lot of hearts.'

'Hell of a way to end a dry spell, losing a good man like that. You two got to know him pretty well last year, didn't you?'

'Yeah, we did.'

'Good thing you didn't catch it, then.'

'Amen to that,' Langer murmured. 'Your partner said you did the walk-through from the front, Frankie. That right?'

'Yep. Tony covered the back. We started out looking for a shooter, ended up looking for a body.' His gaze drifted reluctantly to the bloody sofa. 'Still can't believe we didn't find one. That much blood, you wouldn't think the guy could get very far, especially at his age.'

Langer's eyes were sweeping the room while Frankie talked, noticing the little things: the high gloss on the hardwood floor, the precisely fanned magazines on a polished side table, the careful alignment of leather-bound classics in a bookcase. Nothing was disturbed; nothing seemed out of place here except the obscenity of the sofa. That, and the three large, glossy books stacked on the floor next to the coffee table. His eyes stopped there. 'What was the scene like when you got here, Frankie?'

'Well, the housekeeper – her name's Gertrude Larsen – was standing on the front steps, totally hysterical, out of control, flapping her arms, wailing . . . hate to see what she'd have been like if there'd actually been a body in here. Anyhow, I finally got her calmed down and brought her out to the squad, but she's starting to drift big-time. She must have taken a pill or something. You should probably talk to her before she goes comatose.'

'Did she move anything in here?'

'I doubt it. The picture I got was she walked in,

saw the blood, went nuts. She called from her cell instead of the inside phone, so I don't think she made it much past the front door.'

'Thanks, Frankie. Tell the housekeeper we'll be right out.'

'You got it.'

Langer walked over and looked down at his reflection in the surface of the coffee table. 'This isn't right.'

McLaren joined him and studied the table for a long moment, frowning. 'Okay, I'll bite. I see a nice shiny coffee table, no gouges, no blood, no big smeary fingerprints. So what am I missing?'

'The books on the floor. They're supposed to be on the coffee table.'

'So? Are you telling me that every little thing in your house is exactly where it belongs all the time?'

'Lord, no, not in my house. But in this one? I think so. Take a look around this room. They're the only things out of place, Johnny.'

McLaren gave the room the once-over, considering. 'Gotta admit, the damn place looks like a magazine picture, doesn't it?'

'Yes, it does.'

'Except for the sofa.'

'And the books on the floor.'

McLaren sighed and shoved his hands in his pockets. 'Okay, then maybe they got knocked off the table in the struggle.'

Langer shook his head. 'If that happened they'd be

scattered, at least a little. Look at them. These things are in an almost perfect stack. Someone lifted them off the table and put them there.'

'Someone being the shooter.'

'That's what I'm thinking.'

Jimmy Grimm's head popped up from behind the sofa, startling McLaren and putting a lie to the general consensus that Grimm never heard a thing when he was working a crime scene.

'Jesus, Jimmy, I forgot you were even here. What the hell are you doing hiding back there?'

'I got an exit hole in the fabric I'm lasering up with the entrance in that front cushion. Looks like we're going to find a slug in that bookcase somewhere.' He peered over at the coffee table, then grinned up at Langer. 'Nice call on the books, Langer. I'll bag them as soon as I finish this, put them on the top of the list at the lab.'

'Thanks, Jimmy.'

McLaren scratched at the red haze of whiskers sprouting along his unshaven jaw. 'Still doesn't make sense. You walk into this place, pop a guy sitting on the couch, then you turn around and take a stack of books off the coffee table and set them on the floor. Now why the hell would you do that?'

'Good question.'

Gertrude Larsen was obviously long past retirement age, and she looked pathetic, wrapped up in a sagging, faded cardigan and shivering in the backseat of the squad in spite of the sun warming the car's interior. When Langer approached the open door she looked up with bleary, narcotics-glazed eyes. A few tears traveled the wrinkled valleys down her cheeks, but there was no emotion attached to them.

Langer had seen the look many times, on tranquilized survivors of murder victims, on kids flying on their parents' Valium, but the shivering concerned him. He knelt down next to the car and touched the elderly woman's arm. 'How are you feeling, Ms Larsen?'

She smiled weakly and raised a quaking, arthritis-curled hand to cover his. He couldn't imagine this work-worn woman still scrubbing and sweeping and keeping a house. 'A little better.'

'Did you take something?'

She nodded, a little embarrassed, and handed him a small plastic prescription bottle. 'One of those pink ones.'

Langer opened the bottle and raised his brows when he looked inside. There were pink pills, blue pills, yellow pills, and a dusty cluster of Tums. The pink ones looked like Xanax, but he couldn't be sure.

'I take one of those if I get really upset,' she explained.

'I understand.' Langer made a note of the clinic address on the bottle and handed it back to her. She tucked it in a little-old-lady purse with a metal clasp at the top. 'Are you feeling well enough to answer a few questions for me?'

She nodded slowly, dabbing at her eyes with a damp handkerchief with a lace border.

Langer was exceedingly gentle with the old woman, and it was a slow-motion interview, but eventually they learned that she'd been Arlen Fischer's housekeeper for thirty-two years, came three times during the week by bus and every Sunday morning, also by bus, to help him get ready for the nine o'clock service at St Paul of the Lakes Lutheran. She was well compensated, cared for him like a brother, and couldn't imagine who would want to hurt him. And yes, those books were supposed to be on the coffee table, along with a lovely tapestry runner she'd bought him for his eightieth birthday, and no, she hadn't moved anything.

'Was the tapestry runner very valuable?'

Her watery eyes crinkled. 'Well, you don't often find one with birds on it; certainly not bluebirds; and yes, it was a bit pricey. Eighty dollars plus tax.' She leaned a little closer to him and confided in a whisper, 'But I got it on clearance. Nineteen ninety-nine.'

Langer smiled back at her. 'Quite a bargain.'

'Indeed it was.'

Langer thanked her, gave her his card, then asked Frankie to drive her to the Hennepin County Medical Center, stay with her until she'd been examined, then drive her home.

Frankie sighed miserably. 'You know what the ER at HCMC looks like on a Sunday?'

Langer shrugged apologetically. 'She lives alone, Frankie, she's self-medicating, and she's still shivering in that hot box of a car. I'm a little worried about shock.'

'Okay, okay, but you should have been a missionary or something.'

He and McLaren stood in the driveway and watched the squad pull away.

'So now what are you thinking?' McLaren asked. 'That the shooter moved the books to steal a twenty-dollar tapestry runner?'

'Don't forget, it had bluebirds on it. You don't often find those.'

'Jeez, Langer, was that you trying to be funny?'

'Maybe.'

'Well stop it. You're scaring me.'

An hour later, Jimmy and his crew were still at it, but things were wrapping up. Langer and McLaren found him prone on the living room floor with a tape measure and a notebook, scribbling down figures.

'Hey, Jimmy,' McLaren said with as much cheer as he could muster after spending Sunday morning in a murder house. 'You got this thing solved yet?'

Grimm gave him a tired smile and got to his feet with some effort. 'At this point, I'm not even sure we have a homicide. Next time, try to get a body, guys. It'll make things a lot easier. You hear back from the hospitals?'

McLaren thumbed through his notebook. 'Yeah.

Only gunshot wounds reported last night were from a couple of sixteen-year-old gangbangers trying to pop each other with .22's. The best they could do was soft tissue stuff, no artery hits . . .'

'It wasn't a .22.' Jimmy held up a little bag with a slug inside. '.45 caliber, and some nice rifling, by the way.'

'.45, huh? Well, in that case, whoever got shot here last night didn't make it to any hospital or clinic we know about.'

'Then he's dead,' Grimm said matter-of-factly, looking at the sofa.

Langer followed his gaze, feeling a little queasy. 'That's a lot of blood.'

Jimmy shrugged. 'Looks worse than it is. I'll have to run saturation tests to be sure, but at first blush I'd say your victim left this house alive. There's not nearly enough blood for a heart shot. I'm guessing an extremity. But arteries don't heal themselves. He'd bleed out in a hurry without medical attention of some sort, and there's not a drop of blood anywhere else in the house.'

McLaren grunted. 'So somebody shot him, bagged him, and carried him out, which means we're looking for a sumo wrestler. According to the housekeeper, Arlen Fischer weighed over three hundred pounds.'

Jimmy Grimm was rocking back and forth on his heels, grinning at them. 'Nobody carried him out.'

'Yeah? What then? Aliens sucked him up from the couch?'

'Better than that.' Jimmy smiled, enjoying his secret.

'Jesus Christ, Langer, throw him down, I'm going to take the pliers to his nuts,' McLaren grumbled.

'God, the Irish are so impatient,' Jimmy sighed, pointing to a section of wooden floor marked off with tape. 'We found wheel marks. From the couch, through the kitchen, out the door and into the garage. Four wheels, not two. Your shooter brought a gurney.'

'Whoa.' McLaren's red eyebrows shot up. 'Premeditation with a capital *P*.'

'I'd say so.' Jimmy's plump arms reached for the ceiling in a stretch. 'Well, we're about to clear this place and head back to the lab. Apparently they're bringing in a ton of trace from that scene down at the tracks . . .' He stopped in midsentence, his hands falling to his sides. 'Oh, for God's sake. Did you say Fischer went three bills?'

Langer nodded. 'At least.'

Jimmy closed his eyes and shook his head. 'Man, that blew right past me. My tech said the guy on the tracks was a beefer.'

'Do they have an ID on him?'

Jimmy shrugged, and Langer pulled out his mobile. 'Tinker and Peterson caught that, right?' he asked McLaren.

'Right.'

Langer punched some buttons, put the phone to his ear, listened for a few seconds, then said, 'Tinker, this is Aaron. Tell me about your man on the tracks.'

No one had ever accused Tinker Lewis of being reticent. You asked him how he was, you got the story of his life with no hope of a reprieve. Langer tried to interrupt a couple of times, finally gave up and listened in resigned silence, his face infuriatingly expressionless.

McLaren fidgeted and paced for as long as he could stand it, then finally cozied up to Langer and tried to get his ear near the phone.

'Okay, Tinker, thanks,' Langer said. 'I have to go now. McLaren is making a move on me.' He signed off, tucked the phone away, then simply stood there, rocking back and forth on his heels with a grim smile.

McLaren flapped his arms in frustration. 'Goddamnit, Langer, you want me to beg?'

'There was no ID on the body at the tracks. The man was elderly, easily three hundred pounds, with a big hole in his left arm, just above the elbow.' He gave Jimmy Grimm a nod. 'Artery hit, just like you said, Jimmy.'

'So he bled out?'

Langer's lips tightened, erasing the remainder of his smile. 'No, he didn't. They think he had a heart attack, probably when he saw the train coming.'

'Oh, Christ,' McLaren muttered, seeing too vividly the picture of an old, injured man tied to the tracks, looking up and seeing the single headlight of a moving train, heading toward him.

'But if he'd lived,' Langer continued, 'the ME says he would probably have lost the arm. Somebody put a tourniquet on it, way too tight, and it was on there way too long.' He raised his brows at McLaren. 'It was a tapestry thing, Tinker said, with little bluebirds all over it.'

McLaren blinked at him, then blew out a silent whistle. 'So their guy is our guy.'

'Looks like it.'

'Jesus.' McLaren looked over at the couch and shivered a little, absorbing the totality of what had happened here. 'This is really sick, Langer.'

'No argument there.'

'What we've got is some sadistic son of a bitch coming in here, shooting the poor old guy in the arm, strapping him to a gurney and rolling him out, then driving him over to tie him to the train tracks . . .'

'. . . making sure to keep him alive the whole time so he would know what was coming,' Jimmy Grimm finished. 'God in heaven.'

6

Magozzi watched them load Morey Gilbert's body into the ME wagon, wincing when the bag bounced hard as the gurney wheels folded. He'd seen a lot of bodies go into that wagon over the years, but he never got used to that final bounce as they all left home for the last time.

It was a relief when the wagon's doors slammed shut and the children masquerading as Medical Examiner assistants climbed in and drove away.

'Who are those kids?'

'Just a sec,' Gino said into his cell phone, then held it against his chest. 'Those are not kids. Those are grown-ups with medical degrees. They're starting to look like kids 'cause you're starting to get so damn old.'

'I'm in the prime of my life. Forty's so far away I can't even see it from here. How come we got assistants anyway? Where the hell's Anant?'

Gino sighed. 'Doing the old guy tied to the train tracks, that's where. And the kids did just fine. I watched them. They wore gloves and everything. Can I finish my call now?'

'Are you having phone sex with Angela?'

'No. With Langer. And you interrupted at a critical

point. Do you mind?' He put the cell phone to his ear again. 'Sorry about that, Langer. Leo's having a midlife moment.'

Magozzi kept silent for exactly five seconds. 'The train track guy was old, too?'

'Jesus. Hang on, Langer . . . Yeah, Leo, he was old. Way old.'

'That's three in one night, Gino. Morey Gilbert, whoever bought it in the bloody house, and the train track guy.'

'Actually, it looks like it's only two, and if you'd give me a second to finish this call, I'll find out everything you ever wanted to know about old dead people. Jeez. You're like a little kid, tugging at my pants leg.'

'You don't have a pants leg.'

Gino gave him a nasty look and stomped away across the parking lot, cell phone pressed to his ear.

Magozzi found a bench in the shade at the front of the greenhouse and sat down next to a stack of bulging plastic bags that smelled like chocolate. Sunday-morning traffic was picking up on the parkway, but he could barely hear it through the dense evergreen hedge that blocked all but the driveway from the street. It made for a nice, quiet piece of real estate in the middle of a city; nice for shopping, living, or shooting an old man in the dead of night without fear of being seen.

A couple of crime-scene techs were still inside, processing the area around the table where Lily

Gilbert had laid out her husband. Two more were around the side of the building, trying to find a scene on the rain-washed asphalt where she said she'd found him, but as far as Magozzi was concerned, they were all just going through the motions. Intentionally or not, Lily Gilbert had washed away any evidence the rain missed.

He hated this case already, because he knew where it was going. Nobody just popped geriatrics for the fun of it. Unless robbery was involved, the suspect list was always short, and almost always family. He'd take a drug-crazed psycho any day over relatives murdering each other. There wasn't a monster in a closet any bigger than that.

Gino was heading back toward him across the lot, his broad face already pinking from the sun, his holstered 9-mm bouncing a little against the plaid Bermuda shorts. He slumped down on the bench and wiped the gathering sweat from his forehead. 'Can you believe it was snowing last week? Man, it's hotter than hell out here. Gotta be eighty already and it's not even noon. Wish the son would get here so we could blow this pop stand.'

'What's Langer got?'

Gino leaned forward and rubbed his hands together. 'Now that one's really interesting. He and McLaren have this bloody house and no body, and Tinker and Peterson out at the train tracks have this body and not enough blood. Thanks to the miracle of cell phones they communicate, and *voilá.* Turns out the old guy that owns the bloody house is probably the guy tied to the tracks. They're going to get an ID from the housekeeper, but it looks good.'

Magozzi straightened a little on the bench, frowning. 'Well that's a puzzler.'

'No shit. From what they can put together so far, somebody shot this old man in his house, hit an artery in his arm, then get this. They put a tourniquet on him so he wouldn't bleed to death before they could get him to the train tracks. Spooky, huh? They wanted him alive to see the train coming. Anant's got him on the table now, but he's thinking heart attack.'

'Jesus.' Magozzi thought about that for a long time, didn't like anything his brain came up with. 'They scared him to death.'

'Looks that way. Anyhow, he was shot with a .45, our guy here was hit with a small caliber, and the m.o. sure as hell doesn't tie any knots.'

'So no connection between ours and theirs.'

'Just that they were both old men, living in the same neighborhood.'

Magozzi rubbed his eyes, felt the sweat collecting on his lids. 'I don't even like that much.'

'Yeah. Me either. But nothing else fits, so on the face of it, we're looking for two killers.' Gino eyed the plastic bags next to the bench. 'Are these the ones the old lady moved all by herself?'

Magozzi closed his eyes and smiled. 'No. Those are the ones she made me carry. Thirty pounds each. I thought I'd die.'

'Fine homicide detective you turned out to be, doing hard labor for a murder suspect.'

'She's old. She asked. Respect for your elders and all that. And there was a little machismo involved, since she was carrying the fifty-pounders filled with potting soil.'

'So you think she could have moved the body.'

'As much as she had to. She used the wheelbarrow to get him inside.'

'Jesus, that's creepy. Pushing your dead husband around in a wheelbarrow. Not as creepy as giving him a bath and shaving him, though. I'm telling you, that part bothers the hell out of me. And don't tell me that's how they did it in the old days, because I know that. But this isn't the old days, and it's weird.'

Magozzi shrugged. 'Maybe it's still the old days for some old people. But it bothers me, too. I think there might be something there.'

Gino's brows lifted. 'Yeah?'

'I don't think she killed him, but there's something else here we're not seeing.'

'Like what?'

'Don't know. It's just a feeling. Why do those bags smell like chocolate?'

'Cocoa bean mulch. You put it around your plants, on garden paths, like that. Smells like Hershey bars every time it rains. Great, huh?'

'I don't know. How do you keep the neighbor kids from eating it?'

'You gotta shoot 'em.'

They both looked up as a brand-new Mercedes convertible swerved into the nursery driveway and screeched to a stop less than an inch away from the squad that was blocking it. The driver looked harmless enough – middle-aged, a little soft around the middle, dressed in an expensive suit that still looked good despite all the wrinkles – but when the cop stationed at the driveway entrance tried to intercept him, he started dancing around like a troll with a hotfoot.

'Must be the son,' Magozzi said.

Gino was staring at the man with a silly little smile on his face. 'Holy shit. I never put it together. You know who that is, Leo? That's Jack Gilbert.'

'Yeah, the son. That's what I said . . .'

'No no, he's *the* Jack Gilbert. That bottom-feeder PI attorney with all those hokey TV ads. Don't-let-them-jack-you-around Jack Gilbert. That one. Jeez, poor Marty. Can you imagine having a sleazeball like that for a brother-in-law?'

Gilbert was yelling at the officer now, punctuating his verbal assault with wild, flailing gestures that made him look like a psychotic windmill.

'Christ, look at him. Goddamn attorneys think they own the world.'

Magozzi stood up and motioned for the officer to let Gilbert through. 'Try to reel it in a little. This guy just found out his father was murdered, and his own mother wouldn't call to tell him.'

'Doesn't make him any less of a sleazeball.' Gino

stood reluctantly as Gilbert made a beeline toward them, taking a quick step back when the man swooped in on them so close he could see every single vein in his very bloodshot eyes.

'You guys the detectives?' He eyed Gino's shorts suspiciously.

'Yes, sir. I'm Detective Rolseth and this is Detective Magozzi.'

Gilbert stuck out a palm slick with sweat and pumped both their hands while he bobbed back and forth on his feet. 'Jack, Jack Gilbert.'

Magozzi was about to go through the standard condolences, but he didn't get a chance.

'So what the hell happened here, guys, what do you think? Robbery? Drive-by?'

'It's pretty early in the investigation, sir. We haven't even finished questioning . . .'

'Jesus Christ.' Gilbert pressed the heels of his hands into his eyes. 'I can't believe this happened. There are a hundred people in this city who want to kill *me,* including my own wife, and it's my father who gets shot.'

Gino's brows lifted. 'Mind if I ask who wants to kill you, Mr Gilbert? Other than your wife, that is.'

'I'm a PI attorney – I'll fax you a list. Goddamnit, he was just an old man. Who the fuck would shoot an old man? Where's my mother? Where's Marty?'

'They're back at the house, Mr Gilbert, but if you don't mind, we have a few questions . . .' Magozzi's mouth hung open on his last word as Gilbert sped away without a backward glance.

'Interesting interview technique,' Gino commented. 'Pumped that sucker dry, is what you did. Still, I think we might want to do a little follow-up. You know, a couple of routine questions you forgot to ask, like where was he last night, did he kill his father, stuff like that.'

Magozzi glared at him, then noticed an older uniform he hadn't seen before ducking under the crime-scene tape across the driveway entrance, walking toward them. 'You know this guy?'

Gino squinted across the lot. 'Oh, hell, yes. Al Viegs. Don't say anything about his hair.'

'Huh?'

'He just got his first set of plugs. Looks weird. Little tufts of hair and lots of bare space.'

Magozzi caught himself staring at the man's head as he drew closer. 'Damnit, Gino, this is like not looking at the elephant.'

'Yeah, I know . . . hey, Viegs.'

The officer nodded a somber greeting while Magozzi stared at his bizarrely patterned pink scalp.

'Berman and I just finished the door-to-door for the whole block. We'll have to come back and hit a few who weren't around, but most of them were home. Sunday and all.'

'Let me guess,' Gino said. 'Nobody heard anything, nobody saw anything.'

Viegs nodded. 'Right. But . . . it was weird.' He

looked around, cleared his throat, shuffled his polished shoes. 'We must have hit about twenty places, houses and businesses . . . man, it was really weird.'

Magozzi dropped his gaze from Viegs's head to his eyes. 'What do you mean?'

Viegs shrugged helplessly. 'A lot of them cried. And I mean a lot. The minute they heard Mr Gilbert was dead, they started to bawl. Men, women, kids . . . it was awful.'

Magozzi's gaze sharpened. This was starting to get really interesting.

'I just don't get it. I mean, this is the city. Half the people who live here don't even know their neighbors by sight, and then you look at what's going on out there' – Viegs jerked his head toward the street – 'and you gotta wonder.'

Gino got to his feet and looked over Viegs's shoulder at the empty drive. 'What are you talking about?'

'You been out to the street lately?'

'Not since we got here.'

Viegs cocked his thumb toward the driveway. 'Take a walk, then. You'll want to see this for yourself.'

Gino and Magozzi walked across the parking lot, through the opening where the driveway cut into the hedge, and then stopped, dumbfounded. The sidewalk in both directions was jammed with people of every age and race imaginable, some weeping quietly, others stern and stoic, all standing perfectly still, perfectly silent. Magozzi felt the hairs on the back of his neck stand up.

Gino watched as more people crossed the street and slipped quietly into the ranks of mourners. 'Jesus,' he whispered. 'Who the hell was this guy?'

A tall blond kid next to the tape kept raising his hand just a little, trying to attract their attention. Magozzi walked over and leaned in close to him. 'Something I can do for you, son?'

'Um . . . are you the detectives?'

'That's right.'

The kid was probably good-looking under other circumstances, but now his face was blotchy and red and puffy around the eyes. 'I'm Jeff Montgomery? And this is Tim Matson? We work here, and Mr Pullman told us to stay home, you might want to talk to us? But . . . we had to come, you know?'

Magozzi thought they looked like a couple of lost puppies. He raised the tape and gestured them under, suppressing the instinct to pat them on their heads and tell them everything would be all right.

7

When there were no obvious suspects, the first day of any homicide investigation was a blur of interviews and fact-checking that ate up the precious golden hours between a murder and the probability of it ever being solved. If you were lucky, you caught a spark – a tiny scrap of information that might lead you in the right direction, but Magozzi and Gino hadn't been lucky today. Fourteen hours into the Gilbert case without a glimmer.

Magozzi parked the car on the street next to City Hall, and for a moment he and Gino just sat there in the dark.

You know your big problem, Leo? You take every murder so goddamned personally.

It was the one thing his ex-wife had said to him that still left him dumbstruck, all these years later. Even her end-game confession of all her infidelities had lost its punch as time passed, but not that. It was the very first time he'd ever considered the possibility that murder wasn't personal to everyone, and he still couldn't get his head around that.

It had something to do with empathy for the victim, he supposed. Not once had he ever been able to look at a body with the mental distance that would allow him to see it as 'just' a body. Some cops could do that. Some cops had to do it, or they'd go nuts. Magozzi had never been able to manage it. To him, it was never just a body; it was always a dead person, and there was a big difference.

But this one was worse than most. Only one day into the investigation and he wasn't just feeling sorry for the victim; he was starting to feel sorry for himself because he hadn't known the man, and that had never happened before.

'Long day,' Gino finally sighed.

'Too long. Too many sad people. You know, just once I'd like to work a case where everybody hated the dead guy.'

Gino grunted. 'That ain't gonna happen. Nobody hates a dead man. It's not allowed. You could be the meanest son of a bitch on the planet, but once they put you in the coffin and lay you out in front of the people who hated you when you were alive, they all seem to find something nice to say. It's like a miracle.'

Magozzi scowled out the windshield at the deserted street. Maybe Gino was right. Maybe Morey Gilbert had been just like anybody else, somehow elevated by death. But in his heart, he didn't think so.

Gino was silent for a minute. 'Except I think this one might be a little different, Leo.'

'Yeah, I know. I was just thinking the same thing.' Magozzi closed his eyes, remembering all the mourners outside the nursery. It was the kind of impromptu gathering you expected to see when a celebrity died, or a beloved public figure; not some average Joe nobody had ever heard of. The media had covered it, but mostly because it had snarled traffic on the boulevard. They'd never heard of Morey Gilbert either, and most of their attention was focused on the delicious, ratings-grabbing horror of another old man being tortured and tied to a train track.

Beethoven's Fifth sang out from the pocket in Gino's shorts. He ripped his pocket pulling out his cell phone before the irritating melody started again. 'Damnit, I'm going to ground that kid. Teach her to have a little respect for her father and classical composers.'

'You should get one of those cell phone holsters for that thing.'

'Oh sure. A cell phone in one holster and a gun in the other. I'd end up shooting myself in the ear. Yeah, Rolseth here.'

When Gino turned on the map light and started taking notes, Magozzi got out of the car and leaned against the door, pushing speed-dial on his own phone, waiting for the answering machine beep on the other end. 'Hey, it's Magozzi. We've got something going here, and I'm going to be a little late. I'll try to make it by ten. Call back if that's too late; otherwise, I'll see you then.' He flipped his phone closed and got back into the car, praying that ten o'clock wouldn't be too late; that his phone wouldn't ring in the next few hours.

Gino waggled his notebook at him. 'That was the night manager at the Wayzata Country Club. Jack Gilbert was there last night, just like he said. Apparently he's there almost every night, solo, which tells you a little about his home life. But the place shuts down at one, and Anant put time of death between two and four, right?'

'Right.'

'So he had plenty of time to get to the nursery and pop his father. Which means we don't have one person in that family we can clear. The old lady's alone in the house, and the son and the son-in-law are both supposedly three sheets to the wind and can't remember a damn thing.' He sighed and tucked his notebook in his shirt pocket. 'Nobody has alibis anymore. I hate that. So what do you think?'

Magozzi reached into the backseat to grab one of the two grease-stained bags that were probably leaking onto the seat. 'I think this car is going to smell like barbecue for the next year. Tell me again why we had to pick up dinner.'

'Because if we'd sent Langer he'd have come back with carrots and sawdust or some such vegetarian crap, that's why.'

Minneapolis was dressing itself for the evening with a sparkle of lights. It was a pretty city, Detective Langer thought, staring out at the yellow rectangles in a distant tower, climbing into the night sky like some kind of golden ladder. Not the kind of place you'd expect to produce such a killer.

McLaren, as Minnesotan as he was Irish, was convinced that whoever had murdered Arlen Fischer was certainly from somewhere else; Chicago, maybe, or New York, or wherever it was that people like the Sopranos lived. Langer had smiled at that, but had to admit there was an old-time mob taste to the way the elderly man had been killed. You didn't see creativity like that in many other arenas.

He glanced back at his monitor, jiggled his mouse to bring the report he was writing back to life. He hated writing reports. Hated the arcane, affected cop-speak that mangled the brain and tied the tongue. You never went into a house; you entered a residence. People were never shot to death; they sustained mortal wounds inflicted by such-and-such-caliber firearms. And Arlen Fischer had certainly not been tied to a train track to be turned into oatmeal by the midnight freight to Chicago; he'd simply been 'secured to the southbound tracks by means of barbed wire.' You couldn't even mention that the train was due, because that would imply the alleged perpetrator had actually premeditated a means of death not in evidence. Some junior-high-school defense attorney would jump all over that. Genteel, legalese gobbledygook is what it was. If a cop ever talked like that in real life, he'd be laughed off the force.

He looked out at the lights again, dreaming of

his last sentence, wondering if Chief Malcherson would suspend him if he wrote that Arlen Fischer had been left on the tracks to get filleted by a train.

'C'mon, Langer,' McLaren chided him. 'Goose the mare, would you? The caterers have arrived.'

Langer looked up with the guilty start of the grade-school kid who should never be given a desk by a window. McLaren, Gino, and Magozzi were at the big table in the front of the Homicide room, pulling white cardboard containers out of a collection of smelly paper bags. 'Almost finished,' he said, turning back to his computer.

'Well hurry up,' Gino said good-naturedly. 'My stomach thinks my throat's been cut.'

Magozzi gave him a look. 'Where do you get that stuff?'

'What stuff?'

'All those pithy little sayings.'

'My father. He's a very pithy man.'

McLaren found the bag of garlic rolls and stuck his nose in the top. 'What's "pithy" mean?'

'Like in "pithed off,"' Gino said deadpan. 'Say, how come Tinker and Peterson aren't here? You're doing a tandem, right?'

'Nah. We're catching media bullets on this one, and the chief hasn't let Peterson near a camera since he told that arrogant prick from Channel Three he was an arrogant prick.'

Gino sighed happily. 'That was a beautiful moment.'

'That it was,' McLaren agreed. 'Anyway, Tinker was signed out for vacation starting tomorrow morning anyway, so it worked out. Now I get all the glory as soon as Langer solves this thing.'

Langer smiled as he keyed in the command to print, then stood up and stretched. This was good. Being in the office after hours, working an active case, listening to the guys banter . . . for the first time in what seemed like years, he was beginning to feel as if everything might be all right again.

He was halfway through his fifth barbecued chicken wing, trying to remember if he still had that bottle of Maalox in his bottom drawer, when Magozzi asked a question that reminded him that there might not be enough Maalox in the world.

'You were pretty close to Marty Pullman, right, Langer?'

He held up one finger and continued chewing, buying time. No one expected Aaron Langer to talk with his mouth full. When he finally swallowed, it felt like a small, hairy dog going down his throat. 'Barely knew him until I ran the case on his wife.'

'Sure dogged us on that one, though,' McLaren put in. 'Not that you can blame the poor guy. Man, those were some bad days.'

'I don't doubt it,' Magozzi said. 'He was at our scene today, you know.'

'Figured he would be,' Langer said. 'He really loved that old man.'

'Well, the thing is, Marty looked pretty bad . . .'

'Walking dead,' Gino agreed.

'. . . which is why I brought it up. Gino and I talked about it. We both got some bad feelings from him, think he might be in one of those holes you can't get yourself out of, and we thought if you'd been close . . .'

'We weren't,' Langer interrupted, glancing at McLaren for confirmation. 'Neither one of us.'

'Nah, he was totally shut down,' McLaren said. 'Truth is, he's been walking dead since his wife got killed. He still putting it away?'

Gino nodded glumly. 'Said he woke up this morning on his kitchen floor next to a Jim Beam empty and has no clue where he was last night. And I says, "Gee, Marty, you been drinking like that since you left the force?" And he thought about it for a second, then said, "Well, that would explain the blackouts."'

McLaren winced and pushed away the remains of whatever animal he'd been eating. 'I kind of figured he was headed down that road. Can't remember seeing him sober once during the whole investigation. Seemed like Morey was the only thing holding him together.'

Magozzi's brows shot up. 'Morey? You knew him well enough to call him by his first name?'

McLaren gave an uneasy shrug. 'You met him once, you knew him that well. He was that kind of a guy, you know? Really bummed us out when we heard the news this morning. As if that family hadn't been through enough. And I'll tell you another thing. Your killer was a stranger, because nobody who ever met that man would want him dead.'

Magozzi crumpled his napkin and pushed away from the table. 'Yeah, that's what everyone says, but we're having a little trouble with that. Morey Gilbert caught it once in the head, real close. It doesn't look like an accident or some kind of impulse shooting. What it looks like, and what it feels like, is an execution.'

Langer shook his head. 'Impossible. Morey couldn't have made an enemy if he tried. You can't imagine how much good that man did in his life.'

'Oh, we're getting an idea,' Gino said. 'You saw the crowd outside the nursery today?'

'Yeah. We got stuck in the jam on the way back from our scene.'

'Well, we worked it a little, talked to some people, got an earful of good deeds.' Gino licked some barbecue sauce off his thumb and started paging through his pocket notebook. 'I got a list here of down-and-outs he gave money to, homeless people he dragged off the street and took home to dinner, if you can believe that, some guy with a gang tattoo and a Perry Ellis suit who claimed Morey Gilbert got him out of the life just by talking to him . . .'

That made Langer smile. 'Talking is what he did best.'

'And most.' McLaren grinned. 'Man, he could talk your ear off. But it wasn't small talk, you know? I mean, this guy thought about the weirdest things in ways you never thought of.'

'Like what?' Magozzi asked.

'Oh, jeez, a million things. Like the day Langer and I went over after the case was all wrapped up, and Morey found out I was Catholic – remember that, Langer?'

'Oh, yeah.'

'Anyway, he sits us down at the kitchen table, gives us a beer, and then starts asking me all these questions, like I was a priest or a scholar or something . . .' McLaren shook his head a little, smiling, remembering.

So, Detective McLaren. They have saints, the Catholics. You know about these?

Sure, Morey.

Well, it just seems funny to me, the ones they picked. You know, Joan of Arc, she stabbed people with swords, and then there was St Francis who talked to birds . . . what is the connection there? There's no consistency. And these are the people who are supposed to be putting in a good word with God when you can't reach him directly, am I right?

Well, yes . . .

So my question is this: Now Moses, he had this one-on-one relationship with the big guy, you know? He talked to him personally, just like I'm talking to you. So if anybody should be interceding for anybody, you'd think it would be Moses. But they didn't make Moses a saint. Now why do you think that is?

Uh, I think you have to be a Christian to be a saint.

Ah! You see what I'm saying? There's no sense to the way you pick these people.

Hey, I don't pick them . . .

Maybe you could talk to the people who do that sort of thing, eh? Because the thing is, they based their whole religion on Jesus and even he *couldn't be a saint because he was Jewish, not Christian. You see? No sense. I need your help understanding this.*

Gino was smiling a little. 'So he was a pretty religious guy, huh?'

McLaren thought about that for a minute. 'Not religious, exactly. He just thought about that stuff a lot, like he was trying to figure it out, but I suppose that goes with the territory. He was in Auschwitz, did you know that?'

Gino nodded. 'We knew he was in one of the camps. One of the assistant MEs showed me the tattoo at the scene.'

'Gotta tell you, it just about blew my mind when I found that out. I mean, I never knew anybody who was in the camps before. Seems like that stuff happened a million years ago, you know? So here's this guy who lives through God knows what kind of hell, and he comes out the other side loving his fellow man. I'm telling you guys, he was something. You would have liked him a lot.'

'Aw, don't say that.' Gino got up and started shoving empty containers into a bag. 'I don't want to like dead people. There's no percentage in it. Langer, are you just going to leave those chicken wings?'

'You bet I am.'

Gino grabbed one and ripped off a bite. 'So tell me. When you were getting all cozy with the Gilberts, what kind of vibes did you get off the son?'

'Jack?' Langer shrugged. 'He was never around. Kind of the black sheep, I guess. Marty said he'd had some kind of falling-out with his folks.'

Gino tossed a decimated chicken wing into the bag. 'Must have been a pretty major falling-out. The old lady still isn't talking to him.'

'Must have been,' Langer agreed. 'Jack didn't even stand with the family during his sister's funeral.'

'Oh, Christ.' McLaren winced. 'That was tough to watch. I'd almost forgotten. Here's this middle-aged guy bawling his head off, literally falling apart, and he stumbles over to Morey with his arms out, and Morey just looks at him, then turns and walks away. Left Jack standing there alone, crying, arms stretched out to nobody . . . man, I'll tell you, it was pathetic.'

Magozzi felt a prickle on the back of his neck. 'Well, that's interesting. Loves his fellow man and turns his back on his own son at a time like that? And that's everybody's Mr Nice Guy?'

Langer spoke softly. 'That's the thing, Magozzi. He really was Mr Nice Guy, and that business with Jack at the funeral was so totally out of character, you just had to wonder . . .' He stopped, frowning.

'What you had to wonder,' McLaren finished for him; 'is what the hell did Jack do?'

8

The thing was, Magozzi liked to look at her, and sometimes he couldn't get past that.

'You're staring at me again.'

'I can't help it. I'm very superficial.'

Grace MacBride smiled, but only a little. If she had a full-blown, many-toothed smile, Magozzi hadn't seen it yet. 'I have a favor to ask.'

'Yes.'

'It's a big one.'

'I can handle it.' And he could, of course. He'd do anything for Grace MacBride, and all he asked in return was a few of these nights every now and then, when they'd sit at her kitchen table and drink wine and talk about nothing in particular while he looked at her black hair and blue eyes and dreamed of things that might be, if only he could be patient long enough.

'I want you to look in on Jackson.'

Oh, now that wasn't good. Jackson was a foster kid who lived down the block from Grace, and he would only need looking in on if Grace were planning to leave town. Goddamnit, maybe he'd overdone this patience thing.

Magozzi decided to be strong and silent and

pretend he didn't care, but then he opened his mouth and the truth fell out. 'Grace, you can't leave. I've got this whole seduction plan going.'

Another little smile. 'This is a seduction? Six months and you've never even tried to kiss me.'

'It's a long-term plan. Besides, you weren't ready for that yet.'

She reached across the table and touched his hand then, and Magozzi froze. With only a very few exceptions, Grace never touched people if she could avoid it. Oh, she'd grab your hand and pull you toward something she wanted you to see, but to touch simply for the sake of making contact – that was a rare thing. 'Everything's ready, Magozzi. We've been working on it for months. And now Arizona has something for us.'

'Oh, for God's sake, Grace, no one from Minnesota goes to Arizona in the summer. That's totally backwards.'

'Five women missing from the same small town in the past three years, and all they've got is a mountain of paperwork. It's made to order for the new software program.'

Magozzi felt a sudden, unexpected rush of anger coloring his face, and turned his head so she wouldn't see it. Grace MacBride had spent half her short life on the run from murderers, and what did she do when she was finally safe? Damn fool looked high and low for another murderer, then ran right toward him. She had this bizarre notion that confronting your demons was theraputic, which made a lot of sense when you were dealing with something like fear of flying, and no sense at all when your demons were armed and dangerous and probably insane.

'The back of your neck is really red, Magozzi.'

He turned and looked at her, struggling to keep his voice even. 'There is absolutely no reason for you to go there. Your program can crunch all the information from here.'

'Magozzi. The five investigations have generated thousands of pages of paper and hundreds of tips, with new information coming in every day, and not a scrap of it is on computer. It would take a month just to transmit everything.'

'So take a month.'

She shook her head once, sending waves of black hair swinging over her shoulders. It was an intentional distraction, he thought. He shouldn't have told her he was superficial. 'We don't have that kind of time. This guy takes a woman every seven months, like clockwork. It's been six months since the last one.'

Magozzi thought about slamming his fist down on the table. It seemed like such an Italian thing to do, but he just couldn't see himself doing it. Apparently the gesticulation gene had passed him by on its hereditary journey. 'You want to tell me how the hell you managed to find a police department in this country that isn't computerized?'

Grace put her chin in her hand and looked at him. 'You have no idea how many of those are out there. This one is a four-man office, one of those is the chief, and even he does double duty on patrol.'

Damnit, he hated it when she had good answers for every question. 'Okay, then where are the State boys? The FBI? The Texas Rangers? Whoever the hell fills in down there when they've got a serial going?'

Grace made a face. 'The Feds and the State were in it big-time at the beginning, but technically, all the cases are still classified as missing persons, not homicides. No bodies, no crime scenes, not a lot of press interest after it came out that most of the victims weren't exactly model citizens. Most of them had a history – runaways, drug users, prostitutes – so they went down on the priority list real fast.'

Magozzi felt the first stab of hope. 'So if there are no bodies, what makes them so certain they have a series of homicides at all? Runaways run, after all. It's what they do. Maybe they're still all out there.'

Grace was getting impatient. 'That's exactly the stone wall the chief is running into. When these kinds of women disappear and no one finds a body right away, the State and the Feds back off because everybody's thinking, gee, they just probably went somewhere. But the chief believes he has a serial operating in his town, and he convinced us. The last victim wasn't a user, a prostitute, or a runaway, although the State boys wrote it off that way. She was eighteen years old, driving to a grocery less than two miles away to pick up some ice cream for her father. She was the chief's daughter, Magozzi. The man is looking for his kid, and no one will help him.'

And with that sentence, Magozzi felt himself lose the battle before it ever really began. Grace wasn't running toward a murderer; she was leaving on a crusade. He closed his eyes and sighed.

'This is the kind of case where the new software could really make a difference.'

Magozzi tried not to look miserable, because he had a vague idea that misery probably wasn't macho. It wasn't as if he hadn't known this day was coming. Grace and her three partners in computer wizardry had been knocking themselves out since last October, working on the new program, getting ready to take it on the road, and now that the news was out, Arizona was just the beginning. This thing was really going to snowball.

He'd seen the article in a couple of the recent issues of law enforcement magazines that hit just about every department in the country, and couldn't imagine a single cop who wouldn't jump all over it, especially since the service wouldn't cost them a dime.

The FLEE program was basically a computerized detective. It scanned in every single scrap of paper generated in a homicide case, saved it to memory, then examined itself for repetitions and similarities.

Nothing was lost; nothing was forgotten, and that nightmare happened all too often when a dozen cops were reading and trying to remember thousands of pages of data. The software constantly cross-referenced incoming information with countless databases, identifying in a matter of hours connections that might require weeks or months of a detective team's legwork.

Grace had explained the technical side to him once – he'd walked away with a monster headache. Magozzi could get around a keyboard pretty well, but what went on inside a hard drive made about as much sense to him as waving a wand over a kettleful of toads' eyes. Finally, she'd made it simple.

Look at it this way, Magozzi. Say you have a victim who wrote a check to some antique dealer up north a few months earlier. And say on that day a deliveryman with a record of minor assault drops a load at the antique store. The program will tell you that in minutes, and you can take a closer look at the man. Now a good detective with a lot of free time might make the same connection eventually . . .

And he might not, Magozzi had thought then. There wasn't enough manpower in the National Guard to do that kind of detailed legwork in a timely fashion.

Apparently he hadn't said anything in a long time, and apparently that was worrying Grace, because she was trying to mollify him with food. He looked down at the plate of chocolate-covered strawberries she'd set in front of him and thought what a dirty fighter she was. He'd sell out his mother for a chocolate-covered strawberry, and Grace knew that.

'Annie's been in Arizona for over a week now,' she told him, eliciting a small smile.

The mention of Annie Belinsky – one of Grace's partners, and certainly her best friend – did that to most men. Profoundly overweight and unbelievably sensual, a single glance from the woman was like attending an orgy.

'She's looking for a house for us to rent, setting things up with the chief.'

His smile vanished. 'You're renting a house? Just how long do you think this is going to take?'

Grace shrugged. 'We'll rent by the month.'

Magozzi closed his eyes and sighed.

'I have to go, Magozzi. I have to do *something*.'

'What about the work you're doing here? That program of yours has closed at least three Minneapolis homicides that have been open for years. You don't call that something? Three families who finally have some closure. Three murderers identified . . .'

'Magozzi.'

'What?'

'They were old cases.'

'I know that. And we got a million of them. Gino brought over another file just this morning . . .'

'Two of the murderers were dead, the third was in the vets' hospital drooling in front of cartoons.'

Magozzi scowled and reached for the bottle of

wine. Maybe if he got her drunk she'd stop making sense.

'Don't get me wrong. I'm glad we could help, and those cases were good tests for the software. Helped us work out the kinks. But there are people out there killing right now, and here we are, working your cold cases, sitting on a program that just might be able to save some lives.'

Magozzi looked her straight in the eye. 'I'm Italian. I'm absolutely immune to guilt. You, obviously, are not.'

'Meaning?'

'Meaning that this is your penance. You all still blame yourselves for the Monkeewrench murders.'

Grace winced. Monkeewrench had been the name of their software company, at least until it also became the media name for a killer, and a series of senseless murders that had nearly paralyzed Minneapolis last fall. They'd been trying to think of a new name ever since.

'Of course we blame ourselves,' she said quietly. 'How could we not? But whatever our motivation, this is a good thing, Magozzi, and you know it.' She held a strawberry up to his mouth and watched, mesmerized, as he took a bite. This was the most intimate, overtly sexual moment Magozzi had ever had with Grace, and it scattered his frustrations like a shotgun blast. God, he hated being so shallow.

She almost smiled again. 'So you will look in on Jackson?'

One more strawberry like that, and I'll adopt him, he thought, but what he said was, 'I can't believe you're going to abandon that poor, motherless child.'

'He has a very nice foster mother. He says she's growing on him, even if she is white.'

'That kid worships you, Grace. He's here every single day. You can't just run away from attachments like that . . .' And then he stopped talking, wondering if that wasn't also part of the reason she'd decided to take the software company on the road. Attachments were the most dangerous things of all, because someday they might lead to trust and maybe even love, and in Grace's brutal past, people you loved and trusted almost always tried to kill you.

'It won't be for a few days,' Grace tried to appease him without a strawberry. 'They finished the custom work on the RV today, but Harley and Roadrunner still have to install all the electronics.'

Magozzi drained his wineglass and reached for the bottle again. 'A few lousy days? Goddamnit, Grace, people give employers more notice than that. It's too soon. I could hurry up the seduction thing. I haven't even seen your ankles yet. Do you have ankles?'

Her eyes dropped to the tall English riding boots she'd worn every day of her life for over ten years, because back then there had been a man who slashed the Achilles tendons of his victims so they couldn't run away. 'I'll come back, Magozzi.'

'When?'

'When I can take off the boots.'

Harley Davidson lived less than half a mile from Grace, in the only neighborhood in the Twin Cities he deemed suitable for a man of his wealth and taste.

Nowhere was St Paul's reverence for the past more apparent than on prestigious Summit Avenue, a broad, tree-filled boulevard that rambled from the river bluffs to the edge of downtown.

At the turn of the century, timber, railroad, and milling barons had settled in this area, erecting vast, imposing mansions on the bluffs and up and down Summit, each newcomer trying to outdo those who had come before. A century later, many of the mansions were still intact and lovingly restored, either by descendants who hadn't squandered the family fortune, the Minnesota Historical Society, or the newly wealthy.

Harley was one such newly wealthy Summit Avenue homeowner, much to the dismay of some of his ultra-conservative neighbors. He often stomped the streets on pleasant evenings, an enormous, muscular man in leathers and motorcycle boots, his full black beard and ponytail bouncing with the weight of his steps. A frightening visage to residents, and that was before they got close enough to see the tattoos.

His house was a turreted, red sandstone monstrosity that was surrounded by a tall, wrought-iron fence with spikes large enough to skewer a bull elephant, but a step inside the massive front doors was like walking into a Bavarian castle from a Grimm brothers' fairy tale. Ten thousand square feet of imported crystal chandeliers, exquisite antique furniture as oversized as the man who owned it, and dark, hand-carved wood from a bygone era that gleamed like 'a Spanish whore's eyes,' as Harley put it, which explained a lot about why his neighbors took offense at his presence. He had a sound system that would knock your socks off piped through the entire mansion, which played non-stop hard rock or opera, depending on whether or not he was alone, because sometimes opera made Harley Davidson weep.

Last October, after the bloodbath at the Monkeewrench loft office, they'd moved the company to temporary quarters on Harley's third floor while they worked on FLEE. Up until the day Annie had taken off for Arizona last week, he'd had Grace, Annie, and Roadrunner in his house all day every day for almost six months, and now he was pushing to make the arrangement permanent. Even after everyone left in the evening, the scents and sounds of all of them seemed to linger in the big old house, making it feel as though a family lived there, and Harley liked the feeling.

Tonight he and Roadrunner were in the carriage house – a two-story marvel with a cobblestone floor and tongue-and-groove oak paneling that ran up the walls into the arches of the cathedral ceiling. There were crystal chandeliers in here, too, which Roadrunner found ridiculously excessive. Besides, he missed the horse stalls and second-floor grooms' apartments that had been in here when Harley bought the place.

Right now the enormous space that had once housed carriages, cutters, and the animals to pull them, was home to a very different kind of horsepower. The RV had been delivered today, custom work finally completed. It was a silver-skinned, tinted-glass behemoth, and it just looked wrong in this place.

'It looks like a bus.' Roadrunner was standing in front of the vehicle, spider arms akimbo, his eyes almost level with the vast expanse of the windshield, which was six and a half feet off the ground. He'd ridden his old ten-speed over from Minneapolis, just for the extra workout, and was wearing one of the Lycra biking suits he wore every single day – a black one tonight, because he was anticipating dirty work.

'It is not a bus. Do not call it a bus. Technically, it is a luxury motor coach, and her name is Chariot.'

Roadrunner rolled his eyes. 'Why do you have to name inanimate objects all the time? I hate that. Everything from your house to your dick.'

'My dick is not inanimate.'

'Sez you. If you're going to spend all your free time thinking up names, think up a new one for the company, why don't you.'

'I've been racking my brain over that one for six months. How do you rename Monkeewrench? It's like . . . sacrilege, or something.'

'Yeah, I know. Like renaming a ten-year-old kid.'

'Exactly.'

'But we have to do it.'

'I guess.'

None of them was happy about changing the company name. They'd been Monkeewrench for over ten years now, and the moniker had become part of their identities.

'Gecko,' Roadrunner said abruptly.

'Was that a sneeze?'

'Gecko. We should call it Gecko, Incorporated.'

Harley's mouth made a circle of disbelief in the black frame of his beard. 'Are you out of your friggin' mind? It's a goddamned lizard.'

Roadrunner shrugged. 'It continues the animal theme. I think it's good.'

Harley opened the big hydraulic door and stomped up the steps in disgust. 'Yeah, well if that's the direction you're going, then I think we should just name it after you and call it Dipshit.'

Roadrunner pouted up the stairs after him, but quickly forgot about his wounded pride the minute he stepped inside the plush interior and took a look around. Thick, buttery soft carpets covered the floor, overstuffed down sofas huddled around a gleaming wooden table like silk-covered marshmallows, the spacious kitchen had granite countertops and sparkling chrome fixtures, and there was polished teak everywhere.

Harley folded his arms across his massive chest, a size extra-large smile plastered across his face. 'So what do you think, little buddy? Looks more like Buckingham Palace than something with wheels, huh?'

Roadrunner's eyes were as wide as a kid's on Christmas morning. 'Wow, this is awesome. I really like all the wood.'

Harley shrugged modestly. 'I was sort of going for a yacht look without all the nautical crap. Come on, I'll show you the rest. We haven't gotten to the best part.'

Roadrunner followed him down the length of the RV, stopping briefly to marvel at a large bathroom complete with a full-sized shower and tub. At the far end of the rig was what Harley called the pièce de résistance – an enormous bedroom that had been stripped out and converted into an office. There were four computer workstations, a wall of equipment racks, and a mini-kitchen outfitted with a wine cooler and cigar humidor for Harley; a top-of-the-line, pro-model coffee/espresso maker for Roadrunner.

'This is where our mobile command center is going, my friend. We are going to kick some ass and bust some balls from right here. Bad guys all across the country are quaking in fear as we speak.'

Roadrunner finally managed to tear himself away from the coffeemaker. 'Man, Grace and Annie are going to freak when they see this thing. Where is Grace, anyhow? I thought for sure she'd be over here to check it out.'

'Couldn't make it tonight. She's at her love palace with the Italian Stallion.'

'You mean Magozzi?' Roadrunner asked skeptically.

'Yeah, who else?'

He thought about that for a minute. 'You think they're in love?'

Harley gaped at him in disbelief. 'You just get a news flash, genius? Where the hell have you been for the past six months? Of course they're in love.'

Roadrunner's lower lip curled down in that tragic, wounded expression he always got when he thought he'd been left out of something. 'I've never even seen them hold hands. I thought they were just friends.'

Harley rolled his eyes. 'Jesus Christ, this isn't think-tank material, Roadrunner. It doesn't take more than a heartbeat and one functioning brain cell to know there's something up the minute you see them together, getting all dopey and sloe-eyed on each other.'

'Oh, for God's sake. *That's* why you think they're in love? Honestly, Harley, you're such a hopeless romantic. You only see what you want to see. Magozzi gets all dopey and sloe-eyed. Grace always holds back, and if you had *two* functioning brain cells you would have seen that. I know Magozzi's in love with Grace, and I really feel sorry for the man, but

Grace just isn't ready to let herself go down that road. Maybe she never will be.'

Harley glowered at him. He didn't like what Roadrunner had said, so he decided not to believe him.

'Do not *ever* quash anyone's dreams of romance. Love is a mysterious and unpredictable force, and stranger things than Grace and Magozzi getting together have happened. Hell, who knows? One day a human female might actually find *you* attractive. The world is just full of surprises.'

9

'Puff! Here kitty, kitty, kitty!' There was a tremor in Rose's voice, and for good reason. It was dreadfully late and that useless beast was still sauntering around the yard, pretending to be deaf.

She'd always hated the dark, even as a little girl, and the fear had only grown worse with age. Now, some seventy-odd years later, it had morphed into an irrational, debilitating phobia that made no sense at all. She wasn't afraid of the mundane dangers that might befall an elderly woman living alone, things like burglars or murderers or rapists; or even of falling down and breaking her hip, all concerns her daughter voiced at every opportunity. It was the dark itself.

She took another tentative step out onto the back porch and caught a brief glimpse of white in the farthest corner of the tulip bed. Puff obviously assumed that all the hard work Rose had put into the gardens today was for his benefit – the world's largest litter box.

'Puff, come here!'

He responded with an irritated twitch of his tail, letting her know he'd come in when he was good and ready and not a minute before. His tiny kitty brain just didn't understand that once darkness swallowed the backyard, it wouldn't matter if he were being eaten alive by the neighborhood dogs before her very eyes – she still wouldn't be able to go out to save him.

God, she hated being like this, hated the tears of frustration that prickled behind her eyes. Why couldn't that damned cat just come *in*? . . .

'PUFF, COME *HERE*!'

And at last, Puff did. He trotted up to his mistress as if he'd just noticed her presence for the first time, tail flagging in a cheerful greeting. Rose scooped him up into her arms, cooing admonishments as giddy tears of relief splashed onto his fur. Once she retreated into the safety of her bright, cozy kitchen, her silly tears dried and she poured a dish of cream for him, a glass of sherry for herself.

The phone rang as she was settling into a sofa almost as old and lumpy as she was. It was her son-in-law – not the brightest fellow on the planet, and a lousy dentist, she'd always thought – but he was a good husband to her Lorrel, and Rose supposed a mother couldn't ask for much more.

'Hello, Richard. Yes, I'm fine. I suppose Lorrel is working late again? Of course I remember tomorrow night, I haven't lost my mind yet, Richard. Five o'clock. Kiss the girls for me and tell them I can't wait to see them. I baked cookies.'

Rose smiled as she hung up the phone, and was still smiling as she clicked on the TV, coaxed Puff onto her lap, and started to doze. Her granddaughters were home from college, and tomorrow night they would all go out for dinner.

Rose woke up much later, disoriented and aching from her arduous day of gardening. Puff had deserted her lap, but she could feel his fur tickling the back of her neck. He'd retreated to his favorite perch on the back of the couch, where he liked to sit and look out the window. She reached behind to pat him, but her hand froze in midair.

Puff was growling.

She groped for the remote and eventually found the mute button. 'What's wrong, kitty?' After a few moments of silence, she heard a faint rustling coming from behind her, outside in the bushes.

Juncos in the arborvitae, that's all it is, she told herself. At night the little birds sheltered in the soft evergreen, making fluttery noises as they hopped from branch to branch.

But this wasn't a fluttery noise, exactly. It sounded . . . bigger.

Someone is out there.

Rose felt it in those good senses people never pay attention to until it's too late: the little hairs standing up on the back of her neck, the goose bumps rising on the loose, checkered skin of her old arms, and when the low rumble of Puff's growl jumped in pitch, she knew . . .

. . . *Someone is out there, on the other side of the glass, looking in at me.*

She turned her head slowly, slowly, and then she saw a pair of eyes hanging there in the dark just outside the window, staring in at her.

There was a brief moment when her body reacted the way it was supposed to – when her heart leaped and started to hammer, when the blood rushed from her brain to her legs in an ancient preparation for flight, leaving her face cold and clammy. But it was over almost as soon as it began, and Rose simply turned her eyes back to the muted television screen and sat there quietly, waiting to wake up from this very bad dream.

It isn't a dream.

The rustling stopped and a few minutes later, when she'd finally summoned the courage to turn around again, there was nobody at her window.

She didn't breathe until her lungs screamed for air, and by then, she was feeling a little silly, because it probably *had* been just a dream. The mind always played tricks on you in that twilight netherworld between sleep and wakefulness; especially old minds.

And then the front door rattled in its frame and Rose started shaking so badly, she feared her old bones might shatter like glass.

Call the police.

She reached for the phone on the table beside her, but her hand wasn't working the way it was supposed to, no, not at all, and there was nothing she could do but watch helplessly as the useless appendage spasmed and flailed and twitched and knocked the phone to the floor.

The noise at the front door finally stopped, but the silence was much worse, because she was terribly afraid that she might have forgotten to lock the back door, and even more afraid to get up and look.

She sat frozen on the sofa, a pathetic old woman deluding herself into believing that if she remained perfectly still, if she didn't breathe, whatever was coming would simply pass her by. In the next instant, she heard the back screen door open, then close with a click, and still, she couldn't move.

The heavy inside door closed, sucking a little air from the room.

Rose never turned to look at him, so he walked into her line of sight and waited for her eyes to rise to his. When they did, he pulled a large handgun from his jacket pocket and pointed it at her.

Oh, God. It wasn't going to pass her by; this time it was going to kill her.

In that dreadful moment of realization, she became young and strong and fearless again, and she vaulted upward at the precise moment the bullet left the muzzle, ruining his killing shot. Fire tore into her stomach instead of her heart and Rose looked down to see a blossom of red spreading across the front of her little-old-lady dress.

'Goddamnit,' he said, and shot her again.

10

Chief Malcherson was one of those tall, well-built Swedes with thick white hair, lake-ice eyes that made him look mean, and a hangdog face that made him look mournful. Sort of like a homicidal basset hound. He was wearing pinstripes this morning – for him, a daring foray into edgy fashion.

'I like the suit,' Gino pronounced, flopping into a chair next to Magozzi. Magozzi shot him a warning look, but Gino was oblivious. 'It's real zippy. Kind of a mob look.'

Malcherson froze in the middle of taking off his suit jacket and closed his eyes. 'Not exactly the kind of image I was hoping to project, Rolseth.'

'I meant it in a good way.'

'That's the frightening part.' Malcherson settled behind his desk and tapped one manicured finger on a stack of two bright red file folders. He always kept his copies of open homicides in red folders, probably because this ultra-conservative man found the color almost as offensive as the crime. Magozzi hadn't seen one on his boss's desk in over four months. 'The media would like to know why our senior citizens are being tortured and murdered.'

Magozzi's brows shot up. 'Someone actually said that?'

'An intern from Channel Ten.' Malcherson waved a pink phone message slip.

Gino snorted. 'That is such bullshit. This is what happens when you do your job and you don't have a homicide for a while. The minute two guys get offed in one night some idiot in the media tries to scare the hell out of the city by talking spree, or serial killer, or some such Hollywood crap. Besides, only one of them was tortured, and it wasn't ours. Morey Gilbert was dead before he hit the ground, and he didn't have a mark on him except for that one little bullet hole.'

'So there's no reason at all to suspect a connection between the two murders.'

Magozzi shrugged. 'If there is one, we can't see it yet. They were both old, they lived in the same neighborhood. That's about it. Arlen Fischer's name didn't ring any bells with the Gilbert family or employees; neither did his description, and I'm guessing they'd remember a three-hundred-pound ninety-year-old man.'

'Good. We can quash the serial rumor, then. We're going to get enough pressure on the Gilbert murder the way it is. The desk logged over three hundred calls last night and this morning.'

Magozzi raised his brows. The number was unreal. Twenty calls on a case were enough to make the brass nervous; three hundred could break careers. 'On Gilbert, or the train track guy?'

'The "train track guy" has a name,' Malcherson admonished him. 'Arlen Fischer. Most of the calls on that case were from the media, and the stack is pretty slim compared to Gilbert's, which is amazing when you consider the horrendous nature of Fischer's murder. So what I'd like to know, gentlemen, is who on earth was this man?'

Gino shook his finger at the ceiling. 'That's exactly what I asked when I saw all those people outside the nursery yesterday. Of course, I said it a little more colorfully.'

'I'm sure. I saw a flash of that crowd on the news last night. Just a flash – there didn't seem to be a lot of media interest, until they did a little research on the man. Now Channel Three is putting together a documentary, and you know what they're going to call it? *Saint Gilbert of Uptown.*'

Gino chuckled. 'Oh, that's rich. McLaren told us Morey Gilbert was putting the screws to him once about why Jews couldn't be saints, and now here you go; they finally slap the label on the very Jew asking the question, and he's not around to enjoy it.'

'I'm quite certain the designation is secular, absolutely not Catholic, but real or imagined, the Minneapolis Police Department should not allow saints to be murdered. That was the gist of most of the calls. Frankly, I found it a little embarrassing that I knew nothing about a man who had done so much for others, especially when he was the father-in-law of one of our own.'

Gino slid down in his chair and laced his hands across his stomach. 'Yeah, well, Marty Pullman was never much of a talker. Kept his family life close to the vest. But from what we've heard so far, Morey Gilbert was a one-man charity. Helped more people than you can shake a stick at, and if that's not saint-like, I don't know what is. Trouble is, that doesn't make him a real likely candidate for murder.'

Malcherson turned his eyes on Gino. 'I read your Q & A with Detective Pullman. How was he?'

'He looked like hell, if that's what you mean. I didn't put it in the report, but he pretty much fessed up to being on a toot since the day he walked out of here last year. Couldn't even remember where he was the night his father-in-law was killed. Said he woke up on the kitchen floor holding an empty bottle, and that's all he knows.'

'You didn't seriously suspect him.'

'Marty? Jeez, no. But I had to ask. We gotta look at the family, and he knows that. Funny thing is, his brother-in-law? Jack Gilbert? First off, he hasn't been on speaking terms with his folks for who knows how long – seems he married a Lutheran instead of a nice Jewish girl, which I'm guessing didn't go over too well – so that's interesting. And the night his dad bought it he was running the same deal as Marty, only in a better part of town. Got himself looped up at the Wayzata Country Club, woke up in his driveway next morning, and the people at the club say it's almost an every-night thing. It's like that whole damn family fell to pieces when Hannah got killed.'

Chief Malcherson looked down at his hands, and for a moment, no one said anything.

Even after a year, the mention of Hannah Pullman's murder still had the power to stop any conversation in this building. Random violence was not unknown in Minneapolis, particularly in those few neighborhoods where gangs clung to a tenuous foothold and innocent bystanders were occasionally caught in the crossfire – but it was a rare thing, and always set the city on its ear. But the murder of an officer's spouse had multipled the shock value a thousandfold, and everyone on the force had been deeply affected.

Sometimes cops were killed; that went with the job; but that risk was absolutely not supposed to extend to their families. The murder of Detective Martin Pullman's wife had been a gut-wrenching wake-up call for every one of them, because Marty had been carrying, standing right next to Hannah when her throat had been cut, and still, he hadn't been able to protect her. It made them all think of their families as a little more vulnerable, made them all feel a little more helpless, and the sad truth was, a lot of them resented Marty for that.

Why didn't he shoot the bastard when he had the chance?

Magozzi had heard that question around City Hall a hundred times in the months afterwards, and it always made him feel bad, especially when Gino said it.

‘Did either of you know Hannah?’ Chief Malcherson was asking.

Magozzi shook his head. ‘Just to say “hi” to in the hall. She used to pick Marty up sometimes.’

‘I can’t stop thinking about Mrs Gilbert. Her daughter, and then her husband, both murdered within the space of a year. I don’t know how you survive something like that.’

‘Well, don’t get all touchy-feely about the old lady just yet,’ Gino said. ‘She didn’t have an alibi either.’

‘Gino didn’t care much for Mrs Gilbert,’ Magozzi explained.

‘What I didn’t care for was that she trashed a crime scene, she didn’t seem all that broken up that her husband was dead, and she’s got this *attitude*.’

Malcherson frowned at him. ‘What kind of an attitude?’

‘Pretty hostile, if you ask me. We’re just doing our job, trying to find out who killed her husband, so I ask her a couple of questions and she’s all over me.’

Malcherson slid a weary gaze over to Magozzi for a translation.

‘Gino asked if Mr Gilbert had had any “unusual business dealings,” and she took offense.’

‘Oh.’

‘She actually snapped at him.’

‘Ah.’ Malcherson looked back at Gino, and for one fearful moment, Magozzi was afraid the chief might actually smile. ‘In summary, then, you questioned her late husband’s integrity, and her response was less gracious than you thought you deserved.'

Gino started to blush, and his head seemed to be sinking into his neck. 'You kind of had to be there.'

'I'm very sorry she hurt your feelings, Detective Rolseth.'

Magozzi wiped his hand across a smile, and Gino saw it.

'Aw, come on, Leo, it was a whole lot more than that and you know it. There's something going on with that old lady. Forget that she didn't shed a tear and she's got a mouth like a whip. Did she fall to pieces when she found her husband dead? No. She gets him into a wheelbarrow – a *wheelbarrow*, for God's sake – pushes him around, flops him on a plant table, then washes him with a garden hose and dresses him up for company. This is not your average grieving widow, and if we get caught up in that scenario, we close our eyes to the possibility that she might also be a killer who did her damnedest to destroy evidence.'

Malcherson leaned back in his chair and sighed. 'You interviewed her, Detective Magozzi, and you listed her as a nonsuspect in your report.'

'I'll stand by that, at least for now,' he said, but he was frowning, thinking about Gino's image of events – Lily Gilbert dragging her husband around like a sack of grain – and his own picture of a distraught, elderly woman struggling to get her husband out of the rain, to make him 'presentable.' Either one worked; he just wasn't a hundred percent sure which one was accurate, and in the long run, it might make a whole lot of difference. 'But like Gino said, I agree that there's something there. She's a tough lady, and she's pretty closed off. Could be she knows more than she wants to let on. Could be she's protecting someone. I just don't know yet.'

Gino brightened immediately. 'Hey, I like that. Maybe she's covering up for that sleazebag son of hers. Sure, she hates his guts, but she's got that maternal thing going. So picture this. Jack Gilbert at the club, sucking up scotch like a Wet-Vac. Pretty soon he starts ruminating about his life and the appalling state of his familial ties, and he gets a little maudlin. The old man isn't getting any younger, and Jack's thinking maybe it's finally time to patch things up. So when he gets kicked out at bar time, he decides to pay him a visit and bury the hatchet once and for all. But things don't go so well, and next thing he knows, his father is dead and he's holding a smoking gun.'

Malcherson raised one white brow. He was used to Gino's off-the-cuff theories. 'I don't suppose you found any actual evidence that led to that postulation.'

'Not a scrap,' Gino said happily. 'Just came up with it this minute.'

'Does Jack Gilbert have a history?'

Gino shook his head. 'Nah. Just a couple DUIs and some speeding tickets. No gun registered in his name or his wife's name. But that doesn't mean anything. And he's a PI attorney,' he added, apropos of nothing.

'So give me a quick summary of the time line.'

Magozzi shuffled through his dog-eared mess of frayed spiral notebook paper. 'Same routine as always, according to Mrs Gilbert – she went to bed right after the news, and Morey stayed up to do some paperwork and a few extra chores in the greenhouse. She said he usually turned in around midnight, but she can't confirm that on the night of his death.'

Malcherson frowned his question.

'They had separate bedrooms, sir. She said she slept straight through the night and woke up at six-thirty A.M. as usual. Found him outside the greenhouse shortly after that. But the ME estimates time of death to be between two and four A.M.'

Malcherson's brows shot up. 'A little late for an elderly man to be outside gardening.'

Magozzi nodded. 'That's what we thought, sir. Either something kept Morey Gilbert up and outside past his bedtime, or something brought him out there later.'

'Or someone, like maybe his son,' Gino pushed his latest pet theory. 'Or if you don't like the son, how about the wife? I could go either way.'

Malcherson gave him one of those long-suffering looks you see on the faces of parents confronting a problem child for the hundreth time. 'Your empathy for grieving relatives gives me hope for mankind, Detective Rolseth.'

'The thing is I'm not seeing a lot of grieving from that quarter, Chief. You give me grieving, I'll give you empathy.'

'What it boils down to,' Magozzi interjected, 'is that we have to find out a whole lot more about Morey Gilbert, see if anything points us in a different direction. Seems unlikely at this point that he made a lot of enemies, but obviously he made one, and no one we've talked to so far will even admit that's possible – including Langer and McLaren, who got to know him pretty well when they were investigating Hannah's murder. He had some close friends – the funeral director, for one – and we'll talk to him again.'

The red light on Malcherson's desk phone started flashing.

'Probably another reporter,' Gino said. 'Want me to take it?'

Malcherson almost smiled. 'Excuse me for a moment, gentlemen. Don't go anywhere.'

He picked up, listened for a few moments, then took a pristine legal tablet from his center desk drawer and laid it carefully on his leather blotter. He seemed to have an inexhaustible supply of these brand-new tablets – Magozzi had never seen him use one that looked even remotely used, and he often wondered if the chief had a closetful of tablets he'd discarded because they were missing the first sheet.

He and Gino watched with growing apprehension as Malcherson scribbled away with his Montblanc.

Benign phone calls did not require copious note taking.

'This is not good news,' Malcherson said when he finally hung up. 'Officer Viegs just called in, responding to an elderly woman found shot to death in her home this morning.' He ripped off the sheet of paper and handed it to Magozzi.

'Same neighborhood?' Gino asked.

'Good guess, Detective Rolseth.' Malcherson looked down at his tablet – the second page was marred with pen impressions, sullied by the details of a murder. One more for the closet.

11

Magozzi and Gino pulled up in front of a tidy little rambler with gleaming white shutters and a cheery, robin's-egg blue paint job that made Magozzi instantly sad. Houses like this weren't supposed to have ugly yellow crime-scene tape clashing with the color scheme.

The yard did nothing to alleviate his melancholy. It was filled with meticulously prepared flower beds that would probably be weed choked and forgotten within the week, and the sort of kitschy lawn ornaments only a grandmother could get away with. There were birdbaths encrusted with playing marbles, resin frogs with foggy, rhinestone eyes, and smiling troll statues that wore brocade coats of colorful, broken glass. One of the trolls held a painted plaque that read GRANDMA'S GARDEN.

Gino stared at that troll for a long time, then finally turned away.

Officer Viegs was waiting in the sun near the front door, little droplets of sweat sparkling between his hair plugs.

'Viegs, you show up at any more murder scenes, we're going to have to put you on the suspect list,' Magozzi said.

'Detective, you get any more murders like this on my beat, I'm going to be taking some time off to move my mom someplace safe, like the Bronx. She lives in the senior condos just off Lake, and she and her neighbors were ready to pack up after the two yesterday. This one is going to send them over the edge, and I can't say I blame them.'

'I hear you. But for what it's worth, nothing we've got so far pulls those two together.'

Viegs raised his brows, and all his hair plugs moved. 'Except that now we've got three, they were all old, they all lived in this neighborhood, and they were all shot.'

'Yeah. There is that. What do you have for us?'

Viegs sighed and pulled out his notebook. 'Rose Kleber, with a *K*. Seventy-eight, widow, lived alone. Two shots, one to the stomach, one to the chest, no obvious signs of burglary or sexual assault. Her two granddaughters were home from college on spring break, came over to surprise her this morning, found the back door open and their grandmother dead inside. They called nine-one-one, then their mom.' He paused and took a breath. 'They were all pretty messed up, so I had Berman drive them home after we got their statements. Nothing much there, though. I mean, she was an old lady. She gardened, she went to the senior center, she baked cookies, for chrissake . . . well, shit. Sure took them long enough.'

Gino followed his gaze to see the Channel Ten

van pulling up to the curb. 'A fuel tanker rolled on 494 about an hour ago. Every reporter in town was standing around with the cameras running, waiting for the damn thing to blow up. Guess it didn't. Put up a wall and play dumb, will you, Viegs?'

'Sure. You might want to go in the back door. Jimmy's crew is working the front room.'

Just inside the back door, Magozzi and Gino ran into Jimmy Grimm, whose expression was as solemn as they'd ever seen it.

'Hey, guys. Long time, no see.'

Magozzi clapped him on the back. 'And we liked it that way.'

Gino brightened a little, grateful for the distraction. 'Hey, Jimmy. I thought you were going to retire.'

'Yeah, right. You obviously haven't looked at your pension fund lately.'

Magozzi nodded toward the fistful of evidence bags he was clutching. 'Got anything for us?'

His shoulders seemed to slump under the weight of a question with no good answer. 'Not much. No brass. Some dirt, probably from the gardens here, plenty of cat hair, and one 9-mm slug we found drilled into the couch cushion. That was a through-and-through; the other one's probably still inside the victim. Looks like she took it in the stomach first. But how the hell you could miss a kill shot at close range is beyond me.'

'Maybe he planned it that way.'

Jimmy shook his head. 'Then the bastard is a real sadist.'

'Viegs said there was no forced entry, no robbery.'

Jimmy shook his head. 'Doesn't look like it. Her purse was out in plain view with a wad of cash in it, and we've got no jimmy marks anywhere. She either let him in, or the door was open and he let himself in.'

'Or maybe he had a key, or knew where she kept a key,' Gino added, making a note to check on repairmen, lawn service, anybody who might have had access.

Jimmy nodded. 'Could be. By the way, the TV was on when we got here, but I turned it off after we dusted.' He shrugged apologetically. 'Jerry Springer was on, and there was something obscene about listening to him while we were working this scene. Anyhow, I just turned her over to Anant, if you want to take a look before he moves her. I think he's waiting for you.'

'Thanks, Jimmy. Be in touch.'

He tried for a smile, but it never quite made it to his lips.

As they walked through the kitchen, Magozzi noticed a plate of homemade cookies sitting on the counter, carefully wrapped in plastic, violated by a dusty layer of black fingerprint powder.

Dr Anantanand Rambachan was standing quietly, almost prayerfully, over Rose Kleber's crumpled body. She was slumped facedown on the floor in a large circle of rusty brown, close to a blood-splattered telephone. Even Anant seemed utterly bewildered by what he saw, which made Magozzi's heart sink, because if there was a person alive who could make sense of the nonsensical, it was Dr Rambachan. If he was having trouble with this, there wasn't any hope for the rest of them.

He looked up and gave them a sad, gentle nod. 'Detectives Magozzi and Rolseth. I am delighted to see you both again despite the circumstances.'

'You're always saying that, Doc,' Gino said kindly. 'I think we all need to go out for a beer sometime, break the cycle, you know?'

'Indeed, Detective Rolseth, I do know.'

'Good to see you too, Dr Rambachan,' Magozzi said.

He reciprocated with a broad, white smile that did wonders to improve everyone's mood. 'Detective, you have obviously been practicing your Hindi, because I am hearing marked improvement in your accent since last we met.'

'Yeah, well, those night classes really help.'

Dr Rambachan cocked a brow at him, then smiled again. 'I think you are joking. Very good.'

And then he was all business, slipping on a pair of latex gloves and crouching next to the body. 'I'm going to turn this dear lady over now, and I must warn you, it might be difficult to look at. She has been dead for some time, and I'm sure you know that blood pools where gravity takes it . . .' – he searched their faces, and added – 'and uncirculated blood eventually turns black.'

They knew it, and Anant *knew* they knew it, but even with the warning, Gino recoiled when he saw Rose Kleber's splotchy, blackened face.

They watched and waited for about a thousand years while Dr Rambachan did the on-site, punctuating the silence with an occasional observation, but there was nothing particularly strange about any of it, except for the fact that someone had gunned down an elderly woman in cold blood, in her own home, while she was watching TV.

Gino, who'd never quite achieved Anant's or even Magozzi's level of comfort with corpses, started to fidget. 'Where's the cat?' he finally asked. 'Jimmy said he got a lot of cat hair. That must mean there's a cat somewhere.'

Dr Rambachan looked up. 'I have not seen a cat.'

'Wonder if the family took it home? What if they forgot?'

Magozzi gave him a wry glance. 'Gee Gino, I don't know. It'll probably starve to death. Better go look for it.'

'That's just what I was thinking . . .'

'This is curious,' Dr Rambachan mumbled, stopping Gino in his tracks just as he was about to make his escape.

The doctor pushed back onto his heels and pointed to the inside of Rose Kleber's arm. 'Take a look, gentlemen.'

Gino and Magozzi both got closer than either of them wanted to, squinting as they tried to make out the details of a marking that was nearly obliterated by discoloration.

'It would appear that this lady was also in a concentration camp, just as Mr Morey Gilbert was.'

'Damn,' Gino said, shaking his head. 'I don't like this. I don't like this one bit.'

'Detectives?' One of the crime-scene techs stepped in from the kitchen. 'Might be just a coincidence, but I thought you'd want to know.' He held up a small address book with a faded floral cover. 'She's got Morey Gilbert's phone number in here.'

12

Jack Gilbert was sitting in a lawn chair in the middle of the nursery parking lot, a cooler full of beer at his feet. Some customers actually took him up on his offer of free Bud, but most gave the man in the pink sunglasses and neon yellow shorts a wide berth.

Marty stormed over for the third time in the past two hours, but now he was dragging a heavy-duty garden hose behind him, brandishing the power-wash attachment like a gun. 'Come on, Jack. Get up. Time to relocate.'

'Don't aim that thing, 'less you mean to use it,' Jack drawled with a lopsided grin.

'Don't tempt me. Jesus, what the hell is the matter with you? You're scaring the customers.'

Jack peered up at him from behind pink lenses. 'I'm not scaring anybody. In fact, I'm probably boosting sales by ten percent. I'm telling you, you get somebody buzzed and they buy twice as much. See that fat guy over there, the one with the sweat stains down his back? He came to buy a few basil plants, but after a couple brewskies, I convinced the son of a bitch to buy a whole flat so he could make pesto. Best part is, I don't think he knows what pesto is.'

'Just what are you doing here, Jack?'

'Well, gee, Marty, I don't know. I always thought relatives were supposed to get together and support each other when they were grieving, but now that I think of it, that was pretty dumb since it sure as hell didn't work that way the last time somebody in this family got murdered.'

Martin felt as if he'd taken a hammer to the gut. Every sober moment of every single day he saw his wife bleeding to death in his arms; but seeing it and talking about it were two different things.

Jack eyed his expression with bleary interest. 'Christ, Marty, what do you think? That if we never mention Hannah was murdered she'll be less dead?'

'Shut up, Jack.'

'Oh-h, I get it.' Jack was gesturing with his can, sloshing beer all over the place. 'Hannah's another one of those things this family never talks about, because if you don't talk about it, it never happened, right? Well fuck that. Fuck all of you, because Hannah happened. Hannah was here, and it's too goddamned bad you all want to forget about her, because she was the only Gilbert worth a shit.' He pushed his silly pink sunglasses down his nose and glared defiantly up at Marty. 'And you're not the only one who misses her.'

And that was the one thing about Jack you had to remember, Marty thought. He was loud, obnoxious, in-your-face, and possibly the most irritating human being on the planet – but he loved unconditionally, even though few ever loved him back – and Hannah he had loved most of all.

Marty let out a long-suffering sigh. 'Where's Becky?'

'Becky, my wife? You mean the one no one in this family has ever met? Well, I think she's getting Botox injections in her armpits today. Keeps you from sweating, did you know that?'

'You know what I mean. Why isn't she here with you?'

'You mean like, loving wife supporting grieving husband, that sort of thing? Well, first of all we're not talking, which precludes her being supportive in any way; and second of all, Lily would probably shoot her if she ever set foot on the property; and third of all, frankly, Becky just doesn't give a shit.'

'Oh. Sorry, Jack. I didn't know it wasn't working out.'

'Hell, don't be sorry, Marty. I got exactly what I wanted from this marriage. So did Becky, for that matter. You should see her new boobs.' He popped open a new beer and drained half the can.

'You sure you should be doing that, Jack? I thought you were supposed to be in court this afternoon.'

He shrugged. 'No big deal. It's just this stupid bicycle messenger who claims he got whiplash when a UPS truck hit him. Weasel-faced bastard. He sees deep pockets, and suddenly he broke his fucking neck.'

'So you're blowing off court? Jesus, Jack, you're going to get yourself disbarred.'

'They're not going to disbar me. They can't. I'm on grief leave. My father was *murdered,* for chrissake . . . man, that is just too bizarre, isn't it? I mean, the guy was almost eighty-five and I kind of expected him to keel over one of these days, but Jesus. Shot in the head? Who could see that coming? So what do you think, Marty? Got any ideas, any clues? Anything we can work with here?'

'Just let the cops handle it, Jack.'

'Well, hell, Marty, you are a cop.'

'Ex-cop.'

'Don't give me that. Once a cop, always a cop. It's in the blood, or something. I'll bet that little gumshoe brain of yours is going about a hundred miles an hour trying to figure this out. So who do you think did it?'

'I haven't really thought about it.'

'That is such bullshit.'

'No, it's not, Jack. I haven't thought about it.'

Jack tried focusing on him for a long moment. 'What the hell's the matter with you? He was your father-in-law, for chrissake. Aren't you at least curious?'

Marty took three seconds to examine whatever feelings he had left, and decided no, he wasn't curious at all. 'It's not my job, Jack.'

'Right you are, Marty. It's not your job. It's just your goddamned family, is all.' He turned away, disgusted. 'Christ. You're even more fucked-up than I am.'

'You want to ease up on the language a little, Jack? There are nice people here.'

Jack snorted. 'You want to ease up on the holier-than-thou shit a little, Marty? There are smart people here, and they can see right through it . . . hey, you!' He waved his beer can at a woman examining flowers at one of the outdoor tables. 'Yeah, you in the tent dress! You want to stop fondling those pansies? And then come on over here, meet the biggest fuckstick on the planet.'

The woman gaped at him for a minute, then turned and hurried toward her car.

'Okay, Jack, that's it. You've got to get out of here.'

'Fuck you, Marty.'

'Goddamnit, Jack, Lily is ready to call the cops if you don't get out of the parking lot. One last time, I'm asking nice.'

Jack finished his beer and crushed the can against his leg. 'Listen, you tell Lily if she wants her son out of the parking lot, she can come out here and ask me herself. Otherwise, I'm staying right where I am until the beer's gone.'

For all of his life, Marty Pullman had been a man who got things done, who saw things wrong, and made them right. That Marty Pullman would have grabbed Jack and jerked him out of the chair and carried him away bodily, if necessary. It made him feel a little strange to realize he wasn't that man anymore, and probably never would be again. 'You're making this a lot harder than it has to be, Jack.'

Jack regarded him for a moment, then smiled. 'Gee, really? And I always thought things like this were supposed to be a little hard, and all I'm doing is having myself a little wake, Marty. A little private wake for Morey Gilbert, the nicest goddamned man in the world, the man everybody loved, the man who loved everybody, except his son, of course. And isn't it funny? I'm the only one who showed up. I mean, really, Marty, look at what's happening here. This place shouldn't even be open today, but here you all are, business as usual, life goes on, gee, think we can take out five minutes tomorrow to get him in the ground?'

Marty threw the hose down in disgust, grabbed a can from the cooler and stalked back toward the greenhouse. 'I give up.'

Jack laughed, and then hollered after him, 'So what else is new?'

13

For the first five minutes after they left the crime scene at Rose Kleber's little blue house, Gino sat in the passenger seat like a normal person – out of respect for the dead, Magozzi supposed – but once they hit the parkway, he cranked down the window and somehow manuevered himself so that most of his upper torso was hanging out of the car. It looked uncomfortable, but his eyes were closed and he was smiling.

'You look like a golden retriever,' Magozzi said.

Gino took several gulps of fresh air. 'Another hundred miles and I just might be able to get that smell out of my nose.' He slumped back into his seat, suddenly depressed. 'Shit. Now I feel bad. It's not fair, you know? You die and it's sad, and then to top it all off, you end up smelling so bad, people can't even stay in the same room with you. Dead people should smell good so you can stand around and look at them and feel really rotten about what happened.'

'I'm going to stand around and look at you and feel really rotten no matter how bad you smell, Gino.'

'And I appreciate that.'

Magozzi turned into the nursery drive and nosed past the hedge into a jammed parking lot.

'Well, would you look at this,' Gino said. 'The bereaved widow is open for business. Hey, is that clown in the lawn chair Jack Gilbert?'

'Looks like it.'

'Also looks like he's getting seriously soused. This is going to be a lot of fun.'

Jack seemed genuinely happy to see them. 'Detectives! I just tried calling you. Did you get him? Did you get the guy who killed my father?'

'We're still working on it, Mr Gilbert,' Magozzi said. 'We have a couple more questions for you and your family.'

'No problem.' Jack wiped the foam off his upper lip and tried to look sober. 'Anything you want. Anything I can do. Ask away.'

'Who's Rose Kleber?' Gino asked abruptly, watching carefully for a change in Jack's expression, disappointed when he didn't see one.

'Jeez, I don't know. Why? Is she a suspect?'

'Not exactly. She lives in the neighborhood. We were wondering if she was a friend of your father.'

'Beats me. Probably was, if she lives in the neighborhood. He knew just about everybody.' He frowned hard and tried to steady his gaze on Magozzi's face. 'So who is she, guys? What's she got to do with all this?'

'She was murdered last night,' Magozzi said.

Jack blinked, trying to process the information as it seeped through alcohol-soaked brain cells. 'Jesus, that's awful. Shit, they're dropping like flies around here, aren't they? So what are you thinking? Is there a connection? You think the same guy did both of them?'

'She had your dad's number in her phone book,' Gino said. 'It's just one of the things we have to check out.'

'Shit.' Jack sagged back down into the lawn chair. 'Half the people in the city have Dad's number. He used to pass out cards at the soup kitchen, for chrissakes. The man was totally out there.'

'Then again, for all you know, she could have been someone your dad saw every day, right?' Gino asked casually. 'Seeing as how you haven't been around here much lately.'

Jack tipped his head thoughtfully to one side, and for a moment Magozzi feared it would fall off his neck. 'Yep. You're right about that. Did I tell you I've been persona non grata here for a year or so?'

Magozzi nodded. 'You did. Yesterday. I thought that was kind of a shame. Hate to see rifts like that in a family. It must make this especially hard for you, losing your dad before you had a chance to patch things up.'

'Nah. There wasn't a chance in hell we were going to fix that.'

'Really.'

'I mean, it wasn't like I didn't take out the garbage or something, you know? Never could be what Pop wanted me to be, and like I told you yesterday, to top it off I married a Lutheran. That went over like a pork chop at a Seder dinner.'

Gino nodded sympathetically. 'Sounds like he was a little hard on you, Jack, and I know just where you're coming from. I could never please my father, either.'

Magozzi maintained a poker face. Gino's father thought his only son walked on water.

'No matter what I did,' Gino continued, 'no matter how hard I tried, it was just never enough for that man. Used to really piss me off.'

Jack raised his eyes in drunken disbelief. 'Jesus, Detective, I'm an attorney. Give me a little credit. Did you actually expect me to fall for that load of sympathetic bonding crap?'

Gino shrugged. 'Had to give it a shot.'

'Well for what it's worth, I didn't kill my father, okay?' He collapsed back onto the lawn chair and closed his eyes. 'Shit. You guys might want to step back a little. I think I might actually hurl.'

'So who was she, this Rose Kleber?' Lily was standing at the front window of the greenhouse with her arms folded, staring out at Jack, cluttering the parking lot with his lawn chair and cooler, lying there like a stunned carp.

'She lived over on Ferndale, Mrs Gilbert,' Magozzi answered, 'and a couple of things caught our attention. She was in the camps for one thing, just like Mr Gilbert.' He saw Lily's eyes close briefly. 'And she had his name and number in her phone book.'

Marty was at the counter, rubbing at an old stain with his thumb. 'Sounds pretty thin, guys.'

'It is. Just something we're checking out.'

Marty nodded absently, and Magozzi had the feeling he was barely interested, barely present.

Lily took a breath and turned away from the window. 'People buy plants, Morey gives them a card, tells them to call if they have trouble with them. Do you have a picture? Maybe she was a customer.'

'Not yet. We'll get one to you as soon as we can. In the meantime, you don't recall hearing the name?'

She shook her head. 'Morey was the one who was good with names. Never forgot a name. Never forgot a face. Such a big deal people made over that, like he was giving them a present.'

Magozzi tucked away his notebook. 'Do you have a customer list? A Rolodex, maybe?'

'In the office in the back of the potting shed. But mostly it's numbers I wrote down. Morey never needed to. He heard a number, he remembered it forever.'

'Maybe we could take a look anyway, if it isn't too much trouble.'

Back by the potting shed, they ran into the two employees Magozzi had talked to yesterday when they showed up at the impromptu memorial outside the nursery. They were tossing fifty-pound bags of fertilizer onto a wheeled pallet with a careless ease that made Magozzi long for his youth, but they straightened respectfully when Lily approached. They gave her shy, almost identical smiles, then turned to Magozzi and Gino.

'Good morning, Detectives,' they piped in unison, wiping their hands on their jeans, then holding them out.

Gino looked positively flummoxed by the apparition of two well-mannered young men greeting their elders with almost old-world politeness. 'Hey, yo,' was about the nicest thing anybody under twenty had ever said to him.

'Jeff Montgomery, right?' Magozzi shook the hand of the tall blond kid first, then the shorter, darker one. 'And Tim . . . ?'

'Matson, sir.'

'Either of you remember a woman named Rose Kleber shopping here at the nursery?' Gino asked.

The boys thought about it for a moment, then shrugged. 'We help out a lot of customers, but we don't always get their names, you know?' Jeff Montgomery said. 'What does she look like?'

Magozzi cringed inwardly, remembering the mottled face, the blood-stained dress. 'Elderly, a little heavy, gray hair . . .' he looked at their blank faces and realized this was hopeless. Teenaged boys remembered teenaged girls, and that was about it.

'Actually, that sounds like a lot of the people who come here, sir,' Tim Matson said. 'Maybe she's on the mailing list. Mr Gilbert sent out sale flyers every now and then. Did you check the computer?'

'You know how to run that thing, Timothy?' Lily asked impatiently.

'Sure. It's just a computer.'

'Good. Come with us. Jeffrey, we're almost out of basil on the herb table. Take care of that, would you?'

'Yes, ma'am.' Jeff disappeared in a flash while Lily led the way through the potting shed into a tiny back office.

There was a fine layer of black dust over everything – soil from the adjacent potting shed, Magozzi assumed. It covered a bookcase jammed with catalogs, a paper-cluttered desk, and the old computer and printer that sat on it. Grace MacBride would have had a fit.

'Can't be good for this thing,' Gino tapped a finger on the top of the computer. 'Having it right next to the potting shed like this.'

Tim took a seat in the only chair and booted up the computer. 'It's an old one, sir. They aren't as sensitive as the new ones. Better hardware, if you ask me. And Mr Gilbert didn't use it for much. Just the invoices once a month, and the mailing list.'

'*Hmph.*' Lily folded her arms across her chest in disapproval. 'That's what you think. He played games on this stupid machine. You can hear that beep-beep-beep thing all the way from the front greenhouse, so I come back and take a look one day, and there he is, a grown man shooting down little cartoon spaceships.'

Tim held back a smile as he pulled up an

alphabetized mailing list, then waved his hand at the screen. 'Sorry. No Rose Kleber.'

Gino was lifting some of the loose papers on the desk, peeking under them. 'You got a Rolodex, Mrs Gilbert?'

Her eyes narrowed. 'One of those things with all the little cards?'

'Yeah, that's it.'

She shook her head. 'Silliest things I ever saw. You want to find Freddie Herbert's number? You spend half your day looking at all those little cards, one by one.' She opened a drawer, slapped a thin address book on the desk and opened it to the *H*'s. 'Here. All the *H*'s on one page. No turning, no little cards, Freddie Herbert right there in a second.' She paged to the *K*'s, glanced at the three names listed, then shrugged. 'No Kleber.'

'Anything else on that computer, Tim?' Maggozi asked.

Tim pushed a few keys and called up the main menu. 'Just the mailing list and the invoices, sir. That's it.'

'Okay.'

'Can I turn it off? I should get out there and help Jeff.'

'Go, go, go,' Lily told him, and then turned to Magozzi and Gino, obviously impatient to get back to her customers. 'Anything else?'

'Not for the moment,' Magozzi said. 'Thank you for your help, Mrs Gilbert.'

'What help?' Gino grumbled a few minutes later as they were following the asphalt apron around the greenhouse, back toward the parking lot.

'She showed us the office, she answered our questions.'

'Yeah, but she didn't ask any of her own. We've been here almost an hour and she didn't ask once if we had any leads on who killed her husband, and that just pricks my cynic trigger.'

They paused at the place where Lily said she had found her husband's body.

Gino rubbed the back of his neck. 'You know, it just bothers the hell out of me that she opens this place the day after her husband was murdered. Shouldn't she be home covering her mirrors or something?'

Magozzi raised his brows at him. 'Gino, I am amazed and impressed. You went home and read up on Jewish funeral traditions last night, didn't you?'

'Nah. Movie. Melanie what's-her-name, the good-looking blonde with the baby voice? She was NYPD, undercover someplace with these really religious Jews – can't remember what you call them, but all the guys had banana curls.'

'Hasidic Jews.'

'Whatever. Anyway, somebody died and they covered all the mirrors. She oughta be home doing that.'

Magozzi sighed. 'She's not Hasidic, Gino, or even Orthodox. McLaren said they weren't even religious, remember?'

'You don't have to be religious to show respect.' He looked at his watch and tapped the crystal. 'What time is it? I told Rose Kleber's daughter we'd be there at eleven.'

'Almost that.'

'We better move it, then. Damn, this is going to be more fun than a barrel of crippled monkeys.'

Marty hadn't moved since Lily, Magozzi, and Gino had left the greenhouse. Most of the customers were still outside, emptying the sale tables, and for ten full minutes he'd been alone at the counter, staring at nothing, thinking that another six or seven beers from Jack's cooler might take the edge off the headache that had been with him since yesterday. He'd been stone-cold sober for over twenty-four hours now, and couldn't remember the last time that had happened. Sobriety, he decided, wasn't what it was cracked up to be.

He glanced out the window and saw Jack passed out on his lawn chair, turning red in the sun. He took one step toward the door to holler at him to get in the shade, then stopped.

Let the bastard fry.

14

Detective Johnny McLaren sat behind the stacks of clutter on his desk, tufts of bright red hair barely peeking over the top. Gloria was sashaying down the center aisle toward him, and there was no hope at all of concentrating on anything else when that body was in motion. She was a big, black, beautiful bulldozer of a woman and most of the time she dressed with all the subtlety of a movie marquee. Today she was wearing an intense yellow sari with a matching headdress and Johnny felt like he was staring into the sun.

'What are you looking at, you little Irish twerp?' She poked a pink message slip onto his desk with a long, yellow fingernail.

'Poetry in motion. The woman of my dreams. My soul mate. My destiny.'

'Give it a rest, McLaren.'

'I can't. I look at you, I look at me, I see little red-haired black children . . .'

'Uh-huh. Grand dreams for a little stick man.' She tapped the message slip again. 'That guy called three times this morning. Some Brit with an attitude.'

McLaren's ruddy face wrinkled into a perplexed

frown as he read the message. Just a name and overseas number. 'What the hell would a Brit be calling me for? I don't know any Brits.'

'Well, gee, honey, I don't know. I was hoping it might be your new tailor. Lord knows they would never have sold you that jacket on the other side of the puddle.'

'What's wrong with my jacket?'

'McLaren, madras was over before you were born. Get used to it. And if Langer gets back from the can anytime this century, Chief Malcherson wants you both in his office by three P.M. with some kind of an update on the train track guy he can feed to the media for the five o'clock news. Those jackals are in *love* with that murder.'

'Lucky us,' McLaren grumbled as he pawed through the wreckage on his desk and tried to find the case file.

Gloria moved in a little closer and eyed him shrewdly. 'Pretty strange doin's, that one.'

'Uh-huh.'

Gloria clucked her tongue. 'That Arlen Fischer must have been one nasty piece of work to end up the way he did.' She waited for a response, but McLaren was thoroughly engrossed in a month-old Malcherson memo regarding dress code. 'Honest to God, McLaren,' she said irritably, 'Jimmy Hoffa could be buried under that pile of crap.'

'It's all this inner-office shit. I can't keep up with it. How the hell am I supposed to find time to solve crimes when I've got to read a goddamned five-page memo on profanity every week?'

Gloria arched one perfectly plucked brow. 'Well I am purely amazed. And all this time I thought you weren't reading those at all. Don't know where I got such a silly idea.' She reached under a stack of sales circulars and pulled out Arlen Fischer's file. 'This what you're looking for?'

McLaren blinked at her, amazed. 'Yeah.'

She cocked one hip and made a low humming sound that reminded McLaren of a cello. Gloria always did that when she was fishing for information, and it always worked. 'Well, speaking of Jimmy Hoffa, I don't know what you guys are thinking, but this sure sounds like a mob hit to me.' She waggled the folder under McLaren's nose before handing it over.

McLaren beamed at her. 'I keep telling you, Gloria, we're soul mates. That's exactly what I thought at first. Out-of-state mobsters messing up Minnesota with their nasty little vendettas. Too bad we couldn't make it fit.'

'And why is that?'

'Well, for openers, Arlen Fischer was a three-bill, eighty-nine-year-old with bad hips. Not exactly your average mob type.'

'I got two words for you. Marlon Brando.'

'And I got one word for you. Movie. Besides, this was the king of ho-hum. You know what he did for a living? Fixed watches. Worked at the same damn jewelry store for thirty-some years, lived on social security and a little pension, no family, no friends, no money. I'm telling you, the man was a nobody. Never even made a blip on the radar screen.'

'Hmm. You know what I think, McLaren?'

'I'm all ears.'

'Honey, I don't have time to talk about your physical deformities right now. But what I think is, you don't tie a nobody to a train track and leave him to either die of fright or get chopped in half.'

McLaren sighed. 'Yeah, well, we're having a little trouble with that part.'

Gloria folded her arms under her extremely large bosom. 'You just remember that old Gloria told you to look for a mob connection. And when you end up collaring Tony Soprano for this, you owe me a big, fat lobster dinner.'

McLaren sat up in his chair. 'I'll take you out for a big, fat lobster dinner anytime you want.'

'Who said you were invited?'

McLaren watched helplessly as she glided off to continue her rounds, dropping memos and message slips on other desks in Homicide, all of them vacant with Gino and Magozzi out in the field, and the rest of the guys farmed out to other, busier divisions.

McLaren hated the silence of an empty room. He got enough of that when he went home every night. He breathed a small sigh of relief when Langer came in from the hall, then groaned when he saw the cardboard box he was carrying 'Oh, come on, Langer, you're killing me. Not another one.'

Langer set the box on a working table they'd shoved between their desks. 'This is the last of them.'

'Gloria says it's mob related.'

Langer smiled a little. 'The scary thing about that woman is that she's right more than she's wrong, which is better than our average. I don't know why she doesn't just sign up and get into the job for real.'

'I asked her that once. Said she wouldn't be caught dead in the clothes they make us wear. Do we really have to go through another one of those damn boxes?'

'We do.'

'It's depressing as hell.'

'Tell me about it.' Langer started sorting through more of the detritus of Arlen Fischer's life with little hope of finding anything helpful. So far the contents of the old man's desks and cabinets had yielded little but confirmation that he filed garbage instead of throwing it away. They'd been through four boxes like this already, and the most interesting thing they'd found was an old, empty Chicklets box that had instantly called up childhood memories for both of them. Apparently mothers of all faiths had surreptitiously doled out those precious little white squares of gum to keep their children quiet during sermons.

Johnny stood up and stretched, peered into the box, and plucked out a cellophane packet of crumbled soup crackers. 'Oh boy. Here's a clue.'

Langer looked at the pathetic little package, frowned hard, and looked quickly away. It was the kind of thing he'd found in his mother's house after he'd buried her last year. Single pieces of gum so old and brittle they'd shattered in their tin foil shrouds when he touched them; boxes of candle stubs and scraps of wrapping paper; and the one that still puzzled him – a paper bag of panty hose, all with one leg cut off. The collections of the dead were surely among the saddest things in the world.

'Something the matter, Langer?'

He shook his head and pretended to study an old political flyer he'd just pulled from the box. He didn't talk about his mother's long death to anyone. Not his partner, not his rabbi, not even his wife, who was probably on the schedule as his next failure. His mother had been the first. After a lifetime of love and humor and Chicklets, he'd run from her Alzheimer's, abandoned her to strangers who left her to die alone, just as he had.

'Langer?'

And after he'd failed his mother, he failed the job, watching like a blind fool as the Monkeewrench killer passed him in the parking ramps at the Mall of America, pushing the latest victim in a wheelchair. He was a detective, for God's sake, and he hadn't recognized a killer just a few yards away. He still woke up in the middle of every night, sweating, gasping, thinking of the lives that were lost after that day, and how easily he could have saved them.

And then, of course, came the big one, when he had failed himself, his god, and everything he had ever believed in, and the funny thing was that it had only taken a moment. No, not even that long. Just the few seconds it had taken him to . . .

'Jesus, Langer, what the hell's wrong with you?'

He jumped at Johnny McLaren's hand on his shoulder, and in that instant thought his heart had stopped, and the possibility moved him not at all.

'Hey, what is it, man? You got the flu or something? You're sweating like a pig.'

Langer straightened and wiped at his face, feeling the greasy slick of fear and regret. 'Sorry. Yeah. Maybe a touch of the flu.'

'Well, sit down, for chrissakes, I'll get you some water, and then maybe you better think about going home.' McLaren was watching him with a wary, almost frightened caution. 'You really zoned out there for a minute, you know? Creeped me out big-time.'

Langer smiled at him, just because McLaren had offered to get him water. Such a silly, little thing, and yet it touched him, as if it were a kindness far beyond what he deserved. 'Pigs don't sweat,' he said.

'Huh?'

'You said I was sweating like a pig. But pigs don't sweat.'

'They don't?'

'No.'

McLaren looked absolutely flummoxed. 'Well that's so stupid. Man, that really pisses me off. Why the hell do they make up sayings about pigs sweating when they don't sweat?'

'I just don't know.'

By the time McLaren returned with a chipped mug of water and two little white pills, Langer was sitting quietly at his desk, watching the grass turn green across the street from City Hall.

'You look better.'

'Actually, I feel fine now. Normal, in fact. What are these?' he pushed at the little pills.

'Aspirin. Well, not aspirin, exactly. Couldn't find any of those, but Gloria said they have aspirin or aceta-whatever in them, you know, just in case you had a fever.'

Langer flipped a pill over and smiled when he read the marking he recognized from the pills his wife took for PMS. 'Thanks, Johnny. I appreciate it.'

'No problem. You know, I was thinking, you opened that box and then boom, you got sick. Could be some kind of spores living in all that old junk, like when they opened the Egyptian tombs? And you just got a big whiff.'

'Ah.' Langer nodded sagely. 'So we should close that box and forget it, because there may be life-threatening spores inside, right?'

'Good idea.' McLaren started to close the box flaps, then stopped, releasing a miserable sigh. 'Trouble is, that pretty much leaves us with nowhere to go. I suppose we could talk to the housekeeper again, but I don't know what more she could tell us.'

'Probably nothing.' Langer glanced over at the abandoned box. 'There doesn't seem to be much to tell about that man's life.'

'Yeah, that's what I was telling Gloria, that he was kind of a nobody, and she said basically that a nobody didn't die the way he did, and that's the kicker, isn't it? Somebody knew Arlen Fischer existed, and apparently he really, really pissed them off.'

Langer thought about that for a minute, then pulled a fresh tablet from his drawer and clicked open a ballpoint. 'Okay. Who tortures people when they get really, really pissed off?'

McLaren started counting them off on his fingers. 'Well, you got your mob types, which we've already eliminated because there's absolutely nothing to support it . . .'

'Right.'

'. . . and then there's your sicko serial killers, a bunch of foreign dictators, military intelligence in a couple hundred countries, bad cops, hate groups . . .' McLaren stopped and blinked. 'Jeez. That's kind of a long list, isn't it?'

Langer nodded. 'The sorry world we live in.'

'McLaren!' Gloria poked her head around the edge of her cubicle. 'That Brit is on line two; and Langer, pick up line one right now. Your downstairs toilet is backing up.'

Langer grimaced at his blinking phone. 'I was supposed to fix that toilet last week. Forgot. Who's the Brit?'

'Dunno. Some guy with an attitude, Gloria says. Already called a couple times. Probably pissed I didn't call him back yet.'

'Not as pissed as my wife.'

It took Langer the better part of ten minutes to calm down his wife and intimidate the plumber she'd called – one of those emergency yahoos who stood in the middle of your flooding house and demanded a thousand dollars to turn a valve. By the time he finished, McLaren had filled three paper napkins with scribbles, and was thanking his caller with uncharacteristic politeness.

'Sounds like your call went a little better than mine,' Langer said, settling his phone into its cradle.

McLaren's grin was a little foolish, close to giddy. 'Man, you are not going to believe this. You know who that was? Interpol. The goddamned friggin' Interpol, for chrissakes. We've got a little action on our .45.'

Langer could almost feel his ears pricking. 'The .45 that put a hole in Arlen Fischer's arm?'

McLaren nodded, beaming. 'They picked up the ballistics we punched through the FBI, and it hit on six cylinders.'

Langer frowned, confused, as always, by McLaren's labryinth-like metaphors.

'Six hits,' McLaren explained excitedly. 'That gun is the murder weapon in six unsolveds over the past fifteen years, and Langer, my man, they are all over the place.'

15

Magozzi pulled the unmarked into his driveway, thinking that talking to Rose Kleber's family had been one of the most difficult interviews he could ever remember. It was disturbing to talk to high-voltage grievers who wailed so loudly you had to shout to be heard; troubling to question the ones whose eyes were still glazed with shock, whose voices were empty monotones; but it had been heart wrenching to interview this small family of gentle people who all cried endlessly, often soundlessly, even as they politely answered every question put to them.

Understandably, the two college girls who had found their grandmother's body seemed to be the most distraught, choking back sobs as they compulsively patted a bewildered cat that huddled between them on the sofa. But their mother, Rose Kleber's daughter, wore an expression of devastation that was far deeper. Her husband fluttered around his little family, patting shoulders and heads, doling out hugs like magic potions, but he too was weeping, even as he struggled for dignity. Whoever Rose Kleber had been, she had been deeply loved.

No, none of them had known Morey Gilbert personally, and as far as they knew, neither had Rose.

The daughter had visited her mother every day, and couldn't imagine being unaware of any friendship between the two elderly people. 'We shopped at the nursery occasionally,' she told them, 'and he might have waited on us once or twice. I honestly can't remember.'

'Any reason for your mother to have his number in her address book?' Gino had asked.

'They stick plastic stakes with the nursery number on it in every plant. I suppose she might have copied it from one of those.'

They'd asked a few more questions after that: what Rose Kleber did with her time, what organizations she belonged to, and the hardest one of all, about the tattoo on her arm. But the family knew nothing about her time in the camps half a century ago. She had always refused to talk about it.

Gino popped his door and propped it open the minute Magozzi stopped the car. 'That was a bummer,' he grumbled, dispelling the gloomy silence that had ridden with them all the way from the house of Rose Kleber's daughter. 'But you know what? *That* was genuine grieving. That's what Lily Gilbert and that drunken sleazebag son of hers should be doing, unless, of course, one of them killed the poor old guy.'

Magozzi sighed and unfastened his seat belt. 'People grieve in different ways, Gino.'

'You know, that's such a load of crap. It might look different on the outside, but you can tell when people are broken up because somebody died, and I'm telling you, I don't see it with the Gilberts – except maybe a little with Marty. I'm beginning to think he was the only one of the bunch that really cared about the old man. Jesus, Leo, have I mentioned lately that this is the scabbiest, sorriest-looking scrap of yard I ever saw in my whole life?'

And with that, Gino set aside the grief of Rose Kleber's family, the murders, the investigation, and stepped into the here and now, dragging Magozzi along with him.

Magozzi took a breath, felt lighter, and grinned at his partner. 'Not lately.'

They got out of the car and walked across spears of green with large patches of dirt between them. 'You know what this looks like? It looks like Viegs's head, with all that scalp showing between the hair plugs.'

'It's supposed to look like this,' Magozzi said defensively. 'It's called xeri-scaping.'

'Zero-scaping?'

'No, xeri, with an *x*.'

'Did you just make that up?'

'No, I did not just make that up. It's a design term, for when you use native plants that don't require a lot of care.'

'You mean like all those dandelions and quack grass?'

'Exactly.' Magozzi unlocked the door and gestured Gino inside. 'Grab the brats while I fire up the grill.'

By the time Magozzi had a nice bed of coals smoldering in the duct-taped Weber, Gino was finished with his kitchen prep and had wandered into the living room. He looked around at the bare walls, the leather recliner, and the single side table with one of those cheapo high-intensity lamps. 'So what do you call this? Xeri-decorating?'

'No, this is Minimalism.'

Gino shook his head. 'This is pathetic. Looks exactly the way it did the day your ex cleaned you out. You need to do something with this place.'

'Hey, you didn't have to come here for lunch, you know. If you don't like the ambience, you can go home and eat.'

'Oh no I can't. First of all, I left my brats and twelve-year cheddar here yesterday, and second of all, the in-laws are only on photo album number three in a series of ten from their last cruise. God love 'em, they're beautiful people, but they've been here for four days and sometimes you just gotta take a step back. Seriously, Leo, how long are you going to live in a place that looks like an abandoned warehouse? It's like you put your whole life on hold the day Heather left, and that ain't healthy.'

'First of all, I put my life on hold the day I married Heather, I started to get healthy the day she walked out, and second of all, single guys do not spend their free time at feng shui seminars at Wally's World of Furniture. It's not macho.'

Gino grunted. 'Well this sure isn't macho. Macho

is a big-screen TV and a wet bar. This is just plain empty, like nobody lives here. You ever hear the expression a man's home is a reflection of the man?'

'From what I've seen, a man's home is the reflection of the woman he lives with.'

'Are you talking about my house?'

'Actually, I was talking about this place when Heather lived here.' But he was thinking about big bad Gino with a gun living in a house of soft upholstery, dried flowers, and herbal wreaths. A girlie house. Angela's house. Not a big-screen TV or a wet bar in sight. It always smelled like the garlic and basil sauce that was forever simmering on the stove, and occasionally, baby powder. 'And maybe yours, too, yeah.'

Gino rocked back on his heels, grinning. 'Which proves my point. My house is a perfect reflection of who I am. I'm the man who loves Angela.'

Half an hour later, Magozzi was finishing his third brat. 'These are unbelievable.'

'Told you,' Gino said around a mouthful. 'The real secret is in the precook – you got to simmer brats in beer and onions before you grill. If you don't, you might as well be eating tofu pups. Want the last one?'

Magozzi put his hand to his heart. 'I think I've done enough arterial damage for one day. I may be a risk taker, but I'm not suicidal.'

Gino gave the remaining brat careful consideration

for about two seconds before plucking it off the serving platter. 'That's why God invented Lipitor.' He paused for a moment, frowning. 'And speaking of being suicidal, how worried do you think we should be about Pullman? He didn't look like he was doing so hot today.'

Magozzi leaned back in his chair and thought about that. 'It's hard to say. There's a big difference between thinking about it and actually doing it, but he could be going that way. If he's really blacking out a lot, he's got a good start on drinking himself to death, that's for sure.'

'Just like his brother-in-law. Christ, what a messed-up family. You know, I really wanted to like Gilbert for popping his dad, but to tell you the truth, I don't think he's got it in him. Doesn't have the schtupa.'

'Chutzpah, not schtupa, and you might want to forget trying out your Yiddish at the funeral tomorrow.'

'Whatever. He ain't got it.' Gino chewed thoughtfully for a moment. 'Besides, I got the case solved, and I'm sticking with my original doer.'

'Lily Gilbert?'

'Who else? Only now we got her for killing her husband *and* Rose Kleber.'

Magozzi rolled his eyes. 'Okay. I'll bite. Why would Lily Gilbert kill an old woman she's never met before?'

'Hul-lo. Because her husband was nailing the

cookie-baking grandma, that's why. Geriatric crime of passion, clear as a bell.'

'Seems to me we just spent half the morning establishing that Morey Gilbert and Rose Kleber didn't even know each other.'

'Just because the families didn't know about it doesn't mean it wasn't happening. Think about it. You don't run around committing adultery and then tell your family about it.'

'Give me a break, Gino. These people are *old*.'

'So? You think old people don't have sex? You want to spend the night at my house? I gotta repaint behind the headboard where Angela's folks are sleeping.'

Magozzi gaped at him for a moment. 'No way.'

'I kid you not.'

'What are they, seventies?'

'Yep.'

'Huh.' Magozzi smiled. 'That's kind of good news, isn't it?'

'I always thought so.'

'It's still the dumbest theory you've ever come up with.'

'Okay, hotshot. You got a better one?'

'Well, if you're looking to connect Morey Gilbert and Rose Kleber, we've got two concentration camp survivors. Hate crime might fit.'

'You mean like some neo-Nazi creeps?'

Magozzi shrugged. 'Maybe. They pop up now and then. We've had our share of synogogue vandalism, that sort of thing. Then there was that group over in St Paul pasting those anti-Semitic posters up all over downtown.'

Gino snorted. 'The bozos who drew the swastika backward? Jeez, Leo, there were only three of 'em, and from what I heard, they shared a brain.'

'They're probably not the only ones in town.'

'More's the pity. We can check hate crimes just to cover the bases, but those idiots leave a note when they piss on the sidewalk, otherwise, what's the point? Besides, according to the families, neither Gilbert nor Kleber ever set foot in a temple, which puts them kind of below the moron radar of your average neo-Nazi. And these were really clean scenes, like a pro, you know? We're not getting any trace, no prints, no witnesses . . . this is one savvy killer, like some sharp old lady in good shape who watches cop shows.'

Magozzi grinned and shook his head. 'Not buying it.'

'Then give me something else.'

'Hell, I don't know. Psycho bag boy picking out victims on Senior Day at the supermarket, trying for his fifteen minutes.'

Gino rolled his eyes. 'Man, are you reaching. We've got two different weapons, victims of both sexes, and name one serial killer who ever preyed on the geriatric set. Hell, the FBI wouldn't even touch that one, and they want a piece of everything. Besides, if we start thinking serial, then we have to consider Arlen Fischer as part of the series, and there's no way that murder fits in with Gilbert's and Kleber's.'

And that wasn't the only problem. Imagining a killer who went around shooting the elderly for some sort of sick thrill was a horror Magozzi didn't want to consider. It was like hurting kids, or puppies. But imagining two old-timers like Morey Gilbert and Rose Kleber involved in something that would make them targets was just as hard.

Magozzi started clearing dishes off the table. 'Maybe we're on the wrong track, trying to tie them together. It's a Jewish neighborhood, a lot of seniors, and so what if Rose Kleber had Gilbert's number in her book? The gardening thing could explain that.'

'So you're saying it's just a coincidence we've got two old Jews in the same neighborhood killed within a day of each other.'

Magozzi blew out a frustrated sigh. 'No. I haven't believed that since we got the call on Rose Kleber. They're connected, all right. I just can't imagine how.'

Gino got up from his chair and stretched, hands pressed to the small of his back, belly jutting forward. 'You know, I had this all tied up nice and neat with Lily Gilbert killing them both, but you just don't want to do it the easy way, do you? Leo, you gotta quit looking for the zebra.'

Magozzi chuckled, started to rinse the plates and put them in the dishwasher. 'If I remember correctly, you had Grace MacBride pretty firmly pegged as the Monkeewrench killer in one of your "nice and neat" scenarios.'

'She was a perfectly logical suspect.'

'But the zebra did it.'

'So just that one time, I might have been a little misguided. Doesn't mean I'm not dead-on with this one. You got a Tums or something? That last brat is talking back in a foreign language.'

'In the cupboard with the glasses.'

'You've got glasses? How come I was drinking soda out of a can?'

'You wanted a glass?'

'Jeez, Leo, I'm not totally uncivilized.' He found the Tums and popped a few, leaned back against the counter and chewed thoughtfully. 'You know, speaking of Monkeewrench, we could ask them to plug Gilbert and Kleber into the software they used on all the cold cases, see if anything pops. Man, that program rocked. Found connections in seconds we'd been looking for for years.'

'Couldn't hurt, I suppose. I'll give Grace the names tonight, ask her to run them.'

Gino gave him a sidelong glance of scrutiny, and Magozzi grimaced. He was going to get another lecture.

'You know I love Grace McBride, right?'

Magozzi rolled his eyes.

'Hey, I don't mean to bust your balls over this, but tell me honestly, what kind of a future do you see for yourself with her? You gotta face it, Leo, she's walking wounded. Paranoid as hell. And her track record for normal relationships stinks. I mean, the last man she loved was a serial killer.'

Magozzi glowered at him. 'She's getting better, Gino.'

'Oh really? Then how come she took her piece to the movies last week?'

'A lot of weirdos go to the movies these days.'

'Leo, you went to a Sunday matinee to see a *cartoon.* Hey, don't get me wrong, I'm all for working with Monkeewrench – they're great folks, every one of them. But I think you need to be careful, maybe keep the relationship about work for now.'

'Are you finished?'

'Yes. End of lecture.'

'Thank you. And don't call them Monkeewrench.'

Gino cringed. 'Oh yeah, I forgot. Damn, I just can't get that name out of my head.'

And neither could the rest of the city, Magozzi thought.

'They come up with a new one yet?'

'Not as far as I know.'

Gino's chin jutted forward. 'I'm going to give that some thought. Help them out.'

16

It was one-thirty and eighty-four degrees by the time Magozzi and Gino arrived at Biederman's Funeral Home, and both of them were miserably hot, back in their jackets to conceal their guns.

Sol Biederman was waiting for them at the front door. He looked a little better than he had yesterday when they'd met over the body of Morey Gilbert, but his eyes were still rimmed with red. Another downer about getting old, Magozzi thought. Tissues took a lot longer to recover from crying jags, and just about everything else.

Sol led them into a vast sitting room filled with furniture that had been fashionable thirty years ago. The air smelled of fading flowers and scorched coffee, and the stale, cloying scent of the cheap cologne someone had worn to the last viewing.

The air-conditioning, if there was any, was turned very low. Gino flopped into a maroon wing-back chair, grabbed a tissue from a nearby box, and mopped his forehead.

'Who would have thought April could be so warm, eh? I have a man working on the air conditioner now, but in the meantime, please take your jackets off, Detectives. Be comfortable.'

'Thanks, we're fine,' Gino said, his reddening face belying his words.

'I'm not expecting anyone until five. We're alone here. No one will see your guns except me, and I'm very good at keeping secrets.'

Gino was out of his jacket before by-the-book Magozzi could give him so much as a dirty look for defying department policy. He'd just decided to shame Gino by sweltering in his jacket when Sol gestured to his own bare arms below the short sleeves of his shirt.

'If you don't remove your jacket, Detective Magozzi, I'll be forced to put on mine. I'm an old man. I could die from the heat.'

Magozzi grinned and slipped off his sports coat while Sol settled in a nearby chair.

'I assume you have some follow-up questions for me. I'm afraid I wasn't much help to you yesterday.'

Gino pulled out his notebook. 'You did fine yesterday, Mr Biederman. And we understand how upset you were. But the problem is, everything got a little more complicated this morning.'

Sol nodded sadly. 'I heard about Rose Kleber. Her daughter called shortly before you arrived. Such a terrible thing, an unbelievable thing, and I had to ask myself, is there a madman out there killing old Jews?' He looked from Gino to Magozzi. 'That's why you're really here, isn't it? You're wondering the same thing.'

'We're looking at a lot of things, Mr Biederman,'

Magozzi said. 'So you knew Rose Kleber? She was a friend of yours?'

Sol shook his head. 'Not a friend exactly, but it's a small community. Everyone passes through here eventually. I took care of Mrs Kleber's husband when he died ten years ago.'

'Was she a friend of Mr Gilbert?'

'Not that I know of.'

'And you would have known that, because you were Morey Gilbert's best friend, right?'

Sol looked off into the middle distance, blinking rapidly. He didn't answer for a moment, as if it had taken that long for the question to travel across the space between them. 'Yes, absolutely. I would have given my life to save Morey's.'

It was such a calmly delivered, matter-of-fact statement that Magozzi believed it immediately.

Gino leaned forward in his chair. 'This is the deal, Mr Biederman. These two killings weren't random. They weren't accidents. Somebody wanted both Morey Gilbert and Rose Kleber dead, and if the same person killed them both, that means they had something in common we haven't discovered yet: something that might lead us to the killer. So any little detail you can remember, even if it was just Morey mentioning her offhand, or recognizing her on the street, anything like that could really help us out.'

Sol thought about it for a moment, then shook his head. 'I'm sorry. I don't think so.'

'They were both in concentration camps during

the war. I'm sure you knew that,' Magozzi said.

Sol raised his left arm, showing the faded numbers on the underside. 'Of course I knew.'

Gino gaped at the old man's arm. 'You know, my whole life I never met one person who was in a concentration camp, and now you're the third in twenty-four hours.'

Sol gave him a small smile. 'We don't exactly advertise, but there are more of us than you might imagine. Especially in this neighborhood.'

'Damn, I'm really sorry,' Gino said.

'Thank you, Detective Rolseth.' He looked down at the ropy veins in his old hands. 'I'm trying to imagine why someone would want to kill people who survived the camps. What's the point?' He spread his hands in a poignant gesture. 'We're all old. Pretty soon we're going to be dead anyway.'

And what do you say to that? Magozzi thought, taken aback by the man's directness. 'We're taking a look at hate crimes.'

Sol met his eyes and held them with a gaze so riveting Magozzi couldn't have looked away if he tried. 'When you hate Jews enough to want to eliminate them, you kill the breeders, Detective, you understand?' Magozzi tried to nod, but it felt like his neck was frozen. 'The Nazis taught us that. That's what they called the young ones – breeders – as if we were animals. Sure, they killed old people, but only because they were useless, they got in the way. This has to be something else.'

Gino hadn't moved since the old man had started talking. Finally he released a long exhale and spoke softly. 'Then we need to find some other connection between your friend Morey and Rose Kleber. Like we said before, something else they had in common that would put them both in a killer's path. Maybe they met each other back in the camps, kept up some sort of contact over the years?'

Sol shook his head. 'Mrs Kleber was in Buchenwald. That was all she would tell me the day she came to make arrangements for her husband, and she could barely manage to speak the name of the place aloud. Morey was in Auschwitz, as was I. He saved my life there, did you know that?'

'No, sir, I didn't,' Gino replied.

'Well that was Morey. He was helping people even then. Maybe someday I'll tell you about it.' He looked over at Magozzi, and then back at Gino, his dark eyes growing moist. 'The man was a hero. Who would kill a hero?'

17

It was almost sunset when Magozzi stood on the pressure pad outside Grace MacBride's front door, listening to the security camera whir in the eave above his head, stilling the impulse to push his hair back off his forehead. It was thick and black and too long now, falling all over the place. He should have had it cut Saturday, before people in Minneapolis had started killing each other again.

There was a soft woof from the other side of the steel door as the dead bolts started sliding back, and that made him smile. Charlie, the great, wiry mongrel mix Grace had rescued from the streets, was only slightly less paranoid than his owner. It had taken weeks before he would wait on the other side of the door when Magozzi arrived, woofing an excited welcome instead of scrambling for a hiding place. Magozzi had tossed more than one shirt ruined by muddy paws and enthusiastic doggy kisses, and cared not a whit.

When the door finally opened he got a freeze-frame of Grace's swinging black hair and smiling blue eyes before Charlie's paws hit his shoulders and the long, sloppy tongue found his face. It always made him laugh; made the world a better place. He wondered if maybe he should start dating the dog.

'Don't let him do that,' Grace always said. 'He's not allowed to jump on people. You're ruining him.'

Magozzi grinned at her over Charlie's shoulder. 'Leave us alone. This is the only hug I've had today.'

'Oh, you two are hopeless. Get in here.'

Grace was wearing black sweats and tennis shoes, which meant they weren't going out – she wouldn't take a step beyond the front door without the English riding boots – but her Sig Sauer was snug in the shoulder holster, a sure sign that they might go into the tightly fenced backyard, where she felt she needed the range and power of the bigger gun. The derringer was her close-quarters-inside-the-house weapon. If she'd been wearing that instead, over the thick socks that kept the ankle holster from chafing, he would have known the evening held no hope of fresh air, since Grace never opened her windows, in spite of the iron bars that made the little house look like a prison.

While Charlie danced around Magozzi, claws clicking on the maple floor, Grace closed the door, latched all three dead bolts, and started keying in the code to rearm the security system.

Magozzi watched the familiar procedure with a sadness that was gradually moving toward reluctant, bitter resignation. The danger that had haunted her life was over now, it had all ended last October in a terrifying salvo of gunfire, but her paranoia was still as intense as ever, obliterating any chance at all of a normal life. Gino was probably right. Getting really close to Grace MacBride, expecting her to take even a baby step in that direction, was surely just an impossible dream. She was never going to feel safe. Not with him, maybe not with anyone.

'It's habit, Magozzi, that's all.' Her back was turned as she punched in the code, and yet she had known what he was thinking.

'Is it?'

She turned and poked a finger gently into his chest. 'You have a Neanderthal macho thing going here, you know that, don't you? You want me to leave the door unlocked because you're here to protect me.'

'That is absolutely not true,' he lied. 'If you left the door unlocked in this neighborhood, I'd be scared to death.'

She turned with a tiny smile and headed down the stark hall toward the kitchen. Magozzi and Charlie followed at a respectful distance. 'I've got a three-hundred-dollar bottle of Burgundy ready to decant, and an eight-dollar Chardonnay chilling in the fridge. What's your preference?'

'Gee, I don't know. They both sound good. Can I mix them together?'

Ten minutes later Magozzi took a step out onto the back stoop, wineglass in hand, and stopped dead.

Grace's backyard looked as it always had – a small patch of scruffy grass enclosed by an eight-foot-high solid wooden fence, with an old spreading magnolia tree in its center, half dressed in buds just beginning to open.

But now there were three Adirondack chairs arranged under the tree, where there used to be only two – one for Grace, and one for Charlie the dog, who believed monsters lived at ground level, and never sat there if there was furniture available.

Get a grip, Magozzi. It's only a chair. It means nothing. And she probably got it because Jackson is over here after school every day.

'I bought you a present,' she said from behind him.

'Oh?' he said with all the indifference he could muster.

'The chair, silly. So Charlie doesn't end up in your lap every time we sit out here.'

'Oh. I figured it was for Jackson.'

'Nine-year-olds don't use furniture, Magozzi. I got it for you because I like having you here, and I want you to be comfortable.'

'Okay.' Magozzi was glad she was behind him, so she couldn't see his ridiculous grin.

Baby step. She's getting better, Gino.

The day's unseasonable warmth lingered for a short time after sunset, and they had their first glass of wine in the backyard under the magnolia tree. They sat in easy silence as they sipped their wine, listening to the occasional noises of night in an urban neighborhood – a door slamming down the street, the clatter of the neighbors' supper dishes coming from their open window, the sudden twitter of a bird so foolish it thought the branches of the magnolia were a safe place to sleep. Not only did Grace not shoot the bird; she hadn't even flinched at the sound.

She is, by God. She's getting better.

'Look up through the tree branches, Magozzi. You can see the stars. Another week and the leaves will unfurl, and you won't be able to do that.'

'I never saw this tree with leaves.'

Grace was silent for a moment. 'You didn't?'

'Nope. It was almost Halloween, first time I sat out here. Poor old tree had about three leaves left, and they were blaze yellow.'

She made a soft sound that had no discernible meaning. 'That's funny. It feels like I've known you for much longer than that.'

He wasn't dumb enough to ask if that was a good thing. He just reached for the bottle that sat on the ground between their chairs, and refilled their glasses. He took a sip, leaned back in his very own brand-new Adirondack chair, and felt the last of the day's stress leak out onto the happily untended grass of Grace's backyard.

He was pathetic, he decided. Happier here, six months into a relationship with a woman he hadn't even kissed yet, than he had ever been in his life. Frustrated, certainly, by the agonizing absence of physical closeness; but happy – absolutely. He was a disgrace to Italian men everywhere, but he couldn't help it. There was a connection here so deep he couldn't begin to understand it. He'd felt it the first time he'd sat in this yard with this woman and this dog – a feeling of being home, even in this place where there were always reservations lingering behind his welcome.

That's why I don't have any furniture, Gino. I don't live there.

'What are you thinking?'

'That I'm happy.' It never even occurred to him to lie.

'That's nice. I've been reading the papers, watching the news. You've got another mystery to solve. You live for that, I think.'

'It has nothing to do with my being happy at this moment.'

'I know. Tell me about the case.'

'Actually, there are two cases. Morey Gilbert, the man who owned the nursery, and Rose Kleber, but we don't have anything to connect them . . .'

'What about the man they found tied to the train tracks?'

'Langer and McLaren are working that one. No connection to ours. We've got elderly Jews, pretty clean hits; theirs was a Lutheran somebody hated enough to torture.'

'All right, two then. And you've got a bunch of homicide detectives with no homicides to work, while you and Gino are running two of them? Sounds like somebody thinks they're related.'

Magozzi shrugged. 'It's a thin connection. We're looking at it.'

'How thin?'

He shifted a little in his chair, suddenly uncomfortable. 'That's part of the information we were holding back.'

'Come on, Magozzi. You want me to plug the names into the new software program, right? See if anything comes up?'

'Gino and I thought it was worth a shot.'

'All right, then. You watched that program work your cold cases. You know perfectly well it sorts through hundreds of databases, looking for connections, and some of them are damn slow. I need any link you've already got to narrow the search parameters, otherwise this could take days.'

It wasn't that he didn't trust Grace. Next to Gino, she was the person he trusted most in this world. Hell, he was sitting under a tree with a possibly dangerous bird overhead, wasn't he? Trusting that Grace MacBride would pull her gun and shoot the thing if it attacked? But violating departmental policy still went against the grain, and Magozzi, to his everlasting dismay, was no rebel.

'I don't have days, Magozzi.' She folded her arms, impatient with him as she always was when he plodded down that narrow path defined by rules. 'We start loading the computers into the RV day after tomorrow.'

He closed his eyes at the reminder that she was

leaving. 'They both had tattoos on their arms. Morey Gilbert was in Auschwitz, Rose Kleber was in Buchenwald.'

He could feel her eyes on him in the dark; and then he felt them drift away.

Grace was silent for a long time. 'It could be a horrible coincidence.'

'Of course it could.'

'But you don't think so.'

Magozzi sighed. 'It's thin, I told you. I'm reaching here.'

'You never reach, Magozzi, unless you have nowhere else to go. So what are you thinking? That someone's killing Jews, or Jews who were in the camps? Which is it?'

She always did that. Said right out loud the things you never wanted to hear expressed, because some of them were just too terrible to contemplate.

He leaned forward, arms braced on his knees, empty wineglass dangling from his fingers. 'I don't want to think either of those things. What I want is for you to plug those two into your program and discover that they were really bad people involved in something that got them killed.'

'A geriatric drug cartel or something?'

'That would be ideal. Besides, the camp connection thing just doesn't work. Like an old man told us this afternoon, why kill old Jews? They're going to be dead soon anyway.'

'Wow. That's pretty cold.'

Magozzi shrugged. 'He was in the camps too. Gives him license.'

Grace was quiet for a moment, tapping shave-and-a-haircut on the wooden arm of her chair with her fingertips. She always did that when she was thinking. 'I don't know, Magozzi. From what I hear on the news about Morey Gilbert, he doesn't seem like much of a candidate for criminal activity.'

'And you haven't heard the half of it. He spent his life helping people. Saint, hero, pick a title, I've heard them all. He was a good man, Grace.'

'Too good to be true?'

Magozzi thought about that for a minute. 'I don't think so. I think he might have been the real thing.'

'What about the other one, Rose Kleber?'

'Grandma Kleber. Cookies, garden, cat, family who adored her.'

'So another noncriminal type.'

Magozzi sighed. 'I'm spinning in circles here, aren't I?'

Grace poured the last dribble of wine into his glass. 'Then maybe it wasn't something they did, Magozzi. Maybe they both happened to be in the same place at the same time, saw something or someone they shouldn't have.'

Magozzi nodded. 'That would be my all-time favorite scenario, but how the hell do you even start looking for something like that?'

'That's what you've got me for.'

He watched her get up from her chair, a graceful spill of black water rising into the darkness.

'No it isn't.'

Grace smiled and stretched, her fingertips brushing a branch of the magnolia.

The bird went nuts.

18

While Magozzi and Grace were sipping wine under the magnolia, Marty Pullman was downing scotch with more serious intent. He was sitting on the bed in a room that had once belonged to Hannah, long before she'd been his wife. The room had changed over the years in a slow conversion from daughter's bedroom to one of those sad places that has no real purpose anymore. There was a desk no one used, a bed no one slept in, a closet with empty hangers that clattered together when you opened the door. And yet Hannah lingered here as she did everywhere, and there wasn't enough scotch in the world to erase her.

He took a deep drink from his glass and stared out the window at the dark. It was only his second night in this house, and yet it seemed a hundred years since he'd sat in his own bathtub with a gun in his mouth.

He hadn't been fooled when Lily had asked him to stay. From any other woman whose husband of fifty-some years had just been murdered, the request would have been perfectly understandable. Grief expands to fill a newly empty house, and Marty knew better than anyone that the only thing worse than being dead was being a solitary survivor. But that's not why Lily wanted him here. Now that Morey's death had finally brought him out of isolation, she was going to keep an eye on him, and they both knew it. Somehow the old bag knew what he was up to. She always had – except for that one time.

He cringed when the shrill whine of the vacuum started up again. For the past four hours, Lily had been cooking and cleaning in preparation for a houseful of mourners tomorrow. He'd tried to help so she could finish and go to bed; at one point they'd almost come to blows over the vacuum cleaner. 'Have a heart, Martin,' she'd said to him then, and that was when he realized that the object wasn't to finish the job at all. Marty had his bottle, Lily had her vacuum, and God help anyone who tried to take their tools of sanity away.

He grabbed the scotch, went to the kitchen for two fresh glasses, and brought them out into the living room, kicking the vacuum cleaner cord out of the socket on his way. 'For God's sake, Lily, sit down and rest. It's almost eleven o'clock.'

He expected at least some resistance, or perhaps a pointed comment about the booze, but apparently, even Lily Gilbert had her limits. She sagged down onto the couch next to him and stared mindlessly at the muted TV. She was still in her child-sized overalls, but she was wearing a blue cotton babushka over her cropped silver hair, as she always did when she cleaned. The scarf baffled Marty. He wondered if she'd worn her hair long as a girl, donning the scarf to hold it back, and if the scarf had lingered as a habit long after the hair was gone. He tried to imagine Lily with long hair, but with her little old face, her eyes magnified by her glasses, and four shots of scotch in his belly, all he could see was E.T. after the kids had put the wig on him.

'I think the house is clean enough,' she pronounced, to dispel any notion that she was sitting down because Marty told her to.

'The carpet is almost bald now. Yeah, I'd say it's clean enough.' Marty poured her out a finger of scotch. 'Here.'

She gave him a disapproving look. 'You don't want to drink alone, is that it?'

'I have no problem with drinking alone. You need to relax.'

'I don't like scotch.'

'You want something else?'

She stared at the glass for a long time, then finally took a sip and grimaced. 'This is horrible. How can you drink this?'

Marty shrugged. 'You get used to it.'

Lily took another tentative sip. 'Morey's scotch is better. Still bad, but better than this. This is cheap, isn't it?'

He smiled a little. 'Yeah.'

Lily nodded, got up, and disappeared into the kitchen. A few moments later, she came out carrying a bottle of twenty-five-year-old Balvenie.

Marty gaped at the bottle. 'My God, Lily, do you know how much that stuff costs?'

'So we shouldn't drink it? You think you can sell a half-empty bottle of scotch on eBay?'

Marty couldn't decide which was more surprising – the fact that Lily had lugged out a two-hundred-dollar bottle of scotch, or that she knew about eBay.

They sat quietly together, drinking scotch and staring at the silent TV, and because the moment was so strangely comfortable, Marty was almost tempted to tell her everything. Just blurt it out, forget the consequences, let her do her worst.

Suddenly, he saw an image of Jack Gilbert smiling back at him from the TV. He blinked a few times, certain that he was hallucinating, but the smiling face didn't go away. 'Hey, that's Jack. Turn it up.'

Lily snatched the remote from the table and turned the TV off.

'Come on, Lily!' He grabbed the remote, flipped the TV back on, and watched in amusement as the commercial cycled through a montage of touching scenes: Jack at a car accident, helping the victim, Jack at a construction site, talking to workers, Jack at a hospital bed, looking earnest and caring. A narrator's voice spoke over the final shot of a dynamic, charismatic Jack in court: 'You need a lawyer who cares about you. Call Jack Gilbert at 1-800-555-5225. That's 1-800-555-J-A-C-K, Jack. Don't let them jack you around.'

'What a schlock,' Lily muttered.

'I don't know. I thought it was pretty good.'

She grunted.

'You never used to think he was a schlock. You used to be proud of him.'

'He used to be my son,' she said sharply.

Marty sighed. He had made the decision to put his own non-life on hold out of respect for Morey, and to do what he could to help Lily. Hannah would have wanted that. But he wasn't going to do it forever, which meant this family feud nonsense had to end. Jack should be taking care of his own mother, goddamnit. 'Jesus, Lily, you're the most stubborn woman on the planet.'

'Why do you do that? Why do you swear? You know I hate that.'

'Oh, come on, we're Jewish. Saying "Jesus" doesn't mean anything.'

'It means something to someone. You could show a little respect.'

Marty took a breath. 'Fine. I'll stop swearing, you stop changing the subject. We're running out of Gilberts here, Lily. It's just you and Jack now, and it's about time you buried the hatchet. So he married out of the faith – why is that such a big deal? You and Morey never even went to temple. Why should you care if he married a Lutheran?'

Lily gave him an incredulous look. 'You think *that's* what this is about?'

'Well, isn't it?'

'Pffft. Your head is filled with things you don't know. Things you didn't bother to find out because you're such a busy retired person.'

Marty gritted his teeth until he could trust himself to speak. 'Don't even try the guilt thing with this one, Lily. We hadn't seen Jack in a while, he kept blowing Hannah off when she called, so I asked Morey what was going on. He said Jack had married a Lutheran, and we weren't going to talk about it. Period. A week or so after that Hannah was killed, and you can just goddamn excuse me for not following through.'

He took a breath and eyed the bottle of Balvenie. Ten bucks a shot, the way he figured it. Seemed a shame to waste that kind of money on the rapid journey into oblivion he was hoping for.

'Go ahead, drink it,' Lily said. 'Better you should die from a diseased liver than holes in your stomach from that drain cleaner you drink.'

If she thought she was going to have to tell him twice, she was crazy. He snatched the bottle and filled his glass and dreamed of blackness.

Lily watched him take a long drink. 'So you want to know about this thing with Jack or not?'

'Sure. Why not.'

She nodded, then leaned against the back of the couch. Her feet didn't touch the floor when she did that, and she looked like an old little girl with her legs sticking straight out.

'Every day Jack would come for lunch, remember? This was before the schlocky ad, when I could still tell people my son was a lawyer and not worry about them seeing the clown on TV. And then one day, poof. He drops off the face of the earth. No lunching, no calling, no nothing. I call his office, I talk to a machine; I call his house, I talk to another machine. Morey said they argued.'

'About what?'

'Who knows? Fathers and sons argue. This happens. So they stay away from each other long enough to forget the stupid things they said when they were mad, and then it's over. Except this time it wasn't. This time Jack sent us a picture in the mail, and there in the picture are little girls in white dresses and little boys in suits and right in the middle is the big schlock himself, and they're all kneeling in front of a cross with that poor, dead Jew hanging on it.'

Marty blinked at her, wondering if the last drink had finally fried his brain, because he was definitely missing something. 'What are you talking about? What picture?'

Lily ignored his question. 'And on the bottom of the picture it says: Jack Gilbert, First Communion, some Lutheran church.'

'*What*? Jack *converted*?'

She sipped from her glass and said nothing.

'That doesn't make any sense at all. Jack never even believed in God.'

Lily looked at him like he was an idiot. 'What are you thinking? This had nothing to do with God. This was Jack slapping our faces and turning his back on his family and who he was because he'd had some stupid fight with his father. And then a couple of weeks later we get a wedding picture. Same place, same cross, a bigger girl in a bigger white dress. Another slap, and the coward did it with pictures.'

Marty raked his fingers through his hair, as if that might stimulate some dormant brain cell that could help him make sense of what he'd just been told. Jack had his fair share of shortcomings, but he'd never struck him as the kind of guy who'd hurt anybody intentionally, least of all his parents. Besides, it made no sense at all for Jack to punish Lily for a fight he'd had with Morey. 'I can't figure this out.'

'Big surprise. I've been trying for over a year, and I can't figure it out either.'

'You should have asked Jack.'

'I told you, Jack wouldn't talk to me. Morey wouldn't talk to me. You men, you do these stupid things, and the women suffer and never know why.'

Marty watched her drink from her glass, foolish enough, even after all these years, to look for a flicker of emotion on the old woman's face. He knew without a doubt that it was in there, but he also knew he would never see it. Probably if Lily Gilbert ever started crying, she'd never be able to stop.

'Well, I'll talk to the little bastard,' he said.

'Good.'

'And I'm sorry he hurt you.'

Lily gave him a smug look. 'And all this time, *I'm* the bad person. By the way, Sol called tonight while you were closing up the greenhouse. You're a pallbearer, you know.'

'I know.'

She smiled a little. 'Morey picked out his casket years ago. He used to go to the funeral home and play poker with Sol, and one day, he comes home and says, "Lily, I picked out my casket today. It's bronze and it's heavy, and the pallbearers are going to pull out their backs carrying me. This will help out Harvey, the chiropractor, whose business has been bad."'

Marty smiled, thinking that sounded just like Morey. 'I didn't know he played poker.'

'He only played with Sol because he could beat him. And sometimes that Ben person.'

'Who's Ben?'

'A nobody.'

'You don't like him?'

'He's a putz. A stinker.'

'And Morey liked him?'

Lily shrugged. 'You know Morey. He was hopeless. He liked everybody, whether they deserved it or not. Besides, they went way back.'

'Funny I never met him.'

'They weren't that close. Mostly they went fishing. Couple, three times a year, maybe some poker sometimes.'

Marty turned his head very slowly to look at her. 'Morey went *fishing*?'

'Of course he did... oh, turn on the sound. Quick.' She squiggled forward to put her feet on the floor and propped her elbows on her knees, eyes fixed on the TV. 'Look, it's extra innings.'

Marty looked at her in amazement. 'You like baseball?'

She snatched the remote and turned on the sound herself. 'Of course I like baseball. These are gentlemen. They hardly ever knock each other down, and they smile a lot when they do something good.'

He watched, bemused, as she got caught up in the game, thinking how little he had learned about Lily in all the years he'd loved her daughter. He'd spent most of his time with Morey, practicing that age-old gender division that happens when families get together. Lily was the mystery in the kitchen; but Morey was the man, the friend, the substitute father he had come to love and know so well.

Except he'd never known about the fishing, and that troubled him. Maybe he hadn't known Morey as well as he thought.

He let his mind travel back to a day well over a year ago, not long before his life had fallen apart. He and Morey had driven Hannah and Lily fifty miles north of the city to an antique shop that charged twice as much as any closer to home. On the way back, they'd stopped at a rural gas station/convenience store for ice cream and drinks.

'Marty, get over here. Look at this.' Morey was standing at an upright cooler that held milk, cheese, and other perishables, looking into an adjacent water tank with a noisy bubbler, shaking his head.

Marty peered into the tank and grimaced at a writhing black mass of leeches. On top of the tank all manner of worms squirmed in cups of sawdust and dirt. 'This is disgusting. What's wrong with these worms? How come the white ones are in sawdust?'

'I should know this?' Morey gestured a young clerk over to the tank. 'This isn't against the health code?'

'Uh . . . are you an inspector or something?'

'No, no, I'm not an inspector, but it's common sense. There are leeches next to the milk.'

'And worms,' Marty added.

'That's just the live bait,' the clerk replied. 'That tank there's the live well, and that's the dry bait on top.'

Morey snorted. 'Of course it's live. It's moving. This is disgusting.'

'Uh . . . we get a lot of fishermen in here.'

'Fishing. Bah. And they call themselves sportsmen. What kind of a sport is it that you impale helpless creatures on a wire hook so you can throw it in the water and impale bigger helpless creatures?

'Well, they're just worms and leeches and stuff.'

'To you, maybe. Tell me. Did you see that Spielberg movie?'

'Oh, hey, yeah, man, I've seen them all.'

'Really. I'm impressed. You saw Schindler's List*?'*

'Uh . . . you sure Spielberg did it?'

'Never mind. The one I'm talking about had dinosaurs.'

'Oh, yeah, Jurassic Park, *sure. I saw that one four times. The sequels kind of sucked, but the first one really rocked.'*

'Then you'll remember where they tied up the goat so the big dinosaur would come?'

'Oh yeah, that was gross.'

'And did you feel sorry for the little goat?'

'Well, sure, sort of. I mean it was scared, crying and stuff.'

'Live bait. Like these worms.'

The clerk gave Morey a blank look.

Morey shook his finger at him. 'There's an important lesson here. Do you know what it is? I'll tell you. One man's worm is another man's goat. Remember that.'

She's wrong, Marty thought as he drifted back from his reverie. No matter what Lily said, no matter what anybody said, Morey Gilbert was no fisherman.

19

The unseasonable heat continued on the morning of Morey Gilbert's funeral, and meteorologists predicted yet another day of sunny skies and temperatures in the eighties. Old-timers in the state sat on sun-drenched porches, paging through their well-thumbed *Farmer's Almanac*s as if they were the writings of Nostradamus, searching history for a similar Minnesota April heat wave, and finding none. But fifteen hundred miles north, deep into the Canadian territories, the belly of an enormous cold front began to sag toward the American Midwest. A change was coming.

The Uptown Precinct had called for five extra patrols to manage the traffic converging on the synagogue where Morey Gilbert's service was held. By ten in the morning there was standing room only inside; by eleven, when the service began, the crowd had spilled out onto the lawn, the sidewalk, and ultimately the street itself. The numbers were in the hundreds, and there was no hope of moving them, and simply no place to move them to, so the street had finally been closed for three blocks in either direction. Not one resident or motorist complained. Even the cops, initially irritated to be diverted to traffic management, were eventually moved by the size and reverent demeanor of the crowd, and became caught up in the sense that they were more honor guard than enforcers, there to witness the passage of a great man. None of them understood it, and later could only say, 'You had to be there.'

Three hours later Magozzi and Gino sat in the unmarked outside Lily Gilbert's house behind the nursery, watching a small army of black-clad mourners funnel through the front door.

'You know, I think half the city showed up at the cemetery. I don't know how the hell she's going to squeeze them all into that cracker box,' Gino commented.

'It's a private reception. Family and friends only. These are the people who knew him best; the ones we want to listen to.'

Gino sighed and started to loosen the knot in his tie. 'You ever seen press coverage that heavy at a funeral before?'

'Not for anybody who wasn't in politics or a rock band.'

'And isn't that a sad comment on the state of the world? But I've been thinking, you listen to all those people who stood up and told their stories about how Morey helped them out? Christ, it was like taking a stroll through a maximum-security cell block. You had your drug dealers, gangbangers . . . hell, pick a felony, they were all there.'

'*Ex*-drug dealers, *ex*-gangbangers.'

Gino snorted. 'So they say. But what if one of them went bad again, came back to good old Morey for a little more monetary support and got pissed when he unhitched him from the gravy train?'

Magozzi looked at him. 'You know, I just figured it out. You're really respectful, almost genteel, until you loosen the knot in your tie, then everything goes to hell.'

'Well, it's possible, isn't it?'

Magozzi sighed and draped his wrists over the steering wheel. 'That one of the people he helped came back on him? I suppose, but if that's the case, we're going to have a hell of a time picking him out. There must have been over a thousand people there today. Besides, that punches a hole in the same killer hitting Rose Kleber, and I'm kind of stuck on that.' He leaned forward and squinted out the windshield. 'Who's that guy in the navy suit hugging Jack Gilbert?'

'Whoever it is, he ain't hugging him, he's holding him up. Didn't you see him bobbing and weaving at the grave? Man, for a minute, I thought he was going to fall in the hole and shake hands with his dad.'

'Yeah, I saw that.' Magozzi sagged back against the seat and watched the man in the navy suit steadying Jack, then just as soon as he had him stabilized, hurrying away as if he didn't want to be anywhere near him when he fell. It seemed that nobody wanted to be around Jack Gilbert. 'He's alone all the time, you notice?'

'Gilbert?'

'Yeah.'

Gino shrugged. 'No surprise there. The guy's a train wreck.'

'Lily wouldn't get within ten feet of him today. Neither would Marty, for that matter. He was just standing there all alone, just like Langer and McLaren told us he did at Hannah's funeral. You'd think at least his wife would have come with him.'

'I heard a couple of people talking about that on the way out of the cemetery. Sounds like she's going to file on him any day, if she hasn't already. No love lost there.'

Magozzi set his jaw. 'She still should have come. It would have been the decent thing to do.'

Gino turned sideways to look at him. 'Come on, Leo. Jack Gilbert is a drunken asshole. You reap what you sow, and all that, so stop feeling sorry for him.'

'I only do it from a distance. When I get closer, I hate his guts.'

'There's the partner I know and love.'

'But it's the chicken-and-egg thing.'

'Excuse me?'

'Well, you have to wonder, is he a drunken asshole because he's been ostracized, or was he ostracized because he's a drunken asshole?'

Gino blew out an exasperated sigh. 'I pick door number two. Can we go in now?'

Magozzi balked. 'Maybe we should wait a few more

minutes before we barge in. Just to be respectful.'

'We've been plenty respectful, Leo. It's not like we're the first ones here, standing at the door with tape recorders and rubber hoses. Besides, in a crowd this size no one's going to notice a couple of extra extremely handsome guys in spiffy funeral suits.'

Within fifteen minutes, Magozzi was questioning the wisdom of attending this reception, even though the reasoning had been sound. The theory was that no one, not even Morey Gilbert, was a hundred percent good, and there was no way a man could live eighty-four years without pissing somebody off. They were hoping that if they listened closely to the people who knew him, they might get a hint of something about the dead man they hadn't heard yet; something worth looking at.

But so far all Magozzi had heard were even more weeping testimonials – if the man hadn't been a saint, he had been damn close, and it was starting to annoy him. Morey Gilbert had given away whatever he had to give – time, money, counseling, food, lodging – and he hadn't only helped the people he'd stumbled upon – he'd gone out looking for them. It was just plain unnatural.

Suddenly, a whirl of motion from across the room caught his eye. Jack Gilbert was careening from guest to guest like a poorly aimed pinball, obliterating any sympathy Magozzi had felt for him earlier, advertising himself as the single most obvious failure of Morey Gilbert's good intentions.

Magozzi followed Jack with his eyes, thinking hard. It felt like his brain was bobbling over a series of speed bumps.

He found Gino loading up his second plate from a buffet table that exceeded even his wildest food fantasies.

'Is this great, or what?' Gino said gleefully. 'You gotta try the noodle stuff with the raisins.' He popped a cocktail meatball into his mouth. 'So, did you get anything interesting?'

'I think we've got to look harder at Jack Gilbert.'

Gino raised an eyebrow, which was the only movement possible with his mouth as full as it was.

'He's the one and only crack in Morey Gilbert's halo, Gino.'

'Yeah, but he's a wuss. And a drunk. And neither one of us got feelings from him.'

'That's just the thing – we considered him as a suspect, and when we didn't like that, we quit thinking about him. But what if he's the connection? What if something he was into got his father killed?'

Gino popped another meatball, decided he could indeed talk around it. 'What did Jack do?'

'Hell, I don't know . . .'

'No, no, that's what Langer and McLaren said, remember? When they were talking about Morey pushing Jack away at Hannah's funeral? So maybe he got involved in something really bad, way below Morey Gilbert's moral radar, and maybe the old man actually tried to get him out of it, and got popped for his trouble. He said himself there were people who wanted him dead. Maybe he really meant it. But how does Rose Kleber fit in?'

Magozzi used a toothpick with cellophane frills on the top to stab a meatball on Gino's plate. 'I've got a new plan. One murder at a time. If Rose Kleber is connected, it'll show up eventually. So let's talk to Jack's mystery wife, maybe check out his office books, take a look at the kind of people he's been representing, that sort of thing.'

Gino nodded thoughtfully. 'You might have something there.' He sidled a little closer and spoke under his meatball breath. 'Besides, I'm getting a little sick of standing around listening to people talk about what a great guy Morey Gilbert was. Two weeks ago I gave twenty bucks to the Humane Society and felt like Mr Charity. Now Morey Gilbert's making me look like a dirtbag. You know that Jeff Montgomery kid who works at the nursery? Well, turns out his folks were killed in a car wreck right after he started at the U, so Gilbert's been paying his tuition. Can you believe that?'

'No wonder the kid's been crying for the past two days.' Magozzi glanced over Gino's shoulder and saw Lily approaching in her long, black funeral dress. Marty was at her side, as he had been all day, picking up the slack for her useless son. Magozzi gave him a lot of credit for that.

Lily stopped and looked pointedly at Magozzi's empty hands, then nodded her approval at Gino's obscenely stacked plate of food. 'You have a good appetite, Detective.'

'This food is amazing, Mrs Gilbert. Somebody told me you cooked most of it yourself.'

'I did.'

'Then I think you should get rid of the nursery and open a restaurant.'

She didn't smile exactly, but it was obvious from the slight shift in her expression that even she wasn't immune to a compliment. 'I saw the picture of that woman who was murdered in the paper this morning.'

'Rose Kleber,' Magozzi said.

'Anyway, I thought I should tell you, her face looked a little familiar, so she might have come in a couple times, but she wasn't a regular. Regulars, I remember.'

'Lily?' Sol Biederman came up behind her and interrupted tentatively. 'Have you seen Ben?'

'Ben who?'

'Come on, Lily. Ben Schuler.' Sol was obviously worried, but a little impatient, too. 'He wasn't at the funeral, and if he's not here, something's wrong. His heart isn't so good, you know, and he's not answering his phone.'

'He's not here because he's not welcome in my house and he knows it,' Lily said sharply.

Sol's smile was gentle as he touched her hand. 'Frightening as you are, Lily, even you couldn't stop him from coming to his old friend's memorial. I'm going to drive over there, just to set my mind at ease, but I won't be long.'

'If he's not dead, tell him he's still not welcome in my house,' Lily said. She turned on her heel, saw Jack moving toward her, then turned and walked in the opposite direction.

Gino let out a low whistle as soon as Sol and Lily had gone their separate ways. 'Remind me never to get on that woman's short list. What's she got against this Ben guy?'

Marty shrugged. 'You never know with Lily. Excuse me, guys. I should get back to her.'

'She's got about fifty people around her right now, Marty,' Gino said. 'Cut yourself some slack and take a few minutes. I just saw a meatball with your name on it.'

It was tough to watch one of your own going down, Magozzi thought. Gino knocked himself out trying to engage Marty in conversation, and because Marty was a polite man, he tried hard to pretend to be interested in what Gino was saying. But the pretense part was painfully obvious, and after about ten minutes, Magozzi began to feel like they were torturing the guy.

'We should get going, Gino,' he said, but at that moment, Jack Gilbert came stumbling up, sloshing a drink almost as red as his face down the front of his white oxford. He draped his arm over Marty's shoulder. 'Hey, guys! What a turnout, huh?' He gestured around the room with his drink, spraying an arc of punch. 'You'd think the fucking Pope died.'

With a suddenness that surprised everyone, Marty spun toward Jack, dislodging the offending arm from his shoulder, and snatched away Jack's drink. For a minute, Magozzi thought he saw a trace of the old Gorilla. 'Don't push it, Jack. Not today.'

Jack stumbled backward and almost lost his balance. 'Jeez, no offense, Marty. You gotta chill. You want a drink?'

A heavyset woman with maroon hair approached and handed Marty a portable phone. 'Somebody's calling for you.' When Marty took the phone and stepped away, she moved in on Jack. 'Jack Gilbert, look at you, sloshing around, spilling drinks, offending people . . . how could you do this to your mother?'

Jack's head wobbled on his neck a little as he tried to bring the woman into focus. 'Jesus, Sheila, is that you? You look like Dennis Rodman. What the fuck happened to your hair?'

She narrowed her eyes and leaned close to him. '*Farshtinkener paskudnyak*,' she hissed, then stormed away.

Gino's eyes were wide open. He didn't know what the woman had called him, but he was absolutely sure Jack had deserved it. 'You know what, Mr Gilbert? You might want to think about reeling it in a little bit. Sit down on the couch over there, maybe get a cup of coffee.'

'Well, that's a hell of an idea, Detective, but you

see, I just poured my best bottle of bourbon in the punch bowl and there's this Jewish tradition that says if you pour alcohol at a funeral, you have to drink it all or it dishonors the dead.'

Gino stared at him for a minute. He was pretty sure he was full of shit, but you never knew with religion. I mean, who would believe the Catholics smear ashes on people's foreheads?

'He was kidding, Gino,' Magozzi said.

'I knew that. Let's get out of here.'

He and Magozzi started to shoulder past Jack when Marty's hand shot out and grabbed Gino's arm. Still a lot of strength in that hand, Gino was thinking as Marty held him fast, murmuring a low reassurance of some kind into the phone before pulling it away from his ear and pushing disconnect. 'Thought you might want to hear this,' he said very quietly, looking around to make sure none of the guests were close enough to overhear him. 'That was Sol. Ben Schuler's been shot.'

Magozzi's face tightened. 'Dead?'

Marty nodded grimly.

'Who's dead?' Jack said much too loudly, bumbling in a little closer.

'Keep it down, Jack,' Marty told him. 'It's Ben Schuler.'

'No shit? Poor old bastard. What was it, heart attack?'

Marty hesitated, maybe in a remnant of every cop's reluctance to share information with a non-cop. 'No,' he finally said. 'He was shot. Once in the head. Just like Morey.'

With those few words, Jack Gilbert became frighteningly sober, and every drop of blood drained from his drunken, red face. 'Suicide?'

Marty shook his head.

Jack Gilbert got a strange look on his face then – one that Magozzi had only seen a few times in his life – a look of genuine fear. 'Jesus Christ,' he whispered.

'Did you know him?' Gino asked.

Jack nodded. 'Yeah. I knew him.' And then he turned and walked away in a perfectly straight line.

Marty found him a few moments later standing over the kitchen table, staring down at the picture of Rose Kleber in the morning paper. His whole body was shaking.

20

There were a lot of neighborhoods in Minneapolis that had once been moderately fashionable, until freeways started taking big bites out of the city's real estate. Ben Schuler's house was in one of these, perched on a hill where hundred-year-old elms used to shade a boulevard the city had filled with flowers every spring. Dutch elm disease had taken most of the trees within the past twenty years, a new freeway ramp system had taken the rest, and now the locals had little to look at except the six lanes of traffic at the bottom of the hill. Magozzi and Gino could hear the roar of an eighteen-wheeler shifting on an upgrade the minute they got out of the car.

'Used to be nicer up here,' Magozzi said, looking at a long crack in the stucco of Ben Schuler's house; the sagging porch of the two-story brick next door. 'My great aunt had a big old Victorian a few blocks over.'

'Then why the hell did it take you so long to find it?' Gino grumped, peeling off his suit coat and tie and draping them over the seat.

'Haven't been up here in years. We only came a couple of times, when I was about six or seven. She was a scary old broad. Never met a person she liked, according to my folks, and that included family. Refused to speak English, and my dad refused to speak Italian, just to piss her off. Last time we came she slapped me right across the face for picking up my fork before she said grace.'

Gino's mouth tightened into an unforgiving line. Striking a child was one of the few things utterly beyond his comprehension. 'Goddamnit, I hate that. I hope your dad slugged her.'

'My dad wouldn't raise a hand to a woman if she was flaying him alive.' Magozzi smiled a little, remembering. 'My mom decked her, though.'

Gino grinned and blew a kiss eastward toward St Paul, where Magozzi's parents still lived in the house he'd grown up in. 'I always did like your mother.'

'And she likes you. Are you going to take off all your clothes, or can we go in now?'

'You know what it costs to get a suit dry-cleaned?'

Magozzi shook his head. 'Never paid attention.'

'Boy, sometimes I hate single people. I just paid a pretty penny to get this thing cleaned, and I sure as hell don't want it smelling like a murder house.'

'You're still wearing your pants.'

'Yeah, well I can't figure a way around that.' He slammed the car door and they headed up the drive.

'Looks like Anant and the BCA boys beat us here.'

'Small wonder.' Gino glanced at the ugly ME wagon in the drive, and the BCA van snugged up behind it. 'GPS in both those vehicles, and we don't even get a working air conditioner. There is no justice in this world.'

Jimmy Grimm met Magozzi and Gino at the back door of Ben Schuler's house. 'You gotta stop this guy,' were the first words out of his mouth.

'Gee, good idea, Jimmy,' Gino said. 'Why didn't we think of that?'

Jimmy stepped aside to let Gino pass into the small kitchen. 'What got his nose out of joint?' he asked Magozzi.

'The high cost of dry cleaning, mostly. Also, you have a GPS and we don't.' Magozzi's eyes strayed to a crayon drawing on the refrigerator door. He had no clue what it was, but obviously no one had stifled the kid's creativity yet, because the colors were good. 'How bad is it in there?' He tipped his head toward a hallway he assumed led to the bedroom.

Jimmy puffed his cheeks and unsnapped the collar of his white clean suit. 'We've got a minimum of gore and a maximum of pathetic. Anant's really getting bummed out. He's got this reverence-for-the-aged business going, which doesn't help. Is that a Hindu thing?'

'That's a decency thing,' Gino said.

'Well, whatever it is, I think it's cumulative, and I'm telling you, this creep popping old people is even getting to me. I walk into these houses and look around at pictures of grandkids and prescription bottles and Medicare bills and things like that, and I see my folks' place, you know? I mean, these people are at the end of their lives, just trying to get by . . . it just doesn't make any sense. And this one is the worst yet.'

Gino was shaking his head. 'Can't be worse than Rose Kleber. I see that GRANDMA'S GARDEN sign in my dreams; that, and the plate of cookies she'd just baked for her granddaughters.'

Jimmy looked at him for a minute. 'I think he took one of those cookies.'

Magozzi's brows shots up. 'I didn't read that in the report.'

'I didn't put it in. It was supposition, pure and simple. Inadmissible. No evidentiary value. She just had them arranged so neatly on that plate, covered up with plastic, but it was lifted on one side, and there was this space where a cookie should have been. It was just a mental picture I got, that bastard killing an old lady, then helping himself to a cookie she'd baked on the way out.' He tried for a weak smile. 'That's what really gets you after a while, you know? The mental pictures that stay with you. And this one is a zinger. Ben Schuler knew what was coming, and he was scared out of his mind. Looks like the killer might have played with him a while; maybe chased him around, maybe talked to him, I don't know. But the poor old man crawled all over the damn bedroom trying to get away, and that's the picture I'm taking away from this house.'

Gino was scowling at him, working hard at erasing the picture Jimmy Grimm had just put in his mind.

He'd get his own picture when he looked at the scene, and the trick was, you saw this stuff, you sorted out the details that would help the investigation, and then you forgot the rest. If you spent too much time dwelling on images of whimpering, scared old men crawling away from a killer, it pushed you down, turned you to mush, and then you couldn't do the job. And Grimm knew that, damnit. 'Jeez, Grimm, you're starting to sound like a chick flick. You bucking for meter maid, or what?'

'Right now that doesn't sound half bad.' He headed down the hallway. 'Stay right behind me. We've got an entry cleared, but that's about all we've had time for so far. Anant wants you to get a look at the scene before we start taking photos and dusting and bagging.'

Aging floorboards creaked beneath their feet as they walked past an enormous collection of black-and-white family photographs that had to be at least fifty years old. Halfway down the hall Magozzi and Gino both stopped and looked back at the pictures they'd passed, then forward at the ones ahead.

Jimmy glanced back over his shoulder. 'What's the holdup? You're not touching anything, are you?'

'Yeah, we're dragging our hands down the wall, smearing fingerprints,' Gino grumbled irritably. 'Jeez, Grimm, ease up a little. What's the deal with these photos? This is the weirdest thing I ever saw.'

Jimmy walked back to join them. 'Tell me about it. They're all prints of the same picture. Sixty of them in all. Creepy, eh? His friend – the old guy who found him?'

'Sol Biederman.'

'That's him. He was still here when I arrived. Said this is the only photo Ben Schuler had of his family. His folks, him, and his little sister. Apparently he framed another print every year.'

'He say why?'

Jimmy shrugged. 'They died in the camps; he didn't. Survivor's guilt, memorial, who knows?'

Magozzi and Gino exchanged a sorry glance.

'Ben Schuler was in a concentration camp?' Magozzi asked.

'That's what Biederman said.' Jimmy Grimm met Magozzi's eyes. 'Three and counting.'

Anantanand Rambachan stood in the middle of Ben Schuler's bedroom, his head bent, his palms pressed together just beneath his chin. He looked more like a mourner than a medical examiner, Magozzi thought, hesitating in the doorway, wondering if Anant were praying, and if it would be some unforgivable breach of Hindu etiquette to interrupt.

Gino was a little less sensitive. 'Hey, Anant. You in a trance, or what?'

Anant smiled only a little as he turned toward them. No teeth; not tonight. 'Good evening Detective Rolseth, Detective Magozzi. And to answer your question, Detective Rolseth, I was not in a trance. Had I been in such a state, I would have been unable to hear your question. I was merely . . .' His slick, dark brows furrowed as he opened his hands, then closed them and brought them to his chest.

'Taking it all in?' Gino asked.

'Yes. Yes, that is precisely the phrase that describes what I was doing. Thank you.' He gestured them into the room. 'Straight from the door to where I am standing, if you please. Do you see where the floor is a darker color?'

Magozzi glanced down at a three-foot-wide strip in the hardwood where the gleam of old varnish lingered, unfaded by sun and wear. 'There was a runner here?'

'Yes. Mr Grimm removed it for examination before we came in, so we would have a path into this terrible story.'

Magozzi and Gino stepped carefully, walking single file, directly in the center of the path the runner had left. Halfway into the room they stopped and looked around without saying anything, reading Anant's terrible story with their eyes.

The bedroom was a mess, and mercifully, smelled more like cheap aftershave than anything else. Whatever bottles had been on the dresser were now merely a litter of broken glass and spilled liquid on the floor. A nightstand next to the bed was overturned, with a broken lamp nearby, its green glass shade shattered. What was left of the smashed phone was over in a far corner, and a faded chenille bedspread had been dragged from the bed.

The shoes were a standout in the midst of all this

wreckage, somehow untouched by whatever violence had happened here. They were black, highly polished, and neatly placed in front of a hard-backed chair, waiting for feet.

Gino blew out a long sigh. He was looking into the open closet, at a jumble of clothes on the floor that had been pulled from the hangers. 'Where is he? In there?'

Anant followed his gaze. 'No. Not anymore. Mr Schuler is under the bed.'

Magozzi closed his eyes briefly and envisioned a terrified old man dragging himself from one useless hiding place to another in a sick, human version of cat and mouse, trying futilely to save his own life up until the end. Or perhaps he'd already accepted his fate and had sought out the shelter of the bed instinctively, like an injured animal, so he could die out of view and in relative peace – if such a thing were possible when you were being pursued by a sadistic psycho with a gun. 'I don't see any blood. He was shot under the bed?'

'I believe you are correct, Detective,' Anant said, kneeling down and gesturing for them to do the same. He withdrew a mini-Maglite from his coat pocket and illuminated the hidden carnage under the bed. 'Please, gentlemen, if you will.'

Magozzi and Gino crouched down beside him and stared at what was left of Ben Schuler's head. The top of his skull had been reduced to blood and pulp and bone fragments, but his face, ghastly white in the intense halo of the flashlight, was still horribly intact and frozen in a grotesquely twisted expression, as if someone had taken a blowtorch to a Picasso portrait.

Gino turned away briefly. 'Jesus . . . his *face.* Why does it look like that?'

'That is the expression he died with, Detective, frozen in time for us to decipher. I believe you are seeing terror.' Anant swept the light downward to focus on Ben Schuler's clothing – a worn, woolen blazer, the blood-spattered shirt beneath it, and a partially knotted necktie. 'It appears he was preparing to go somewhere.'

'Morey Gilbert's funeral,' Magozzi said quietly. 'He was going to his friend's funeral.'

Jimmy Grimm poked his head through the doorway. 'We've got media outside, guys. All four stations and both papers. Things are heating up.'

21

The news of Ben Schuler's murder had spread quickly through the crowd of mourners at the Gilbert house, quieting voices, sharpening senses, whispering an evil warning. The police might still be floundering, searching for the definitive thread that tied these murders together, but every man and woman in that house knew the truth. Someone was killing Jews.

Not one of them spoke this terrible thought aloud, but they stayed longer than they might have otherwise, huddled together in small groups, seeking the comfort of safety in numbers. It was full dark by the time they started to leave, and even then, they lingered at the door with long last condolences.

While the line of nice people made their way out the front door, Jack slipped out the back and disappeared into the shadows of the backyard.

There were plenty of obstacles on the way to the equipment shed behind the greenhouse, like blades of grass and sundry little bumps in the lawn, but Jack finally reached his destination with only a few scrapes and grass stains. At least he hoped they were grass stains, and that he hadn't fallen on a frog.

He paused at the door and pressed his back against

the rough wood, listening. It was very dark out here, and once you got past the raucous croaking of all the goddamned frogs in the yard, it was very quiet. The only things he could hear were the slamming of his heart against his chest and the scrape of splinters destroying the fine wool of his suit as he slid down to a crouch and put his head in his hands.

Jesus, he had to get a grip, had to relax, had to get a plan, and then, he had to get another drink.

He was unsteady on his feet when he finally stood and pushed the door open, cringing when the hinges squeaked. He stumbled into the center of the room and batted his hands around his head until he found the chain to the bare, overhead bulb.

Illuminated, the shed was as tidy as it had always been. He looked around at all the things that had scared him as a kid: the shovels with their knife-like edges, the gleaming clipper blades, the pointed trowels and garden rakes whose tines glinted like teeth in the swinging light. All monsters when Jack had been six, coming into the shed for the very first time after dark.

His father's hand was big – fingers halfway down his tiny chest, thumb halfway down his back – but oddly weightless. Just warm and comforting.

'Go on, Jackie. Go on in.'

A firm head shake. Six-year-old stubborn.

'No? Ah. It looks different at night, doesn't it?'

And then a little, jerky nod.

'And all the tools, they look a little scary, am I right?'

Another nod, a little braver now that the scary part was out in the open.

'Ha! You think I would let something hurt my son, my golden boy?'

And then there were strong arms scooping him up, lifting him high, holding him close against a scratchy wool shirt that smelled like sweat and soil and air. 'Nothing here will hurt you. Nothing anywhere will ever hurt you. I won't let it. You believe me, don't you, Jackie?'

Jack didn't realize he was crying until he heard the horrible, wrenching sounds of his own sobs. He clamped his hand over his mouth to muffle the noise and stumbled, half blind from the potent cocktail of bourbon and tears, over to the corner where bags of sheep manure were stacked on a pallet. It took him ten minutes to unload the heavy bags off to the side so he could pull the wooden pallet away from the wall, and by then the tears had stopped.

He found the crack in the cement floor right away, grabbed a trowel, and started to pry up the chunk of concrete, feeling beads of nervous sweat pearl up on his forehead.

The plastic bag was dark with oil, the rags inside slick and sweet smelling. Evil wrapped in swaddling clothes.

Jack stared down at the gun that felt so familiar in his hand, fascinated by the way the overhead light glinted off the barrel. He popped open the chamber and counted the bullets, and was about to pocket it when he heard the door squeak open behind him.

Without thinking, he gripped the gun and spun around in a shooter's stance. He knew how to do that very well.

One of the kids who worked at the nursery was standing in the doorway, his eyes the size of fried eggs and fixed on the gun. 'Omigod omigod . . . Mr Gilbert? It's me, Jeff Mongtomery? Please don't shoot.'

Jack collapsed onto his butt and closed his eyes, feeling the tremors as the adrenaline tried to find a place to go. Jesus Christ, he'd almost shot the kid. 'Oh, for fuck's sake,' he mumbled, adrenaline gone, alcohol back, slurring his words. 'I'm not gonna shoot you. Didn't anyone ever tell you not to sneak up on a guy with a gun?'

'I . . . I . . . I didn't know you had a gun? I just saw the light on and thought I'd better check it out?'

Jack lurched to his feet on jellied legs and saw the kid still frozen in the doorway, his eyes darting back and forth, looking like a rabbit about to run. It occurred to him then how bad this probably looked.

'Listen, kid. This isn't what it looks like. I fucking hate guns, but there's some crazy son of a bitch running around shooting up the neighborhood, so I need this, understand?'

'Yessir, yessir, I sure do. Uh . . . I think I'll go now?'

'No, no, wait a minute.' Jack gestured wildly with the gun and the kid shrank back against the door, terrified. Jack looked from the kid's eyes to the gun in his hand. 'Oh, Christ, I'm sorry.' He shoved the gun in his pocket and held out his open hands. 'Don't be afraid, kid . . . Jeff, isn't it?'

The boy nodded cautiously.

'Okay, Jeff, now listen. I'm really sorry I scared you, I'm just a little drunk, and pretty scared myself, and I've just got this gun to protect myself, see? But the thing is, it's not exactly legal, you follow? So it wouldn't be cool if anyone found out I had it. Especially Marty. For God's sake don't tell Marty, okay?'

'Okay, sure, no problem, Mr Gilbert.'

'Excellent. Just excellent.' Jack clapped his hands together and the kid jumped. 'So! Want to give me a hand stacking those bags back on the pallet?'

'I sure do, Mr Gilbert.'

Jack gave him a wonderful smile. 'You're a good kid, Jeff.'

22

After the last of the mourners had left Lily's, Marty found Jack slumped behind the wheel of his Mercedes, staring into the dark beyond the windshield, an empty silver flask dripping its last precious drops of bourbon on the buttery leather seat. Marty bent down to the open window and nearly passed out.

'God, Jack, what the hell is that smell?'

Jack didn't even look at him. 'Sheep manure. You oughta air out the equipment shed, Marty. The place reeks.' He sounded oddly sober for a man who had probably been drinking since sunrise.

'What were you doing in the equipment shed?'

'Just . . . taking a trip down memory lane, I guess. Pop used to take me out there when I was a kid. Let me hang out while he sharpened the tools. You know what? I think I've had a little too much to drink to actually start this thing, and I could really use a shower. Feel like driving me home, Marty?'

'Not in that car.'

Twenty minutes later they were in Marty's '66 Chevy Malibu, top down to disperse the smell, heading west on the freeway past downtown Minneapolis. The traffic was light, the night air had an almost sexual warmth, and Jack was uncharacteristically quiet in the passenger seat.

Finally Marty said the words he'd thought would never come out of his mouth. 'Okay, Jack. Start talking.'

'No problem, buddy. Pick a subject.'

'Let's start with what you did to your mother.'

'Excuse me?'

'Don't give me that crap, Jack. You've got about as much interest in religion as a fern, and all of a sudden you're filled with the spirit and decide to chuck the yarmulke and become a Christian? Bullshit. That stupid confirmation picture – and probably your marriage, too – was a direct shot at your folks.'

'So?'

'So it was childish and spiteful and damn near unforgivable.'

Jack sighed noisily. 'You finished?'

'No, goddamnit, I am not finished. So you had a fight with your dad. Lily didn't even know what it was about, so why'd you shut her out?'

'It's complicated. And you don't want to know.'

'Yeah, I do want to know. I want to know what the hell Morey said that made you lash out like that.'

Jack straightened a little in the seat and looked at Marty with something like amazement. 'You know what, Marty? You're the very first person who ever thought I might have had a reason for what I did, that I wasn't just being an asshole.' He faced front again and shook his head. 'Man, you cannot imagine what that feels like.'

'Great. Glad I made you happy. So what was the reason?'

'I really love you for that, Marty.'

'Oh, for chrissake, I can't talk to you when you're like this.'

'Well that's good, Marty, 'cause I didn't want to talk about that shit anyway. Water under the bridge, spilt milk, bygones . . .'

'Damnit, Jack, it isn't any of those things, because it's still hurting Lily. And you, for that matter. You gotta fix it.'

Jack shook his head strongly. 'Can't.'

'Well then, tell me what it is. Maybe I can fix it.'

'God, you are such an arrogant prick, which is pretty funny, when you think about it. What the hell have you got to be arrogant about? You can't even fix your own life, so just leave it alone. I'm not going to talk about it.'

Marty's fingers tightened on the wheel as he took the tight cloverleaf onto the freeway that led to Wayzata. 'Fine. You don't want to talk about that? Then let's talk about Rose Kleber.'

Jack folded his arms across his chest. 'I didn't know her.'

'Don't give me that shit, Jack. I saw your expression when you were looking at her picture in the paper.'

Jack didn't move for a minute, didn't say anything,

but Marty could feel him tense. 'Okay, okay. So I met her once. So what? I meet a lot of people. Doesn't mean I know them. I don't think I ever even heard her last name. It was just a shock, that's all. I mean, Jesus. Three old Jews get capped in three days, and it turns out I know all of them.'

'How'd you meet her?'

'Christ, I don't know, what the hell is this? What's with all the questions?'

Marty knew better than to give him time to think. 'Well, it's like this, Jack. The cops are looking for a link between the victims, and it's starting to look like you might be it.'

'That's bullshit. I'll bet you could find at least a hundred people who knew all three of them.'

'They were close, weren't they? Morey, Ben, and Rose?'

'How the fuck should I know?'

'Because you DO, goddamnit. You were scared shitless when you heard about Ben Schuler getting shot, and Gino and Magozzi saw that. You think they aren't going to wonder why? And they didn't even see you freak out when you saw Rose Kleber's picture. Jesus, Jack, you know something about these murders. Why aren't you giving it up? People are dying.'

Jack turned on him. 'What the hell is this? Yesterday you couldn't have cared less who killed your own father-in-law, and today you're Mr Cop again. What's that about?'

'Oh yeah? Well you forgot something, Jack. Yesterday you were all over me for *not* trying to find out who killed Morey, and now that I'm asking a couple of questions, you're the one who doesn't want to talk about it. What's *that* about?'

Jack slammed his head back against the seat in frustration; read the big white-and-green freeway sign as they went under an overpass. 'Goddamnit, Marty, that was Jonquil. You missed it. Take the next exit.'

'You gotta talk to me, Jack. This isn't going to go away.'

Jack was silent for a moment, then bizarrely, just as they were slowing on the freeway exit and about to hit the safer surface streets, he buckled his lap belt. 'Take a right. Three blocks up, the road forks at a creek, and that's where you bear left.'

Marty looked at his right hand curled around the steering wheel. It looked like a fist, and he wondered what it would feel like to slam that fist into Jack's face. It took all his willpower to keep his voice calm and nonthreatening. 'Listen to me, Jack. You're not thinking straight. If you know something that might help the cops stop these murders, you have to tell them. Because if you don't and somebody else dies, you might as well have pulled the trigger yourself.'

Jack turned to him with a strange smile that seemed to flash on and off as they passed under streetlights. 'That's not going to happen, Marty.

Don't worry about it. You still got that .357 you used to have?'

Marty looked at Jack in disbelief and almost clipped a parked car. 'Goddamnit, Jack, you're driving me crazy. I don't even know who you are anymore.'

'Yeah, me either. But what about the gun? Have you still got it?'

Marty slammed on the brakes, flinging Jack forward, and the car screeched to a halt in the middle of the street. 'Yes, I've got the goddamned gun! You want to borrow it? Put a bullet in your head and save me the trouble?'

'Jesus, Marty, take it easy.' Jack shook the hand he'd used to brace himself against the dashboard. 'You nearly broke my wrist. Good thing I had my seat belt on. Did you know that ninety percent of car accidents happen on surface streets? Everybody thinks the freeways are the killing fields, but it just ain't so.'

Marty closed his eyes and leaned his forehead against the steering wheel.

'Now, back to the gun. I want you to do me a favor. Go home, pick it up, keep it close, and stay with Ma for a few days. Can you do that?'

Marty rolled his head to look at him with an expression of hopeless resignation. 'Jack, you have to tell me what's happening.'

'People are getting shot, that's what's happening. Old people. Jews. Like Ma. Just keep an eye out, that's all.'

Marty sighed and moved the car slowly forward. Left at the creek, around the sweeping curves of a heavily wooded development, all the time feeling as if he were driving through a dream, powerless to change anything.

'You don't really think I'd let people die if I could do anything to stop it, do you, Marty?'

Marty didn't even have to think about it, and that surprised him. 'No. I guess I don't. But I think you're in trouble, and you won't let me help you.'

Jack chuckled. 'I've been past help for a long time now, Marty. But it was goddamned nice of you to offer.' He leaned his head back on the seat and looked up at the golden bottoms of night clouds, reflecting the distant city lights. 'Boy, Hannah used to love this car. Sometimes when you were working nights we'd take it down to Porky's for hot fudge cake, then drive around the lakes with the top down. Those were really good days.'

Marty squeezed his eyes shut for a moment, thought that if he kept them closed, eventually they'd run off the road and into a tree and both die, and maybe the world would be a better place.

'Her world turned on you, Marty, you know that? That's the other reason I love you. You made Hannah happy.'

Marty pressed his lips together, went to that dark place he visited every day. 'I got Hannah killed.'

'No you didn't, Marty. Don't take that on yourself.' Jack reached over and ruffled Marty's hair in a strangely paternal gesture, and for the first time in over a year, Marty thought he might cry.

Jack stood at the end of his tree-lined driveway and watched Marty pull away. He waited until the taillights disappeared around a curve before gingerly pulling the gun from his pocket. He'd spent the whole ride home worried about the damn thing firing and blowing his dick off, because he couldn't for the life of him remember if he'd set the safety back in the equipment shed.

He still had the gun in his hand when he heard a soft *snick-snick* in the trees behind him. Deer, he thought, or maybe those damn raccoons, but still, the hair on the back of his neck stood up.

23

Gino and Magozzi caught the last half of the ten o'clock news from a dark booth in the back of the Sports Bar with No Name. Gino was eating an enchilada the size of a baseball bat, drenched in hot sauce; Magozzi was eating a bowl of chicken noodle soup. His stomach was a mess.

On the overhead screen they watched a saccharine five-minute segment on Morey Gilbert's funeral that was a blatant plug for their upcoming focus piece, *St Gilbert of Uptown,* then location shots of Ben Schuler's house that bled into a close-up of Magozzi, giving the standard ambiguous statement: They had no suspects in custody, they were pursuing all possible leads, and no, they had not confirmed a definitive connection between the murders of Morey Gilbert, Rose Kleber and Ben Schuler. At that point the shrill voice of Kristen Keller, Channel Ten's blonde Barbie doll, called out from somewhere off-camera, 'Detective Magozzi! All three murder victims were concentration camp survivors. That certainly looks like a definitive connection from where I'm standing.'

'Look at that.' Gino jabbed his fork at the screen. 'Straight to commercial after she kicks us in the balls.

Goddamnit I hate that woman. You know what we ought to do? Catch her in a dark alley some night and shave her head. That'd keep her off the air for a while. What blows me away is how they found out Schuler had been in the camps that fast.'

'Neighbors, probably,' Magozzi said, dipping into his soup. 'Jimmy said the camera crews were knocking on doors for thirty minutes before we came out.'

'Malcherson ain't gonna like that interview.'

Magozzi put down his spoon. 'You have any Tums?'

It was almost eleven o'clock by the time Gino and Magozzi slogged up the steps to City Hall. Their suits were rumpled, their ties loosened, and remnants of Lily Gilbert's cooking and the more recent enchilada decorated Gino's once-white shirt. The wide corridor that led to Homicide was deserted, the lights were on dim, and the building was so quiet they could hear Johnny McLaren's voice before they opened the office door.

He was talking on the phone at Gloria's station, probably because he couldn't find the phone under the landfill on his own desk. He gave them a grin and a wave, and they followed his thumb toward the back of the room, where Langer was daintily ripping the last flesh off a chicken wing.

'Whoa,' Gino said. 'Langer's eating barbecued chicken wings again. It's the end of the world.' He looked down at the decimated bones piled neatly on a napkin. 'I thought you were a vegetarian.'

'I was, until last night. I love these things. Want one?' He poked the greasy white bag sitting on his blotter.

'No thanks. What are you two doing here so late?'

Langer patted the corners of his mouth with a napkin. 'Overseas calls to a few cops we couldn't reach during the day. McLaren's trying to connect with some guy in Johannesburg, if you can believe that.'

McLaren hung up the phone and walked back toward his own desk. 'Next time we get a lull in Homicide we should all pack up and go to South Africa. Every time I try to call those guys, they're out on another murder.' He slapped a message slip on Langer's desk. 'And you are calling this one, because I do not know how to pronounce a name with no vowels. I asked for the guy, they hung up on me.'

'What's going on?' Magozzi asked. 'What's with the overseas calls?'

McLaren's face fell. 'You're kidding me. You didn't watch the six o'clock news? Oh, man . . .' He threw up his hands. 'The one time we give a really killer press conference, you miss it. Malcherson actually let us talk this time, and I was great, even if I do say so myself. Wasn't I, Langer?'

Langer rolled his eyes up to Magozzi. 'He wore the madras jacket.'

Magozzi winced.

'They tried to trip us up, of course' – McLaren

waggled his eyebrows – 'especially that dipshit new guy with the permed hair who does the late news. But we were rocks. Cool, tough, kind of your basic hero types. I got a tape . . .'

'So what the hell happened?' Gino asked, one arm diving deep into the chicken wing bag. 'Something break on the train track guy?'

'Oh yeah, did it ever,' McLaren grinned. 'Seems the .45 that damn near took off Arlen Fischer's arm is one hot piece. Got a shitload of hits on that gun from Interpol. Let's see, there was Johannesburg, London, Paris, Prague . . . and a couple of others.'

'Milan and Geneva,' Langer reminded him.

'Right. Anyway, Channel Three has a source in the FBI who caught the Interpol connection, and the press went nuts. International intrigue in the heartland, that kind of stuff.'

'So what are you thinking?' Magozzi asked.

Langer shrugged. 'Interpol's always had them pegged as contract killings. They've got six murders spread out over fifteen years – seven, counting Arlen Fischer – and it looks like the same shooter using the same gun. In and out clean, no witnesses, no forensics, single shot to the head.'

'Except Arlen Fischer wasn't shot in the head,' Magozzi reminded him.

'That's the best part. There's always a chance the gun traveled without the shooter, of course – maybe he dumped it after the last hit and it ended up over here in someone else's hands – but what Interpol's hoping is that it's the same killer, and that the Arlen Fischer hit was personal. Contract killers don't usually torture strangers.'

Magozzi nodded. 'So he knew Fischer.'

'That's the theory. That Fischer and his killer crossed paths at one point, and if we can find that connection, we might be able to put a name to this guy.'

'Jeez, guys,' Magozzi said with a bemused smile. 'You're going to nail an international hit man.'

'Wouldn't that just be roses?' McLaren grinned. 'But the bad part is that Interpol wants us to let the FBI in on it. They got a real hard-on for this guy. Chief Malcherson is keeping them at bay until we check out the six overseas victims, see if we can't tie them to Fischer somehow. Speaking of which' – McLaren handed Langer the message slip – 'here's Mr Consonant. I ain't calling him, I told you.'

'He probably speaks English, McLaren.'

'That's not going to do me a whole lot of good if I can't get him on the phone because I can't pronounce his friggin' name.'

'All right, all right.' Langer took the slip and passed another one over. 'You do Paris, then. I swear those people pretend they can't speak English just to be irritating.'

Gino snorted. 'Like McLaren can speak French.'

Langer smiled at him. 'McLaren is fluent.'

'No way.'

'Just in the Romance languages,' McLaren said.

'I got them hammered down pretty well, but those Slavic dialects are a bitch.'

He trotted over to his desk and started punching in a long series of numbers. Gino and Magozzi gaped at him when he started babbling in a language neither could hope to understand.

'Unbelievable,' Gino murmured. 'And all this time I thought McLaren was just another pretty face.'

'So what are you guys doing here?' Langer asked.

Gino and Magozzi traded gloomy expressions. They were tired, discouraged, and underneath it all, maybe a little scared, both feeling as if things were getting away from them. 'We lost another senior,' Magozzi said.

Langer's face sagged. 'You've got to be kidding.'

'Wish I were,' Magozzi said grimly. 'Eighty-seven, shot in his own house, another tattoo.'

Langer blew out a pained breath and looked off to the side, shaking his head. 'What the hell is going on out there?'

'The TV talking heads are starting to ask the same thing,' Gino grumbled. 'You got the six o'clock edition; they gave us the ten. Pretty much chewed us up and spit us out.'

'I'm going to make the calls,' Magozzi told Gino as he headed for his own desk. Gino nodded, but lingered behind with Langer.

'So who's your victim?' Langer asked.

'Guy called Ben Schuler. Ever hear of him?'

Langer shook his head. 'I don't think so.'

'Well, apparently he and Morey knew each other pretty well.'

Langer's brows peaked. 'You found your thread.'

'The beginnings of one, maybe, but just between Schuler and Gilbert. Rose Kleber's still the odd man out. We talked to her family yesterday, looking for a connection between her and Morey Gilbert, but there was nothing there. Now Leo's checking with them to see if she knew Ben Schuler. Maybe we can tie them all together that way.' He glanced over at Magozzi. The phone was still pressed to his ear, but he was shaking his head and held one thumb down. 'Or maybe not.'

Magozzi hung up the phone and pulled a rolling chair close to Langer's desk. He didn't look nearly as depressed as Gino thought he should. 'Rose Kleber's family never heard of Ben Schuler.'

'Yeah, I got that.' Gino was an unhappy man.

'But I've been thinking how weird it is, we've got a string of killings, and now it turns out the murder Langer and McLaren are working has a string behind it . . .'

'Do not go there,' Gino warned him. 'We're busting our balls trying to connect three murders and now you want to bring in another one? Come on, Leo, we looked at it, then we shit-canned that idea the first day. The murders were just too different, and so were the victims.'

'They were all old, Gino, three of them lived in the same neighborhood if you count Arlen Fischer.'

Langer was regarding Magozzi, chin in his hand. 'Guns don't match. Victim profiles don't match. Yours were Jews, camp survivors; ours was a Lutheran.'

Magozzi grimaced and scratched the back of his neck. 'Yeah, I know. You look at this thing head-on, you see four old people, all executed within a few days and a few miles of each other; but then you look at the details, and they shoot it all to hell. But it's still weird. They're as much alike as they are different.'

Langer frowned at him. 'No way we could justify running this as a tandem with all the holes.'

'Yeah, I know that. Let's just keep the lines of communication open, okay?'

Gino was looking frighteningly shrewd, tapping a plump forefinger against his lips. 'You know, come to think of it, I could like this a lot. Jack Gilbert, kingpin of a gang of international assassins.'

Langer laughed out loud. 'Jack Gilbert? You've got to be kidding.'

'Ah, I don't know. Something's just not right with that guy. When he heard Ben Schuler was shot, the blood drained out of his face so fast I thought he was going to keel right over.'

'Well, maybe he knew him.'

'He said he did, but it was more than that. You should have seen him, Langer. Jack Gilbert was scared to death.'

24

Marty walked into his house and felt like a trespasser. He'd only been gone for two days, but already the kitchen looked strange and unfamiliar, like a place somebody else lived.

You should sell the house, Marty. Get a condo, maybe. Or come to live with Lily and me. We could use the help at the nursery, anyway.

I can't, Morey. I belong here.

No. You and Hannah belonged here. The two of you. Now you have to find where you belong without her.

It isn't over.

Of course it's over. The case is closed. The animal who murdered my daughter is dead. This is as it should be. I thank God for this. I dance around his grave in my heart. And now we can live again.

That had been months and months ago. He'd never seen Morey alive again.

The .357 was still in the hamper, buried beneath the mildewed, shower-drenched clothes he'd thrown in there when Jeff Montgomery had come to tell him Morey was dead.

He went down to the basement and spent thirty minutes cleaning and oiling and checking out the gun before it was fit to carry and shoot. It wasn't department issue. It didn't fit in the smaller belt holster he'd worn on his hip for over half of his fifteen years on the force, so he stuffed it in his suit jacket pocket.

He'd never planned on carrying this gun around. He'd bought it for one reason, and one reason only, and holstering the thing after it had served that purpose wasn't part of the package. Dead men didn't need holsters.

But he couldn't tag around after Lily all day with a .357 flopping in a jacket pocket. Not that he really believed he needed the gun, or that she needed his protection. He was half convinced that Jack had already taken a giant leap over that line between sanity and madness, and was seeing imaginary demons everywhere, but it wouldn't hurt to humor him for a while, until he could figure out what was really going on.

He frowned as he put his cleaning tools and oil back into the kit, trying to figure out the logistics of making a trip to the gun store for a holster without leaving Lily alone, and without frightening her by lending credence to Jack's paranoia. It seemed an insoluble dilemma, and he decided to deal with it in the morning.

He carried the hamper out to the curb for the garbagemen, ruined clothes and shoes inside, and then went to the big back bedroom to pack. He'd already worn almost everything he'd hastily tossed in a duffel on the morning of his aborted suicide. If he really intended to stay close to Lily for a while, he might as well take the job seriously, and that meant he wouldn't want to leave her every day to run home for fresh clothes.

The closet smelled like Hannah. It was a light citrusy scent, and yet it nearly knocked him over when he opened the folding doors. He stood there with his big hands hanging helplessly at his sides, massive shoulders hunched forward as if he'd just taken a hard punch to the stomach, staring at whispery silks and soft cottons that moved in the breeze the opening door had created. Sad, empty shells of gentle colors that had once held his wife's body. The man who had killed her, dead for seven months now, was still killing him. Over and over again.

She was wearing the long white gauzy dress that made it look like she was floating when she walked. He'd seen it in a store window that very day, hanging lifelessly on a mannequin, longing for Hannah's slender curves to give it form. She was halfway into her old black suit when he carried it into the bedroom, draped over his muscular arms like some gossamer altar cloth. She cried when she put it on, which only made Marty smile. Hannah always cried when she was happy.

They were celebrating life that night. After seven years of trying, Hannah was pregnant.

'Don't call it that,' she told him.

'Why not?'

'Because I don't like the word. It has a hard g. *Why would you use such an ugly-sounding word to describe such a*

wondrous thing? I'm not going to be pregnant, I've decided. I'm going to be with child.'

'Very biblical.'

Her laugh was music in the nearly empty parking ramp. They'd lingered too long at the restaurant after dinner, and now shadows were everywhere. One of them jumped from behind a pillar and grabbed Hannah from behind, laying the evil gleam of a serrated knife against her white throat.

He'd been so smart, that desperate, lanky, wild-eyed kid with the greasy blond hair and the needle-marked arms. He'd taken Hannah first, knowing it would stop Marty cold.

But Marty was a cop. A narcotics detective, for God's sake. He dealt with people like this every day of his life. He knew what they wanted. He knew how to handle them.

'Take it easy, son. I've got almost fifty bucks in my wallet. It's not much, but it's all I've got, and it's all yours. Just let her go.'

'Money first. Toss it over here.'

'No problem. I'm going into my inside pocket, okay? See? I'll go really slow, I'll throw down the money, then we'll turn around and just walk away. Is that all right with you?'

The kid had blue eyes brightened by a hunger few would ever understand, and for an instant, just an instant, Marty thought he might be making a mistake. The kid's eyes were too blue; too intense; too narrowly focused. Heroin didn't do that; neither did crack. He began to think it might be something much worse, like one of the new lethal mixes that made nuclear explosions in burned-out brains.

He opened the lapel of his good jacket slowly, to show the pocket inside, the rectangular shape of a wallet against the silk.

But he'd forgotten. Jesus Christ, he'd seen the knife against Hannah's throat and he'd forgotten everything he knew. He'd forgotten to tell the kid about the gun he had to wear, on duty or off, and then he saw the shock and fear in the kid's too-bright eyes, and then the flash and bite of the knife, and then the gush of Hannah's life in a flood he wouldn't have believed possible.

He held Hannah in his arms as her white dress turned red, frantically punching numbers into his cell phone, calling it in, then tossing the phone aside and rocking her gently. The gash across her throat was so deep it took her voice, but she managed to move her hand to her stomach and ask him with her eyes.

'It's all right, Hannah,' he told her, one hand pressed as hard as he dared on her throat, trying to hold the life inside. 'The baby's all right. The baby's all right.'

He kept telling her that, over and over, until her eyes went flat and her hand slipped lifelessly to the concrete.

The ambulance arrived within five minutes. It was only three minutes too late.

Marty had never even heard the smack of the kid's footsteps as he ran away. But he remembered his face.

He stood very still in front of the closet for many moments, just breathing, coming back. The pictures of that night were always with him. To one degree or another, he visualized pieces of it every day. But never had the recollection been that complete, the images that cruel and vivid. He'd always known the complete memory would resurface eventually in all its horror, and he'd lived with the certainty that when it did, he would finally be able to pull the trigger.

It took his breath away when he realized that he'd been wrong. He had a gun in his pocket, and absolutely no inclination to use it. He'd seen the worst his mind had to offer, and now, miraculously, he felt himself letting it go.

Lily was sitting in her chair with a book in her lap when he got back to the house. She was bundled into a purple terry robe, sipping water from a glass with multicolored stripes. She patted the arm of the couch next to her chair. 'Sit a minute. You were gone a long time. I worried.'

Marty settled onto the couch and sank into cushions that had been softened over the years by all the dead people he'd loved.

'Minneapolis isn't so safe anymore, that you can be out at all hours. Of course you probably have nothing to worry about with that gun in your pocket.'

Marty smiled a little. Lily didn't miss a trick.

'Then again, guns are dangerous. It could go off, you could shoot yourself accidentally.'

'I'm not going to shoot myself, Lily.'

Lily cocked her head and stared at him for a moment. 'That's good to hear, Martin. Then all these months, I've been worrying for nothing.'

Marty looked into bright blue ageless eyes, and wondered what would happen if anyone in this family ever told the truth. 'I thought about it,' he said, testing the waters.

'You must still be thinking about it if you're carrying a gun.'

The truth thing seemed to be working out. Marty thought he'd try it again. 'Jack asked me to go home and get it. He's worried about the murders, and wants me to keep an eye on you.'

Lily sipped from her glass without looking at him. 'He said that?'

'He did.'

'Hmph. So I have a bodyguard, now? You're going to move in, stay here forever? That's a very big suitcase you brought in.'

Marty gave her a tired half smile and looked down at the old tweed Samsonite he and Hannah had gotten for their honeymoon. 'I'm going to stay until the cops find out who's killing people.'

She set her glass down very carefully on the table, then pushed herself up out of the chair. 'Then you might as well unpack that thing.'

Marty was hanging up his last pair of khakis in the bedroom closet when he heard a soft rap on the door. Without waiting for an answer, Lily entered with a stack of neatly folded clothes and set them down on the bed.

He looked uncertainly at the blazing white boxer shorts on the top of the pile. 'Are those mine?'

'All day I had to soak these in bleach. Have you heard of bleach?'

He walked over and held them up. There were

razor-sharp creases in the front. 'You ironed my underwear?'

She shrugged. 'Are we animals? Of course I ironed them.' She toddled over to the closet and examined the row of khakis he'd just hung up. 'You can't fold slacks like that,' she said, pulling each pair off the hanger and refolding them along the crease.

When she'd finished, she turned to find Marty sitting on the bed, watching her with a sad smile.

'What?'

'Hannah used to do that.'

Lily folded her lips together, looked away, and nodded. 'We all walk around with holes in our hearts.' She looked back and met his eyes. 'But we still walk around.'

'Sometimes I'm not sure why we do that. Why we hang on when things get so bad.' He glanced at the fading, bluish tattoo on her arm. 'There had to have been times when you wondered if it was worth it.'

She squared her shoulders beneath the puffy purple robe and eyed him steadily. 'Not once. Not for one single minute. Life is always worth it.'

Marty remained sitting on the bed for a long time after the door clicked shut behind her, a little shamed by this tiny old woman who was so much stronger than he was.

Finally he went to the old rolltop desk in the corner, pulled out the chair, and sat down. The top drawer was mostly empty, except for a legal tablet and a package of ballpoint pens. With great care, he centered the tablet on the desk, selected a pen, and then just sat there, waiting. Eventually his hand moved almost of its own accord, picking up the pen, drawing a circle with lines radiating from it, like a sun. In the middle of the sun, he wrote 'JACK.'

An hour later, he leaned back and rubbed his burning eyes, and for the first time in a long time, he was craving coffee instead of scotch. He'd filled three pages with notes and questions, and still, jumbled thoughts ricocheted through his head, demanding transfer to paper.

This is what he used to do when he was working a particularly troublesome case, and the familiarity of it reminded him of many a late night when Hannah would creep into his office quietly, drape her arms over his shoulders, and chide him gently for leaving her alone in that big, cold bed. He could almost feel the weight of her soft arms, smell the lemony soap she used to wash her face, feel the tickle of her silky hair on the back of his neck.

An amazed smile formed slowly on his lips. For an entire year, his only memories of Hannah had been of her death. Now, for the first time, he was recalling a piece of her life.

I'm getting better, he thought, flipping over a new page.

25

The sun was just beginning to rise over the river bluffs when Magozzi and Gino crossed the Mississippi on the Lake Street Bridge. The streaks of pink and gold in the sky reflected on the dark surface of the water, rippling like shimmering ribbons of champagne.

'Boy, would I love to be able to put that on canvas,' Magozzi murmured. 'Look at the water, Gino. It's beautiful.'

Gino grunted. He had some serious bags under his eyes this morning, and his cropped blond hair looked angry. 'Beautiful, my ass. You wouldn't think so if you'd had my night. The Accident got into a box of that kids' cereal with all the different-colored animals, and threw up rainbows for about three hours. Looked just like that water.'

'The kid's kind of young to be eating that stuff, isn't he?'

'The kid will never eat that cereal, if Angela has anything to say about it. It was my secret cache. You know those rubber-bandy things you kid-proof your cupboards with?'

'Nope.'

'Well, they don't work, or else the Accident's a genius.'

'You have to quit calling him that. He's going to get a complex.'

'I would never call him that to his little, sweet, drooling face. Man, I'm starving. Would you please tell me why traffic is stopped dead in the middle of this bridge at six o'clock in the morning?'

The legendary body of water they were suspended over was the geographical division between Minneapolis and its twin city, and after Magozzi had seen a repeat of Kristen Keller's report this morning, he'd understood why Malcherson had chosen a hole-in-the-wall diner in St Paul as the venue for this morning's emergency briefing. Word was that the press had already set up a full ambush at City Hall in Minneapolis. St Paul was the last place they'd be looking for them.

'Oh, man, would you look at this?' Gino grumbled, getting out of the car. 'There are people trotting around all over the road up there. Slap on the roof light, I'm going to go push my weight around.' He stalked away up through the lines of motionless cars, and Magozzi said a silent prayer for all the motorists who had come between Gino and his breakfast.

He was back in under five minutes, sliding into the car, wearing a silly little smile. 'That was pretty cool.'

Magozzi gave him a sidelong once-over. 'You've got feathers on your shirt.'

'Huh. How about that.'

'You didn't eat a bird or anything, did you?'

'Nah. It was one of those suicidal mother ducks,

leading her kids across the bridge like she owned the place. You got any idea how fast those little yellow buggers can run? We had a heck of a time catching them all. Some guy had an empty beer case in his truck, so we stuffed them all in there and he's taking them to the other side. Traffic should start moving in a minute.'

Basil's Broiler was a dimly lit greasy spoon that catered to all-night types, most of whom had already straggled home to bed if the empty stools and tables were any indication. The only person at the front counter was a spike-haired kid with an unbelievable amount of metal bristling from his ears, eyebrows, lips, and nose. He looked up briefly when Magozzi and Gino entered, then went back to staring into his coffee cup.

'You see that kid?' Gino whispered once they were out of earshot. 'Get yourself a little red ball and you could play jacks with his face. I'm telling you, that's what happens when you let your kid pierce her ears. They start out with a cute little gold button, then it's a hoop, then it's two hoops, and before you know it – jack-face.'

'Helen got her ears pierced?'

'Over my dead body.'

They found Malcherson at a far back table. He had a tablet, two cell phones, and one of those nasty red homicide folders fanned out in front of him.

He looked up when they approached and nodded once. 'Good morning, Detectives.'

'Good morning, Chief,' they replied in unison, sounding like schoolboys greeting a scary headmaster.

'You're late.'

'Mother duck and her babies on the bridge,' Gino explained, earning a rare smile from Malcherson. Anyone who'd lived a single spring in Minnesota knew about ducks crossing the road, freeway traffic coming to a halt, and frazzled motorists who probably wanted to shoot each other morphing instantly into a happy group bent on animal rescue.

'I trust you were able to get them across safely?'

'We did, sir.'

'Good.' He gestured for them to sit, and nudged a metal coffee carafe toward them. 'There is no menu. There is no waitress. There is, however, a hulking brute in the kitchen who said he would bring out three breakfasts. I have no idea what that might consist of.'

'It'll be great,' Gino said. 'Viegs told me about this place. They cook everything in lamb oil.'

Malcherson sighed. 'How . . . unusual.'

Gino poured himself a cup of coffee, took a noisy sip, then studied the chief's suit with a slightly puzzled expression. He was wearing the double-breasted dove-gray this morning with a pale blue tie.

Don't ask, Malcherson told himself, pretending not to notice, but finally he couldn't stand it anymore. 'All right, Rolseth, what's the problem with my clothes?'

'Well, that is truly one of my favorite suits, sir, but . . . it's not one of your murder suits.'

'I see. I have murder suits. Which ones would those be?'

'You know. The aggressive ones. The black for sure, and the charcoal, even the pinstripe works when you're really hot to trot after some lowlife. But this one is kind of upbeat. Hopeful. You usually only wear the dove-gray when we're wrapping things up.'

Malcherson released a weary sigh. 'I find it strange that a man who wears food on forty-dollar sport coats takes such an interest in analyzing the psychology of my wardrobe choices.'

'Well, you're kind of my fashion idol, Chief.'

Malcherson's eyes were the same color as his suit. He turned them toward Magozzi. It was simply too early in the morning to even try to talk to Rolseth. 'I've been getting calls since last night's late newscast. I thought we were going to try to hold back the information on the tattoos.'

'Yeah, well, that was a great idea, but Kristin Keller and her gang of henchmen were interviewing neighbors before we even zipped up Ben Schuler's body bag,' Gino said. 'Besides, we knew from the get-go we weren't going to keep that detail under wraps for long. Anyone who knew any of the victims knew they'd been in the camps. Hell, anyone who ever saw them in short sleeves would have seen the tattoos, and that's the kind of thing that comes out when you get the media interviewing friends and neighbors.'

Malcherson assented with a slight tip of his head. 'True enough. But now the pressure is on. As of last night, the entire city knows that we have three concentration camp survivors killed for no apparent reason, and every broadcast I listened to this morning – including CNN – was either implying hate crime, or suggesting it outright.'

Gino shook his head firmly. 'We've been over that, sir. Hate crime doesn't fit for a lot of reasons. Besides, two of these three people knew each other, and our feeling is that they were involved in something that got them killed.'

Malcherson smiled at Gino, which was pretty terrifying. 'I can hardly wait. Tell me, Detective Rolseth, what sort of nefarious activities do you think these senior citizens were involved in that made them murder targets?'

'Well . . . we don't exactly have a handle on that yet . . .'

He was interrupted by the gunshot sound of the hulking brute's boot hitting the swinging door from the kitchen. The closer he came to the table, the higher Magozzi had to lift his chin to see the guy's craggy, scarred face. Seven feet minimum, he thought, with the coiled musculature of an ex-con who always got the weight bench in the exercise yard. He unloaded the huge tray he was carrying, setting a meat platter in front of each of them. Eggs, sausage, cottage fries, biscuits and gravy towered and steamed.

Gino licked his lips at the feast before him, then looked up at the man, apparently undaunted by his size. 'Jesus, buddy, are those knife cuts all over your face?'

Malcherson and Magozzi both tensed. Gino was happily oblivious.

'Yeah,' the rumble came back. 'Bunch of guys jumped me with shivs.'

'Bummer. Inside?'

'Yep. You?'

Gino stabbed an accordian of potato circles and stuffed them into his mouth. 'Not yet. So far I'm on the other team . . . Omigod, these fries are amazing. Leo, try the fries, then ask this guy to marry you.'

The hulking brute beamed, and assuming that meant he wasn't going to kill them all, Malcherson examined his fork, took a small bite of potato, then blinked. 'Oh my. Fresh rosemary. Wonderful.'

'Thanks. Nobody in this neighborhood ever notices the rosemary. You want ketchup?'

By tacit agreement, none of them spoke for a few moments while they ate. Magozzi and Malcherson had both managed to clear about a third of their plates, then pushed them away simultaneously.

'You aren't going to eat that?' Gino asked, chasing the last skittering bit of sausage across his own barren platter. 'Damn shame to waste it. Besides, I wouldn't want to offend the guy.'

'Good point.' Malcherson nudged his plate in Gino's direction, then glanced at his watch. 'If you two really believe Morey Gilbert, Rose Kleber, and Ben Schuler were connected beyond their common experience as concentration camp survivors, I assume you're examining their records, phone bills, bank statements, that sort of thing.'

Well, yes, they were, Magozzi thought; but not exactly through the proper channels. 'We're handling that, sir.'

'Really. Handling it how? I haven't seen a warrant cross my desk –' He stopped abruptly and looked at Magozzi. 'Never mind. Don't answer that.'

Malcherson knew full well about Magozzi's continuing relationship with Grace MacBride, who could hack her way into any supposedly secure database. He also knew that his best detective – a man who wouldn't loosen his tie on the job because it violated department dress code – had developed a troubling impatience with privacy laws and civil rights and department procedure when he thought lives were at stake. Warrants took time. Checking records took time, and the temptation to take shortcuts was enormous for a cop who thought he was fighting the clock to find a killer. Malcherson understood the temptation as well as anyone, but also understood that once you started breaking the rules, it was hard to stop, and one of the most dangerous things in the world was an officer of the law who thought he was above it. 'Detective Magozzi . . .'

'We're trying to move pretty fast on this, Chief,' Magozzi interrupted. 'We don't know if there are other targets out there.'

'I know that.'

'Old, defenseless, terrified targets,' Gino inserted around a mouthful of eggs. 'Cookie-baking grandmas like Rose Kleber.'

'Detective Magozzi,' Malcherson repeated in a tone that quieted both his detectives. 'If you intend to ask Grace MacBride and her associates to use the program that worked so well finding links on our cold cases, remind her to access only that information in the public domain.'

'I'll do that, sir. But we aren't just waiting for something in the records to pop. Like we said in the report, we think Jack Gilbert knows something, and we're going to hit him hard today.'

'Then I wish you all the luck in the world. As far as the press and the public are concerned, it looks like this killer has a very specific demographic target group, and those people are starting to panic.' He folded his hands together and looked down at his shiny gold watch. 'Do you recall the dire predictions the press was making when the legislature passed the new conceal-and-carry law?'

Gino snorted. 'Oh yeah. They were singing the dark song. Millions of Minnesotans packing, gunning each other down in the streets. And you know what?

I didn't hear a word on the news when the new applications fizzled down to near nothing.'

Malcherson's eyes slid to Gino. 'Yesterday alone there were three hundred seventy-three new applications to carry a concealed weapon. That was in Hennepin County. Our county, gentlemen. Three hundred of those applications were filed by people over the age of sixty-five.'

'Holy shit . . . sir.'

Malcherson flinched at the vulgarity. 'That was before Ben Schuler's murder was reported. I expect the numbers could go even higher today, especially now that we've earned national attention. CNN headlined it last night; the other networks will have it by the evening news, and that, gentlemen, is really going to stir the pot.'

Gino threw up his hands. 'What's the matter with these people? If I was a national reporter sifting the wire reports I'd jump on the old guy who was tortured and tied to a train track.'

Malcherson sighed. 'It was one murder. Sensational, yes, but there are dozens of sensationalistic murders every day in this country. You, on the other hand, are working three murders, and even if no one says "serial" aloud, they're thinking it. That in itself is enough to garner national attention. Add to it the incomprehensible horror of someone murdering elderly survivors of the death camps, and the eyes of the country will be on you.'

Magozzi felt a tickle deep inside his head, as if little

brain cells were standing up and waving their arms, trying to get his attention. He closed his eyes and frowned hard, concentrating.

'What is it, Detective?' Malcherson asked.

Magozzi opened his eyes and looked at the chief. 'I don't know. It'll come to me.'

26

By the time Magozzi and Gino left Chief Malcherson at the diner, the sun had risen high into a hazy, almost-white sky. The air was soupy and oppressive, and the mercury was already courting the eighty-degree mark. When they turned west on 394, they could see the haze starting to gel on the horizon, stirring the sky.

'There she comes,' Gino remarked, looking up from his pointless fiddling with the buttons on the car's useless air conditioner. 'Canadian cold front is finally dropping, and when that baby gets here, we're going to have the clash of the Titans.'

'They said sometime tonight,' Magozzi said. 'The whole state's under a tornado watch.'

'How weird is that? Two weeks ago I was shoveling five inches of snow off the driveway; now we're poaching in our own sweat watching the sky for funnel clouds.'

'Welcome to Minnesota.'

Twenty minutes later Magozzi was guiding the unmarked along the scenic, curving streets of a wooded development that tried hard to look like Minnesota wilderness. It had all the elements – enormous stands of mature trees, the bubbling rush of creeks fed by snowmelt and spring rains – but nature had not groomed these places. This was what some community planner thought nature was supposed to look like.

There was no fallen brush between the trees, no canted branches to mark the passage of the last storm, and if one leaf had dared to fall on the unmarked tar last autumn, it had long since been swept away.

There were no lots in this part of Wayzata. Here, everyone had 'acreage,' and only occasionally could you catch a glimpse of the enormous homes set far back from the street, artfully concealed by strategic landscaping.

Gino was looking out the window with a deeply suspicious expression. 'Okay, now this is just not right. There are no potholes in this road. It's spring in Minnesota, for chrissake. You're supposed to have potholes. And the damn tar looks polished. You get a load of that house we just passed on the hill back there?'

Magozzi shook his head, eyes on the road as he negotiated a hairpin turn that followed the natural course of what was clearly a very confused creek. 'There has to be another way to Jack Gilbert's house. No way he could drive this street drunk.'

'I don't know. Might help to be drunk. Man, this thing twists like an intestine.'

'Really pretty imagery, Gino.'

'Thank you. I kind of like all the curves, actually, and the only place you find them anymore is in some kind of hoity-toity development. Pisses me off how MnDOT straightens all the roads as if none of us had steering wheels. The whole damn state's turning into one big ugly grid pattern . . . Uh-oh. What do we got here?'

Magozzi had seen the first of the flashing lights peeking around the curve ahead, and had already started to apply the brakes. The closer they got, the more vehicles they saw, all with light bars flashing. There were four Wayzata police cruisers, an ambulance, security rent-a-cop cars, the fire department's first-responder truck, and worst of all, a couple of satellite vans from the local TV stations.

Magozzi came nose to door with a WPD car blocking the road. 'What do you bet that's Gilbert's place up there?'

Gino's voice was tense. 'Goddamnit. We should have pinned him down last night. I'm going to hate myself if that drunken son of a bitch is dead.'

A tall, blond, buff patrolman who looked like a *GQ* model walked up to the driver's side. Magozzi held up his badge. 'Minneapolis Homicide. Detectives Magozzi and Rolseth. Is that the Gilbert house?'

'Yes sir, it is. But we don't have a homicide here.'

Gino and Magozzi sighed in a relieved duet.

'Glad to hear it, Officer. So what happened? We were hoping to catch Jack Gilbert for a couple questions on a Minneapolis case we're working. He's not hurt, is he?'

The officer looked back toward the phalanx of vehicles. 'I don't think so. Nothing visible, anyway. The med techs are looking him over now, but he's pretty shook-up. Says somebody tried to kill him.'

Gino and Magozzi exchanged a glance. 'We need to get in there and talk to him, Officer. Any problem with that?'

'I'm sure there isn't, Detective, but you might want to talk to Chief Boyd first, get some background on what's been happening here. Gilbert's version is a little garbled. Hang on, I'll get him for you.'

They barely had time to get out of the car before Wayzata's police chief came over and introduced himself. If anything, he was better-looking than his patrolman, with just a little more age on him. Magozzi decided you had to be a pretty person to live in Wayzata.

'It's a real pleasure to meet you, Detectives.' Chief Boyd flashed a spectacular set of pearly whites. 'You did some amazing work on that Monkeewrench case last fall. You're on the Uptown murders now, right? I read Gilbert's dad was one of the victims.'

'That's right,' Gino said. 'We were on our way to talk to Jack Gilbert, clear up a few things, when we ran into your parade. You got a pretty heavy call-out here, Chief. What happened?'

'Last night, or this morning?'

Gino raised his brows. 'Last night?'

'That's when it started. About eleven P.M. Gilbert dialed nine-one-one in a panic. He said he thought he had an intruder on the grounds, so we sent out a couple of cars to take a look. They went over the property pretty thoroughly, but couldn't find anything, and to tell you the truth, the boys shrugged it off as a false alarm. Mr Gilbert was . . .' He paused diplomatically.

'Drunk out of his friggin' mind?' Gino suggested, and Chief Boyd smiled, almost apologetically.

'Well, he had just come home from burying his father,' he said, making Gino feel like a heartless son of a bitch. 'And I think he's been going through a really rough patch for a while now. We've had some problems; stopped him a few times on the road, saw to it that he got home safely.'

Gino looked at Magozzi. 'I want to live here.'

'Then this morning,' the chief continued, 'we received calls from just about everybody within earshot about gunfire at the Gilbert house. Jack Gilbert was close to hysterical and waving a gun when we got here, and the yard and his wife's car were pretty shot up.'

'Jesus,' Gino murmured. 'Someone really was trying to kill him.'

'Well, we're not so sure about that. There's a lot of damage, and a lot of brass around, but so far it's all 9-mm. Slugs, too. We dug a couple of those out of the garage siding and some tree trunks.'

'Which means?' Magozzi asked, and the chief lifted one shoulder in an awkward shrug.

'The gun Mr Gilbert was holding was a Smith &

Wesson 9-mm, still warm, and he told us outright he'd emptied the clip trying to hit whomever he thought was shooting at him. We'll send everything to the lab, of course, just in case there were two men shooting two different 9-mm's out here.'

Magozzi studied him for a moment. 'You don't think there was another shooter at all, do you?'

Chief Boyd looked down at the polished tar beneath his polished boots and sighed. 'You know, Jack Gilbert's lived here ten years – as long as I've been chief – and he's always been a little . . . eccentric. But overall, a hell of a nice guy. Then about a year or so ago he just started to unravel. A lot of drinking, a lot of complaints from the neighbors, and as I said, we've had to pull him off the road more than once. One time I was driving down the main street in town on my way to lunch, and there's Mr Gilbert strolling the sidewalk in front of the shops in his bathrobe and not much more. I put him in the car in record time, but when I asked him what the hell he thought he was doing parading around downtown in his robe, he looked down at himself and said, "Holy shit." I swear to God, the man didn't realize he wasn't dressed. Almost locked him up right there, just so the Court would order a psych evaluation and get him some help.'

'Might have been a kindness,' Gino said.

Chief Boyd chuckled softly. 'Unfortunately, the residents of this community do not think it's a kindness when their police officers arrest them, no matter how good the intentions. I'll tell you, this job is more political than I ever wanted to be.'

Magozzi nodded in understanding. 'We run into the same thing in the city sometimes. If a patrol gets a judge blowing point-one-oh on the Breathalyzer, you know he's gotta wonder if the arrest is going to come back to haunt him next time he's got a case in front of the bench. Sad but true.'

The chief looked off into a patch of painfully pruned woods. 'My officer tells me you wanted to question Gilbert. He's pretty messed up. I hope you're not going to tell me he's a suspect in the Uptown killings.'

Magozzi smiled. 'You like him, don't you?'

'I guess I do. I get a feeling from him, like he's one of the good people that just got lost somewhere along the way.'

'Well, for what it's worth, we're not looking at him as a suspect right now, but we think he might be holding something back that could help us out. We just want to talk to him.'

They found Jack Gilbert slumped in the back of the ambulance, dressed in shorts and a polo shirt, bare legs dangling over the edge. He looked like precisely what he was – a heavy drinker coming off a long-term toot. Bleary, pouched eyes, sallow complexion, and a looseness around the mouth that made it look like it was melting. There was a butterfly bandage on his forehead, and he was holding a cold pack on his cheek. He looked up as they approached and toasted them with a bottle of water.

'Hey, guys. Welcome to the burbs. Little out of your jurisdiction, aren't you?'

'How are you doing, Mr Gilbert?' Gino asked.

'Doing fine. Little cut up here, little smackeroonie right here.' He wiggled the cold pack. 'Probably ran into a goddamned tree, can't really remember, otherwise I'm just aces.'

Magozzi moved in a little closer until he and Gino had Gilbert flanked. 'Are you going to the hospital?'

'Nah. I just figured I paid about a grand to get this rig out here, might as well sit in it for a while.'

'You want to tell us what happened?'

'I saw you talking to the chief. He didn't tell you?'

'The chief wasn't here; you were,' said Gino.

Jack sighed, pulled away the cold pack and pointed his cheek toward them. 'How's it look?'

Gino leaned forward and squinted. 'A little swollen. A little red, but not so bad. Where'd you get the Smith & Wesson, Jack?'

'Whoa. No foreplay?'

'Not today. The body count's going up a little too fast for that sort of thing.'

Jack held Gino's eyes for a minute while his brain tried to work, then finally shrugged. 'Pop had it forever. Don't know where he got it, but I knew where he kept it. I brought it home last night.'

'After you heard Ben Schuler had been killed. That really scared the hell out of you, didn't it, Jack?'

A defensive glint in the eyes now. 'Yeah, you bet it

did. In case you hadn't noticed, they're dropping Jews, Detective, and I happen to be one.'

Magozzi leaned his shoulder against the ambulance door and said reasonably, 'One of several thousand in the Cities. What made you think you might be a target? You're too young, for one thing, and so far all the killings have been in Uptown, and that's a long way from Wayzata.'

'Oh, come on. First Pop gets it, then one of his best friends? You don't think that's a little too close to home?'

Magozzi lifted a shoulder in concession. 'Okay. I'll give you that.'

'Goddamn right you'll give me that, because some asshole tried to shoot me in my own driveway this morning.'

'You never did fax us that list, Jack,' Gino said.

'What list?'

'First time we met you, you said you'd fax us a list of all the people who wanted you dead. About a hundred, I think you said.'

'Oh, for chrissake, it was a joke.'

'Was it?'

Jack lifted the cold pack back up to his cheek. 'What are you getting at?'

Magozzi shrugged. 'Well, in your line of work, you're bound to run into a few shadowy characters every now and then. Maybe you stepped over the line, got involved in something where the people play hardball.'

Jack blew a raspberry. 'And what? Started killing the people around me? Man, you've been watching too many DeNiro movies.'

'Hey. It's been known to happen.'

'Your father was a real upstanding guy,' Gino put in. 'Bet he wouldn't like his only son swimming below the scum line. Bet he'd turn his back on you quicker than a dog shakes off water, which would explain the estrangement.'

Jack was incredulous. 'I don't believe this. Is that why you came out here this morning? You think something *I* did is getting people killed? I'm a fucking personal injury attorney. My clients are people who slip in spilled pickle juice in grocery stores, not John Gotti types, for chrissake.'

Gino spread his hands. 'You're the wild card, Jack. You're messed up in this somehow, and we're going to look you up and down until we find out what the hell you did.'

Jack threw up his hands. 'Be my guest. I've got nothing to hide.' He eased down from the ambulance and limped off toward the driveway.

Magozzi glanced over at the part of the yard he could see from the street. A heavily wooded hill rose up, blocking any view of the house, and Wayzata cops were crawling all over it. 'Maybe we're on the wrong track,' he said.

'Wouldn't be the first time. We gotta make nice now, right?'

'That's the way it works.'

They caught up with Jack next to a place where cops were using their flashlights in the shadows under the big pines.

'You're limping, Jack,' Gino said. 'Did you hurt your leg, too?'

'Kiss my ass.'

'Hey, I'm trying.'

Jack smiled a little. 'You suck at it.'

'So is this where it happened?' Magozzi asked.

'No, up by the house, but who knows where the guy was shooting from?'

They moved on up the paving-stone driveway until they rounded a curve and got their first look at the sprawling house that Jack built, and the scene in front of the garage.

'Jesus,' Gino murmured. 'What a mess.'

The driveway was littered with shards of bark and little branches. It looked like a tree had exploded. The Mercedes SUV parked close to the garage was pockmarked with what were surely bullet holes, with most of the windows blown out or damaged. The big one in the rear gate had cracked and crumbled to the ground, little patchwork pieces of safety glass glinting on the paving stones.

They stopped a few feet from the vehicle, respecting the crime-scene tape around it. One of the Wayzata officers was inside, tweezing something out of the dashboard and into a plastic bag.

'That's where I was,' Jack said, pointing. 'I was just about to open the rear gate when I heard the shot and felt something whiz by my ear. Scared me shitless, I don't mind telling you, so I pulled the gun out of my pocket and started shooting back.'

Magozzi looked off through the trees to the right. A few twigs dangled from strips of bark. 'The shot came from there?'

'I'm pretty sure.'

'Just one?'

'Jesus, I don't know. I was making a little noise myself by that time.'

Magozzi nodded. 'Okay, that makes sense, but I was wondering about the bullet holes in the back gate if your shooter was off to the side like that.'

Jack frowned at the bullet holes. 'I might have done that.'

'Yeah?'

'Maybe. I was kind of shooting all over the place. I mean, Jesus, I didn't know where the guy was.'

'Nice going,' Gino said dryly. 'You could have killed half the neighborhood.'

To his credit, Jack went pale.

'You look a little wrung out, Jack. What do you say we go inside, sit down, relax, and have a little talk,' Magozzi suggested, but Jack shook his head.

'Can't go inside. Slept in the pool house last night after Becky kicked me out, and she sure as hell isn't going to let me back in after this. I don't want to be in there anyway. I'm going to call a cab and go get my car at the nursery, maybe bunk at the club for a while.'

'We're headed back that way. You're welcome to ride with us if you like.'

Jack eyed him suspiciously. 'Am I under arrest?'

'For getting shot at?' Gino asked. 'Jesus, Jack, we're just offering you a lift. You want it or not?'

'Yeah, I guess. I got a duffel down in the ambulance.'

'We'd better grab it then, before they drive off with it.' Gino caught Magozzi's eye and tipped his head ever so slightly in the direction of the house.

Magozzi glanced behind him and saw a slender woman standing in the shadows of the open doorway, arms folded across her chest. 'I'll catch up with you in a few minutes.'

Becky Gilbert, like the neighborhood she lived in, was just a little too perfect to be entirely natural. Her pretty, bronzed face was smooth and oddly taut, like fabric stretched too tight in an embroidery hoop. She had the lithe, perfectly toned body of a serious fitness club member, and her tennis whites looked as if they'd been tailored to make the most of it. Diamonds flashed on her wrist – probably the only woman in the world who actually wore tennis bracelets while she played tennis, Magozzi thought.

Her arms were crossed angrily over her chest, and her eyes flashed when Magozzi approached. 'Mrs Gilbert?'

'Yes. Who are you?'

'Detective Magozzi, Minneapolis PD. Homicide.'

She glared over his shoulder at Jack heading down the driveway. 'He's not dead yet.'

'You sound disappointed.'

She let out a frustrated sigh and forced a tight smile. 'I'm not disappointed, Detective. I'm just furious. The police were here half the night looking for Jack's imaginary stalker, and now this.'

'So you don't actually believe someone is trying to kill him?'

'Of course not. Jack's burned some bridges in the past year, but nothing that would get him killed.'

'Can you think of anything unusual that's happened recently?'

'Like what?'

'Oh, I don't know, strange cars hanging around, late night knocks at the door, hang-ups, threatening phone calls, that sort of thing.'

'Nothing like that.' Becky Gilbert tipped her head curiously. 'Homicide. Is this about his father?'

'Yes. We needed to ask Jack a few more questions.'

Becky Gilbert's outright anger at her husband seemed to dissipate, like a teakettle steaming itself dry, but bitterness lingered in her eyes. 'That was a terrible thing.'

'Did Jack talk to you about his father's murder?' Magozzi asked.

She shook her head. 'Jack never talked about his father, period. By the time we met, they weren't on speaking terms. I thought it might be a painful subject, so I never brought it up.'

Magozzi looked at this woman who so clearly belonged in this suburb, who so clearly wanted to be here, and thought maybe she hadn't really been all that considerate of her husband's feelings; maybe she just had no use for an elderly Jewish couple who lived in Uptown.

'Do you know what caused the rift between Jack and his father?'

'I have no idea, Detective. He never chose to share that information with me.'

And you didn't ask, Magozzi thought.

He ran into Chief Boyd's genial smile halfway down the driveway.

'Detective Magozzi. Did you learn anything that might connect to your Uptown cases?'

'Not unless Ballistics comes up with something. We'd really appreciate a heads-up when you get some results, Chief.'

'I can do better than that. We don't send those folks at the lab much business, and I'm guessing you might have a little more pull than we do.' He held up a large sealed pouch with a chain of custody log tucked into a plastic insert. 'One Smith & Wesson 9-mm, eleven casings, and nine slugs. I was hoping you might put these in for us.'

Magozzi grinned at him. 'And I was hoping you'd say that. Saved me the trouble of asking.' He pulled out the evidence log sheet, braced it on his knee, and started to sign.

'The elderly woman in Uptown was shot with

a 9-mm, if I remember correctly,' Chief Boyd said casually.

And so was Ben Schuler, Magozzi thought, but there was no reason to put that information on the table just yet. 'That's right.'

'So you'll probably be getting some answers on the gun in that pouch pretty soon.'

Magozzi straightened and looked at him. 'There are a lot of 9-mm's out there, Chief Boyd.'

'I know that. And I'm really anxious to hear that the one we took from Mr Gilbert hasn't killed anybody.'

'I'll call you myself, the minute I hear. We should have something today.'

They walked together down to the street, where Magozzi paused and looked over at the news satellite vans. When the reporters and cameramen scattered around the trucks saw Chief Boyd and Magozzi, they converged in a swarm, cameras running, microphones waving, reporters calling out questions. They all moved en masse toward the curb, then stopped as if the ridge of concrete were the Great Wall of China.

Magozzi looked over at the chief, who was waving congenially at the press. 'You have an invisible fence down there? One of those electric things they use on dogs?'

The chief kept waving like a doped-up prom queen. 'Why on earth would we need one of those?'

'Gee, I don't know. In the city, the media

steamrolls pretty much anywhere it wants to go. I've turned tail and run a couple times myself.'

The chief chuckled. 'The street's public property. They have as much right to be there as anyone else. But the minute they step up on that curb, they're trespassers and they go to jail.'

Magozzi snorted. 'Yeah, right.'

'We told them all that when they arrived, but there was this really attractive young woman from Channel Ten – a little pushy, though – who trotted right after me on the way up Jack's driveway.'

'That would be Kristin Keller, the anchor, and the samurai sword in my side.'

'Could have been. Don't watch the news much. Anyway, the minute we cuffed her and put her in a car, the others backed off in a hurry.'

Magozzi turned to him in amazement. 'You arrested Kristin Keller?'

'I guess.'

Magozzi tried to remain professional, but he just couldn't manage it. A shit-eating grin nearly broke open his face. 'Chief Boyd, you are the man.'

'That's what I told them.'

27

Grace MacBride was in her home office: a narrow, wooden-floored space that looked more like a dead-end hallway than a room. Several computers lined the desk-high counter that stretched the full length of one wall, and she rolled from one to the other in her wheeled chair, checking the monitors, tweaking command lines, cursing the flood of useless information that clogged the Net's public-domain sites. It was easier to hack into any protected site than it was to sort through the drivel jamming the public search engines, and it was time she started to do just that, because this was taking much too long.

She'd plugged Morey Gilbert's and Rose Kleber's names into the new software program first thing yesterday, and added Ben Schuler's name when Magozzi called her last night, but after hours of sifting through the legitimately accessible databases, the only link the program had found between the three was a tendency to shop at the same local grocery. As did everyone else in that neighborhood. It was possible, she supposed, that there was no extraordinary connection to be found – but Magozzi and Gino weren't thinking that way, and she trusted their instincts.

She scowled at the unremarkable grocery store revelation the program had thought worthy of an asterisk, then balled up the paper and tossed it to one side. 'This is nonsense,' she said aloud.

Grace had tried to be legal for months now, breaking through the fire walls of the truly off-limits sites only when it was absolutely, positively necessary. This feeble attempt at walking the computerized equivalent of the straight-and-narrow was a private, silent nod of respect and gratitude to Magozzi and the other cops who had finally ended the reality of her years of terror, if not the haunting, lingering aftereffects. Then again, she rationalized, it was cops of another sort who had put her in jeopardy in the first place, and by respecting Magozzi's dogged adherence to law, wasn't she also respecting theirs?

It took only moments to reconfigure one computer's operating system and initiate the search parameters for bank and phone records for the three victims. Bank and phone company sites were fair game as far as Grace was concerned. Bastards sold every detail of their customers' lives to the highest bidder, then got all self-righteous and privacy oriented when the cops asked for information. It didn't make sense to her that the police had to have a warrant and the telemarketers didn't, so she broke into those sites regularly and gleefully. Besides, Magozzi knew damn well she was going to do this when he asked for her help, whether it was spoken aloud or not.

The other sites she was about to access – the IRS, the INS, the FBI – were a little dicier to justify, but that didn't slow the speed of her fingers as she rolled down to the big IBM and happily started clattering away on the keyboard. She was still pissed at the FBI, and sometimes she hacked into their sites for no particular reason other than pure spite. But this was different. This time she was doing it for Magozzi. Not that she'd tell him, of course. No reason to torment the man with personal knowledge of computer crime.

The phone rang just as her printer began spitting out little droplets of ink in the shape of asterisks. Grace picked up, smiled when she heard country music and raucous laughter in the background. 'Hey, Annie. What are you doing in a bar in the morning?'

A warm, syrupy drawl answered her. 'I am not in a bar, I am in a cantina, and they have the best *huevos rancheros* in town.'

'It sounds like a bar.'

'Honey, the library sounds like a bar down here. These people really know how to have a good time. Grace, you have got to get your pathetic, skinny little butt down here. You are not going to believe it. I'm lookin' at a roomful of men in boots and honest-to-God cowboy hats, and you know what?'

Grace's smile broadened. 'I'm afraid to ask.'

'These good old boys open doors, they pull out chairs, they tip their hats, and they just plumb knock a woman off her size sixes. And the very best part is that I am the fattest woman in Arizona.'

'You must be very proud.'

'What I am, is the one and only package on the shelf for any man who likes a Renaissance woman. What the hell was I doing in Minnesota for so long? Up there I was just another hippo in the *Fantasia* chorus line; down here I'm the big fat lush peony in a row of scrawny daisies. God, I love the Southwest, but I miss your face. Hell, I even miss Harley and Roadrunner.'

'I miss you too, Annie. You could call a little more often.'

'I'll do better than that. I'm flying back up there this weekend. I talked to Harley last night; he said the rig should be ready to ride any day now.'

'You're making the road trip with us?'

Annie chuckled deep in her throat. 'Wouldn't miss it. Besides, that'll give us a chance to go over what I've managed to pull together down here so far. You told Magozzi you were going, didn't you?'

'I told him.'

'Did he cry?'

'Actually . . . I only told him about Arizona.'

For a moment, all Grace could hear from the phone was some cowboy crooner singing about leaving his heart at the Tulsa Greyhound Station. 'You little weasel,' Annie finally said. 'You can't string that poor man along like that. We already committed to those missing child cases in Texas, and Harley says the requests are really starting to pile up. We are going to be on the road a long time, Grace. You've got to tell him . . . unless you're thinking of staying up there, maybe marrying the guy and getting a place without bars on the windows so you aren't raising your kids like zoo animals.'

'Don't be silly, Annie. Magozzi and I don't have that kind of relationship.'

'The hell you don't. You two have sex every time you look at each other; sleeping together is just a formality you haven't gotten around to yet.'

Grace was silent for two seconds, which was a big mistake.

'Lord God,' Annie said. 'You're thinking about it, aren't you?'

'I'm thinking about a lot of things lately. But I'm coming to Arizona.'

After the phone call with Annie, Grace found Charlie, who was better than any barometer, sitting in the hallway facing the basement door, staring at the knob.

Bad weather coming, Grace thought.

Annie hung up the phone and drummed her fingernails on the rough-sawn oak bar. They were periwinkle today, because there weren't many women in the world who could wear that color, and Annie liked to stand out. Besides, she'd wanted to wear her periwinkle contacts, and the idea of her fingernails not matching her eyes was insupportable.

It had been a genuine hardship preparing for today's color choice; there was no doubt about that. She'd had to rush to the salon first thing this morning to get a black rinse in her hennaed bob, because there would never, ever be a day when Annie Belinsky wore red highlights with her periwinkle silk kimono; but as she looked around the cantina at the thirty pairs of male eyes ogling her, she decided it had been worth the effort. How on earth working women with families ever managed to keep themselves looking presentable was beyond her.

She smiled – just a wee bit wickedly – and wriggled her big, silk-clad fanny a little deeper into the bar stool and swore she heard the sound of thirty sighs of longing.

There were women with some of the men, of course, and Annie suspected that several of them were plotting her demise. Everything they ever saw in magazines or on television had taught them that there was absolutely nothing remotely alluring or fashionable about being overweight, and a lot of them probably spent a lot of time doing aerobics and calculating calories to ensure they would never achieve such a state. For the most part, they were all tanned and slim and athletic-looking in their butt-hugging jeans and little bitty T-shirts. But Annie's presence – her open flaunting of every excess inch as if it were gold – had them totally flummoxed, and totally pissed, since men who normally lusted after Barbie dolls in bikinis were now in drool stage two over a fat woman.

Annie could have told the miffed women that men didn't respond exclusively to any particular body type – in her opinion, the gay male designers had perpetrated that myth – they responded to how a woman *used* her body and her eyes and her voice, and oh, honey, Annie had that down pat.

'Miss Belinsky?'

Lord in heaven, she'd never seen him coming, and Annie rarely missed anything. He'd just sneaked up right behind her and nearly knocked her off the stool with that earthy, cowboy, slow-motion way of talking. The accent of the Deep South, like Annie's, was syrup on a platter, but it only sounded good coming from women. If you were a man and wanted your voice to work for you, you just had to come from cowboy country.

'Well, hello, Mr Stellan. You are one of the few men who ever succeeded in startling me.'

He stood there with his cowboy hat held respectfully at his chest, looking for all the world like Gary Cooper in some of the old movies – except his eyes were too intense. 'Miss Belinsky, I will use any method available to plant myself in your memory.'

Annie gave him a tiny smile of mystery, rewarding his appropriate response. Not that the man had a chance with her, of course. He had the look and the voice and the manners, but he was, after all, a real estate agent. Sleeping with a real estate agent was a ride down the slippery slope to mediocrity – almost as bad as sleeping with a lawyer. 'So tell me, Mr Stellan. Do we have the hacienda?'

'Indeed you do, ma'am, terms and price that you specified.' He laid a rental agreement on the bar for her to sign. 'The owners were a little reluctant to lift the no-pets clause, until I explained about him being a police dog 'n' all. He doesn't attack on sight, or anything, does he?'

Annie touched the corner of her mouth with a periwinkle-tipped finger. 'No. He most definitely is not an attack dog.' She signed the agreement with a flourish.

'Well, that's surely good news. I suspected he was a tracker, being that you're here to help the chief find his daughter.'

Annie smiled at the notion of Grace's dog tracking anything except Grace, which was almost as funny as the notion of Charlie as an attack dog. 'You're a well-informed man, Mr Stellan. I don't recall mentioning that we'd be working with your fine local police department.'

'Ah, heck, everybody in town knew that about three minutes after you showed up. It's a real small place, Miss Belinsky.'

A real closed place, Annie thought as she strolled down the sidewalk toward the chief's office a little later, feeling a lot of eyes on her. If one little old heavyset woman in a dress could turn this many heads, these locals would purely have a fit when they saw Harley on the streets.

Chief Savadra was the single exception so far, and the minute he gave her his standard morning sad-smile, she felt totally at ease, free to be herself. He was surely the ugliest man in town, with his rough-cut, sun-seamed face and a wiry body that didn't seem to know where most of its parts were going at any given time; but there was something special about him Annie had liked the minute they met.

'I hear you got the hacienda.'

Annie went straight for the watercooler she'd had delivered on her second day. 'I swear, news travels faster in this town than I can walk.'

'The way I hear it, you do not walk at all, Miss Annie. You sashay.'

Miss Annie. She liked that. Reminded her of Mississippi. Liked it especially because there was no flirtation behind it; just a friendly tease. 'Wait till this town sees the other three. I'm the conservative one.'

Chief Savadra leaned back in his creaky wooden chair and watched her start packing files into her briefcase. 'I thought you weren't leaving until Friday.'

'I've done about all I can do before the computers get here. Now that I've signed on the hacienda, I can head back a little early.'

'You miss your people.'

Annie gave him a sidelong glance. 'I didn't expect to, at least not this much, but I do. Don't tell them.'

The chief smiled. 'I'll take a run out to the place next week; make sure the a/c is turned on and the pool is filled before you get back.'

'Thanks, but Joe Stellan has some people coming out to take care of that.'

'I'll still take a look, flash my badge in front of the help, put the fear of God into them.'

Annie smiled. 'That's nice of you.'

'Are you kidding? No way in this world I'll ever be able to repay you all for what you're doing for me. What I don't get is why you're doing it. What prompts a group of people to travel halfway across the country to give away technology that's probably worth a million bucks?'

'That's kind of a long story.'

'I look forward to hearing it.'

28

Gino was quiet until they'd passed through Wayzata and were on the freeway, probably because he was afraid Jack Gilbert might jump out of the back if they started questioning him again at anything under seventy miles an hour. He actually leaned over to look at the speedometer before unsnapping his seat belt and turning around to face Jack.

'Okay, Jack. I'm going to give you another chance to do the right thing. Who do you think is trying to kill you?'

Jack's head lolled back against the seat. 'I knew you guys were going to do this. "We're just offering you a lift" my ass. You wanted to get me alone in this crappy piece of shit car with no air-conditioning and try to sweat something out of me.'

Gino managed a puzzled expression. 'Gee whiz, Jack. I'm pretty confused here. Now if I thought somebody was hell-bent on putting me in the ground, I'd be tickled pink to have a couple of cops driving me around, keeping me safe. And you know what else? I'd be telling them everything I knew, helping them any way I could so they'd have a chance to nail the guy before he nailed me. But that's not what you're doing. You're just sitting back there all quiet and hostile with your lip zipped, and I gotta tell you, Jack, I can only think of one reason for that kind of attitude, and that's if you're the shooter we're looking for. Maybe you just staged that dog-and-pony show back there to throw us off.'

'Oh, for chrissake, back off, Detective. I'm not some mouth-breathing, brainless dirtbag you picked up for lifting Twinkies at a 7-Eleven, and I don't have to answer any of your stupid questions. Think whatever the hell you want. I could give a shit.'

Magozzi glanced quickly to his right, and was pleased to see that Gino's gun was still in its holster. Still, it was time for him to jump in. 'We're trying to help you, Jack,' he said reasonably. 'Look at it from our side for a minute. We don't want to believe you're a suspect in your father's shooting, but we are dead sure that you know something that explains why these people were killed, and why you think the murderer is after you.'

'What makes you think it's the same person?' Jack scoffed.

'Because you do.'

That shut Jack up for a minute. 'All right,' he finally sighed. 'This is straight shit, Detectives. I have absolutely no idea, not the slightest clue, who killed my father, Ben, or that Rose woman, and I don't know who was shooting at me this morning. You don't think I'd tell you if I did, just to save my own ass?'

Gino shrugged. 'Maybe you would, maybe you

wouldn't. Who knows? Maybe you're trying to save someone else's ass.'

Jack laughed out loud. 'That's good, Detective. Jack Gilbert, the hero. I should hire you to do my P.R. Crack a window, would you? It smells like barbecue back here.'

Magozzi drove a full half mile in stony silence before saying, 'I didn't suggest that you knew who the killer was, Jack. I said you knew something about *why* these people were killed. There's a big difference.'

Jack met Magozzi's eyes in the rearview mirror, but he didn't respond.

They made a courtesy stop halfway back to the Cities. Jack said he had to use the can, but when they pulled up to a gas station, he got out of the car and veered left toward an adjacent liquor store.

Magozzi shook his head. 'Oh, this looks good. Detectives run shuttle service to liquor store. I'm not putting this in the report.'

'Goddamned son of a bitch beat us bloody,' Gino grumbled.

'He did that.'

'I hate lawyers. Goddamned hate 'em. So what was the wife like? Did she give you anything?'

'I don't think that woman gives anybody anything anytime. She was really cold. Minnesota ice. She didn't know anything about why Jack and his dad were fighting, and never cared enough to ask, as far as I could tell.'

Gino leaned his head back and closed his eyes for

a minute. 'Tell me we've got enough to throw him in jail for an obstruction of justice charge.'

'We don't.'

'So where the hell do we go from here? He's not going to tell us anything.'

'Maybe Pullman can help us out.'

The front two rows of the nursery parking lot were full by the time they pulled in, and a surprising number of customers were moving through the outdoor display tables, pulling flat wooden wagons that sprouted flowers and greenery.

'Looks like the flower business is booming,' Magozzi said.

Jack was already sitting forward in the backseat, anxious to get out. 'It's eighty-two degrees. This time of year, you get an extra two cars in the lot for every degree the temperature rises over seventy.'

'No kidding?'

'No kidding. Stop this thing and let me out, will you?'

Magozzi glanced at him in the rearview mirror. Two seconds at his mother's place and the cockiness was gone. 'Hold your horses. I'm looking for a spot.'

Gino was scowling out the passenger window, still fuming over the abysmal failure of his efforts to get information from Jack. 'Who are all these people? Why don't they have jobs? And why can't they park between the lines? Every one of these goddamned cars is taking up two spaces, at least.'

Magozzi pulled into a slot that faced the big greenhouse just as Marty and Lily came out the door, pulling loaded wagons toward a customer's pickup. Marty spotted their car immediately and gave them a questioning look and a tentative wave. He looked even more puzzled when he saw Jack climb out of the unmarked and make a beeline toward his Mercedes convertible at the back of the lot.

'Gee. He didn't even say good-bye.'

'Scummy bastard,' Gino muttered.

They waited in the car, watching Marty load flats into the pickup while Lily supervised.

'Pullman looks better today,' Magozzi observed.

'Hard labor and a female overseer. Builds character, according to my mother-in-law, or at least that's the line she was feeding me last weekend when she had me up on a ladder cleaning out the gutters. She looks like a little kid in those overalls, doesn't she?'

'Who? Lily?'

'Yeah. Let's go in and rough her up a little. Maybe she's an easier takedown than her kid.'

Magozzi snorted. 'She'd eat you alive.'

'I know. You take care of her, I'll talk to Marty.'

They followed Marty and Lily into the greenhouse, then waited politely until a customer at the counter had checked out and left. There were other shoppers in the greenhouse, but all were out of earshot. Magozzi stepped up to the counter, but Jack barged in before he could say a word.

'I need my keys.' He glanced briefly at his mother, then at Marty. 'Where are they?'

Marty looked blandly at the bruise on Jack's cheek and the bandage on his forehead. 'You mouth off to the wrong person, Jack?'

'Ran into a tree.'

'Figures.'

'Trying to get away from the person who was shooting at me.'

Lily's eyes jerked toward her son, and for the first time, Magozzi saw the mother inside the woman. 'Who tried to shoot you?' the words snapped out.

Jack almost shuddered. His mother hadn't addressed him directly in a very long time. 'I don't know.'

And now the old woman straightened, and her eyes grew hard again.

Shit, Magozzi thought. *She knows something, too.*

Marty was staring at Jack, wearing a lot of expressions on his face. Anger, disgust, frustration, and maybe a little fear, too; but there was concern behind all of them. It surpised Magozzi a little to see that Marty Pullman actually cared for Jack.

'What do you know about this?' Marty asked Gino.

Gino eyed a woman in purple capri pants approaching the register with her cart. 'Let's take a walk. I'll give you what we've got.'

'Keys,' Jack demanded just as they started to move away.

Marty turned around and pointed a finger at Jack. 'No keys. You're staying right here.' He looked straight at Lily as he added, 'All day, all night, from now on, until I say otherwise.'

Jack and Lily both blinked at him like startled children.

'I mean it,' Marty warned as he and Gino went out the door.

Jack opened his mouth to speak just as the woman in purple capri pants tapped him on the shoulder. 'Excuse me, sir. Could you tell me if this is the right fertilizer for rhododendrons?'

Almost without thinking Jack turned around and looked at the green plastic jug she was holding. 'Oh no. That's too alkaline. You need something more acidic for a rhododendron. Should be something on the same shelf where you found this.'

'Really? Do you think you could show me? There were so many brands of fertilizer there . . .'

Jack pinched his nose while he slipped from one dimension into another. 'Okay. Yeah. Sure, I can show you.'

'Sounds like he knows the business,' Magozzi said to Lily.

'He should. He grew up with it,' she said absently, her eyes following her son past a crowd of customers overloading their wagons from a sale table of impatiens. 'So tell me about this shooting business. Who was shooting at Jack?'

'Maybe you should ask Jack about that.'

'I'm asking you.'

Magozzi sighed. 'Jack thinks somebody took a shot at him in his driveway this morning, so he shot back.'

Lily turned her head slowly to look at him. 'He *thinks*? He's not sure?'

Magozzi shrugged. 'He is. We're not. At least not yet. There were a lot of slugs and casings around, but they might all be from Jack's gun. We're checking on that.'

Lily was giving him one of her Yoda stares through her thick glasses. 'Jack doesn't own a gun. He hates guns.'

'He says it was Morey's, and that he took it home from here last night after he heard Ben Schuler was killed.' Magozzi watched her face carefully as he asked, 'Did you know Morey had a gun?'

Her stare never faltered. 'If he did, he didn't tell me about it.'

Magozzi leaned his forearms on the counter, which put his eyes on a level with hers. 'Listen, Mrs Gilbert,' he said quietly. 'We think Jack knows something about these murders – including your husband's.'

Lily's eyes flickered at that.

'He almost fainted at the reception yesterday when he heard Ben Schuler was shot, and not just because he was shocked. He was scared to death, and we think it was because he knew he was next. He knows something, Mrs Gilbert, and we can't help him unless we know it, too.'

‘You want me to talk to him,’ she said flatly.

Magozzi straightened and spread his hands. ‘He won’t talk to us. Maybe he’ll talk to his mother.’

Outside, Gino and Marty were perched on the front bumper of the unmarked, slamming bottled water Marty had pulled out of a cooler near the entrance. ‘He’s all we’ve got at this point,’ Gino was saying; ‘and he won’t give us diddly squat. My preference, slam him in a cell with a couple of Bubbas until he decides to talk, but Magozzi’s got this ethics problem. I was thinking because you were family and all, you could get away with beating the shit out of him.’

Marty started a smile, then thought better of it and just shook his head. ‘I tried last night, Gino, and I pushed hard. I know he’s holding something back. The funny thing is, I get the feeling he thinks he has a damn good reason. But I’ll try again. Later tonight, after Lily goes back to the house.’

‘You’re really going to keep him here?’

‘If someone’s really trying to kill him, he’s probably safer here than anywhere else.’

‘How do you figure? Morey wasn’t very safe here,’ Gino pointed out.

Marty turned to look at him squarely. ‘Because I’m not leaving, and I’m carrying. Last night Jack asked me to go home and get my gun. He was worried about Lily. Now I’m worried about both of them. I think he’s really scared, Gino.’

Gino nodded. ‘So do we. But he might have shot

up his yard all by himself, Marty. We won't know until we get something back from Ballistics, and maybe not even then. If we get a positive on something that came from a gun other than the one Jack was waving around, we can put a car out here.'

They stopped talking when they saw Jack rushing across the lot toward them.

'Where the hell are the Big Boys, Marty? They're supposed to be on the same table as the Early Girls, and I've got a customer freaking out back there because she can't find any.'

Marty rubbed at his forehead, trying to shift gears from murder to plants. 'I don't have the slightest idea what you're talking about, Jack.'

'I'm talking about fucking tomatoes, for chrissake. Now where are they?'

'Oh. I think I put a bunch of those in the shade over there by the small greenhouse.'

Jack gaped at him. 'You put tomatoes in the shade?'

'I guess. If those things over there are tomatoes.' He jerked a thumb to the right, and Jack looked in that direction.

'Oh my God.' He started to hurry off, then turned around and walked back to Gino. 'I think I forgot to thank you for the ride, Detective.'

'Yes, you did.'

Jack nodded, shoved his hands in his pockets and looked off to one side. 'And there's another thing.'

'Yeah?'

'Sometimes I'm kind of a prick.'

'You think so?'

'And in spite of everything, you and your partner have been pretty decent to me. I wish I could help you out.' He raised his eyes to meet Gino's. 'I really mean that.'

Gino watched him walk away with a miserable expression. 'Goddamnit. Now I'm really conflicted.'

Marty chuckled. 'Jack turns everybody upside down.'

29

Gino was mobbed the minute he pushed through the door to Homicide. Langer, McLaren, Gloria, and Peterson all moved toward him like a pack of slobbering puppies. A lesser man, he thought, might have been fearful. 'Lars, what are you doing here?' he asked Detective Peterson. 'I thought they bumped you over to Narc until Tinker got back from vacation.'

Peterson was zipper thin and had just a little more color than most of the corpses they'd seen in the last few days. 'Just for yesterday. And you know how I spent it? Sitting in a methadone clinic waiting for Ray the Mouth to show up. God knows what I caught there . . .'

Gloria pushed Peterson aside with a gentle nudge of her hip that nearly dropped him. 'Yadda yadda yadda, come on, Rolseth, spit it out.'

'What?'

'Are you kidding?' McLaren asked. He was wearing a navy-and-white houndstooth check jacket that looked like an eye test. 'You've been all over the news all morning, and you don't even call in. So what happened at Gilbert's place? Where's Magozzi?'

'Leo's dropping off some stuff for Ballistics, and nothing happened at Gilbert's.'

'No dead people?'

'No dead people. Looks like Gilbert killed his wife's car emptying a clip at a phantom assassin. That's about it.'

Peterson's bony shoulders sagged beneath his white shirt. He looked sadly down at his empty desk, probably dreaming of homicides, the bloodthirsty bastard. 'Sounded like Waco on the news.'

Gloria spun in a swirl of rainbow silk, cornrow beads clattering. 'I told you fools there was nothing to it. You flick a Bic in Wayzata, everybody gets all worked up. Peterson, you've got about three minutes to sign off with Narc before Harrison leaves, or you belong to them.'

'Oh shit.' Peterson beat a path to the door.

'So nothing broke for you?' Langer asked Gino as they all drifted back toward their desks.

'Don't ask. Another twenty steps forward and we'll be back to square one. How about your case?'

Langer shook his head and stabbed at a thick pile of printouts on the edge of his desk. 'This is everything we could get on the six Interpol victims. Dull as dirt, most of them, ordinary people living ordinary lives.'

'But Interpol had them pegged as contract hits, right?'

'So they say, but they're the unlikeliest targets I ever came across.'

'Just like all the people getting bumped off around here.'

Langer raised an eyebrow. 'Good point. But we still can't come up with a connection to Fischer, except for the gun.'

'And the Feds are nipping at Malcherson's ass,' McLaren said miserably. 'The way they figure it, we're a couple of cow tippers who can't see shit in a sewer, so they'll just take our case, solve it in their lunch hour, and get all the glory. Which means Langer and I are probably going to be giving safety lectures at some grade school tomorrow.'

'Huh.' Gino made a feeble attempt at tucking in his shirt. 'What's Malcherson say?'

Langer shrugged. 'We've got until the end of the day to come up with something, then he's letting them in. And to tell you the truth, I'm not so sure it isn't a good idea. We're pretty much at a dead end.'

Gino shook his head. 'If they want it, they've got something you don't have.'

'Probably.'

Magozzi came into the office like a stiff breeze, moving swiftly down the aisle with his cell phone pressed to his ear, listening hard. He greeted everyone with a wave as he passed, thumbing Gino toward their desks in the back.

While Magozzi finished his call, Gino pawed through his desk drawer looking for food. He was examining a soggy, lint-covered cough drop, trying to decide if it was edible, when Magozzi said, 'Thanks,

Dave,' into the phone and flipped the cover closed.

'Dave? As in Ballistic Dave?'

'That's the one. He had a little news. Rose Kleber and Ben Schuler were killed with the same 9-mm.'

'Oh, yippy-ki-ay, our first solid connection, and please, God, tell me it was the 9-mm Wayzata took off Jack Gilbert so I can throw his ass in jail.'

'Sorry. Dave did a quick test-fire. It wasn't Jack's gun.'

'Crap.'

'He also scoped all the slugs from Gilbert's place. All of them came from Jack's gun, except one.'

'Whoa.' Gino leaned back and laced his fingers over his belly. 'So somebody really was trying to kill him.'

Maggozi nodded. 'They dug the odd slug from the inside of the roof, about an inch in from the back of the wife's SUV. Jack said he was standing back by the gate, remember? And *that* slug came from the same gun that killed Kleber and Schuler.'

Gino thought about that for two seconds, said, 'Oh, for chrissake,' then got up and grabbed his handcuffs from the desktop.

'What are you doing?'

'I'm going to go arrest Gilbert, that's what I'm doing.'

'For what? Getting shot at?'

'Material witness, protective custody, public drunkenness, I don't care. I just want him in a cell. That goddamn stupid son of a bitch knew it was coming, and that means he knew *why* it was coming, and maybe even who the shooter is. And does he tell us? No. He just sits around with his mouth shut while other people are getting killed. Goddamnit, why do they put these handcuff clips way in the back I can never reach the damn things . . .'

'Gino. Calm down.'

Gino snorted out a furious exhale and looked at his partner. 'What?'

'We can't arrest him.'

'Please.'

'He didn't actually witness anything, so he's not a material witness. Protective custody is voluntary, and as for the public drunkenness . . .'

'Yeah, yeah, I know.' Gino flopped back down into his chair, thoroughly disspirited. 'We could go over there and question him again, though. Maybe pick up a cattle prod on the way, because without one, that guy is not going to tell us a thing.'

'Call Marty. Tell him what we know, give him a little more ammunition. And have him tell Lily, too. I gave her a nudge this morning. Maybe between the two of them they can break him down.'

Gino reached for the phone. 'We're going to have to put a patrol out at the nursery if Jack's staying there.'

'Right. You take care of that, I'll call Chief Boyd in Wayzata and have him put a car on the wife, just in case.'

Magozzi's cell burped as he was ending his call with Chief Boyd. 'Hey, Grace.'

'Call me back on a landline. I hate cells.'

He blinked when she hung up abruptly, but called her back on the desk phone. 'Why didn't you call the office number in the first place if you hate cells so much?'

'Because I have to go through Gloria, that's why. Gloria hates me.'

'What are you talking about? Of course she doesn't.'

Grace actually laughed out loud, there and gone in a flash, then she was serious again. 'The program is starting to kick out some things. They may not be important. I'm not sure.'

'I know for an absolute fact that Gloria doesn't hate you.'

Gino looked up from his phone call with hiked eyebrows, but Magozzi ignored him.

'Oh, for God's sake, Magozzi, it's certainly more important than that,' Grace said impatiently. 'Listen, I wasn't getting any matches on expenditures for your three victims through the regular channels, so I expanded the search parameters a little.'

'Oh dear. What does that mean exactly?'

'I pulled everything for all three of them. Bank records, credit cards, investment portfolios, tax returns . . .'

Magozzi dropped his head in his hand and covered his eyes while the list of Grace's computer crimes went on and on.

'Magozzi? Are you still there?'

'I'm here. Maybe this would be a good time to mention that Chief Malcherson asked me to remind you to access only information in the public domain when you're helping us out.'

'Okay. Here's your public domain information. Morey Gilbert and Rose Kleber shopped at the same grocery store.'

'That's it?'

'That's it.'

'Oh.'

'Look at this way, Magozzi. You've got legal access to most of this information already at two of the crime scenes. All you have to do is go through every single sheet of paper in Rose Kleber's and Ben Schuler's houses and compare them all, and then in a couple of weeks you'll know what I know right now.'

'Okay, Grace. Point taken. I'm listening.'

'All three of your victims – Morey Gilbert, Rose Kleber, and Ben Schuler – spent a lot of money on plane tickets. As soon as I made that connection, I looped their records into the airline databases and found out they took a lot of trips together. And I mean a lot. Same planes, adjacent seats, same destinations, same dates.'

'What kind of trips? You mean like vacations? Senior tours, that sort of thing?'

'I don't think so.'

'So where'd they go?'

Magozzi sat and listened for a second, his brow furrowed at first, then slowly clearing. 'Wait a second.

I've got to change phones. I'm going to put you on hold, okay?'

Gino looked up when Magozzi jumped out of his chair and held his own phone against his chest. 'What's up?'

'Maybe everything,' Magozzi threw over his shoulder as he made a beeline for Langer's desk.

Gino said a few words into the phone, hung up, and hurried after him.

Magozzi swooped in on a startled Langer, grabbed his phone, and punched the red blinking button. 'Grace, you still there? Hang on . . . Langer, give me the sheet with the Interpol hits.'

Gino heard the undercurrent of excitement in his partner's voice; saw the tightness in his face, and moved to look over his shoulder while Magozzi bent over the desk, a pen poised over the paper Langer had just shoved in front of him.

'Okay, Grace. Give them to me again.' And then he put pen to paper while Gino and Langer watched.

'What's going on?' McLaren whispered, rolling his chair over from his own desk, closing in on Magozzi's other side. Langer shrugged, so McLaren watched Magozzi write, his red brows furrowing more with every stroke of the pen.

He was circling the cities of the Interpol killings – London, Milan, and then Geneva, and all the rest – and next to each of them he printed 'MRB' and a series of numbers. 'Got it,' he said into the phone. 'Thanks, Grace. I'm going to have to get back to you.'

Gino was poking a fat finger at what Magozzi had written on the paper. 'What is this? What's MRB?'

Magozzi took the pen and checked off the letters one by one. 'Morey. Rose. Ben. Grace found some flights our victims took together. She started rattling off the destinations, and they rang a bell.' He nodded at the paper. 'Those are the trips. The numbers are dates. They were in and out of those cities within twenty-four hours of each Interpol murder.'

No one said anything for a moment. Gino was rubbing his forehead, massaging his brain. 'That's a hell of a coincidence, isn't it?'

'I'd say so. Especially when the trips are so short. Who goes to Paris for a day and a half?'

'Business travelers?' Langer suggested.

Magozzi's lips tightened. 'Maybe if their business is contract killing. These people made six trips to six cities on the exact days that your Interpol murders went down.'

Gino wrinkled up his face. 'That's really weird.'

'It's a little more than weird. Looks to me like we just jumped from coincidence to circumstantial evidence.'

McLaren looked at him in disbelief. 'Do you hear what you're saying, Magozzi? That we've got a ring of geriatric assassins living in Uptown. That's a little too far out there, even for me. You couldn't sell that to Hollywood.'

Magozzi looked to Gino, who was scowling hard,

working every one of his brain cells. 'I hear you, Leo, and you know I like an off-the-wall theory as much as the next guy, but Jesus. Saint Gilbert whacking people in Europe? Grandma Kleber in her little old orthopedic shoes hitting the cobblestones after she caps somebody? I mean, what are we saying here? That these people hit sixty-five and decided to supplement their retirement with a little murder-for-hire sideline?'

Langer spoke quietly. 'Morey Gilbert would be absolutely incapable of such a thing. You didn't know him, Magozzi.'

'Maybe nobody did.'

'There has to be another explanation,' Langer persisted.

'And we'll keep looking for that. But come on, Langer. You can't close your eyes to the obvious just because you don't want it to be true.'

Langer went still, replaying that sentence over and over again in his mind, because it was a perfect summary of what he'd been doing for the past year – closing his eyes, keeping the secret, trying to pretend it had never happened because he wanted so desperately for that to be true.

McLaren wouldn't give it up. 'Langer's right. I don't know about the other two, but I did know Morey Gilbert, and that man freaked when a ladybug died. No way he'd kill anybody. Besides, just because they were in those cities doesn't mean they killed anybody. Say I take a trip to Chicago Friday. What do you think the odds are that somebody's gonna get murdered in Chicago on a Friday night? But that sure as hell doesn't mean I did it.'

Magozzi smiled a little to pacify McLaren, who had obviously been more attached to Morey than he realized. 'Maybe not one trip and one murder, but six? We have to look at it, McLaren.'

That took the wind out of McLaren's sails, but only for a moment. 'This is crazy.' He flapped his arms. 'It doesn't make sense. The Interpol killings go back what, fifteen years? That means these people were in their seventies when they popped the first one. Who waits until he's old to decide he's going to be a hit man?'

'Maybe that wasn't their first kill, McLaren,' Magozzi said, and everyone went silent. 'Grace says they made a lot of other trips before that year, and a lot more since. Some of them overseas, some domestic, some to Mexico, Canada – all of them short, a couple less than twenty-four hours. Grace is faxing what she's got so far, then we'll make some calls, see if we can tie those trips to murders, too.'

'Jesus,' Gino said. 'How many more trips were there?'

'Besides the Interpol cities?' Magozzi blew out a breath. 'Over a dozen in the past decade that all three of them made together. She's still tracking. Computer records only go back so far, so we may never know the full number.'

Langer sighed, leaned back in his chair, and looked

wearily at the ceiling. 'I don't know. None of these people were rich. Where's the money?'

Magozzi shrugged. 'Offshore, Swiss accounts, buried in Rose Kleber's garden, who knows? Just because we haven't found it doesn't mean it isn't there.'

'Okay, fine.' McLaren folded his arms irritably. 'I'll play your silly game. You think Morey and his friends were killers because they were in the same cities as our Interpol murders. Well, the Interpol victims were all killed with the same .45 that shot Arlen Fischer. So that means your victims killed our victim. And they didn't just kill this one; they tortured him.'

'Well, that part makes sense,' Gino said. 'Interpol thinks the Fischer murder was personal anyway, and these people lived in the same neighborhood for years, which means there's a really good chance Fischer crossed paths with at least one of them at some point. Beyond asking the Gilberts if they knew him, we didn't go anywhere with that. I don't know one person who doesn't want to kill at least one of their neighbors, and let's face it, if you were killing people all over the world for money, you've got a little sociopathic bent going anyway. What's to stop you from taking care of some personal business with a guy who really pissed you off?'

McLaren kicked at the floor and rolled his chair back to his desk, dropped his chin in his hands. 'I hate this. I absolutely hate this. I really, really liked Morey Gilbert.'

Langer gave him a sad little smile. 'Everybody did.'

30

'I feel like somebody dumped a load of bricks on my head,' Gino said, elbows on his desk, hands rubbing at the blond brush on his head as if such a thing had actually happened.

'I know what you mean,' Magozzi replied. There had been too much information, too fast, coming from a totally different direction than what he'd expected. Two years ago a twister had dropped down in rural Minnesota, sending a farmer scrambling from his tractor to race toward his storm cellar. He was running hell-bent for leather across the field, looking back over his shoulder at the tornado bearing down, when he ran smack-dab into the side of the pickup his wife was driving out to the field to get him. He died instantly, so focused on the twister chasing him that he'd never seen the truck.

That's what Magozzi felt like now, chasing after the killer of his victims, and running smack-dab into the fact that his victims were killers. He'd never seen the truck coming, and it had knocked him flat.

The Homicide room was quiet. Everyone else had gone to lunch. Gloria had rolled calls back to the switchboard so she could tag along with the rest of them, supposedly to give Gino and Magozzi some quiet, but more likely to pump the hapless for information.

'You got a car to cover Jack Gilbert, right?' Magozzi asked.

'Becker was close. He's at the nursery as we speak. Marty's carrying, watching Lily and Jack like a hawk, and he told Jack he'd shoot him if he tried to leave, so Becker won't have to do any fancy tailing.'

'What else did Marty say?'

'That he's been hammering at Jack since we left, but not getting anything. He's going to close the nursery early, get Jack drunk, and beat the truth out of him if nothing else works.'

'So we're covered.'

'Like flies on a cow pie. We got an ex-cop on site, a unit hanging close, a contained scene, and you know what? While we're knocking ourselves out, that stupid asshole's just sitting there with his mouth shut while some psycho is tracking him down, lining him up in his sights, and maybe that's not half bad. I'd never set it up, but this might be the only way we catch the guy.'

Magozzi raised his eyebrows. 'Live bait?'

Gino shrugged. 'Not our doing. But we're ready. What really pisses me off is that we just solved Langer and McLaren's case because our victims killed their victim. So they're out probably drinking their lunch while we sit here trying to figure out who killed our killers. It's like trying to catch fog with your fingers.'

Magozzi rubbed the back of his neck and looked

down at his empty tablet. 'It's got to be here. I feel like it's been right in front of us all along and we just haven't seen it yet.'

Magozzi and Gino always kept their desks pushed together, facing each other, partly because it made passing paperwork easier, partly because Gino had once pronounced that all thought traveled in a straight line from the forehead, and he wanted Magozzi to be in a position to intercept anything he forgot to say out loud. It had been the most frightening thing Magozzi had ever heard his partner say.

They'd been sitting in silence for about two minutes when Gino asked, 'What are you doing?'

Magozzi looked up from his tablet. 'Same thing you are. Taking notes, pulling it together, laying out our next step.'

'So what have you got?'

Magozzi looked down at the idle doodling that always helped him think. 'Two sunflowers and a butterfly. How about you?'

Gino held up a page that was filled with a large unidentifiable stick figure. 'Horse.' He turned the page toward him and frowned at it. 'You know, we should draw masculine stuff when we do this. Guns, cars, shit like that. This looks bad.'

'Shred it.'

'Good plan.' Gino tossed his paper in the shredder basket and looked down at a blank page. 'I don't think my brain wants to go here. I try to think about it, and I see packs of geriatrics with holsters on their little old bony hips. I may never go to the market on Senior Day again. This thing just blows my mind.'

'It's still just circumstantial, Gino.'

'Maybe. But you know what, Leo? It feels right.'

Magozzi nodded. 'Yeah. It does. But it's goddamned unbelievable.'

Gino rubbed his chin thoughtfully. 'You know, I couldn't even find a guy to clean out my roof gutters, so how do you find a contract killer? And what kind of an outfit would employ a bunch of geriatrics? Bob's Discount Assassinations?'

'You think they were working for an agency?'

'Maybe. I can't see two old guys and a little old grandma hanging out in the kinds of sleazy places where you can get a secret word about that kind of thing. Besides, they were pretty busy for freelancers, and these hits were slick. Pro, all the way.' He blew out a long sigh. 'As much as I hate to say it, this is a little out of our venue.'

'Then don't say it.'

'It's their kind of ball game, Leo. They were hot for the Interpol murders already. If we really think we've a got a team of assassins operating here, we've got to bring in the Feds.'

Magozzi started filling in the petals on his sunflower. 'That's just it. We don't know that. At least not for a certainty. If we bring them in too early, they're going to mess up our case.'

'If we don't bring them in and it turns out these people were assassins, there's going to be hell to pay.'

'No there won't. It's not our job to prove Morey Gilbert and his group were killers. It's our job to find out who's killing *them.* Hang on to that. Besides, we've got a lot of reasons to doubt the contract killer theory, and only one coincidence to support it – the overseas trips. And the triad thing really bothers me. Three killers for one hit? Never heard of anything like that.'

Gino threw down his pencil. 'The longer you think about this, the wronger it gets. We just spent half an hour convincing McLaren and Langer our trio of elders were killers, and now we're spending another half hour convincing ourselves they weren't.'

Magozzi smiled a little. 'It's a hell of a merry-go-round, isn't it?'

'I guess.' Gino reached across the desk and dragged over the Arlen Fischer murder file Langer had given them before he left. 'This one really freaks me out. Sure, everybody wants to kill somebody, but what the hell did Arlen Fischer do to deserve this? Knock a plant over at the nursery? Put a door ding in Grandma Kleber's car? I mean, Christ, this was brutal.' He Frisbeed a glossy across the desks to Magozzi. 'Have you seen these shots? They tied the guy to the tracks with barbed wire, for God's sake. Talk about your premediation. You can't pick that stuff up at the corner market. They got it way ahead of time. Torture was a big part of the plan.'

Magozzi centered the glossy in front of him and stared down at it, keeping his brain very still so that one thought, the one that had been nagging at him since breakfast with Malcherson, could start to creep forward. Maybe the thought had been there from the beginning of the investigation, when his mind recorded what he wasn't ready to look at yet, a sad, unpretty thing festering in the dark until it was time to show itself.

And then it did.

'Jesus, Gino. There it is.'

Gino rose slowly to his feet, peered across at the upside-down photo, trying to see what Magozzi saw. 'What? For chrissake, *what*?'

Magozzi looked up at him with the most miserable expression Gino had ever seen on his face. 'Barbed wire. Trains. Concentration camps. They were Jews, Gino. Holocaust survivors.'

Gino eased his bulk slowly back down into his chair, never taking his eyes off Magozzi.

'They weren't contract killers,' Magozzi said sadly. 'Ten cents against my badge, Morey, Rose Kleber, Ben Schuler – they were killing Nazis – the ones who got away. And this one' – he jabbed a finger at Arlen Fischer's photo – 'this one, they knew personally.'

Gino looked down at the photo again, then turned his chair sideways and stared at the wall for a minute. 'Angela made me watch this thing on public television once. Somebody was interviewing Jews. Concentration camp survivors. A bunch of old men and women, and they were talking about the Nazis they'd hunted down and whacked after the war. Not one of those official things like Simon What's-his-name . . .'

'Wiesenthal?'

'Yeah. That sounds right. But it wasn't anything like that. These were underground groups, little death squads, and they said there were a lot of them.'

'You believed them?' Magozzi asked.

'I don't know. At first I thought it was just some sensationalistic bullshit they put on during pledge drive to suck people in, but the thing is, these people had lists of the ones they said they killed, and they knew stuff about some unsolveds the locals had been holding back. By the time the show was over the hair was standing up on the back of my neck.'

31

When Langer and McLaren got back from lunch, Magozzi and Gino sat them down and laid out the whole thing.

Langer knew he wasn't taking it well – maybe because he was Jewish, maybe because it made so damn much sense he couldn't talk himself out of it. The notion of Morey Gilbert as a contract killer had enough holes to give him hope it might not be true; Morey Gilbert as a Nazi killer closed most of them.

For the first thirty-some years of his life Langer had listened closely for stories his mother never told, trying to understand the empty places that lived in her eyes, wishing she would tell the terrible secrets he knew she kept. Alzheimer's finally loosened her tongue and granted his wish, and in her last months of sporadic, time-traveling recall, she forgot he was her son and remembered instead the horrors of her eleven months in Dachau, sixty years before.

Be careful what you wish for.

Her disease had delivered its ultimate blow, erasing every memory except Dachau, and her mind spent its last functional moments on a narrow, splintered wooden bunk in a foulness of smell and sound and spirit that left Langer weeping in the chair beside her bed.

Morey Gilbert, Rose Kleber, and Ben Schuler had shared her experience, had kept their silence just as she had, but maybe for them, justice and morality had different parameters.

He glanced over at McLaren, sitting at his desk with his arms folded, his face closed, angry and sad all at once. Contract killers, Nazi killers, it probably didn't make a whole lot of difference to him. McLaren had idolized Morey Gilbert. The idea of him killing anyone for any reason was simply incomprehensible.

But now Langer believed it. He even understood what would compel the hunted to become the hunters, had understood the moment he'd relived Dachau with his mother. And he suddenly realized that that ability to understand had probably been his downfall.

He looked up at Magozzi. 'If you're right about this, in order to close our case, McLaren and I have to prove a man we both liked very much killed Arlen Fischer.'

'That's about the size of it. And Gino and I need that information, too, because whatever Morey and his friends were tangled up in is probably going to point the way to who killed them.'

'So in a way, we're working the same case.'

'That's what we're thinking.'

McLaren was slumped over his desk, his head

pillowed on his arms. When he raised it, Magozzi thought he looked like a kindergartner who didn't want to wake up from his nap. 'I don't know what to do with all this,' he said. 'I've spent half my life trying to catch bad guys, and all of a sudden, I can't tell who's who. I thought Morey Gilbert hung the moon.'

'For a lot of people, he did,' Langer reminded him. 'He saved a lot of lives, Johnny.'

'Right. During the week he saved lives, then on weekends he went out and killed people, and I'm having a little trouble with that. How many people do you have to save to cancel out taking a life? And the worst part is, half of me says, okay, if that's what he was doing, I get it. He was in Auschwitz, for chrissake. Who knows what he went through? Maybe I'd do the same thing. And then the other half of me – the homicide cop half – can't believe what the first half was thinking.'

'You gotta put all that aside for now, McLaren,' Gino said. 'We're all in exactly the same place, but we've got to stop worrying about dead killers and start worrying about the live one. He's still out there.'

McLaren sighed, then straightened up. 'Okay. I hear you. So where do we go from here?'

Gloria had been standing in the center aisle, filling it up with her big bad black self, listening without talking for the very first time in her life. McLaren had surprised her, the pathetic little dweeb, first by being flat-out heartbroken, which indicated genuine feelings; and second, by saying it all out loud, laying himself open like that. He had a sad little face when he was depressed, she thought. Didn't look quite so much like a leprechaun in a kid's storybook. She slipped quietly back to the reception desk when Magozzi started to get down to business.

'We've got three possibilities here that I can see,' Magozzi was saying. 'Either Morey Gilbert, Rose Kleber, and Ben Schuler were Nazi killers, contract killers, or totally innocent victims of some local psycho bumping off concentration camp survivors, and the trips were just some bizarre coincidence.'

'Goddamnit, Magozzi, stop jerking us around,' McLaren said. 'You've got every single one of us believing they were killing Nazis. Why don't we just go from there?'

'Because we've got a shooter operating in the Cities right now. Job number one is to identify him and stop him before he hits somebody else. If the Nazi-killer scenario is right, we look for a family member who saw our old people kill one of their relatives, or maybe somebody they went for and missed, coming back for a little gotcha-first.'

'You mean like an old Nazi?' McLaren asked.

'Why not? We've got old people killing on one side; why not the other?'

Langer closed his eyes, thinking that it just kept going around and around. It never stopped.

'But if they were contract killers,' Gino put in, 'we might want to look for a mob connection, and if it's a psycho serial, we've got a whole different set of rocks we gotta turn over.'

'Right.' Magozzi nodded. 'And we don't have the time or the resources to cover all three possibilities at once, so we've got to make damn sure we're headed down the right path before we focus the resources we've got, or this guy could walk right past us. Since we all like the Nazi connection, we'll cover that one first. We need to confirm it, or disprove it, and the way I figure, we've got about a couple of hours to find out either way, because this boy's been killing one a day, and we could be looking at another body by the ten o'clock news.'

'And how the hell do we do that?' McLaren asked.

'Gino and I are heading over to Grace MacBride's with the files. I gave her the Nazi scenario, and she thought she might be able to help us with that. In the meantime, we've got two open crime scenes – Rose Kleber's and Ben Schuler's.'

'BCA hit them already.'

'Yeah, but our bodies were just victims then, not potential killers. You're going to be looking at their places with a whole different point of view. Split up, pull some floaters from the roster to help, then each of you take a team and turn those houses upside down. We want the .45 in a big way, but some kind of documentation would work, too.'

'Oh, come on,' McLaren scoffed. 'No matter who they were killing, they'd never keep records that could come back and bite them.'

'Not if they were pros,' Langer interjected quietly, 'but if they were killing Nazis, they just might. That would have been their legacy.' He glanced up at Gino and Magozzi. 'We should search the nursery, too,' he said, regret in his voice.

Gino nodded. 'Yeah, we talked to the county attorney about that when you were at lunch. Kleber and Schuler are still secured crime scenes, and we can crawl all over them, but the Gilbert place is something else. Technically, we never had much of a crime scene, and what we had – the greenhouse and the area around it – was released after the BCA boys covered it. That means we need a warrant, and no way he's going to sign off on it with what we've got.'

'We could ask Lily,' McLaren suggested.

Gino snorted. 'Right. Hey, Mrs Gilbert, we think your husband was a mass murderer. Mind if we look around?'

McLaren's face screwed up in frustration. 'So if our only proof is at the nursery, we're screwed anyway.'

Magozzi sighed. 'We try the other two places first, before we waste time trying to put together reasonable cause for a warrant. If we come up empty, we'll go to Malcherson, see if he has any big strings he can pull.'

Gino jumped off the edge of the desk he'd been sitting on. 'We gotta get moving here.'

Magozzi held up a finger. 'There's one more thing you should know. We've got something going with

Jack Gilbert. Turns out someone really did take a shot at him in Wayzata this morning, and the gun they used was the same one that killed Rose Kleber and Ben Schuler.'

Langer blinked at that and came to attention. 'Wait a minute. They're trying to kill Jack Gilbert? That doesn't even make sense . . . unless you think he was in on this thing.'

'Family business?' McLaren offered.

Gino shook his head. 'Doesn't feel right, even to me, and I hate the guy. But he sure as hell knows something he's holding back – maybe even who the shooter is – which makes him a prime target. Marty's making him stay at the nursery, and we've got a car covering them, just in case.'

McLaren's brows made little red mountains. 'Jesus. You set a trap for the guy, and Jack Gilbert's the bait.'

'Do not even say that out loud. We did no such thing. We'd have him in a cell in a second if we could make anything stick, just to save his worthless ass. As it is, we've got Marty as on-site protection, and a patrol hanging close. That's the best we can do. If it turns out the guy does come for him, we'll make the best of a bad situation.'

32

It was almost two o'clock by the time Gino and Magozzi pulled to the curb in front of Grace MacBride's house. The thermometer in the car – which ironically worked perfectly when the air conditioner wouldn't at all – read eighty-seven degrees. The air was breathlessly still and thick, and Gino's forehead was dripping as they walked from the car to the house.

'Man, you almost gotta do the breaststroke to get through this stuff. I feel like Frosty the Snowman when he got locked in the greenhouse with all the poinsettias.'

Charlie was all over Gino when Grace opened the front door. He didn't just jump up and lick his face; he whined while he was doing it, licking so hard that he nearly pushed Gino off the steps.

Magozzi folded his arms across his chest and watched the annoying display. Damn dog was making a fool of himself, the stub of his ravaged tail wagging so hard he couldn't keep both hind feet on the ground at once.

'Charlie, Charlie, my man.' Gino was laughing, hugging the stupid dog as if he were a person.

Grace was standing in the open doorway, hair pulled back into a ponytail, wearing the ubiquitous black T-shirt and jeans. The derringer was snug in its ankle holster, and she wore a smudge of flour on a sour expression. 'Charlie, get in here.'

Charlie wasn't moving, so Gino picked him up and carried him inside.

'That was pretty disgusting,' Magozzi said.

'Bite your tongue. That was pure, furry adoration. This dog loves me to death.'

'That's always bothered me,' Grace said irritably, closing the door, resetting the security system.

'You think it bothers you?' Magozzi tried not to look wounded. 'Took weeks before that dog came out from hiding to meet me at the door. First time Gino ever showed up here he damn near knocked him down.'

'I got doggie pheromones,' Gino said.

Charlie was pressing against Magozzi's leg now, trying to apologize. 'Slut,' Magozzi grumbled down at him, managing to resist for almost a full second before dropping to one knee and settling happily for second best.

Grace was standing with her hands on her hips, shaking her head. 'What is it with men and dogs?'

'Similar morals?' asked Gino, earning a very small smile before Grace reverted to business mode, holding out her hand to Magozzi.

'Did you bring Arlen Fischer's pictures?'

'Right here.' Magozzi got to his feet and handed her a thin file. 'Crime-scene photo from the tracks and a morgue shot.'

Grace opened the folder and took a quick look. 'These should work, but you realize it's still a long shot. Even if Arlen Fischer was a Nazi, there might not be any photodocumentation on the Web. There aren't a lot of photos of the low-level camp guards, for instance, because those weren't the big guns the war crimes people were looking for. If he was an officer, we've got a chance.'

Magozzi handed her another file. 'I brought the photos of the overseas victims that Interpol faxed over, but the quality sucks. They were photocopies in the first place, and you said you wanted originals.'

Grace glanced at them and wrinkled her nose. Magozzi thought it was about the cutest thing he'd ever seen happen to a human face. 'We'll start with Fischer then, and if we don't get any hits, I can try the photocopies. It's a slow program. I'll get it started.'

They followed her up to the doorway of her office, but didn't go in. Charlie and Magozzi had seen her roll her chair at high speed from one end to the other when she was working more than one computer, and knew better than to get underfoot. Gino avoided small rooms with computers as a matter of course, convinced they emitted some kind of radiation that might have a deleterious effect on cherished body parts.

Grace settled in front of a large computer Gino thought looked particularly dangerous, and proceeded to do confusing things with a mouse, which he could identify; and with another machine, which he couldn't. 'What is that? Looks like a teeny-weeny mangle.'

'What on earth is a mangle?' Grace asked without looking up.

'You know. One of those ironing machines. You stick wrinkled clothes in one end and they come out the other all pressed and flat. Sheets and tablecloths and stuff. It's kind of cool, actually.'

'That's a scanner, Gino,' Magozzi informed him.

'What's a scanner?'

Grace snapped them a look. 'You two want to know what I'm doing or not?'

'Absolutely,' Gino said.

'I just scanned Arlen Fischer's photograph into the new face-recognition program I'm working on.'

'We've got one of those,' Gino said, glancing at Magozzi. 'Don't we have one of those?'

'I don't think so.'

Grace rolled her eyes and kept typing. 'If you had one, which you don't, it would be the Flintstone version. Some of the facial-recognition programs out there draw on a single database – like the setups they've got at some of the airports. They've got one database with photos of known terrorists, criminals, and anybody else who's red-flagged; the machine takes a digital photo of the guy walking through the security line, and checks it against all the photos in their database.'

Gino was pretty impressed. 'I get it. The facial-recognition program is like a witness, and the database is like a mug book. It looks at all the pictures and picks out the bad guy.'

'Exactly.'

'Well that sounds simple enough.'

'It would be, if there were a single database with a picture of every single Nazi in it, but there isn't. What we've got is hundreds of individual Web sites with archive photos of *some* Nazis. So what we're left with is entering each site one by one, pulling out each picture one by one, and entering those into the recognition software that runs comparisons with Arlen Fischer's picture. You could spend your life on that kind of a search.'

Gino sighed. 'I should have brought my pajamas.'

'Not necessary, thank God,' Grace said, her fingers busy. 'Instead of pulling photo images off the Web and entering them individually into a recognition program, I put together a program that would go into the Web instead, and do the search that way. It's still slow – I can only route it to about ten sites at a time – but it's a hell of a lot faster than the old way. I'm going to run Fischer's photo through the Nazi watch group sites first, because that's our best chance to get an early hit – they've archived more photos of the period than any of the historical sites.'

Magozzi frowned. 'Fischer would have been a lot younger then.'

'Doesn't matter. Skin sags, chins fall, people get fatter, thinner, have cosmetic surgery, whatever; but the bones remain essentially the same. The program focuses on thirty-five key structural points in the face. So even if you had your jaw and your cheekbones reconstructed, for instance, that still leaves twenty-some identifiers the program will jump on. It's never wrong.'

'Never?'

'Not unless somebody put their head in a mangle and had the whole thing rebuilt.'

Gino smiled and elbowed Magozzi. 'She's quick.'

'Like a bunny,' Maggozi agreed.

'It's still pretty primitive,' Grace conceded. 'But eventually you'll be able to slap a school photo of your fifth-grade sweetheart into a scanner, push a button, and if there's a picture of her anywhere on the Web, the program will find it.'

Grace rolled down to another computer and held out her hand. 'Give me the stats on the overseas victims. I'll start the standard search program on them while we wait.'

Gino's stomach made a noise that sounded like a large volcanic eruption. 'I'll give you my first-born son for a cracker.'

Grace raised an eyebrow. 'The Accident?'

Gino frowned and thought a minute. 'I'll give you a *picture* of my first-born son for a cracker.'

Grace shooed them away with a wave. 'Give me five minutes alone to work this, and I'll get you a cracker. Go sit in the dining room.'

Gino, Magozzi, and Charlie took their seats at the

dining room table while Grace finished up in the office.

Gino kept eyeing the dog in the chair at the head of the table. 'Jeez, he really does sit in chairs like a person. That's kinda creepy.'

Charlie turned his head to look at him.

'Shit. Does that dog understand English?'

'Hell, why not? McLaren understands French.'

Gino's stomach let out another rumbling protest. He leaned sideways to peer through the archway to the kitchen. 'Maybe I could just go in there and rummage around until I found a crust of bread of something.'

'The cupboards are all booby-trapped.'

'Oh.'

Magozzi rolled his eyes. 'Kidding, Gino.'

'Well, I believed it. She's still got the house locked up tighter than a drum.'

'A lot of people have home security.'

'Most of them don't run around in their own house with a gun strapped to their ankle.'

'She's getting better, Gino.'

'You keep saying that, but personally, I don't see it.'

'She bought me a chair.'

Gino arched a brow. 'You mean for here? Your very own chair?' He looked over his shoulder into the living room. 'Where is it?'

'Outside.'

'And that doesn't tell you something?'

'You don't understand.'

Grace came from the hall into the kitchen then and started making little domestic noises. A minute later she walked into the dining room balancing four plates. Three held mounds of glistening greenery topped with large, snowy chunks of lobster. The fourth held kibble buried under some kind of chunky gravy that smelled like the greatest hotdish ever made.

Gino looked pointedly at that one. 'Smells terrific,' he said, saddened a little when she set it in front of Charlie. 'But jeez, Grace, this is some cracker.'

'I figured you hadn't had a chance for lunch with all that was going on today. We might as well eat while we're waiting for the program to kick out something.'

Gino looked down at the generous pile of lobster on his plate and almost wept. 'This is the nicest goddamned thing . . .' was all he managed to get out before his fork found his mouth. When he was finished, he patted the corners of his mouth with a napkin. 'Grace MacBride, I will tell you this. Aside from Angela's marinara, this is, without a doubt, the best food I have ever eaten in my life.'

'Thank you, Gino.'

'And I like the way you decorated the plates with all this green stuff, too.'

'That's not decoration. You're supposed to eat that.'

'No kidding.' Gino prodded warily at the greenery.

‘So what are these little round things that look like worms?’

‘Eat one.’ Grace pointed with her fork. ‘Then I’ll tell you.’

Gino sorted through the meadow on his plate, finally stabbed one of the scary little green coils, and eased it carefully into his mouth. He chewed tentatively a couple of times, then scooped up another forkful. The real measure of Gino’s eating pleasure was taken by the number of times he chewed. Steak got three chews, pasta got two, dessert got one, but this time Magozzi could have sworn he swallowed it whole. ‘Man, this stuff rocks.’

Grace looked on in satisfaction; Magozzi looked almost alarmed. ‘I don’t think I’ve ever seen you eat anything green before. Am I going to find a pod in the car?’

Gino looked offended. ‘I eat green stuff sometimes.’

‘Like what?’

‘Lime popsicles.’ He grinned at Grace. ‘Okay. What is this stuff, ’cause I gotta get some.’

‘Fiddlehead ferns in a champagne vinaigrette with Comte cheese.’

Gino nodded. ‘That explains it. I’d eat Leo’s shoes if you poured champagne on them. There is no culinary road I won’t travel.’ He pushed away from the table and laced his hands over his protruding stomach, looking at Grace. ‘You are going to make some lucky man a wonderful wife someday.’

Grace stared at him for a second. 'That is the most sexist thing I ever heard anyone say. You do know I'm armed, right?'

Gino grinned. 'That was just my little attention-getting intro.'

'Okay. You've got my attention. Intro to what?'

'Well, I've just been wondering what your intentions are.'

Grace's blue eyes widened a little, which made a startling change in a face so normally devoid of expression. 'Excuse me?'

'Toward my buddy here. I'd like to hear your intentions. And you see? I'm not sexist at all. Usually you ask the guy that question.'

Magozzi dropped his head in his hands. 'Oh, for God's sake.'

Grace's eyes went back to their normal size. Gino had done the near-impossible by catching her off guard, but she recovered quickly. 'And that would be your business because . . . ?'

'Because he's my partner and my best friend, and partners and friends look out for each other, and because you two have been seeing each other for damn near half a year and I'm guessing neither one of you ever brought up the subject of where this thing is going, or whether you'll ever get there.'

Magozzi looked up, embarrassed and angry. 'Jesus, Gino, shut up.'

'I'm doing you a favor here, Leo. You'd do the same for me.'

'Not in million years.'

A faint chime sounded from the office. Grace was still staring at Gino with that flat, emotionless expression that had bothered him the first time he'd met her. He couldn't read her at all, and it made him wary. When the chime sounded again, she got up from her chair. 'I'm going to get that. There's dessert and coffee in the kitchen, Magozzi. Bring it in, would you? Feel free to dump it on Gino's head.'

A few minutes later Gino had forgotten the mysteries of Grace MacBride as he gazed happily at a layer cake with a gleaming shell of chocolate. 'Jesus, Magozzi, cut the damn thing. I'm dying here.'

'You're lucky I didn't dump it on your head. What the hell was that all about?'

'That was about me, taking care of you.'

'Well, stop it. Grace is right. It's none of your business.'

'Well, that's about the dumbest thing you ever said.'

Now Magozzi was staring at him, and Gino didn't have a bit of trouble reading his expression. He raised his hands in surrender. 'All right, all right, maybe I went a little too far. I apologize. I want to make up. Let's cut the cake and toast our reconciliation with chocolate.'

Grace walked in and tossed a printout on Gino's cake plate, intentionally, he was sure. 'We have a couple of hits, the first on one of the Interpol victims. Charles Swift, retired mason murdered in Paris during one of the trips your victims made together. His real name was Charles Franck.' She pointed to a place halfway down the page. 'Convicted at Nuremberg; served fifteen years for war crimes.'

Gino and Magozzi were silent as they read the pertinent paragraph a few times, letting it sink in.

'Anything on the others?' Magozzi finally asked.

Grace shook her head. 'This one had been caught. He was in the system, so when he changed his name after he served his time, he had to do it legally, which made the records easy to find. If the others were Nazis, too, they were probably under pretty tight cover.'

Gino sucked in air through the side of his mouth. 'I told Langer if the Feebs wanted this case they had something he didn't. What do you bet it was the goods on this Swift character. Really nice work, Grace.'

'Don't try to make up with me, Gino.' She placed another printout on the table, this one with an old black-and-white photograph of several men wearing the unmistakable garb of the S.S. Grace had circled one of the faces. 'That's Heinrich Verlag, bad boy at Auschwitz, a.k.a. Arlen Fischer, sixty years and a hundred and fifty pounds ago.'

Magozzi looked down at the picture. The pieces were finally coming together. 'Morey Gilbert was at Auschwitz. So was Ben Schuler.'

It was the confirmation they had been hoping for and dreading, all at the same time, and Grace saw the conflict in their faces. 'I will never understand cops,' she complained. 'You come here looking for information, I give you exactly what you ask for, and now you're depressed. Your old people were Nazi killers. That's what you thought, wasn't it?'

Gino nodded, his face glum. 'Yeah, that's what we thought. But we were kind of hoping they didn't kill anybody. That we had this nice, normal psycho serial killer bumping them off instead.'

Magozzi's mouth turned down in unhappy resignation. 'These were nice people, Grace. Ben Schuler was a lonely old man who passed out ten-dollar bills to inner-city kids on Halloween. You should hear his neighbors talk about him. Rose Kleber was this sweet little old grandmother who loved her family, a cat, and her garden. And Morey Gilbert did more good for other people in a day than I'll ever do in a lifetime. We prove they were cold-blooded killers, and all that is gone.'

Grace's sigh was irritated. 'You know as well as I do that people are not always what they seem, Magozzi. Besides, they weren't killing innocents. The Nazis were the bad guys.'

It startled him a little, the way she said that – flat-out, pragmatic, a casual justification for vigilantism. It threw a light on the great differences between them, and Magozzi could almost feel his heart squinting at the sight. 'You know the worst thing about bad people, Grace? It's what they make good people do.'

A little later, when they were leaving, Grace touched Gino's arm at the door, holding him back as Magozzi started down the walk toward the car. 'I'm trying, Gino,' she said very quietly, following Magozzi with her eyes.

Gino wasn't a hundred percent sure he knew what she meant, exactly, but when she looked up at him, he got a glimpse of what Magozzi saw – this haunted little excellent woman treading water as fast as she could, and it made him very sad.

Langer called Gino's cell when they got in the car. 'We've got something from the Schuler house.'

33

Chief Malcherson was standing with Langer and McLaren at the long table in the front of the Homicide room when Gino and Magozzi walked in. Gino was pleased as punch to see that he was now wearing his charcoal double-breasted suit and a flame-red tie.

'Gee, Chief,' he said happily. 'You went home and changed into a murder suit. Cool.'

Malcherson looked at him. 'I did not go home to change into a "murder suit." I spilled coffee on the other one.'

Gino kept smiling, because that was a load of crap. Malcherson never spilled anything, ever. 'You know, a lot of men couldn't pull off that tie with that suit without looking like a drum major, but you nailed it.'

'Thank you so much.' Malcherson stepped away from the table to let Gino and Magozzi move closer. 'Langer and McLaren filled me in on where you're going with this. It looks like Langer found the confirmation you were looking for at the Ben Schuler house.'

Magozzi looked at the sixty identical photographs of Ben Schuler's family, still in their frames, spread out on the table. 'We saw those at the house; thought it was weird. Jimmy Grimm thought they might have been some kind of memorial for his family, because they died in the camps and he didn't.'

Gino was frowning. 'I don't get how this is confirmation that Schuler and the rest of them were killing Nazis.'

Langer took a picture off the table and started dismantling the frame while he talked. 'I thought it was weird, too, so I took down one of the frames and opened it, just because people hide things in pictures sometimes. This is the first one I opened.' He pulled the picture free of the cardboard backing and turned it over to expose small, spidery writing on the back side. 'I didn't recognize the name, but I certainly recognized the date and the place.'

Magozzi squinted at the writing. 'Milan, Italy, July 17, 1992.' His eyes flew up to Langer's. 'Is that the date of the Milan Interpol murder?'

Langer nodded. 'We've checked the backs of six photos besides that one so far, and they all have the same kind of notation: a name, a place, and a date. One match to the Interpol list, all the others were on the list Grace MacBride faxed over of the domestic trips Gilbert, Kleber, and Schuler took together. I'm guessing that when we call the locals in those cities and give them the date, they'll have a murder that went down, probably an unsolved.'

Magozzi's eyes swept over all the pictures, seeing a body behind each one. 'Jesus,' he whispered. 'These pictures aren't memorials. They're trophies. One for every Nazi they killed. We're looking at sixty bodies here.'

'Sixty-one,' Langer said. 'He never had time to put one up for Arlen Fischer.'

Malcherson picked up one of the photos and looked down at the faces of people who had been dead for over half a century. 'Not trophies, Detective Magozzi. They were offerings to his family,' he said quietly. 'A body a year.'

Gino sighed and shoved his hands in his pockets. 'Man, I was blown away before, but this is mind-boggling. These people have been on a sixty-year murder spree.' He glanced over at McLaren, who was dismantling the frames, removing the photos, and placing them on the table in what looked like chronological order. He hadn't said anything since they came into the room, but he didn't look so depressed anymore. Just focused and maybe a little angry, which was good. Depressed cops were pretty useless. 'You find anything at Rose Kleber's house, McLaren?'

'Oh, yeah. About a thousand pictures of her grandkids, every single greeting card she ever got from anybody, you know, grandma stuff. Nothing like this, and no gun. A couple guys are still over there. I came back when Langer called.'

'We picked up a couple of things at Grace's, too,' Magozzi said.

And then he laid Grace's printout of the S.S. officers down on the table, showed them Arlen

Fischer as a young man named Heinrich Verlag, and told them all about it.

Langer picked up the picture and looked closely. 'Fischer was the prize catch for somebody – Morey or Ben Schuler, I suppose, since they were both at Auschwitz with this animal.'

'Yeah,' Gino said. 'I don't even want to know what he did to them to deserve the death he got.'

'But the thing that puzzles me,' Langer went on, 'is that he was right under their noses for decades. Why did they wait so long to kill him?'

Magozzi shrugged. 'Maybe they just found him. We still don't know how they tracked these people down, but they obviously had an edge over Wiesenthal and the rest of the groups that were looking – Fischer's been on the watch list since the fifties. Or maybe it was something as simple as serendipity. Fischer was something of a shut-in, remember; the only place he went regularly was a Lutheran church, and it's not likely that Morey Gilbert or Ben Schuler would have run into him there over the years. But maybe he took a walk a few weeks ago, and one of them just happened to be driving by. We'll probably never know.'

Gino nodded. 'So Morey Gilbert and the rest of them go over to Fischer's house Sunday night. They've got it all planned, what they're going to do to him, right down to bringing along a gurney. But maybe Fischer fought back or tried to run away. Whatever happened, somebody panicked and let off a shot, and there's Fischer bleeding to death before they can get him to the train tracks.'

'So they grab the runner off the coffee table and make a tourniquct,' said Langer.

'Right. Then they take him to the tracks, do their thing, and a few hours later Gilbert's dead. Next day Rose Kleber is killed, Schuler the next. I'm thinking maybe somebody close to Fischer saw what went down and went after them to even the score.'

McLaren shook his head. 'Everything fits but the last part. Nobody was close to Fischer. No wife, no kids, no friends that we can find, and I sure can't see the old housekeeper toddling after a bunch of killers for a little payback.'

'Then we have to go back farther than Fischer,' Magozzi said. 'Could be someone's been tailing them for a while – maybe a family member of one of the earlier victims – and took his shot when Morey came home late that night. We've got to start calling the cities listed on those pictures, see if we can match up murders to the dates, and then start looking hard at their families.'

They all moved in on the table and started helping McLaren disassemble the pictures. Gino was shaking his head while he worked. 'Calling all these places, sweet-talking the locals, tracking down families . . . this could take forever.'

'I know,' Magozzi said. 'Where the hell's Peterson?'

'Damnit,' McLaren muttered, heading for the

nearest desk and phone. 'He went along to Rose Kleber's house to help with the search. I'll get him back in here.'

'I'll do it,' Malcherson said quietly from the doorway, making McLaren jump. He'd forgotten the chief was there. 'You need to get back to what you were doing.'

And that was the very best thing about Malcherson, Gino was thinking. He'd jump in and take care of the small stuff when things got heavy, because he trusted his detectives to do their jobs, and knew when to back away and let them get to it. He threw a little salute to the chief as he walked out.

Five minutes later they had all the pictures in chronological order, barely glancing at the cities, except when they rang a bell, like the ones on the Interpol list, and one just last year in Brainerd, Minnesota, which creeped Gino out because he went to Boy Scout camp there when he was a kid. Five minutes after that, Peterson hustled in, his pasty face flushed.

McLaren gaped at him. 'How the hell did you get here so fast?'

'Sixty miles an hour on the surface streets. I feel like I'm going to have a heart attack. Malcherson had me on the cell all the way, bringing me up to speed. Give me somebody to call.'

Magozzi handed him a photograph. 'We're starting with the most recent dates and going backwards. You know what to do?'

'You bet. Call the locals, find a murder for our date, track the families.'

'Right. But remember, the name on the photo probably won't match the name of the victim. If these guys were Nazis, they were hiding.'

'Got it.' Peterson snatched the photo and headed for his desk.

'Holy shit, Leo, take a gander at this one.' Gino shoved a photograph under his nose. '1425 Locust Point, Minneapolis, fourteen April, 1994. You know who that is? That's the plumber somebody turned into a sieve. The cold case I brought over to your place Sunday, remember?'

'Valensky?'

'Gotta be. The name's different, but unless there was another murder at that address on that date and nobody told me, that's our guy.' He took a beat and looked at all the pictures. 'I'll bet we're going to solve a lot of cold cases for a lot of departments before we're finished with this mess.'

McLaren straightened from the table, his normally affable face furious. 'Okay, that tears it. Goddamn that son of a bitch, that really pisses me off. The whole time Morey Gilbert's convincing me and Langer he's God in a pair of overalls, he's out killing people in our city.'

'He had reasons we'll probably never understand, Johnny.'

McLaren looked at his partner as if he were out of his mind. 'Our city, Langer. If anybody has a problem with people in our city, they come to us and we take care of it. That's the way it's supposed to work.'

Langer looked at the conviction in Johnny McLaren's face, remembering when things had been that clear for him. *Murderers are bad, catching murderers is good.* So simple. So black and white. It was examining the gray areas that got you in trouble. At that moment he realized that of the two of them, McLaren was the better cop.

'Let's get moving,' Magozzi said, grabbing the most recent pictures and passing them out. His phone was ringing by the time he got to his desk.

Dave from Ballistics had a reedy voice so distinctive you could recognize it immediately, and right now it sounded tight and strained. 'I'm backed up to my balls here, Leo, but you and Gino need to know this right away.'

Magozzi motioned for Gino to pick up the line. 'Okay, Dave, we're both on. Go.'

'I just got a chance to run Jack Gilbert's Smith & Wesson through the system, and got a hit. The same gun killed a resort owner in Brainerd last year. I'm pushing the fax button now.'

'Okay, Dave, thanks.'

'Hold on a second. There's something else. Is Langer there? Or McLaren?'

'Both here, both on the phone.'

'Well pass this on, will you? Tell them I'm really sorry about this, I don't know how it happened, it's been a goddamned zoo down here this week, but that .45 in their Arlen Fischer case?'

'Right. The one used in the Interpol hits.'

'Yeah, well that wasn't the whole of it. Another match came in a little later and somehow got lost in the paperwork. Just laid eyes on it about three minutes ago, and I faxed that up, too. Tell them their .45 killed Eddie Starr.'

Magozzi squinted, pulling the name up from his good memory. 'The same Eddie Starr who killed Marty Pullman's wife?'

At his desk a few feet away, Langer's head jerked up and his face went cold.

'That's the one,' Dave said. 'Marty Pullman's wife, Morey Gilbert's daughter, Jesus, guys. What the hell is going on with that family?'

'We're going to have to get back to you on that.'

McLaren looked over, his phone hooked in his shoulder. 'I got Muzak. What was that about?'

'Ballistics Dave says the gun Wayzata took off Jack Gilbert this morning killed a guy in Brainerd last year.'

'The Brainerd guy on the back of our picture?'

'Don't know yet,' Gino said. 'But your .45 just got even more interesting. The same gun brought down that Eddie Starr kid who killed Hannah Pullman.'

The phone slipped from McLaren's shoulder into his lap. 'You are shitting me.' He looked over at Langer who was still on the phone, but staring at Gino with an intense expression.

'I wonder if I could call you back, Sergeant?' Langer said politely into the phone, and then hung up without waiting for an answer.

'Looks like we just wiped another unsolved off the books,' Gino said. 'And the sad truth is it makes perfect sense. Morey Gilbert had been killing people for years with that gun. Why not the kid that killed his daughter?'

'I wonder how the hell he found him before we did,' McLaren said.

'Are you kidding? Morey was finding Nazis missing for sixty years. Eddie Starr was probably a cakewalk for him. Besides, he was only an hour ahead of you. Starr was still pretty pink when you found him, right?'

McLaren nodded. 'Real pink.'

'So there you go. What do you think about Jack's gun popping the guy in Brainerd, Leo?'

Magozzi shrugged. 'He said he got the gun from his dad's, and after getting a look at his dad's history, I'm inclined to believe him.'

'Me, too,' Gino said. 'I'm going to get on the horn to Brainerd since we've got a ballistics tie-up along with everything else. Besides, that one's still fresh as a daisy. Langer, you get anything from the guys in L.A.? . . . Jesus, Langer, you don't look so good.'

Langer gave Gino a sickly smile, then got up and quickly left the office.

'What's the matter with him?'

McLaren shrugged. 'He had some kind of a flu

yesterday. Must have relapsed.' He pushed the disconnect button on his phone and hit redial. 'I'm going to call these jokers back and tell them I'm FBI. Maybe they won't put me on hold this time.'

'Go for it,' Magozzi said.

34

Marty hadn't taken a relaxed breath since Gino and Magozzi had dropped Jack off that morning. The cops might have thought that Jack was shooting at phantoms in Wayzata, but Marty had that twist in his gut he used to get on the job when things were about to go bad. He'd handed most of his chores over to Tim and Jeff and spent all his time tailing Jack, his gun stuck in the back pocket of his jeans, his shirt hanging over it to keep from scaring the customers.

Lily, as usual, had complicated everything. She wasn't about to talk to her son, but apparently she wasn't going to let anyone kill him either. The minute Magozzi and Rolseth left, she'd planted herself within two feet of Jack, and there she had stayed ever since, mother on a tether. Also mother in the target zone.

Marty had caught himself balancing on the balls of his feet once, ready to dart in front of them both in case the lady in the straw sandals suddenly dropped her basket of flowers and morphed into a mad gunman. Two things about that moment had surprised him: first, that he was looking at everything with a cop's eye again, seeing the potential for danger everywhere; and second, that he could still balance on the balls of his feet. As far as he could remember, he hadn't been able to balance flat-footed for a year. He'd laughed out loud at that, and Lily and Jack had both looked up and stared at him with strange expressions, probably because he didn't laugh very often these days, or more likely, because being followed by a laughing gunman might be a little disturbing. So he'd slipped back into his stone-faced demeanor by remembering how damn irritating this whole thing was, and the two people he was guarding so assiduously were the cause of it. Jack should be in protective custody, telling the cops everything he knew, and Lily should be making him do it. They should be taking care of each other instead of relying on him for everything. Christ, this was exhausting. Three days ago he'd been in a drunken stupor with a gun stuck in his mouth; now he was a pseudo-cop, a pseudo-bodyguard, and the hardest-working man in the nursery business.

And goddamnit, he'd thought then, nearly laughing aloud again, it almost felt good.

But those hours had been more like playing cop than the real thing. When Gino called shortly before 2 P.M. and told him that someone really had taken a shot at Jack that morning, pseudo-anything flew out the window, and Marty started thinking like the man he had once been, not so long ago.

He shouldn't be trotting around the nursery after Lily and Jack like a guard dog on a leash. He should be beating the truth out of Jack, finding out who killed Morey, doing the job he had been trained to do, and most important of all, he should be closing the goddamned nursery.

'What do you mean, you're closing the nursery?' Lily and Jack demanded almost in unison.

They were all in the front of the greenhouse, unloading plants from a pallet onto an outside table. The place was packed in spite of the sweltering weather, and the plants disappeared almost as soon as they set them down. Jeff and Tim were manning the outside registers, and there was a long line at each counter.

Marty kept his voice low. 'Ballistics came back on the slugs at Jack's house this morning. The same person who killed Rose Kleber and Ben Schuler took a shot at him. So just in case this asshole decides to try again, we're going to get these customers out of the line of fire, close this place down, and you two are going to do exactly what I say from this moment on.'

He waited for one of them to protest, but it never came.

'I'll start getting the customers out of here,' Jack finally said.

'No you won't. Come with me.'

Marty led them both to the bench at the greenhouse entrance, sat them down, then stood in front of them like some burly Colossus, facing the parking lot.

Lily had been acquiescent for about three minutes.

Marty figured that was an all-time record. 'For heaven's sakes, Martin, do you expect us to sit here all day?' she asked.

He didn't even turn around to look at her. 'Gino's sending a car over. When it gets here, Jack goes back to the house and stays there with the officer, you hear me, Jack?'

'I hear you.'

Officer Becker pulled into the parking lot a few minutes later, got out, and introduced himself to Marty. He was young, blond, and deceptively fresh faced, but Tony Becker had been at the warehouse when the Monkeewrench firefight went down last fall. It had hardened him in a hurry, made him watchful and sharp, and Marty liked the way his eyes kept moving, checking everything out.

'This is Jack Gilbert,' Marty explained quickly. 'He's the target. Take him back to the house and stay with him.'

After they left, Marty called Tim and Jeff over from the registers. 'We're closing the nursery. I want you two to get all the customers out of here.'

'You're closing the nursery?' Jeff Montgomery asked.

'That's right.'

Both boys looked over his shoulder at Lily, who nodded slightly.

'Okay.' Tim Matson shrugged his broad shoulders, glancing back at the line at the registers. 'We'll just finish checking these people out . . .'

‘No. We’re closing now. This minute. Apologize, tell them it’s a family emergency, get them out of here. And then I want you two out of here. Don’t bother with the till, don’t bother with the tapes, just go.’

Marty knew he was scaring them – they looked like a couple of teddy bears with their eyes wide and suddenly worried – but that was what he wanted. Two scared kids hightailing it out of here, back at their own places, safe.

‘Is there a problem, Mr Pullman?’ Jeff asked. ‘Because if there is, maybe we could stay and help you out?’

‘You can’t stay,’ Lily said from the bench. ‘Somebody might be trying to shoot Jack. I don’t want you here. I want you safe.’

Tim and Jeff looked at her in disbelief, trying to take it in, and Marty knew they were thinking about Morey getting shot just a few days ago, wondering how and if it all pieced together, and what kind of an animal would try to destroy the family that had been so good to them. He prepared himself for a barrage of questions, but as it turned out, he’d underestimated them both, forgetting that they were nearly men, and that the protective instinct blooms early, pushing everything else aside. They both straightened, squaring their shoulders, puffing up.

Jeff, who’d been driving Marty crazy for days by ending every sentence with a question mark, suddenly looked like a man instead of a boy, his blue gaze steady, his mouth set and determined. 'Is that why the cop came?'

Marty nodded.

'One cop to guard this whole place? Let us stay, Mr Pullman. Let us help.'

Great, Marty thought. Just what I need. A couple of adolescent heroes. 'Listen, kid, I appreciate the offer, but we don't really think anything's going to happen here. We're just being extra-careful. Officer Becker and I have it under control, and the only thing that might mess it up is having to worry about the two of you on top of everything else. If you really want to help, get rid of the customers – right now – and go home.'

Tim, his dark hair dripping sweat, went immediately to the bench and sat next to Lily. 'You shouldn't stay here either, Mrs Gilbert. If we have to leave, I want you to come with us.'

Lily smiled at Tim and patted his hand. 'You're good boys. Stop worrying. Tomorrow we'll put Jack in a safe place, and everything will be back to normal.'

Marty looked at her as Tim and Jeff started clearing out the customers. 'How are we going to do that?'

'Do what?'

'Get Jack to a safe place? '

'Easy. You're going to talk him into it.'

'You don't have enough scotch for that.'

'Pfft. I have a case in the basement.'

35

It took Tim and Jeff half an hour to clear the nursery greenhouses and grounds of every customer. They'd been good about it, very professional, Marty thought, using the family emergency line, saying it with mournful expressions that quashed any shopper's irritation almost before it took form. 'I'm so sorry to hear that,' was a response he heard over and over as people filed obediently to their cars. Most of them probably knew about Morey's murder on Sunday, and the idea of more misfortune striking this family had a sobering effect. A surprising number asked if there were something they could do. It wasn't just Minnesota Nice – it was people nice, reminding Marty that the big scale still tipped way over to the side of good, and the bad was just a sprinkle. When you spent most of your life as a cop, most of your days on the dark side, it was good to be reminded of that once in a while.

Right up until the last minute, Tim and Jeff were still trying to stay on. They offered to patrol around the grounds all night, if not to stop trouble, to at least watch for it. The idea of these two kids walking the property in the dark made Marty shudder, because the feeling that something could happen was growing stronger by the minute.

It was the weather, he thought, when he finally put the kids in their beater cars and shooed them out of the drive, locking the gate behind them. You couldn't see the big clouds yet – just a filmy white haze that lay over the sun like a cataract – but you could feel them coming deep in your chest, like when they put that heavy lead apron on you before X rays at the dentist's office. The air was thick and hard to breathe, and leaves hung limply on every tree and bush.

Marty looked around the parking lot one last time – saw only his Malibu, Jack's Mercedes, and Becker's patrol car – and then, satisfied, walked around the big greenhouse to the planting beds in the back.

Lily Gilbert had always hated the straight lines that men were forever drawing all over the world. Lines were bossy, unforgiving things; harbingers of tyranny. Rows of crops, rows of buildings, and eventually, rows of people standing mute and still and fearful.

The front of the nursery had that kind of rigid order – the main greenhouse aligned with the street, the hedge aligned with the sidewalk, white lines in the parking lot telling the cars where to go. She had to put up with them in the front of the greenhouse, because that's the way it was when they bought the place. But in the back, where the previous owners had lined up pots and plants like subjugated servants, Lily had destroyed the order of straight lines and created happy chaos.

Pea gravel walkways meandered like sleepy drunks

through stands of potted trees and flowering shrubs, arcing around the perennial beds that provided cutting stock – the 'mother beds,' Morey had called them, where the seeds from a single flower produced hundreds of seedlings they would sell the following spring. And in high summer, little forests of ornamental grasses crowded some of the walkways, towering over giggling children who ducked beneath bobbing, seed-heavy heads as they followed the twisting paths through the lovely disordered maze of nature Lily's hatred of lines had created.

She waited for Martin on a bench circled by potted lilacs. She'd forced blooms on a few of the shrubs so customers could see the color, but most were still flowerless, rather ordinary-looking plants with unremarkable leaves. The peasant plants, she called them, secretly pleased when for two short weeks every spring, the lowliest of these dressed themselves like gaudy monarchs.

Martin moved lightly for such a big man, but the nursery was so quiet Lily could hear his shoes crunching on the pea gravel long before she felt his weight on the bench next to her.

'I'm going to try to get Jack to stay in a hotel for a few days,' Marty said.

'Good. I could use a vacation. So could you. Get a suite with a kitchen.'

'I'd just as soon you kept your distance from Jack until this is over, Lily.'

She turned to look at him. Most of the time Lily

was moving so fast it was impossible to think of her as an old person. But the strain of this week was wearing on her, and he could see the age in her face, wiping away the illusion of strength. It was the first time he'd ever thought of her as a frail mortal, just like the rest of them. 'Jack goes to a hotel, I go to a hotel.'

Marty gave her a little smile. 'So you're a mother again.'

'You have kids, even a schlock, you're always a mother, no matter what. This is not a voluntary thing.'

Marty thought about Lily and Jack locked in a hotel room, a cop at the door. He liked the picture.

'The only bad part about the hotel is that this has been good for you, Martin, being here. You want to know how I know this?'

'No.'

'I know this because you're drinking like a normal person again. A little tipple at night, maybe, that's all.'

'Can't think and drink.'

'So what are you thinking about?'

'I want to find out who killed Morey.' He turned and looked at her hard. 'Don't you?'

She tightened her mouth, so spare of flesh now that it almost disappeared.

'You know, it's funny, Lily. Most of the time when someone gets killed, the family's all over the cops, calling, coming down to the station, how's the investigation going, do they have a suspect . . .'

'Like you and Morey did, when Hannah was killed,' she said with an odd chill in her tone.

Marty closed his eyes for a second. 'You never came with us. You never asked. It was like Morey and I were all alone in that. And now you're doing the same thing again. Morey's been dead for three days, and not once have you shown the slightest interest in who might have killed him. I just don't get it.'

Lily filled her lungs with the sodden air and looked at the lilacs, not at him. 'Let me tell you something, Martin. For me, if it's cancer or war or a man with a gun or a knife, dead is dead. Dead is the end. It's been seven months since the man who murdered Hannah was killed. Now you tell me, is your life so much better, now that he's in the ground? Because it's not better for me. This person, he was a nothing. Bury ten thousand more just like him and still' – she tapped her chest – 'this is empty.'

Marty braced his elbows on his knees and dropped his head into his hands. 'I'm still glad he's dead,' he whispered.

Lily shook her head. 'You men. You always want to know who did this or that terrible thing, so someone can find them and make them pay. Always it's been like this for men, the eye for the eye, as if it would make any difference.'

Jack was well on his way to a fine toot by the time Marty and Lily got up to the house, the weight of the weather and their conversation weighing them down, slowing their steps.

He was sitting at the kitchen table, a bottle of Glenlivet in one hand, a glass in the other, dispensing unwanted legal advice to Officer Becker. The young cop was standing off to one side, watching his charge, the windows, the doorway. Marty figured he'd had them made before he and Lily ever got anywhere near the house.

'Marty, ole' buddy, glad you're here. Tony here's a hell of a nice guy, but he's a little stiff, you know? And he's making me nervous, hopping around peeking out windows and all that.'

'That's his job, Jack. Saving your sorry life.'

Jack giggled. 'A little too late for that.'

'We're all going to a hotel. Right after supper.'

Jack raised his glass. 'Whatever you say, Marty. In the meantime, grab yourself a glass, I'll make your world a better place.'

And it was a little too late for that, too, Marty thought, watching Lily shoot a sharp glance in Jack's direction that sent him slinking away into the living room, Becker close behind.

They ate myriad cold salads and meats contributed by thoughtful friends and neighbors. 'Funeral food,' Lily called it, making a plate to force on Officer Becker while Marty made one for Jack he probably wouldn't eat.

After supper Marty went upstairs, showered, dressed, and started packing a few clothes in his duffel. In the contained environment of a hotel with an officer posted at the door, Jack and Lily would be perfectly safe. There was no logical reason for him to go with them – except for this sudden sense that that was where he belonged. This was his family, dysfunctional though it was. It was all he had; all he'd ever had, really.

When he went to the closet to get his favorite shirt – a short-sleeved white linen Hannah had gotten him for his birthday last year – it slipped from the hanger and fell on the floor. When he bent to retrieve it he saw an old red metal tackle box tucked into the back corner.

'I'll be damned,' he murmured, pulling it out, remembering his disbelief when Lily told him Morey had gone on fishing trips with Ben Schuler. He flipped the hasp, opened the lid, and saw an array of lures, hooks, and bobbers, still encased in unopened plastic, tucked into the neat compartments of the upper tray. Marty didn't know much about fishing, but he did know you probably had to take the lures out of the plastic to use them. This was not the tackle box of a real fisherman.

He caught himself smiling. In his heart he had known that Morey, who revered all life, was incapable of pushing a barbed hook through a live worm, but Lily's assertion had been so unequivocal, it had planted a troubling seed of doubt. What he was looking at now seemed to prove that Morey had been exactly the man he appeared to be. He may have sat on a dock or in a boat with Ben Schuler, but Marty would bet his life that he never dropped a line in the water. As a matter of fact, he probably freed the minnows when Ben wasn't looking.

He lifted the top tray by its handle, and stared curiously at what lay beneath – a clear plastic sandwich bag, and inside it, a passport.

Morey Gilbert smiled at him from the photo on the inside of the front cover. Not the young Morey who had come to America in the late forties, but Morey as Marty had known him. He checked the date of issue – eight years ago – and flipped through the pages, his frown deepening with every entry stamp, then he tucked it into his pocket.

There was a small, dirty cloth bundle on the bottom of the tackle box. Marty tugged at a corner of the fabric, then scrambled backwards when the thing inside fell out, his heart pounding, his mind seeing Morey again, standing at his front door holding out a paper grocery bag. It had been exactly one month since Hannah's murder.

This is for you, Martin.

What is it?

Jack's inheritance back when he was my son. He didn't want it; now it's yours.

I'm not taking Jack's inheritance, Morey . . . Jesus. Where did you get this?

Beautiful, isn't it? Government Model 45-A Colt. Custom pearl handle. It's over sixty years old. I took it off a dead Nazi who probably killed an American officer to get it. This is the most valuable thing I own, Martin. This is my legacy.

Marty sat on the bedroom floor, catching his breath, staring at the pearl-handled .45 preposterously kept in the bottom of a tackle box. He'd never expected to see that gun again.

He didn't know he was reaching for the gun until he felt the smooth mother-of-pearl against his palm. The texture, the weight, the little indentation in a curve of the trigger – it was all the same. Exactly the same as it had been last time.

He smelled urine in the room, smoke, and the unmistakable acrid odor of someone cooking death. A rat crossed his path, stopped and looked at him, then moved on at a leisurely pace. He watched his own shadow move along the wall he approached, darkening the long, stringy blond hair of the noncreature who slumped there as he slid a needle into his arm.

And then he saw the eyes he would never forget, the pale, sinewy hands that had slashed Hannah's throat, and then the Colt, rising into his line of sight, pointing at Eddie Starr's forehead like an accusing finger. Fire seemed to jump from the muzzle when he pulled the trigger, but it didn't startle him. He stood there for many moments, watching with empty eyes as red blood dripped down the wall.

The next morning Marty had gone to the nursery and given the gun back to Morey. It was too valuable, he'd said; too much a part of family history; he couldn't keep it. That afternoon he'd bought the .357 and started planning his suicide.

He was calm now, maybe calmer than he'd been in months. He carefully wrapped the gun, put it back in the tackle box, and tucked that back in the closet corner where he'd found it. At some point in the last three days he'd decided he still had a family, he still had obligations, and amazingly, he still wanted to live.

So he'd turn in the gun, he'd turn in himself, and he would pay the price for what he'd done, because that was the way it was supposed to work.

But not just yet.

36

By five o'clock Magozzi could see thunderheads piling up in the distance outside the window, as if someone had dumped a bag of cotton balls on the western horizon. Langer had come back from his hasty exit from the office a few minutes later, looking a little pale, but solid, and they'd all been hitting the phones ever since.

They'd confirmed unsolved murders that matched the dates on the twenty most recent photos pulled from the Schuler house, put the locals to work tracking family members, but now they were hitting a wall. Farther back than that a lot of law enforcement records were archived in dusty boxes in a warehouse someplace, and most of the detectives who had worked them were long since retired.

Magozzi wasn't particularly worried. The way he figured it, if some vengeful family member wanted payback for a relative Morey, Rose, and Ben had killed, they weren't likely to wait that long anyway. If it was a family member at all. There were no guarantees with that theory. Maybe they were just spinning their wheels in a rut that went nowhere, and that did worry him.

But ten minutes ago he'd come upon something

interesting, and now he was drumming his fingers on his desk, waiting anxiously for the phone to ring.

'Son of a bitch,' Gino said, slamming down his phone. 'The Brainerd sheriff's been out of his office for two hours, and you want to know why? He's out on some lake with damn near every other officer in the county, trying to save some deer that went through ice.'

Magozzi looked out at the city sizzling under the day's heat. 'They've got ice?'

'Are you kidding? It's April in Brainerd. They'll have ice for another month. Besides, they're north of the warm front, haven't gotten any of the heat we're getting. You know what this reminds me of? Hansel and Gretel.'

'You're going have to explain that to me.'

'Come on, it's obvious. The old witch keeps the kids for a while to fatten 'em up before she eats them. That's just what these guys are doing. Saving a deer one of them's going to pop next fall and turn into link sausage. And in the meantime I'm here sitting on my thumbs trying to solve sixty murders while they're out on a venison rescue . . .'

Magozzi's phone rang, cutting Gino's rant short. He listened for a minute, then held the phone to his chest. 'Get everybody off their calls. We may have caught a break.'

A few minutes later Langer, McLaren, and Peterson had rolled their chairs over to hear what Magozzi had to say.

'According to Grace's list, Morey Gilbert, Rose Kleber, and Ben Schuler made a trip to Kalispell, Montana, a few years ago, but there was no Montana kill on any of Schuler's pictures. So I called law enforcement up there, just to check it out. There was no homicide the day our threesome was there, but there was a shooting. Some old kook who lives in the woods with his adult son – apparently they're survivalists or something like that – comes into the hospital with a .45 slug in his leg. The only thing he could give the cops was that a black pickup pulled up to the cabin, and someone inside opened fire on him and his son while they were sitting on the porch. Neither one of them got a make or a plate.'

Gino thought about that. 'Or maybe they did, and just didn't share it with the law. I can't see a couple of survivalists waiting for the cops to take care of their business. Those guys hate us.'

McLaren whistled softly. 'Wow. So maybe they left one alive.'

'It's possible. The old guy was the right age. And the best part is that the sheriff just took a run out there, and when there was nobody around, he talked to a neighbor. Seems the old man and his son took off in their camper a couple weeks ago, supposedly to Vegas, but the neighbor thought that was a little peculiar since they hadn't left the property in over twenty years, and as far as he knew, they weren't gamblers.'

Langer got up from his chair. 'Did you get a plate?'

'And the names.' Magozzi passed over a scrap of paper. 'Langer, why don't you take Vegas, get an APB out on the plate, try to sweet-talk somebody down there into checking the campgrounds. McLaren, you get an APB on the air here, the rest of us will hit the yellow pages and split up the campgrounds around the Cities.'

The sheriff in Brainerd caught Gino between campground calls, and kept him on the phone for fifteen minutes.

'The good news,' Gino told Magozzi after he'd hung up, 'is that the deer's okay.'

'That's a load off.'

'The bad news is the sheriff was tickled to death we might have a lead on who killed his resort owner, and depressed as hell when I told him they were dead. He wanted to wring their necks personally.'

'He knew the victim?'

'Yeah. Salt-of-the-earth, hardworking type. The old guy had a wife and two sons, one in high school, one in college in California. Six months after he bought it the resort folded and the wife killed herself.'

'Jesus.'

'It gets worse. The college kid died in a car wreck on his way home for his mother's funeral.'

Magozzi stared at him. 'Are you making this up?'

'I wish. Anyway, the high school kid had some kind of a breakdown after that, and went to live with some of his dad's relatives in Germany, see if he couldn't get a life together.'

'Germany?'

'Right. Ties in with the Nazi thing. The sheriff's going to pull the file and fax us everything.' Gino blew out a sigh and pushed away his notebook. 'But you know what? Maybe the old guy was a bad-ass and the world's better off without him. But his wife and kids? What did they do? Makes you wonder if Morey and his crew ever stopped to think about the wreckage they were leaving behind.'

Magozzi thought about sixty pictures, sixty groups of children who might not have known that Dad was a Nazi – only that he was Dad.

'Did you get a contact for the surviving son?'

'Better than that. The kid called the sheriff yesterday. They got kind of close after everything started to go bad, and still keep in touch. He gave me the number. Think I should call?'

'I think we'd better. Just to make sure he's still there, cross him off the list.'

Gino picked up the phone. 'Oh, happy day.'

Outside the window, the thunderheads were piled even higher, turning dark, moving in. Langer got up from his desk and turned on the lights.

37

It was hard for Marty to leave the bedroom where Hannah had slept as a child. Even though nothing of her remained in that room, he'd been able to look at the walls and the doorknob and the old wavy glass in the windows, knowing that she had seen the same things a thousand times; that wherever he walked, she had walked before him. After he'd put Morey's .45 back in the tackle box, he couldn't feel her around him anymore. It was almost as if she'd seen the gun and the story behind it, and had left the room forever.

He sat cross-legged on the floor for a long time after that, letting himself feel empty as the world darkened outside the windows. He had to turn the light on to finish packing his duffel, then turned it off as he headed downstairs, leaving the room dark behind him.

He found Lily alone in the living room, her face stark in the light of a table lamp. She was watching a baseball game with the sound muted. A weather warning scrolled across the bottom of the screen next to a miniature map of the state. Almost every county was colored orange.

'Where're Jack and Becker?' he asked her.

‘They went out to the greenhouse. Jack left his bag out there.’

‘How long ago?’

‘Right after you went upstairs.’

Marty glanced at his watch and frowned, trying to remember what time it had been when he went up to shower and pack.

‘They’ve been out there about an hour,’ she told him. ‘You took a long time up there, Martin . . . Where are you going?’

‘Out to get Jack. I want to talk to him a few minutes before we leave.’

‘So talk in the car, or at the hotel.’

‘No offense, Lily, but if he knows something about who killed Morey, I don’t think he’ll talk about it in front of you.’

Lily snorted. ‘He hasn’t exactly been running off at the mouth with you, either, has he?’

‘I think I have a little more leverage now.’

That got her attention. ‘You found this in the shower?’

‘Lock the doors after me.’

‘Don’t be silly. Nobody shot at me. I’m the good person in the family.’

Marty smiled. He couldn’t help it. And that had probably been her intention. ‘I mean it, Lily. I already locked the back, and I’m going to stand outside the front door until I hear you turn the lock. And pack an overnight bag while I’m out there.’

Lily sighed in annoyance and got up to follow him

to the door. 'I already packed. Five minutes. You men are so poky, it's a miracle you ever get anything done.'

Marty felt the sweat bead up on his skin the minute he stepped outside. It was still breathlessly hot and oppressive. The clouds to the west had blackened, bringing on an early twilight in that eerie, grayish green that always precedes a summer storm, distorting the true colors of the world like cheap sunglasses with yellow lenses. The winding path from the house through the back planting beds was shadowed, grayed, and dulled by the strange light.

He'd helped Morey put down that gravel, running the Bobcat, dumping the loads, trying not to tip the thing over backwards when he lifted the blade. The gravel itself was a wild extravagance, trucked from some pit near the Canadian border, where quartz and agate and other minerals had colored the rock with sparkling streaks of pink and purple and yellow. He'd nearly passed out when Morey had told him what it cost.

But the cheap rock is all gray, Martin, and the old woman hates gray. This is from the camp, I think. Everything was gray there, and nothing sparkled. You see how this gravel sparkles in the sun? This, she will like. This will make her happy.

It was the one and only time Morey had ever said anything about their time in Auschwitz, and Marty had felt privileged to hear it. More privileged to know the reason for the colored sparkles in the gravel path.

Hannah didn't like it much, thought it looked unnatural, even though it was the opposite; and Jack simply thought it was gaudy. But Marty knew the story, kept it close like a gift, and Lily raked the path almost every day.

He'd never been able to define the relationship between Morey and Lily. If it was love, it was a different kind than what he had found with Hannah. He tried to remember if he had ever seen them kiss, or hug, or even touch hands, and came up empty. And yet there were these strange little kindnesses between them – the colored gravel for Lily; the strange spicy cucumbers she made every single morning of her life for Morey, who was the only one who would eat them.

He found Jack and Officer Becker in the windowless office behind the potting shed. The lamp on the desk was turned on, casting long shadows on the walls, leaving absolute patches of darkness in the corners.

Jack was sprawled on the cracked vinyl sofa shoved against one wall, his face silly and red from booze and sun, the omnipresent glass in his hand; Becker was standing in the outside doorway, half in and half out of the building, so that the first fat raindrops splatted on his uniformed shoulders. The inside door that led to the potting shed was closed and bolted.

'Hey, Marty!' Jack patted the cushion next to him, making the vinyl crackle. 'Take a load off.' He produced another glass from the floor by the sofa, and a bottle of Morey's Balvenie that he'd obviously filched from the house.

Officer Becker stood aside so Marty could pass. 'Detective Rolseth told me you'd be armed, sir. Are you carrying now?'

Marty nodded and lifted the hem of the white linen shirt, exposing the .357 uncomfortably tucked in the waistband.

'Not the best place to holster that, sir.'

'Tell me about it. You missed the shift change.'

The young cop talked without looking at him, his eyes constantly on the move through the deepening shadows outside. 'I thought I'd get you all settled in the hotel, then call my relief.'

Marty nodded, pleased. He liked the way Becker handled himself, the way he was taking his assignment seriously. 'I'll be glad to have you with us.'

'Thank you, sir. Is everyone ready?'

Marty glanced over at Jack, who was more intent on his drink than their conversation. 'I'd like to take a private minute here with Jack, if that's okay with you.'

Becker didn't seem too happy about that, and lowered his voice. 'To tell you the truth, Mr Pullman, after spending the afternoon with Mr Gilbert, I was looking forward to having him safely locked in a hotel room with a man at the door. He pretty much hops all over the place, and he doesn't seem half as concerned as he should be, for a man who dodged a bullet this morning.'

‘Relax, Supercop,’ Jack slurred from the sofa, who had apparently been listening more closely than Marty thought. ‘This guy doesn’t like an audience. Shoots old women alone in their houses, or hides behind a tree and takes potshots, cowardly bastard.’

Becker, who probably knew very little beyond that someone had taken a shot at Jack, raised a questioning eyebrow at Marty, who nodded.

‘That’s the history so far.’

‘All right then. I’ll step away from the building, give you gentlemen some privacy, but I’ll keep the door in sight at all times.’

‘Thanks, Becker.’ Marty watched him move out among the rows of potted arborvitae until he looked like just another shadow, thinking that at least he wouldn’t get wet. Those first few raindrops had made it look like the sky was going to open, but it had stopped almost as soon as it began.

He closed the door, crossed to the desk, and sat down in the chair, shaking his head at the glass Jack was holding out for him at a precarious angle, sloshing good scotch all over the floor. ‘No thanks.’

Jack shrugged and started drinking it himself, even though he held his own glass in his other hand.

‘Did you call Becky to tell her where you’d be?’

‘Becky, my wife?’

‘That’s the one.’

‘Well, gee, Marty, that would be like calling Mr Filcher at the butcher shop and telling him where’d I’d be, and he’d say what the fuck do I care? So if you want me to call somebody just to listen to that, I think I'll go for the butcher.'

'You're not making a lot of sense.'

'Probably not. Half a bottle of scotch'll do that to you. The way I figure it, I'll be dead of alcohol poisoning in about ten minutes, and shooting me will be redundant.'

'Not funny.'

'Sure it was. Lighten up. The thing is, Becky gave me the one-finger salute last night – and that was before the gunfight at O.K. Corral. Sayonara, fuck off, see you in court. Wouldn't even let me in the house, so I slept in the pool house, took a shower with the garden hose.'

Marty blew out a breath and reached for one of the partially full glasses Jack was juggling. 'Sorry.'

'No prob. I hated that house anyway. Faggot designer Becky hired did the whole master bath in a frog motif. Can you believe that? S'like trying to take a shit in the middle of a Budweiser commercial.' He drained his glass, filled it again. 'You want me to top that off for you?'

'No. I want you to tell me why Morey went to London.'

Jack looked at him. 'Excuse me?'

'Or Prague. Or Milan. Or Paris.' He tossed over Morey's passport, and Jack jumped when it hit his lap.

'What the hell is this?'

'That's Morey's passport. I found it in a tackle box in a closet.'

'Dad had a passport?' Jack opened it up and squinted hard. 'God, this is small print . . . Is this Paris or Prague? Goddamn Frogs can't even use a stamp without blurring it . . .'

'It's Paris. He was there for a day. Not much longer in any of the other places. Since when was Morey a world traveler?'

Jack kept drinking as he flipped through the pages. 'Jesus. He went to *Johannesburg*?'

'Are you telling me you didn't know about those trips?'

'These?' Jack tossed the passport on the cushion next to him. 'Nope. Didn't know about them. Is that it? Can we get out of here now? It's hotter than hell with the door closed.'

'Why would Morey hide his passport in a tackle box? Why would he make a bunch of overseas trips and then turn around and come back the next day? What the hell was he doing in all those places, Jack?'

'I knew it. I *knew* this would happen. Was I right? You can take the man out of the cop, but you can't take the cop out of the man, and now you're doing all that detective shit. So what now, Marty? Are we going to play interrogation again? You want to move to the equipment shed? We got a bulb hanging from a wire in there. You could swing it back and forth, do the movie thing . . .'

Marty closed his eyes and took a sip out of the glass without thinking. 'I was thinking maybe we could skip all the crap and you could just tell me the truth,

Jack. I know it's not normally done in this family – hell, maybe not in any family – but I tried it on Lily the other night and it turned out okay.'

Jack giggled. 'Oh yeah? What truth did you tell her?'

Marty looked straight at him. 'That I thought about killing myself.'

Jack's glass stopped halfway to his mouth. 'Jesus, Marty. Because of Hannah?'

'Not exactly.'

That seemed to surprise Jack more than anything. 'Well then why, for chrissake?'

Marty took another drink, then set the glass on the desk and pushed it out of reach with one finger. The alcohol was still seductive. Prison would cure that, he thought with a grim smile. 'That's a really big secret, Jack. Quid pro quo. A truth for a truth.'

Jack set his own glass on the floor and hunched forward, bracing his elbows on his knees. 'I should have been there for you. I let you down, buddy. On the list of a hundred regrets I've been piling up over the past couple years, that one goes on the top.'

'The truth, Jack. What do you know about who killed your father?'

Jack smiled at him without moving. 'Truth isn't what it's cracked up to be, you know, Marty?'

'Whoever did it is killing other people, Jack. You've got to help.'

'Nah. He's finished. 'Cept for me.'

'And how the hell do you know that?'

Jack looked down into his glass, took a breath, then blew it out hard. 'I think I have to start this at the beginning.'

Sometimes you spitfired questions, hammered them home fast, non-stop; but there was a time in every interrogation when you stopped asking and just went quiet. Marty kept his hands still on the arms of his chair, kept his eyes on Jack, and waited.

'I kind of hate to do this to you, Marty. I know what that old bastard meant to you.'

'He was a good man, Jack.'

'This is going to be like Elvis.'

'You lost me.'

'Well, do you remember what it was like when you found out the King was a drug addict? I mean, here was this guy, the one true King, and what does he turn out to be? Some potbellied, pill-popping junkie. Man, the idol crumbles, and that just rocked my world. You ready for that?'

'Jack . . .'

'Pop put a gun in my hand for the first time on my ninth birthday. Did you know that? You have to be ready, he said, and every Saturday morning from then on he took me out to the Anoka Gun Club and we did some target shooting. Ma thought we were going to McDonald's for some father-son bonding, and I wasn't allowed to tell her different. Boring as hell. I hate guns. But I was a dumb kid. As long as I was with him, it was great.' He picked up his glass again and leaned back against the cushions. He took a long drink, then smiled. 'I'm a hell of a shot, Marty. But I was nothing compared to Pop.'

Marty stared at Jack's white legs sticking out of his shorts, the little potbelly, the sunburned arches on his forehead where hair had once been. While the idea of Jack as a good shot scared the hell out of him, the image of a gun in the good and gentle hand of his father-in-law was absolutely unbelievable. 'Is this going somewhere, Jack?'

'Sure it is.' Jack's head wobbled a bit as he tried to bring him into focus. 'You want to know who would want to kill Pop, right? 'Cause he's this great guy, loved everybody, everybody loved him . . . Shit, Marty. I spent the last couple years ruining my life so I wouldn't have to tell anybody, and now you just want me to spit it out.'

Marty heard the rumble of distant thunder. 'Whatever it was, the cops will put it together eventually.'

Jack giggled. 'Those bozos aren't ever gonna figure it out, and if they did, they wouldn't believe it anyway.'

'Figure out what?'

Jack tried to think and keep Marty in his line of sight all at the same time. It was almost too much for him. 'That somebody finally caught up with them, that's what. Only it wasn't the cops, 'cause we'd all be on Jerry Springer right now. But you can't get away with that kind of thing forever without pissing somebody off, right?'

‘What kind of thing?’

‘Christ, Marty, pay attention, would you? Killing people, of course. Near as I can figure, a couple a year for a long time.’

Marty didn’t bat an eye. ‘You are so full of shit, Jack.’

Jack nodded, a dangerous move in his condition. ‘Yep. I am that. But not about this. This, I know for a fact.’ He leaned forward to grab the bottle of Balvenie off the floor and filled his glass right to the top, spilled some when the thunder clapped a little closer. ‘’Bout six months before Hannah died Pop took me up to Brainerd one weekend – said he was going to take me fishing, get me away from the office for a while. When we got to this big old lodge a couple other cars pull up, and there’s Ben Schuler getting out of one, and Rose Kleber out of the other.’

Marty’s eyebrows arched. ‘So you did know her.’

‘First time I saw her, last time I saw her. Sweet little old white-haired lady in this dress with purple flowers on it and these big clunky shoes, and I wondered what the hell she was doing there, fishing with a couple of old guys like Pop and Ben. Never knew her name. Pop just called her a friend. So we go into this lodge, I’m guessing to check in or something, and there’s nobody in the place because there’s some kind of contest going on at the lake, except this old geezer at the registration desk, and what happens then is that Pop pulls a gun out of his jacket pocket and reaches across the desk and shoots the guy in the head.' He closed his eyes and just breathed for moment while Marty's mouth sagged open and his heart started hammering at his chest, as if it were trying to get out. 'I think I might have screamed then, but I can't really remember. Next thing I know, Pop hands the gun to Ben, and that old bastard walks around the desk and shoots the guy on the floor, and then he hands the gun to sweet little grandma, and she plugs him a few more times, cool as a cucumber. She got blood and some other stuff all over her dress and those black shoes. Funny, what you remember, isn't it?' He gave Marty a lopsided, sad little smile.

Suddenly Marty's throat was bone-dry, and for a second he marveled at that, and then at the way his voice cracked when he finally spoke. 'Who was he? Who was the man they killed?'

Jack shrugged. 'Just another Nazi, like all the others. And you know what happened next?'

Marty stared at him, shook his head mindlessly.

'Well then, Marty, my man, after Rose was finished, she handed the gun to me.'

38

Jeff Montgomery was sweating beneath the black rain slicker he wore over dark jeans. It was uncomfortable, but necessary. Before the night was over the cold front would push hard against this monstrous heat layer, the winds would howl, the temperature would drop twenty degrees, and the rain would pour down. Every good Minnesota boy knew when to wear a slicker.

Personally, he was wishing the cold front would get a move on. Hottest April on record, they kept saying, and although he didn't mind the heat himself, the cool-weather plants were suffering. The other problem was that this kind of heat often broke with a hailstorm, and he didn't even want to think about that. It was going to be bad enough coming to work tomorrow and dealing with the mud; the thought of hail damage to the tender young plants almost made him sick to his stomach.

And that was funny, he thought – him worrying about plants, when just a few months ago, he wouldn't have known chickweed from a hydrangea. Engineering was the ticket. His father had been pushing that on him his whole life. But then his folks had died, the dream of college in the East dying with them, and he ended up taking a few classes at the U of M and working for Morey and Lily Gilbert.

He'd learned more about plants from Mrs Gilbert than anything he picked up in classes so far, found he had a knack for it, and before he knew what was happening, he was hooked.

He loved working the soil, testing it in the little tubes for nutrient content, deciding which additives and how much of each were necessary for whatever seedlings he was trying to germinate. That was the engineering part of his brain kicking in, he supposed. But he also loved feeling the soil in his hands and under his nails, seeing the morning dew in a tulip cup, and watching new growth sprout from the sharp, clean cuts of his knife on the candles of a Black Mountain spruce. If he were granted one wish when his work was done, it was to work in this nursery forever, learn from Mrs Gilbert, maybe buy into it when he could put some money together.

Funny, the ways things happened; the way the horror and shock of his parents' deaths had led him, unwittingly, to the place and the life he was meant for.

The streets around the nursery were completely empty now – everyone in the neighborhood was probably glued to their TVs, waiting for tornadoes and the excited weathermen to tell them when to take cover. Everyone but him, of course. He couldn't afford to let a little weather scare him off, because he was on a mission, and sometimes missions were very dangerous.

He'd already circled the block around the nursery three times, and found everything as it should be. No armed figures crouching in the bushes, the single squad car that arrived this afternoon still in its original place in the parking lot, and most important, Mrs Gilbert still safe in the house.

A rumble of distant thunder made him jump a little, and he covered a nervous giggle with his hand. The sky was getting blacker by the minute, and off to the west, webs of cloud-to-cloud lightning flashed, followed by more ominous thunder, charging the air with excitement. God, this was fun. Meek, quiet Jeff Montgomery slinking around in the near-darkness, eyes sharp and busy checking all the shadows, strangely titillated by the possibility of danger.

When he reached the nursery's hedgerow, he pressed himself into the greenery and moved slowly and stealthily, inch by inch, along the screen. He rotated his head, covering all directions, keeping a sharp eye out for anything suspicious, maintaining his cover. He couldn't afford to be seen – if Mr Pullman or the officer spotted him, it'd be all over and they'd send him packing, or even worse, they might shoot him by accident. He had to be very, very careful.

At this moment, it didn't seem at all odd to be thinking of all the things the Gilberts had done for him – paying him twice what other nurseries paid their help, covering the cost of his classes, even helping him out with rent if he came up a little short on the first of the month. He knew she didn't expect it, but someday he was going to pay back every dime to Mrs Gilbert. It was the least he could do.

He felt a secret thrill when he realized he was now on the nursery property, and so far, no one had spotted him . . . *made* him, he amended. Darn, he was good at this. Maybe he should quit school and join the CIA.

The last time Marty Pullman had felt this way – like someone had flicked a switch and shut off his brain – he'd been sitting on the cold cement of the parking ramp, looking down at his dead wife.

A lot of the emotions that had gone through him that night were fighting for their place in line again – disbelief, outrage, shock, and finally, a sadness beyond measuring. Jack was right about that stupid Elvis analogy, and now his world was rocking and he didn't know which end was up. How do you get past learning that a man you'd worshiped, idolized because he was so much better than you could ever hope to be, had been every bit as flawed as you were? And maybe a little bit more, he thought, if you looked at it numerically. A silly part of his mind looking for distraction had tried to estimate how many men Morey had killed during the years when he'd had his son-in-law the cop over for Sunday dinner once a week. And just when the outrage started to set in, the sense of betrayal, he almost laughed aloud. Was there really such a difference between murdering Nazis and murdering the man who had killed your wife?

No wonder you loved him so much. You were two of a kind.

Jack had been totally silent for the past few minutes, maybe giving Marty time to absorb what he'd said so far, maybe waiting for the big question Marty was almost afraid to ask. So Rose Kleber had taken her turn shooting the old man behind the fishing lodge counter, and then handed the gun to Jack.

What did you do, Jack? What the hell did you do?

Jack giggled drunkenly, and Marty realized he'd asked the question aloud. 'Actually, I threw up. Hurled all over the floor, the gun, and the old lady's hand. Boy, was she pissed. Not as pissed as Pop, though. He kept telling me to shoot him, "shoot the Nazi bastard" were his exact words, and that was the first time I had an inkling of what was going on. Maybe if he'd been in one of those S.S. outfits torturing somebody I could have done it. I guess I'll never know. But the thing was, I didn't see any Nazi. I just saw this really old, messy dead guy.'

'You didn't shoot him.'

'Jesus, Marty, of course not. What do you think I am?'

'I don't know, Jack. You keep surprising me.'

'Whole damn family's full of surprises, isn't it?' Jack said bitterly. 'Anyway, on the way home Pop told me what they'd been doing all these years, a lot of things about Auschwitz I wish I hadn't heard, and how it was my duty as his son, his legacy to me, for chrissake, and that if he died before the "work" was done, I had to finish it.'

'What did you say?'

Jack looked at him over the rim of his glass. 'I told him I didn't want to be his son anymore, that I didn't even want to be a Jew anymore. And then I set out to make sure I wasn't.'

Marty nodded slowly, remembering the confirmation picture and the wedding picture, Jack's sudden absence from the family, finally making sense of the jumble of his actions that Lily had called slaps in the face. 'You should have talked to Lily about it, Jack.'

Jack smiled and drank all at the same time. 'Double-edged sword, that one. Triple-edged, actually. Hell, for all I knew, she could have been in on it . . .'

'Jesus, Jack, how could you ever think that?'

Jack gaped at him. 'Christ, Marty, maybe because I never would have thought it of my father either, and look how that turned out. I never really bought that Ma could do such a thing, but I wondered, How do you live with somebody for over fifty years and not know something like that is going on? And whether she did it or just knew about it . . .' He shrugged helplessly. 'I couldn't face it. I didn't want to know. And if by some miracle she'd been as fooled by him as I'd been, I sure as hell wasn't going to break her heart by telling her. So I stayed away from both of them, not saying anything, wondering all the while if Pop was out murdering people while I sat there doing nothing, saying stupid things to get through the days like "Gee, Jack, don't worry, they're just Nazis and probably deserve it," trying to figure out if I could live with myself if I turned in my own father and ruined my mother's life, or if I could live with myself if I didn't . . . Christ.' He took a breath, then a drink. 'Gotta tell you, though, the alcohol helped.'

On the other side of the bolted door that led to the potting shed, Lily leaned against the splintered wood, listening, her eyes closed, her face creased with pain. 'Goddamn you, Morey Gilbert,' she whispered, then she turned and walked away.

'You should have come to Hannah and me,' Marty was saying.

'Are you kidding? I couldn't get anywhere near Hannah. She would have had it out of me in three seconds, you know she would have. And it would have killed her, Marty, finding that out about her father. She worshiped that man.'

'Almost as much as you did,' Marty said, leaning back in his chair, looking at Jack the drunk, the schlock, the inconsiderate, irresponsible black sheep who had sacrificed everything to spare the people he loved. Inside, Marty wept for him, struggling to focus on what he needed to know. 'You said the killer was finished except for you, Jack. How do you know that?'

'Oh, yeah, that. I suspected, but didn't know for

absolute sure until the guy took a shot at me. Pop and the others made a lot of trips, killed a lot of people – he was pretty proud of that – but I was only with them once.'

'At the fishing lodge in Brainerd.'

'Right. There was a big old loft up behind the registration desk. Last thing I remember was Pop dragging me out by the arm, everybody yelling at me, and I looked up and saw a shadow move behind one of the big wooden posts up there. Somebody saw us, Marty, and as they say, what goes around, comes around.'

Marty closed his eyes a minute and focused on shutting down his emotions, just as he had when he was on the job. Later, when the killer was caught and Jack was safe, he would pull out the memory of all he had learned tonight and just let himself react, but right now, feelings were a luxury he couldn't afford. It surprised him a little, that he could do it so quickly and so well. Maybe Jack had been right about that, too. Once a cop, always a cop.

'Okay, Jack, this is what we're going to do.' He pulled his cell phone out of its holster and searched the program for Gino Rolseth's number. 'We're going to call Magozzi and Rolseth over here, and you're going to tell them everything you told me so they can do their job and get this guy, because I'm not about to leave you alone until he's locked up somewhere, and personally, I don't like being in the target zone.'

'No?' Jack tried to raise his eyebrows. 'I thought you were suicidal.'

'Yeah, well, things change, Jack. Man, do they change.'

When Gino answered, Marty told him where they were, that Jack was ready to talk, and that he might have a lead for them. The minute he clicked off there was a tremendous boom as lightning struck something very nearby, bringing Marty to his feet, and then the rain and wind hit with a vengeance, hammering on the roof, battering at the door. When it flew open and banged against the wall, Marty spun around, the .357 already in his hand, pointed toward the doorway.

A bedraggled Jeff Montgomery stood there with his blue eyes wide as the rain blew in around him.

Jack looked blearily at the poor kid and figured he'd quit for sure now. The last time he'd seen his eyes that big was the night *he'd* pointed a gun at him in the equipment shed. Too many guns in this family, he decided.

'Goddamnit, Jeff,' Marty shouted at him. 'I told you not to come back here tonight!' Marty was furious, but the kid looked pathetic, like a drowned rat, and he softened a little. 'Oh for chrissake, get in here. Did you see Becker?'

'Uh . . . yes sir?' Jeff took a step inside, but his eyes followed Marty's gun as he jammed it back into the waistband of his pants and pulled his shirt over it.

'Well, call him in before he gets washed away.'

'I'm afraid I can't do that, Mr Pullman,' he said,

taking another step in and closing the door behind him.

Then he pulled a gun from beneath his black slicker and pointed it at Marty's chest.

39

At City Hall, the long-anticipated storm was announcing its arrival. Thunder growled in the near distance and wicked-looking forks of lightning stabbed from one swollen, black cloud to another, like electric children poking at water balloons. A few minutes later, fat drops of rain started blatting against the windows of the Homicide room.

After an hour of working the phones, they still hadn't found the Montana camper. Nothing from the APBs they put out here and in Vegas, and nothing from the local campgrounds Gino had crossed off his half of the list. He was liking the Montana guy more and more, mostly because they couldn't find him. He got up from his desk and stretched, took a walk around the office while Magozzi finished the last of his calls.

The little TV on top of a filing cabinet was rarely turned on. Even with the sound muted, the changing images caught the eye and, according to Malcherson, mesmerizied the mind.

Not that he needed a whole lot of help in that department, Gino thought, punching the power button. His mind already felt like mush. Besides, he figured if a tornado was bearing down on them, they ought to know about it in time to dodge flying glass. He pushed mute, but within seconds every eye in the room was on the screen anyway, watching one of Channel Ten's animated meteorologists dancing around in front of a computerized map. Little cartoon funnels were spinning all over the place.

Langer covered the mouthpiece of his phone with one hand. 'Anything headed our way?'

Gino ran through all the channels and found all weather, all the time. 'Armageddon, from the looks of that map.' He stood close to the screen and squinted at the red crawl line on the bottom as it ran through a list of warnings. 'Touchdowns in Morris, Cyrus, heading for St Peter . . . nothing here yet.'

He left the TV on and went back to his desk to call Angela to make sure she was keeping an eye on the weather and to give her directions to the basement in case she'd forgotten where it was. 'Under the stairs, remember, if you have to go down there.'

'There's no room, Gino. Mom and Dad are down there.'

Gino glanced at the window. The rain was really coming down now, and sure, there was a lot of lightning and thunder, but that was about it. 'Already?'

'First clap of thunder, down they went. They took a bottle of vodka with them.'

'Oh boy.'

By the time he finished his call, Magozzi was hanging up his own phone. 'Don't tell me you sent Angela to the basement already.'

Gino shook his head. 'The in-laws are down there under the stairs getting sloshed, doing god knows what else. Probably better for the kids to see a tornado than whatever the hell they're doing down there.'

Magozzi looked out the window. 'Are we under the gun?'

'Nah. They've just lived in Arizona too long. There's no weather there. None. They forgot what it's like. I finally got through to that kid from the Brainerd resort who went to live in Germany. Thomas Haczynski, please call me Tommy, sir. Politest damn kid I ever talked to, except for those two who work at the nursery, and that's the nicest thing I can say about this case, meeting some decent kids for a change. Gives me hope for the world. Sad, though. He's still pretty messed up. When I told him we might have a lead on who killed his dad, he said thank you very much for calling to tell me, and then burst out bawling. Had to pass the phone over to his uncle.'

'And what did he say?'

'Don't have a clue. Something in German, I think. Man, I hate overseas calls when you get that delay and end up talking over each other.'

Magozzi sighed unhappily. 'Okay. So the gun Jack said belonged to his dad killed a resort owner in Brainerd last year, presumably a Nazi . . .'

'Right.'

'. . . but the Nazi's wife committed suicide, one

son died in a car crash, and the other one you just talked to is in Germany somewhere.'

'Munich.'

'Shit.'

Gino tossed a pencil across his desk in frustration. 'Which leaves us the guy in Montana that our friends Morey, Rose, and Ben didn't quite kill. And you know what? That one makes a lot of sense to me. Seems a hell of a lot more likely that once a guy took a shot in the leg, he'd figure someone meant business, and decided to hit them before they had a chance to take another stab at it. Besides, the Montana guy and his son are survivalists. If there's a profile for this kind of thing, they probably fit it to a *t*.'

'Sorry, guys,' Langer said from across the aisle, waggling his phone receiver before he hung up. 'The Montana survivalists aren't a prospect. The Happy-Go-Lucky RV Ranch in Vegas ID'd the camper and confirmed it had been there for almost two weeks. I asked about the occupants, and the manager said he was looking at them as we spoke, and that he already checked their licenses. Said as far as he knew, they hadn't been out of the park once – they just sit there and drink beer all day.'

'We're not getting anywhere, either.' Peterson was walking back from the fax machine. He tossed a sheet of paper on Magozzi's desk. 'Those are all the murders from the past ten years, at least the ones listed on the backs of the photos from Ben Schuler's house. If any relatives of those vics came after Morey

Gilbert and his little gang, they did it in wheelchairs and oxygen masks. Most of 'em are in their seventies, half of them are dead or convalescing from bypass or chemo or some such nightmare – damn, this getting old business is a bitch. The few who would have been even remotely capable of planning and executing a multiple homicide had ironclad alibis for when Gilbert, Rose Kleber, and Ben Schuler were killed.'

Gino looked over at McLaren's desk. The young detective's red hair was standing straight up from where he'd been messing with it, and he was talking earnestly into the phone. 'Looks like McLaren's working something.'

'Actually, he's working his stockbroker. We're out of murders, unless you want us to go back further than ten years.'

'Christ, no.' Magozzi sagged back in his chair and pinched the bridge of his nose. 'We've already wasted most of the day. Sorry, guys. I led us down the wrong road.'

'Looking at the families was a good idea,' Gino told him. 'And it's not like we had anywhere else to go. Question is, where do we go from here? We just ran out of suspects.'

Peterson handed over a fat file folder. 'Here's the fax from the Brainerd sheriff. Maybe we'll get lucky with that one.'

Gino tossed the folder aside. 'Not likely. The sole survivor in that family is in Germany. I just talked to him a while ago.'

Peterson flapped his arms. 'So now what?'

Magozzi looked up at him with bleary eyes. Peterson was frustrated. They all were. Frustrated, tired, and hungry, he realized, listening to the growl of his stomach. It was time to call it a day. They'd followed every lead, every theory, cleared them all, and at this point, there didn't seem to be anyplace left to go. But admitting that was an acknowledgment that all they could do was sit on their hands and wait for the killer to hit again, and that was a homicide detective's worst nightmare – when solving a case depended on another body turning up. Jack Gilbert was an apparent target, and they had him covered, but what if he wasn't the only one? What if the killer skipped Jack and went on to the next one on his list? All they could hope for at this point was that whatever Jack Gilbert knew would lead them to a viable suspect, and that Marty could somehow get him to talk.

Over at his desk, McLaren slammed down the phone. 'You know what that son of a bitch did? Put in a margin call on some piece of shit stock out of Uruguay. I fired his ass. So what's up?'

'Absolutely nothing,' Gino said miserably. 'We've trashed every lead.'

'So we're where? Waiting for the guy to take another shot at Jack Gilbert?'

'Gilbert's covered,' Magozzi said. 'I talked to Becker a little while ago. He's shadowing Jack, and apparently they're all checking into a hotel tonight to make Becker's job a little easier. I'm more worried about our killer moving on to another target we don't know about yet.'

Gino's cell burped in his pocket. 'That's Angela, and I'm outta here. She's stuck at home with two kids, a couple of sloshed parents, and a storm on the way.' He took the call and headed out, phone pressed to his ear, then turned around and held up one finger, still listening.

Magozzi started paging idly through the Brainerd fax while he was waiting. Had to be at least a hundred pages of police reports, autopsy results, interviews, newspaper clippings . . .

'You're the man, Marty,' Gino said into his phone, then signed off with a grin for Magozzi. 'Marty pulled through, got Jack talking. They're in the office at the nursery, and he says if we can get there before Jack sobers up or passes out, he'll give us an earful that might point us in the right direction.'

'Thank God,' Peterson said. 'You want us to stick around?'

Gino shook his head. 'Just keep your cells on in case we learn something we want to move on right away.' He pushed speed dial for Angela to tell her not to wait up, and frowned at Magozzi while it rang. He should have been hopping all over the place, halfway to the door by now, but he was just hunkered over the desk, staring at something. 'Hey, Leo, did you hear me?'

Magozzi raised a hand without looking up, picked up a piece of paper and stared at it. It was a photocopy of an obituary from the Brainerd newspaper, showing a photo of the recently deceased William Haczynski, owner of Sandy Shores Resort, with his son, Thomas. The old man and the fresh-faced blond kid had their arms hooked over each other's shoulders. They were beaming for the camera, cradling rifles in their armpits.

Magozzi had only been looking at the picture for a few seconds, but it felt like he'd been swimming in it for hours. He looked once more at the old man's son, the light eyes, and the innocent face of a kid he knew as Jeff Montgomery. 'Jesus Christ, Gino. Thomas Haczynski isn't in Germany.'

They were all over Magozzi in an instant, looking at the picture. Gino saw the Montgomery kid and said, 'That little son of a bitch,' before he realized he still had the phone in his hand, and Angela on the other end. He stepped away from the desk and started talking low and fast, then clicked off.

Langer, Peterson, and McLaren were all frowning at the picture. 'I don't get it,' McLaren said. 'How do you know he's not in Germany?'

Magozzi stabbed at the photo. 'That kid calls himself Jeff Montgomery. He works at the nursery, Lily Gilbert treats him like a grandson, and Morey was paying his tuition.'

Langer exhaled sharply. 'And he's the son of a man Morey Gilbert killed last year?'

'Sure looks that way.'

McLaren shivered. 'He's gotta be our guy. Jesus,

that's cold. Morey's paying his tuition while he's plotting his murder and a few others to boot. The kid's a killing machine.'

'I suspect he had a good teacher,' Langer said quietly.

'Goddamnit I just talked to him this afternoon,' Gino said. 'It was an overseas connection, I swear to God. You can't fake that delay . . .'

'Maybe he's got someone covering for him in Germany, but however he did it, it doesn't matter now,' Magozzi said, his words clipped and urgent. 'We've got to move on this right now. Gino, call Marty back and give him a heads-up and then do the same for Becker.'

'I'll take care of Becker,' Peterson volunteered, hustling over to his desk while Gino punched frantically at his cell.

Magozzi turned to Langer and McLaren. 'The kid's probably at one of two places – his apartment or the nursery – and we need to cover both simultaneously. You two pull together a team and hit the apartment, and don't be shy with the back-up. I have a feeling this kid isn't just going to roll over.'

'Will do.'

Gino was stabbing buttons furiously, listening, then stabbing them again. 'Goddamnit, Marty isn't answering his cell.'

Magozzi was moving fast, checking the load on his 9-mm, holstering it, snapping cuffs on his belt.

'Try the nursery, Lily's house, Jack's cell. Do we have a cell number for Jack?'

'Dispatch can't raise Becker,' Peterson called out, tension in his voice.

Everyone in the room froze for an instant. Becker, like every officer on the job, had a car unit and a shoulder unit, and non-response was one millimeter away from officer down.

Two seconds later Gino and Magozzi were out the door, their shoes pounding on the tile, the sound of panic echoing in the empty hallway.

40

Marty was standing directly in front of Jeff Montgomery, the kid's 9-mm pointed right at his chest, his thoughts slamming against the brick wall of the obvious, bouncing off when they didn't like looking at it.

In the past hour he'd learned that beloved, elderly Morey Gilbert was an executioner, and so, apparently, was this innocent-looking kid with the smooth face and the clear blue eyes. The real question was why should he be so goddamned surprised?

Too many years working in Narcotics, he thought, where meth freaks looked like meth freaks, street dealers looked like street dealers, where everybody looked exactly like what they were. There was a sick kind of security in that particular segment of the underworld, where what you saw was what you got, which was what had drawn Marty to it in the first place. But out here in the real world, almost everyone wore a disguise. He'd known that as a kid, of course; his father had taught him well; but he'd forgotten.

None of that mattered now, and he freed his mind to race at breakneck speed along the path it was trained to take. The hows and whys and motivations of an armed man were totally irrelevant when a cop found himself on the wrong end of a gun – the only thing that mattered was what happened next.

He was too close to the kid, and too far away, all at the same time. Too close to dodge a shot, too far away to disarm him. Talk was the only option he had. 'What are you doing, Jeff?'

'Just taking care of business, Mr Pullman.'

He wasn't ending sentences with a question mark now, Marty thought, trying to push back the feeling that he was racing around some preordained circle that was going to open up at any moment and launch him off in a direction he hadn't imagined. It seemed ironic that his last earnest attempt at suicide had been interrupted by Jeff Montgomery when he came to tell him that Morey was dead, and now that same kid who'd unwittingly saved his life was holding a gun on him.

'What kind of business would that be?' Marty asked, keeping his voice easy.

It surprised him a little when Jeff smiled at him. 'I think you must have been an excellent police officer, Mr Pullman. "Engage the enemy's attention when you find yourself at a disadvantage. Initiate conversation, introduce distraction . . ." That's right out of the handbook.'

'Not any handbook I ever read.'

'Would you please turn around, Mr Pullman? Then lift your shirt with your right hand, and remove the gun from your waistband with your left. Use only two fingers, then turn to face me again and toss the gun over here, well to my right, if you don't mind.'

'You going to shoot me in the back, Jeff?'

'Certainly not, sir. I wouldn't do that. It wouldn't be honorable.'

The funny thing was that Marty believed him, but still, he didn't move for a minute, a little unnerved by the pervasive politeness of this strange boy.

He turned halfway around and looked at Jack, who was leaning forward on the sofa, wobbling just a bit, his hands gripping his knees. The worst part was his eyes – they weren't frightened; just big and sad and apologetic when they met Marty's.

Marty winked at him, then lifted his shirt and eased out the gun with two fingers, just as Jeff had told him to, then turned around to face him again. 'You don't want me to toss this gun at you until I put on the safety, Jeff.'

'You put on the safety before you tucked it in your pants, Mr Pullman. Please don't patronize me.'

Shit, the kid was on top of it, but Marty still stood there holding the gun at his side, thinking how heavy it was when you could only use two fingers, his mind so busy it was falling all over itself trying to sort out the options.

You don't give up your gun. Period. Which left him with two choices. Toss the gun, use that off-balance moment when Jeff reached down for it to leap at him; or crouch a little like he was cooperating, but slide the gun back toward Jack, then surge up and hit the kid. Jack was a good shot by his own admission, and if he was fast, he might be able to use the moment to get off a shot. Then again, Jack had put away a lot of booze, and his reaction time had to be down near zero.

'The gun, Mr Pullman.'

Marty looked at the kid who'd worked by his side for the past three days, the kid who had cried at Morey's funeral after he'd shot him in the head. 'I can't do that, son.'

'I understand and respect that, sir.' Jeff said, but he steadied his aim and his finger tightened on the trigger. 'But if don't give up your weapon I'm going to have to shoot you.'

'You're going to shoot me whether I make it easy for you or not,' said Marty.

'No, Mr Pullman, I am not. I didn't even know you were out here until I walked in the door. I have no argument with you, and I don't want to shoot you. But I will if I have to.'

'So you were in the loft at Brainerd, right?' Jack said conversationally from the sofa. Marty heard the gurgle of Jack filling his glass from the bottle.

Jack, what the hell are you doing? But Jeff's eyes had flickered, just a little. Jack had taken him by surprise, just as he did everyone.

'Excuse me?' Jeff asked, his eyes still hard on Marty, his finger still tight on the trigger.

'Brainerd. The fishing lodge. You were in the loft,

you saw what happened, you saw us. So that guy behind the counter, what was he? Your dad?'

Jeff's eyes darted briefly to Jack, and Marty tensed, feeling the first surge of hope he'd felt since Jeff had pulled the gun from beneath his slicker.

Keep talking, Jack, he sent him a mental message that was absolutely unnecessary, because talking was what Jack did for a living. Distraction, persuasion, bullshitting – those were the lawyer's forte, and now Jack was doing what *he'd* been trained to do. But Jesus, it was still an act of courage. He turned a little sideways, looked at Jack out of the corner of his eye. Thirty seconds ago he'd been hanging on to sobriety with his fingernails; now he was waving his glass, playing the part of a sloppy drunk.

'Kind of old to be your dad, come to think of it. Grandfather?'

'He was my father,' Jeff said stonily. 'Mr Pullman, slide your weapon over right now or . . .'

'Shit. Must have been hell growing up with a Nazi for a father. Christ, I thought I had it bad. Kid, you got my sympathy.'

The 9-mm shuddered slightly in Jeff's hand, and color started to bleed up from his neck into his face.

Too fast, Marty thought, jumping in. 'If you saw everything that happened in Brainerd, Jeff, you know that Jack didn't shoot your father.'

Jeff's smile was absolutely humorless. 'You expected him to tell you anything different? I came out of my room when I heard the shots. Jack was holding the gun.'

'He didn't pull the trigger, Jeff,' Marty insisted. 'The others shot your father. They tried to get Jack to shoot him after he was dead, but he wouldn't. He couldn't.'

Jeff narrowed his eyes at Marty. '*He was there.*'

'You bet your bonnet I was there,' Jack slurred from the sofa; 'and you wanna know why? 'Cause my dad was trying to get me to finish his business, just like your dad got you to finish his. I'm telling you, kid, we got a lot in common . . .'

'Please be quiet, Mr Gilbert.'

'. . . but what I really want to know is just how the fuck did you find us?'

Jeff was still focused on Marty, still in control, but Jack was unnerving him a little bit, momentarily diverting his attention from the .357 Marty still held at his side. Marty started to move his finger ever so slightly toward the safety.

'Your father was foolish enough to drive his own car. I saw the plate, cozied up to the sheriff, waited until he signed onto the DMV for a license check on some speeder, and ran the numbers. Once I found your father and got a job here, all I had to do was wait for the other two to show up. Child's play.'

'Why didn't you tell the cops?' Marty asked, moving his finger a little closer.

'In my family, we take care of our own business.'

'And now your business is to kill Jack.'

'That's correct. An eye for an eye. I'm not an indiscriminate murderer. These are righteous acts, and Jack is the last of them. I don't have to kill you, Mr Pullman, and I certainly don't want to. Originally I'd hoped to stay on at the nursery, helping Mrs Gilbert, maybe even make my life here . . .'

Marty heard Jack's sharp intake of breath behind him, and had a hard time keeping his face expressionless.

'. . . but when I saw you, I knew I'd have to sacrifice that, just complete my mission, and then disappear. I'm happy to do that to spare your life, Mr Pullman. All you have to do is choose to live by passing over your weapon.'

Marty just stood there, eyes steady, finally feeling the safety nudge the side of his finger.

'You've made your choice, haven't you, Mr Pullman?'

'I guess I have, Jeff.'

'Goddamnit, Marty, give him the fucking gun!' Jack yelled, jumping up from the sofa, making Marty start a little, and in that instant Jeff's left foot shot out with amazing speed and accuracy, kicking the .357 out of Marty's hand. It spun across the floor and under the sofa, hitting the wall behind it with a loud clunk.

Marty closed his eyes and kept them closed. Fifteen years a cop, disarmed by a kid. Goddamnit to hell, he couldn't save anybody.

*

The gate to the nursery parking lot had been locked. By the time Magozzi and Gino pulled up, four squads were already lined up at the curb and another two were coming in from Lake Street. No lights, no sirens, thank God. Peterson was doing his job.

Viegs came trotting up to them, his hat protecting his hair plugs from the rain, a hat condom protecting the hat. 'There's a squad in the lot. Two of the guys went through the hedge to check it out. No sign of Becker. Didn't know if you wanted us to go any further. Peterson said to wait.'

'Hold on a minute,' Gino said, pulling out his cell, shielding it from the driving rain. He keyed in a number and listened. 'Pullman's still not answering,' he said.

'Let's move it,' Magozzi said. 'Viegs, cover the perimeter with whatever men you've got; we're going in.'

He and Gino ripped off their rain slickers at the car – too restrictive, too noisy – and started circling the property close to the hedge, heading around the side to where the bushes opened, near the office. The thunder and lightning were easing up – just a flash or two and a distant rumble every few minutes – but the rain was heavy, and the wind was hitting them hard.

Please, please, Magozzi prayed to a god he wasn't sure he believed in: Let Montgomery not be here, let him be at his apartment, let Langer and McLaren be slapping the cuffs on him right now, and let there be no more bodies in this awful war that never seems to end.

They found Becker in the planting beds a few yards from the office door. He was on his back, eyes closed, rain smacking against the young skin of his face, the entire left side of his head oozing blood. Magozzi didn't know if Becker was alive or dead. He pressed hard into where the carotid should have beat against his fingers, and felt a pulse that could have been Becker's, but might have been his own.

Gino was on his feet instantly, cell phone in his hand, racing toward the front of the greenhouse, frantically signaling the officers in the lot with hand gestures he'd learned in the academy and thought he'd forgotten.

Behind him, Magozzi crept closer to the office door alone. Slices of light were leaking out from around the edges.

Jeff Montgomery's kick had had enough force behind it to push Marty back a few steps, and to break his hand. It hung uselessly at his side now, swollen and throbbing and empty.

'I'm sorry I had to do that, Mr Pullman. It was the only way I could think of to save your life.'

Jesus, Marty thought, shaking his head, smiling helplessly. Jeff was focusing as much attention on saving Marty's life as he was on taking Jack's. It was such a bizarre, twisted sense of honor and right and wrong that for a minute, he couldn't get it to gel in his head.

And then suddenly, it did, and he realized that he wasn't just looking at Jeff Montgomery now – he was looking at Morey Gilbert, Rose Kleber, Ben Schuler, and last but certainly not least, Marty Pullman. For the first time in a long time, he felt easy with himself. He was looking at things head-on, seeing them clearly. 'Listen to me, Jeff. I've been where you are; I've done what you're doing; and I am telling you it is not a righteous act.'

Jeff eyed him cynically. 'You do not understand. Killing in the line of duty isn't the same thing.'

'I never killed anyone in the line of duty.'

Now Jeff's brows peaked with interest, and so did Jack's 'Just what exactly did you do, Mr Pullman?'

Marty took a breath and blew it out so the words would have something to float on. 'I killed the man who killed my wife.'

Jack's mouth sagged open and he reached back, found the edge of the sofa and eased himself down. 'You shot Eddie Starr?' he whispered, and Marty nodded without turning around to look at him.

Jeff was smiling at him beneficently. 'Then it was a noble kill, Mr Pullman. You had to do it.'

'I shot an unarmed man when he was sticking a needle in his arm, Jeff, and there was nothing noble about it. It wasn't justice, it didn't elevate me, it just made me a killer, and there's not a goddamn thing I can do to fix that. But you've got a chance that I never had. Walk away from the last one. Make a choice not to kill. Just turn around and walk out that door, and you'll have that to hang on to for the rest of your life.'

The wind was picking up outside, buffeting the side of the building, rattling the door in its frame.

Jeff was looking at him with pity in his eyes. 'It's really too bad, Mr Pullman. You did the right thing, the honorable thing, and you can't even see it.' He took a quick step left to get a clear shot at Jack and pulled the trigger, almost before Marty realized the moment was at hand. Almost, but not quite.

In that millisecond before Jeff's finger tightened on the trigger, Marty had launched himself sideways into the air, feeling right, and good, and suddenly pure as he put himself between the bullet and the only innocent man in the room. *The Amazing Flying Gorilla,* he thought, and he was smiling as the bullet drilled into his lower chest.

'Goddamnit!' Jeff screamed, taking fresh aim at Jack, and then the door flew open, banging against the inside wall, ripping away from its hinges, and Magozzi crouched there in the driving rain and wind, shouting, 'Drop it! Drop it!'

Jeff spun around fast, shooting wildly because he'd lost control, because everything was going wrong. When wood splintered near his head, Magozzi pulled his own trigger again and again, firing repeatedly into Jeff Montgomery's chest, hot adrenaline feeding his muscles and skipping his brain so he wouldn't see the baby-smooth face, the surprised blue eyes of the very young person he was killing.

41

Magozzi rose slowly out of his crouch in the doorway, gun still steady in his hands, pointed at the motionless body of Jeff Montgomery. His eyes darted around the room, taking snapshots: Montgomery off to his left, his chest a ruin; Marty Pullman straight ahead, flat on his back but his eyes still open, even as his shirt turned red; Jack Gilbert vaulting from the sofa to drop to his knees beside Marty. Desk, computer, chair, an empty bottle on its side, dribbling liquid onto the floor.

He allowed himself to breathe then, and let the wind push him into the little office that smelled like booze and cordite and blood. He toed Montgomery's gun away from the boy's curled hand, then felt the heavy comfort of Gino's hand on his shoulder, easing him off to one side. 'Let me by, buddy. Just let me by.'

Magozzi's legs trembled beneath him as the adrenaline drained away. He watched Gino bend to press his fingers against Montgomery's neck, and then rise again, saying, 'He's done.'

By the time they took the three steps over to where Marty lay, there were half a dozen cops outside in the rain, flanking the doorway, weapons drawn. 'Clear?' one of them hollered in.

'Clear! We need a bus here right now!' Gino answered.

'On its way!'

Jack was ripping open Marty's shirt, then peeling off his own to press it hard against the wound. Marty grunted and his eyes creased in pain.

'Christ, Jack, are you trying to kill me?'

'It doesn't look so bad, Marty. You're going to be okay. Just a little hole, we got it under control now, but you bled all over your shirt, you stupid asshole. Do you know how hard it is to get blood out of linen?'

Marty closed his eyes and smiled a little, but he looked bad.

'Let me take that for you, Jack.' Magozzi laid his hand over Jack's, waited for him to pull his away, then put some weight on the polo shirt compress, but not too much. He knew damn well that Marty wasn't bleeding much on the outside because he was bleeding on the inside, and that wasn't good. He was breathing hard, lungs and heart fighting the pressure, and the blood that seeped into Jack's polo shirt was bright red – arterial red.

'Hey, Pullman,' Gino was up by his head, kneeling in close. 'Open your eyes, buddy. You think we're going to write this report on our own, you're out of your friggin' mind.'

'Gino,' Marty whispered, but he didn't open his eyes. 'How bad?'

Gino swallowed hard, making sure his voice would come out light. 'Are you kidding? You took a slug in the chest, you think that's going to be a cakewalk? Way I figure, you'll be flat on your back for about a month, pissing into a tin bowl. Why the hell did you let that asshole shoot you?'

'He was shooting at *me,*' Jack choked out, hands gripped so tightly together they were turning white, holding each other back so they wouldn't touch Marty, wouldn't hurt him. He was breathing fast, talking fast, blinking hard, trying to hold it together. 'Goddamnit he was shooting at me and Marty jumped in the way. Stupid son of a bitch jumped right in front of a bullet and it's my fault this is all my fault why the fuck did you do that Marty why do you always have to be the fucking hero . . .'

Marty's hand shot out and grabbed Jack's wrist and held on. He rolled his head, opened his eyes and looked at Jack. 'I'm not a hero. I'm just like Morey, Jack. Remember that . . .'

'That is such *bullshit* . . .'

Marty's hand tightened on Jack's wrist, and the effort cost him. It was getting harder for him to talk. 'Just like Morey. Just like the rest of them. You gotta tell them. Tell Magozzi and Gino about Eddie Starr. Let them close it down.' And then he smiled. 'All this time, you were the only good guy, Jack. Better than any of us. You're the hero.'

Jack laid his head down on Marty's and started to cry.

Gino pushed himself up, scowling hard, then cleared his throat. 'I'm going to check on that bus,' he said, proud because his voice cracked only a little. When he turned to face the doorway, he saw a sea of blue uniforms standing a silent vigil just outside the door in the rain, faces hard, lips compressed, a few of them touching their eyes, pretending they weren't. Lily Gilbert was pushing her way between them, a little old bulldozer with rain plastering her white hair against her head, running down her glasses, hammering her straight shoulders. The uniforms parted and let her pass. She walked over to where Marty lay and knelt beside Jack, giving not one glance to Jeff Montgomery's body. Magozzi got up and backed away.

She had to get very close before Marty could see her. He was having trouble with his eyes, for some reason, and that seemed all wrong, since he'd been shot in the chest. 'Is that you, Lily?'

'Who else?'

'I'm right here,' she said, laying her old bony fingers on his forehead, feeling a deathly chill.

'Jack has things to tell you,' he whispered, his tongue moving to the side of his mouth, finding blood.

'I know. I'll listen. Be still now.'

'A little late for that.'

Tears were streaming down Jack's face, dripping from his chin to his bare chest, rolling down the swell of his silly little belly. 'Shut up, Marty, goddamnit, shut up. You're going to be okay. I swear to God you're going to be okay . . .'

Marty's eyes fell closed as he tried to speak, his chest lifting with the effort, then falling.

'Jack,' Lily said gently. 'He's not going to be okay. He's dying. Let him say what he needs to.'

Marty's smile was a sad grayish blue, but when he opened his eyes again, they were clear and focused and brimming. 'God, I love you, Lily,' he whispered. 'I tried to make it right.'

She smiled down at him. 'Always, you tried to make things right. That's who you are. A good man. A good son, Martin,' she whispered, and then watched his eyes close for the last time.

A few feet away, Magozzi turned his face to the wall, found a splinter of wood peeling up from the paneling, and stared at it hard. He could hear Jack sobbing, he could hear the sniffling of some of the officers near the door, he could hear Gino outside, screaming, 'Where the *fuck* is that goddamned ambulance?,' and over it all, he could hear the wind picking up again, the rain coming down harder, hammering the world.

Finally, he heard the sirens.

The med techs worked on Marty Pullman for a full ten minutes, doing all the horrible things they did to people they weren't willing to lose, going through all the motions they knew were futile the minute they looked at him, because a cordon of officers and the family were standing around watching, and they all needed that. When they finally packed their gear, got up, and backed away, one of them wept, unashamed. He'd wrestled against Marty Pullman at the State tournament a million years ago, laughing when he lost, because trying to pin Marty's monstrous shoulders had been like trying to hold down a gorilla.

Jack had moved far enough away to give the techs room to work, but no farther. The minute they left, he was back on his knees at Marty's side, because he'd looked so sad, lying there all alone.

One by one, the officers at the door walked in and looked down at one of their own in silent homage, and then filed out and disappeared into the heavy rain. Without their bodies blocking the doorway, the rain blew in on Marty's body, washing the blood from his chest.

Gino, Magozzi, and Lily were standing near the doorway, and somehow Lily's hand had found its way into Magozzi's. It felt tiny and fragile and sad. There would be a few moments of relative calm before the technicians bustled in to turn death into science. Too many moments for Jack Gilbert to sit over there all alone, Gino thought, trying to be grumpy because he didn't like Jack Gilbert, nevertheless pushing himself away from the wall, walking over to stand next to him.

With the blood washed away, Gino saw the long,

ragged scar on Marty's quiet chest. 'Jesus,' he murmured. 'How'd he get that scar?'

'His father,' Jack said, his voice as dead as the man next to him.

'What?'

'His father cut him when he was a kid.'

'Christ.' Gino closed his eyes briefly, thinking of all the history that makes up a man, that you never knew everything about anybody, and that there were monsters everywhere.

He turned his back when a particularly strong gust of wind blew a sheet of rain in through the doorway, making a sickly, smacking sound on Marty's exposed skin. Gino's thoughts shot back to the beginning of this awful case, to Lily Gilbert contaminating his precious crime scene by moving her dead husband's body in out of the rain. When he glanced over at where she was standing next to Magozzi, she was looking at him through those thick glasses of hers, not crying, not saying anything, just looking.

Gino looked back down at the rain splatting against Marty's face and understood a few things.

Magozzi raised an eyebrow when he saw Gino squat, slip his arms beneath Marty Pullman's shoulders and knees, then lift the dead man and carry him gently over to the sofa, out of the rain.

When Gino turned around, Lily was still looking at him. She nodded once, then walked over to stand behind Jack. She placed her hands on his shuddering shoulders, bent to kiss the top of his head, and whispered, 'Come, take care of your mother. Her heart is breaking.'

Chief Malcherson had shown up within half an hour of the shooting to take charge of the scene. He took statements from Magozzi and Gino, relieved Magozzi of his weapon, and initiated all the procedures required whenever an officer used deadly force. Technically, Magozzi was on admin leave until the board cleared the shooting of Jeff Montgomery – Gino would have to sign all the reports generated before the clearance – but Malcherson never once considered sending him home. For one thing, Magozzi would have defied him, which would have been messy and unacceptable – they would both have been forced into posturing positions that could only hurt the investigation; and for another, the Gilberts knew and trusted him, and if there was a key to closing this case, the Gilberts owned it. Sometimes you followed the rules to the letter, and sometimes you didn't. He stayed on while Jimmy Grimm and his crew worked the scene, releasing Gino and Magozzi at ten o'clock so they could go talk to the Gilberts.

They followed the gravel path through the back planting beds to the house. Pieces of colorful quartz sparkled and winked in the beams of their flashlights, in spite of the heavy rain. At least the lightning had moved off to the east for the time being. There was another line of storms moving in from the west

– according to Jimmy Grimm, the supercell that was dumping on Minnesota was going to keep them under the gun all night – but they had a lull before the next batch blew in.

Lily met them at the back door, wearing a dry pair of overalls and a short-sleeved shirt. Magozzi could see the wiry muscles in her skinny arms, and the tattoo down near her wrist. 'Have you heard anything about Officer Becker?' were the first words out of her mouth.

'He's going to make it,' Gino said. 'Montgomery didn't shoot him. Just cracked him over the head.'

'Where did they take him?'

'Hennepin County, I think.'

'He was a nice boy. I have to send flowers before you take us to jail.'

Gino and Magozzi exchanged a quick, puzzled glance. 'We're not here to take to you jail, Mrs Gilbert.'

'Not yet, maybe. Come in. We've been waiting for you.'

She led them into the kitchen, where Jack was already at the table, dry and sober now, wearing an old-fashioned plaid robe that had to have been his father's. The sleeves were rolled up several turns, reminding Magozzi that Morey Gilbert had been a very tall man. Jack's eyes were red and his face was puffy. 'How are you doing, Jack?'

'Okay, I guess. Sit down, guys.'

'This was a terrible night,' Gino said. 'We're sorry about Marty. Really sorry. And we're sorry we have to ask you these questions now.'

'This is your job,' Lily said, moving around the kitchen, getting dishes out of cupboards, filling glasses as if they were a couple of guests who'd dropped by for a snack. 'Here. Eat this.' She put a bowl of aromatic soup in front of each of them. 'That's chicken soup. It fixes a lot of things. Homemade, real schmaltz. The other stuff doesn't work.'

Gino had no clue what schmaltz was, but it didn't sound half as good as the soup smelled. He picked up his spoon, then hesitated. She thought they were going to take her to jail, and she was giving them soup. He wondered if eating it would constitute accepting a bribe.

'Don't fight it,' Jack was watching him. 'She knows why you're here. We'll tell you anything we can. But you still have to eat the soup.'

'First,' Lily added. 'Then we talk.'

Magozzi ate his soup, but unlike Gino, he understood the offering for what it was. Lily Gilbert was finally letting them in.

When they'd finished, she cleared the dishes and sat down next to Jack. 'Tell them about Brainerd.'

Magozzi got busy pulling out his notebook and pen, keeping his face averted in case the surprise showed. *How the hell did Jack know about Brainerd*? He knew the answer before he asked the question, and it sickened him. Jack had been up there at the fishing lodge with his father and the others. Jack had been in on it.

He felt the tension coming off Gino, knew he was thinking the same thing, but they both kept their silence, waiting to hear it out loud.

The real story was almost worse.

It took Jack a long time to tell them about Morey, Rose, and Ben shooting the old man in the fishing lodge, about the shadow he'd seen in the loft that day, and finally about his own refusal to participate.

Magozzi and Gino stopped writing and looked up at Jack simultaneously.

'What?' Jack asked.

'Nothing, Jack. Go on.'

He told them about the ride home that day, the fight with his father, and everything that came after. 'But I never connected Brainerd with Pop's death at all,' he finished. 'Not until yesterday when Ben was killed and I saw Rose Kleber's picture in the paper – I never knew her name until then. That's when I realized what was happening, that whoever had been up in that loft saw what we did, and they were taking us out, one by one.'

'What *they* did, Jack,' Gino corrected him. 'Not you.'

'Whatever. I've got blood on my hands any way you look at it. If I'd told you sooner, maybe you could have figured it out in time to save Marty.'

Magozzi gave him the truth. 'Maybe. But maybe not. Jeff covered himself pretty well.'

He'd thrown him a little bone, but it would never be enough, and Magozzi couldn't offer any more. Half of him wanted to wring Jack's neck, because he had to believe that with a little more lead time they might have been able to save Marty – but the other half of him bled for the guy. What would it be like to have a father who tried to turn you into a killer, then disowned you when you refused?

Jack got up and poured himself a cup of coffee. 'There's something else. Pop said they'd been doing this for years, that they'd killed a lot of Nazis. He said he kept a list on the computer, but I couldn't find anything. He could have erased it.'

'We'll have someone come over and pick up the computer, take a look at it just in case,' Magozzi said.

Jack shrugged. 'It might not even be true.'

'I'm afraid it is true,' Magozzi said. 'We just put that together this afternoon. Ben Schuler kept records of the ones they'd killed on the backs of some pictures he had in his house.'

Lily straightened slightly in her chair. 'How many?'

'Over sixty so far.'

She closed her eyes.

'You had no idea what Morey was doing all those years?'

She took off her thick glasses, opened her eyes, and looked at him. It was the first time that Magozzi had seen her eyes without the barrier of the glasses. They were beautiful, he thought, and tragic.

'This is what I knew. He started talking about this

thing right after the war. Other people, little groups, were hunting these men down, killing them, and he thought this was just. A noble thing. I told him if he ever left our house to kill another human being, not to come back, and he never talked about it again.'

'He took trips without you at least twice a year,' Gino reminded her. 'You didn't think that was strange?'

'You're such a suspicious person, Detective Rolseth. Your wife goes away for the weekend with friends, do you think, aha, she's out killing people? Morey and Ben went fishing every now and then. Was that so hard to believe? So anyway, that's all I knew until the night Morey was shot. I thought he was in the greenhouse, like every night. But then he woke me up at about midnight and said he'd killed the Animal.'

'An animal?' Gino asked.

'*The* Animal. It's what we called him. He was S.S. at Auschwitz.'

'Heinrich Verlag,' Magozzi said. 'Also known as Arlen Fischer.'

Jack's jaw dropped open. 'Fischer? The man who was tied to the railroad tracks? Are you telling me *Pop* did that? And then he *told* you about it?'

Lily nodded. 'Verlag, I knew. Verlag, I had seen in action. Sixty years, I wished for that man's death. So Morey wakes me up like a proud cat bringing home a dead mouse, maybe thinking I wouldn't mind that he had killed this one. All those years, and he never knew me.'

'You should have told me, Ma.'

'You think I wanted my son to know his father was a murderer?'

'But I already knew that.'

Lily gave him a sad little smile. 'Now you tell me.'

Magozzi laid down his pen and rubbed his eyes. It was almost too much information to take in, and almost none of it looked good for either Jack or Lily.

'We're going to have to write all this up, turn it in,' Gino said, echoing his thoughts.

Jack smiled a little. 'Don't look so glum, Detective. You've been trying to get me in a cell for two days, and now you've got your wish. I witnessed a murder, I didn't report it, and I'll sign a confession. It's about time somebody in this family started taking responsibility for what they've done.'

Lily patted his hand.

'Well don't get your hopes up for any luxury accommodations at Stillwater just yet. Lots of extenuating circumstances here. We don't know where the county attorney will go with any of this.'

'One more question, Jack,' Magozzi said. 'Marty wanted you to tell us something that would close the Eddie Starr case.' He glanced at Lily, saw that the name hit her hard. 'He knew that Morey killed him, right?'

Jack just stared at him for a minute.

'It doesn't matter now, Jack. We already had that

anyway – the gun Morey and the others used on a lot of the victims matched the gun that killed Eddie Starr . . .'

'Morey killed the man who killed Hannah?' Lily whispered.

'No.' Jack said quietly. 'Marty did. That's what was killing him. That's what he couldn't live with.'

Magozzi and Gino looked at each other, then leaned back in their chairs, as if the effort of sitting upright was suddenly too difficult.

Magozzi closed his eyes and saw hatred and vengeance everywhere. Morey killing, Marty killing . . . and only Lily and Jack standing apart, standing alone against the violence that had destroyed their lives. He wondered if they realized how very much alike they were, if anyone could sift through the confusion of all their mistakes to see their essential goodness.

And then he remembered Marty's words as he lay dying.

All this time, you were the only good guy, Jack. Better than any of us. You're the hero.

42

Sometime during the night the storm had blown out of Minnesota and into Wisconsin, leaving muddy fields and shattered buildings and ruined lives in its wake. Nine tornadoes had touched down in the state, and for the time being the media was somberly preoccupied with photo-ops of the aftermath.

There had been brief coverage of the shooting at Uptown Nursery, but the press had been too focused on the storm story to do any serious digging yet. But soon, when the public was tired of seeing two-by-fours driven through tree trunks, upside-down trailers, and the flat remains of a pole building near Wilmer that had housed twenty thousand turkeys, the media would come clamoring after Homicide, looking for another ratings grabber. This was not a happy thought for Chief Malcherson as he strode down the hall toward the Homicide office. Then again, there were no happy thoughts in this building today.

Gloria was at her desk in the front, swathed in black, punishing all the mail. Marty Pullman had spent a lot of time in this office when Langer and McLaren were working Hannah's murder, and Gloria had taken a shine to him. Partly because he had bowlegs and she'd never once met a bowlegged man she didn't like; partly because he was always a gentleman in a big way, gave her that quiet kind of friendly respect you could never get enough of. But mostly because that man had been heartbroken over losing his wife and wasn't ashamed to put it right out there. Any man who loved a woman that much deserved mourning.

She looked up when Malcherson stopped at her desk. 'Did you get any sleep, Chief?'

'A few hours, thank you. Who's in?'

'Peterson took the call on that drunken fool they pulled out of the Mississippi this morning. The rest are here. Magozzi and Rolseth came back in about a half hour ago, looking like somebody'd dragged them through a knothole backwards. If you want my opinion, and I know you do, I think you ought to send them back home.'

'I'll give it my best effort, Gloria.'

Malcherson walked to the back of the room, where Langer and McLaren worked at their desks on the left, Magozzi and Gino on the right. He pulled a chair into the aisle between them and sat down, positioning a pristine legal tablet on his knees. 'Gentlemen, we need to go over some things.'

Langer and McLaren looked all right – as far as he knew, they'd finished their reports on the search of Jeff Montgomery's apartment and gone home before midnight – but Magozzi and Rolseth had still been in the office when he'd left at 3 A.M. Magozzi looked gaunt and strained; Gino looked like he was wearing little bags of melting Jell-O under his eyes, but the real measure of his exhaustion was that he hadn't said a thing about Malcherson's suit.

'You've all done some amazing work on these cases, Detectives. Unless I misread your reports, we cleared four homicides last night.'

'The hard way,' Magozzi said bitterly.

'You saved Jack Gilbert's life,' Malcherson reminded him.

'But we lost Marty Pullman. We were ten seconds too late.'

'Every homicide committed in this city means we were ten seconds too late to save somebody, Detective Magozzi. We do what we can.' He pulled his Mont Blanc from his pocket and looked at Langer and McLaren. 'Do we have a final report on the search of Thomas Haczynski's apartment yet?'

'It's coming, but the preliminary pretty much tells the story.' McLaren flipped open a little ragged notebook with doodles all over the cover. 'The kid had a .22 under his mattress that Ballistics confirmed early this morning. Same gun that shot Morey Gilbert. And the nine he used on Marty killed Rose Kleber and Ben Schuler. Plus we got a journal that lays out what he was doing and why, right up to the last entry, just before he went to the nursery last night to kill Jack. It's grim reading, I'll tell you. Gives me the creeps. He'd been planning this for over a year, down to the last detail, even set up that cell phone scam to make it look like he was living in Germany.'

Malcherson looked up from his tablet. 'Explain.'

'We just told Gino and Magozzi about that,' Langer said. 'Montgomery had one of those expensive hybrid phones in his apartment – the kind that works here and in Europe. It was pretty simple, really. All he had to do was set up a German account, complete with German telephone number, and no read-back, including ours, could ever tell the difference. He could take calls or call out from anywhere in the world, and it would still look like he was in Germany.'

'Little bastard,' Gino grumbled, still seething about being fooled. 'Bawling one minute, talking German the next, pretending to be his own uncle.'

Malcherson sighed. 'So essentially, Magozzi's and Rolseth's cases are closed.'

'I'd say so,' Langer agreed. 'The Arlen Fischer case is something else. We know Morey Gilbert and his crew killed him, but it's all circumstantial. A bunch of plane tickets and a lot of conjecture. We can't actually put a gun in the hand of any of them for even one of the sixty-odd murders we know they committed, let alone Arlen Fischer. And as for Morey's confession to Lily, a second-year law student could tear her to shreds. She's old, she was wakened out of a sound sleep, she could have been dreaming . . . like that.'

'Same thing with Jack's story about what happened

in Brainerd,' Gino said. 'From Jimmy Carter, maybe. From a drunken P.I. attorney who walks around downtown Wayzata in his bathrobe – I don't think so.'

'So what's the problem?' McLaren asked. 'It's not like we're going to prosecute these people. They're dead.'

'If we try to close Arlen Fischer based on our conclusions without adequate proof, we *are* prosecuting these people, without a trial,' Malcherson said. 'And I, for one, do not want to try to convince the public to take our word for it that three sweet, elderly pillars of the community, who suffered and survived the horrors of concentration camps only to be murdered in our city, were in fact, a gang of serial killers.'

McLaren threw up his hands. 'So don't close the case. Keep it open forever.'

'That won't work, either,' Langer said. 'Jeff Montgomery's journal is public information the minute we close the Gilbert, Kleber, and Schuler murders, and that journal details those three murdering his father in Brainerd. Then everything unravels, and we take the heat for *not* following through.'

Malcherson touched a finger to one cottonball eyebrow. 'The press is going to have a field day with this. This is the kind of story that journalists dream about. Nazis hiding in plain view, Jewish vigilante death squads . . . the whole city is going to be taking sides over this one on the airwaves for a long time, and we're going to be right in the middle. And that's just what happens locally. When the story hits the wires, this department is going to be caught up in a global media firestorm.'

McLaren slid down so far in his chair his head almost disappeared behind his desk. 'So we're screwed if we try to close Arlen Fischer, screwed if we don't.'

'That appears to be the case, Detective.'

'Well, great. Langer, give the chief your gun. He can shoot us all, then take his own life.'

'I might have another option.' Malcherson had that flinty look in his eyes that meant he might be thinking about smiling in the next six months or so. 'Technically, when we turn a case over to the FBI, it's officially closed in our department. Any and all queries would have to be referred to Special Agent in Charge Paul Shafer. We would no longer be in a position to discuss the case with anyone. Not law enforcement, not Interpol, and certainly not the media. Our hands would be tied, gentlemen.'

One by one they all started to smile for the first time in twenty-four hours. All except Johnny McLaren, who was looking at Malcherson with undisguised awe. 'Chief, you are the sneakiest son of a bitch on the planet.'

'Thank you, Detective McLaren.'

Malcherson was all the way to Gloria's desk when Gino called after him, 'Hey, Chief.' Malcherson stopped in his tracks, but didn't turn around. 'Thumbs-up on the navy suit. The average Joe can get away with black in mourning situations, but a man in your position of power? Might have been a little too much drama. I think you nailed it again.'

Chief Malcherson waited until he was out in the hall, and then he smiled.

Twenty minutes later, Detective Aaron Langer walked into the chief's office just as he was hanging up the phone. Malcherson looked inordinately pleased with himself.

'That was Paul Shafer,' he said. 'He seemed absolutely delighted to hear that we finally realized the Arlen Fischer case was beyond the scope of our investigative abilities.'

Langer smiled. 'What did you tell him, sir?'

'The absolute truth. That the Minneapolis Police Department doesn't have the media skills to manage a case of this magnitude.'

'That had to be irresistible.'

'I believe it was. He's on his way over now to pick up the file. Personally.'

'So as far as we're concerned, the Arlen Fischer case is now closed.'

'That's correct.'

'That's good news, Chief.' Langer removed his sidearm, ejected the clip, and cleared the chamber, then laid it butt first on the desk.

Malcherson stared at it, and then at the badge case Langer laid next to it.

'May I sit down, sir?'

'Absolutely.'

Langer settled in the chair, then looked out the window because he couldn't look the chief in the eye. He hadn't been able to do that for a long time now. 'Marty Pullman was at my desk the day I got that call telling us where we could find Eddie Starr. I wrote down the address, then left the office.'

Malcherson waited, his face still, his expression unreadable.

'Marty overheard the call. He knew whose address that was, and I knew he knew it. So I left the note in plain view and just walked away.'

Malcherson looked down at a fingerprint in the high gloss of his desktop, wondering whose it was. 'What on earth were you thinking, Detective Langer?' he asked softly.

'I'm not sure, sir. Maybe that Marty deserved a chance to beat the shit out of the man who killed his wife before we got there. Or maybe somewhere in the back of my mind I was thinking he might do more than that. I honestly don't know, and it really doesn't matter. The point is that when I saw Eddie Starr's body, I knew damn well what had happened. Marty may have pulled the trigger, but I made it possible when I walked away from my desk that day.'

Malcherson cleared his throat softly. 'Detective Langer, I will never believe that your intent was for Marty Pullman to commit murder.'

Langer's smile pulled at one side of his mouth. 'Really? Well I'm not so sure, and it's been driving me crazy for months. And I'd spent months before that looking at what Morey and Lily and Jack were going through, watching Marty fall apart a little more each day, and all I could think of was how unfair it was that a scumbag like Starr could destroy so many good people . . . you see what I was doing? I was deciding, sir. Deciding who was good and who was bad and maybe even who deserved to die. Just like Marty did, and Morey and all the rest. Then when this case started to unravel and I realized that Eddie Starr was a piker, that if he'd lived another hundred years he wouldn't be able to catch up to Morey Gilbert's body count . . . the good guys and the bad guys kind of blended together until the only thing I was sure of was that I'd never been able to tell the difference.' His eyes drifted down to his badge. 'I should have turned that in, turned myself in, a long time ago.'

He stood up then and patted his pockets, already missing the weight of his life that he'd left on the Chief's desk. Then he met Malcherson's eyes head on and smiled. Strange, he thought, how good that felt. 'You know where to find me, sir,' he said, then turned and walked out.

Malcherson sat quietly at his desk for a long time after he left.

43

Magozzi and Gino were at the big front table in Homicide, making copies of the reams of paperwork they'd all accumulated since the night Arlen Fischer and Morey Gilbert had been murdered. Paul Shafer was in Malcherson's office now with a couple of his FBI henchmen, formalizing the turnover of the Fischer case and all related evidence. They'd be here in a few minutes to collect it.

McLaren wheeled in a dolly with four large boxes he'd retrieved from the evidence room. 'This is the last of the stuff we took from Fischer's place.' He stopped at Gloria's desk and wiped his forehead. 'You want to give me a hand with this, Miss Gloria?'

She held up ten black-enameled fingers and wiggled them. 'Look at these and tell me how much of a fool you are for asking such a stupid question.'

McLaren put a hand to his heart. 'I am a fool. I am anything you want me to be. All you have to do is ask.'

'I want you to be gone.'

'I want you to be my woman.'

'Oh, for God's sake.' She slammed out of her little cubicle and stomped away on her black platforms.

He grinned and wheeled the dolly over to the table. 'I think I'm getting to her.'

'A regular Lothario, that's what you are,' Gino said, grabbing a box. 'You know, McLaren, if you ever lifted anything heavier than a pencil with those little chicken wing arms of yours, you wouldn't have to ask a woman for help.'

'Who's Lothario? And where the hell is Langer, anyway? I swear, that guy finds something else to do every time we've got to bring these boxes upstairs.'

Magozzi stepped away from the table when his cell rang.

'Hey, Magozzi.'

'Hey, Grace.'

'I saw the news. I'm sorry about your friend, Marty. That must have been terrible. Are you okay?'

God, he loved it when she worried about him. 'Not really.'

'Maybe I could come over tonight, cook you supper, we could open a few bottles of wine.'

Magozzi took a few more steps away from the table and lowered his voice. 'You want to come to *my* house?'

'I have a present for you.'

Magozzi's spirits spread their little wings and tried to flap. 'You're not going to Arizona?'

'Sorry, Magozzi. Annie flies in this afternoon, we all leave tomorrow.'

Splat. Spirits squashed under Grace MacBride's boot.

'This is a different present.'

'So it's a going-away present. Goddamnit, Grace, that sucks.'

'You'll like it. I'll be there at seven.'

Magozzi closed his phone and decided that he didn't give a damn if Grace MacBride went to Arizona or the moon. Gino was right. He needed a life. He needed a woman – preferably one who'd help him buy a sofa. Oh, he'd let her come over tonight, they'd eat a little, drink a little, and maybe he'd even bend her over backwards once and kiss her until her boots blew off, but then, by God, he'd kick her ass out. That's what he was going to do.

Gino looked over at him, brows raised. 'Grace?'

'Yeah,' Magozzi growled, sounding like a real man, a man who didn't care, a man who was taking charge. He wondered if the silly grin he felt on his face spoiled the image.

Harley Davidson was behind the wheel of the custom-built forty-five-foot RV, his beefy, tattooed arms draped over the big steering wheel, his solid frame enveloped in a Connolly leather captain's chair specifically designed to accommodate his size. It had cost twenty thousand to have the chair made; another thousand to air-express it over from the small Italian furniture company he'd commissioned for the job; another three grand to install the hydraulics. A white grin sliced through his black beard. It had been worth every penny. 'Goddamnit, I love this thing. I'd drive her to hell and back and be a happy man.'

The storklike man next to him folded long, scrawny arms over his bony chest and pouted. 'It's my turn. I want to drive it. You drove to the airport, I should get to drive back. So pull over.'

Harley's eyes darted right – you couldn't look away from the road too long in this baby or you'd take out a subdivision. Roadrunner was in his customary head-to-toe Lycra, but today it was blaze orange. Harley felt like he was about to talk to a construction cone. 'Roadrunner, you are never driving this machine. Get it out of your head.'

'Oh yeah? Why not?'

'Well, gee, lemme think. Number one, you do not, and never have had a driver's license. Number two, the only thing you've driven for the past thirty years is a bicycle. The brakes are not on the handlebars in this thing, you dipshit.'

'Would you guys quit fighting?' Annie drawled petulantly from behind them, and Harley's gaze jerked to one of the seven mirrors. He had three of them adjusted so he could see three different angles of Annie Belinsky sprawled languidly on one of the couches. She was wearing this skin-tight fawn-colored suede thing with fringe on the bottom and beads on the top and omigod, cowboy boots with spurs. 'Christ, Annie, I can almost feel those spurs in my flanks.'

Annie glared at his back. 'Imagine that. I've only

been gone for two weeks, and yet somehow I managed to totally forget what a disgusting pig you are, Harley.'

'He missed you,' Grace said. She was slouched on the opposite couch, booted feet stretched out in front of her, crossed at the ankles. 'We all did.'

Roadrunner spun his chair around and faced Annie. 'Did you bring me a present?'

'Honey, I sure did. It's in that little black bag right there.'

Roadrunner's face lit up, and he started digging in the bag until he found a tissue-wrapped parcel. He ripped it open and held up a lime green Lycra cowboy shirt, complete with piping on the yoke, mother-of-pearl snaps, and a cow skull appliqué on the pocket. 'Oh, man, Annie, this is great. Where did you find a Lycra cowboy shirt?'

'Let me tell you, Phoenix is a shopper's paradise if you're into the Urban Cowboy look. They put a cactus, a cow skull, or a piece of fringe on damn near anything. That came from a specialty bike shop a few miles out of town.'

Roadrunner stood up, his head almost brushing the seven-foot ceiling, and peeled off his orange Lycra top.

Harley glanced at him, then did a double-take. 'Jesus Christ, Roadrunner, is that your chest or did you swallow a xylophone?'

'A man with boobs your size shouldn't be criticizing.'

'These are not boobs, they are pecs.'

Annie put her head in her hands. 'Are you two going to be like this all the way to Arizona?'

'You should have heard them when they were putting this rig together,' Grace said. 'Couple of old bickering hens.'

Roadrunner was beaming, now newly dressed in his southwestern finery. He posed in his blaze orange stick legs and his lime green shirt. 'How do I look?'

Harley glanced at him. 'Are you kidding? You look like a goddamned carrot.'

Annie rolled her eyes and looked at Grace. 'How'd that thing you were working on for Magozzi turn out?'

'Turned out great,' Harley boomed, loath to be left out of any conversation within shouting distance. 'Our Gracie cracked the case with that face-recognition software she put together.'

'You go, girl. That thing's going to make a jillion dollars when you get it down to idiot level and put it on the Web. So what was the case all about?'

Grace closed her eyes. 'Don't ask.'

'The lady wants to know,' Harley said. 'And I'm the man to tell her. You see, Annie, this is the way it went down. First the Nazis killed the Jews, right? So you know what happened right here in our fair city? Three old ass-kicking Jews got themselves a Nazi. Is that righteous, or what?'

Roadrunner gaped at him. 'I think that's the most horrible thing I've ever heard you say.'

'What?'

'*Har*-ley, they tied a ninety-year-old man to the train tracks so he'd get smushed.'

Harley shrugged, genuinely baffled. 'He was a Nazi, for chrissake. What's your problem?'

'Like most civilized men, Harley, I have this little problem with murder. They should have turned him in, sent him to The Hague. Courts, lawyers, fair trial, does any of this ring a bell? It's not exactly a new concept . . .'

'Ah, bullshit. The only good Nazi is a dead Nazi. You don't believe me? Ask any German and they'll tell you the same thing.'

'How do you know what the Germans think?'

'Because, Mr Chickenshit I Won't Fly, I go to Germany at least once a year to buy wine and party with some of the most hospitable people in the world who happen to live in one of the most beautiful countries in the world, and that's not even getting into the exceptional quality of their lager, or the *cars* . . . and those people hate Nazis.'

Annie leaned across the aisle and whispered to Grace. 'I am not riding all the way to Arizona with those two madmen.'

Grace sighed and smiled, totally happy to be right here, listening to Harley and Roadrunner snipe at each other, Annie complaining – the absolute sounds of family, she thought. Sometimes she loved these people so much it hurt. And some days, when she was feeling really good about herself, she felt that way about Magozzi, too.

Annie was reading her mind again. 'You're going to miss Magozzi, aren't you?'

'He's a nice man, Annie.'

'He's a prince,' Harley bellowed. 'A hail-fellow-well-met. I love the guy. Every time I see him, I want to kiss him on the lips. How's the old bastard doing, anyway?'

Grace shrugged. 'It's been a bad week.' She looked at Annie. 'There was a shooting last night. All part of the Nazi-Jew thing, I think. He lost a cop, and had to kill a kid.'

'Oh, Lord. Magozzi does dearly hate to kill people. Poor man.'

Grace nodded. 'I'm going over to his place tonight. Sort of a bon voyage dinner.'

'You should sleep with him,' Annie decided. 'That always makes men feel better.'

Harley actually turned his head around to look at Grace. 'Are you kidding me? You haven't slept with him yet? I thought this guy was Italian.'

'I think we should paint the name on this bus,' Roadrunner piped up, changing the subject abruptly.

'This is not a bus, dumbshit, but putting the name on it isn't a bad idea. I can see it now. "Chariot" in big scripty letters on the front and sides . . .'

Annie looked appalled. 'You renamed the company Chariot?'

'No, no, Harley named the bus that isn't a bus Chariot. He names everything. You want to know what he calls his dick?'

'God, no.'

'And that's not what I meant, anyway, Harley. We should paint the name of the company on the bus. Gecko, Incorporated. I see green letters, and maybe the *g* is a curled-up lizard's tail.'

Annie and Grace looked at each other. Harley just dragged a big hand down his face.

'We are not renaming this company after a creepy little reptile,' Annie said firmly.

Roadrunner pouted. 'Well I don't see any of the rest of you coming up with a new name.'

'I've been thinking about it,' Grace said quietly, and everyone looked at her. 'Let's call it Monkeewrench.'

No one said anything for a minute.

'That name's had some pretty bad press, Grace,' Harley said.

'So has the USA, and nobody suggested changing that name.'

Annie mulled it over for a bit, then reached over and patted Grace's knee. 'I like it,' she said with a smile. 'It's who we are.'

44

Pleasantly warm days, cool, cool nights. That's what the Canadian cold front had left behind when it had pushed the storms out of the state last night. By six-thirty the temperature had already dropped to fifty-five degrees, and Magozzi stood on his front porch in a heavy black sweatshirt, wondering what it would be like to live in a place where the temperature didn't leap or drop forty degrees in any twenty-four-hour period. Boring, probably. For a lot of Minnesotans, conversation would grind to a halt.

Bodies sunburned by the weeklong heat wave were encased in sweats and windbreakers as they took their evening jog, or walked tongue-lolling dogs along the sidewalk before hurrying home. There was a stiff, chill wind tonight, and Magozzi could already smell wood smoke rising from nearby chimneys.

It was a good night for a fire. He'd laid one in his own house earlier, then stood on the empty expanse of carpet in front of the hearth, trying to figure out where he and Grace would sit. He'd remembered to decant the red wine and chill the white, lay the table in the little kitchen, right down to forks, knives *and* spoons, even though he'd always thought spoons were pretty useless utensils, and then he'd imagined a cozy, languorous evening in front of a roaring fire. The one thing he'd forgotten was that he didn't have any furniture to speak of, and he had never once seen Grace MacBride sit on the floor. She wouldn't like that. It would take too long to jump up and shoot somebody if you had to, and Grace spent her life assuming she would have to.

'Let me give you two words,' Gino had said this afternoon when he'd learned Grace was actually going to visit Magozzi at his house for a change. 'Bower birds.'

'Thanks, Gino. I'll cherish those two words forever.'

'Don't be a wiseass. I'm trying to educate you.'

'Okay.'

'The male bower birds – there's a whole bunch of different kinds – build these elaborate nests on the ground, like little portable caves made out of twigs and branches and vines and shit like that, and then they go find pretty stuff, like flower petals, or sparkly bits of stone, and they scatter that all around so the place looks great. That's how they attract females. The guy with the prettiest bower wins. Now the unhappy moral of this little story is that, Leo, my friend, you got the ugliest bower in town.'

Magozzi sighed and looked out over his scabby lawn with the dying spruce, at the single chaise on the porch and the Weber grill with its duct-taped legs. He considered digging around in the dirt for a few sparkly stones, but in the end, he just picked up the roll of duct tape that was still lying next to the grill and went inside. It was the best he could do on short notice.

At precisely 7 P.M. he opened his front door and looked at Grace MacBride standing on his porch, and felt pretty pleased with himself. He'd gotten her here without a single sparkly stone.

She was wearing a full-length fringed buckskin coat he'd never seen before over her English riding boots, somehow making the clash of cultures look right. Black hair curling a little over her shoulders, blue eyes smiling at him, even though her mouth wasn't.

He took the grocery bag she was holding in one hand, and looked down at the laptop she was carrying in the other. 'Are we going to play computer games?'

'Later,' she replied, striding in like she owned the place, taking possession of all the air. 'I want to give you your present first.'

He closed the door and faced her in the little foyer, which was fast becoming his favorite room in the house. It had a little table on one wall where he tossed his keys, and he considered it fully furnished.

Grace set down her laptop, straightened, and gripped the front plackets of the coat, elbows out. 'Ready, Magozzi?'

'I don't know. Are you going to flash me?'

The smile made it down to her mouth as she

opened the coat and let it slide to the floor, and in a way, Magozzi thought, she had flashed him. Even in her jeans, boots, and black silk T-shirt, she had to feel naked, because she wasn't wearing the Sig.

His eyes darted automatically to her ankle, looking for the derringer she strapped on whenever she didn't wear the shoulder holster, but it wasn't there. 'All right, Grace, where is it?'

'At home in the gun safe. Both of them.'

'You drove all the way over here without a gun?'

Her eyes sparkled like a kid's. 'I did. But oh, Magozzi, I thought I'd die.'

He was hugging the grocery bag hard, feeling something soft mush between his arms, grinning like a fool. 'It's a great present, Grace.'

'I told you you'd like it.'

Magozzi figured there probably wasn't another man in the world who would consider it an amazing, hopeful gift when a woman agreed to have dinner with him unarmed, but they just didn't understand. Grace had just given him a giant step.

Magozzi poured the wine while Grace unloaded the grocery bag and turned on the oven. He eyed a shallow casserole dish covered with tin foil. 'That smells fantastic.'

'Beef Wellington.'

'Excellent.' Magozzi couldn't remember the exact components of Beef Wellington, but figured it was some kind of hotdish with delusions of grandeur.

'Why don't you clear a space on the table and plug in my laptop. I'll show you what I pulled from Morey Gilbert's computer while we're waiting for this to heat.'

Magozzi hesitated, feeling like he'd been suddenly flung into another dimension. Mentally, the case had ended for him the minute he'd fired the first shot at Jeff Montgomery. He'd completely forgotten having Morey's office computer sent over to Grace.

Her fingers flew over the keys and pulled up a cartoon fish on a hook, with the legend *Go Fish* beneath it.

Magozzi grunted. 'Lily said he played computer games every night.'

'I had to restore this. Probably Jeff Montgomery tried to wipe it out the day after he killed Morey Gilbert – but it's not a game.' Grace clicked the icon, and the page filled with three columns – names in the first, locations in the second, and a date column that was empty. Magozzi scanned the names, but didn't recognize any of them from the list of victims they'd gotten off the pictures at Ben Schuler's house. It took him a second to put it together. 'Jesus. These are the ones they hadn't hit yet.'

Grace nodded. 'That's what I thought, so I cross-checked with Wiesenthal's site. We need to send this out, Magozzi. Most of these guys are on their list as unfound.'

'Then how the hell did he find them?'

Grace's fingers got busy on the keys again. 'That's the beauty of it – or the horror, depending on your point of view. I don't know how he tracked the earlier ones, but the worldwide Web made his job a lot easier.' What seemed like an endless series of Web-site addresses started to scroll by at high speed. 'When I checked the logs of all the Web-site visits he deleted, it made the hair stand up on the back of my neck. Every single one of them was a neo-Nazi or white supremacist site – he spent hours in the chat rooms on those sites, Magozzi, and he posted the same message on all of them.' She stopped the scrolling on a bold-faced message.

WARNING! JEWS ARE KILLING OUR BROTHERS! PROTECT YOURSELF!

Magozzi stared at the message, and then at the e-mail address that Grace was pointing to.

'That was a blind account Morey Gilbert set up – password protected. And there are about a thousand replies on his hard drive. A lot of them are garbage, but some of them are the real thing.' Grace leaned back in her chair and sighed. 'They came to him, Magozzi. They read the warning, or someone told them about it, started a correspondence, and the ones who had reason to be scared eventually agreed to a personal meeting with the man they thought could save their lives. It's all in the e-mails. He set himself up as the bait, and once they took it, he had them.'

Magozzi rubbed at his forehead with his palm,

almost more disturbed by Morey's systematic stalking of his prey than he had been by the murders themselves. He wondered if his mind would ever be able to put that man, and the philanthropist the city mourned, in the same body.

'Yin and yang,' Grace said softly, reading his face, seeing his thoughts. 'There's some of that in all of us, Magozzi.' She folded up her laptop, put it aside, and reset the table, giving him time. 'Food or wine?' she finally asked.

'Wine.'

They sat on the top step of the front porch as dusk deepened into twilight, letting the wine stave off the evening chill. Not that Magozzi needed it. Grace's shoulder was actually touching his, and he didn't think he'd ever be cold again.

There were still a few people about in spite of the fading light. One of them paused in the shadows at the edge of Magozzi's property, catching his eye.

He didn't think about it, he didn't analyze it, he just responded instantly to that gut-wrenching, mind-screaming instinct that this was very, very wrong. That particular figure should not be here. For the first time all day, he felt a great void on his hip where his gun should be.

He turned his head and buried his lips in Grace's hair next to her ear, just a man whispering sweet nothings to the woman he loved. 'Get up quietly, Grace. Go into the house, then out the back door, do you understand?'

'What's happening, Magozzi?' she whispered back, just a trace of panic in her voice, but by then someone was approaching the front walk, head turned, watching them, and Magozzi's demeanor changed. He shoved his wineglass at her and spoke loud enough to be overheard.

'Fill it up to the top this time, will you?'

Every muscle in Magozzi's body was tensed to the point of pain. It eased up just a little when he heard the screen door slam behind Grace. *Safe*, he thought. *Please, God, be safe, run, run out the back door, run to a neighbor's, don't do anything brave, Grace, don't do anything stupid . . .*

The figure was on the walk now, features taking on their familiar shape as he moved closer, and there sat Magozzi with a lame smile of greeting on his face, trying to look natural, rational thought telling him there was nothing to worry about while his instinct told him he had only a few seconds to live. The instinct had already made its plan. Whatever happened was going to happen out here. Grace would get away. The thought gave his lame smile a hint of authenticity as the focus of his entire life boiled down to the most important contribution he would ever make to this world – saving Grace MacBride.

Inside, pressed against the wall next to the door, Grace's hand reached automatically for the Sig that wasn't there, and then came the real panic. She couldn't breathe; she could barely see, and her legs were threatening to collapse beneath her. Her thoughts flashed back to six months ago – the last time genuine terror had left her frozen and helpless in the loft of the Monkeewrench offices – frantically seeking the remedy she had found then, remembering the hope of salvation, the aura of calm settling over her only when she felt the empowering weight of the Sig in her hands.

She heard steps on the front walk coming closer. She had no idea who the person was, no clear vision of his intentions except what she had seen in Magozzi's eyes, heard in his voice, and that was all she needed.

Her mind raced up the stairs to Magozzi's bedroom – was that where he kept his guns? They'd taken his service weapon last night, but he had to have another – all cops had another – but where would he keep it, and how in God's name would she find it in time? Her mind was stuck in the rut guns made. Goddamnit, it was all about guns, all the time, blinding her to any other choices.

'Hello, Detective Magozzi.'

She heard the voice through the screen, angled her eyes so she could see the figure right there, stopping a safe distance from Magozzi, his hands in his jacket pockets. One pocket bulged more than the other with a distinctive muzzle shape aimed at Magozzi's chest.

'Please get up, Detective. Slowly. Then go into the house.'

No gun, no gun, no gun – it was a paralyzing mantra that wouldn't let her go, and then she heard Magozzi answer, 'Sorry. I'm afraid that's not going to happen' – and then suddenly her mind opened and filled with Magozzi. Magozzi sitting on the Adirondack chair in her backyard, Charlie in his lap; his silly little half smile when he told her about his long-term seduction plan; Magozzi saving her life all those months ago, and then showing up again and again at her door, refusing to leave her alone, hanging on.

Grace MacBride had never had much of a life, but she knew absolutely that whatever chance she had for one was sitting out there on the porch steps, prepared to die for her.

She scooped up the two wineglasses from where she'd set them on the floor, then butted her hip against the screen door, sending it crashing against the outside wall as she stumbled out onto the porch. 'Hey, honey, guess what? . . . oh. Hi, there. I didn't know we had company.'

So fast, she toddled down the steps, wine sloshing in the glasses, a slightly drunken grin plastered to a face that had never worn one before, an impossible vision of Grace MacBride as the ditzy suburban housewife, so unexpected that it made empty seconds where there had been none.

For just an instant, the figure on the walk looked at her, startled, and in that instant, Magozzi flew off the porch in a vault that covered the distance between life and death, his head ramming into Tim Matson's chest, knocking him backwards onto the hard cement of the sidewalk.

45

The first squad arrived less than five minutes after Tim Matson had gone down on Magozzi's front walk. He was still wriggling violently, fighting the yards of duct tape Grace had wound around his arms and legs while Magozzi held him down, making furious muffled sounds behind the strip she'd slapped over his mouth.

Gino was there a few seconds later; McLaren a few seconds after that. Magozzi sat on the ground next to the trussed Matson, utterly exhausted, thinking that pretty soon the whole damn department would be there.

He glanced over at Grace, looking small and lonely on the front-porch steps, staring at the ground, and in that second he knew they would never make it. He'd been an idiot to think they'd ever had a chance. Everything Grace had always been afraid of was what Magozzi did for a living, and sometimes, goddamnit, it followed you home.

For the next hour he and Grace answered questions, gave statements, told their story to McLaren, the crime-scene techs and the first responders while Gino sat in the squad with a cuffed Matson doing God knew what. After everyone else left, Gino came inside and sat at the kitchen table with Grace and Magozzi.

'You two doing okay?'

Magozzi and Grace looked at each other, but neither one of them said anything, and Gino couldn't read their expressions. He waited for a while, growing more uncomfortable by the second. There was an open bottle of wine on the table with what looked like French words on it. McLaren would know; Gino didn't care. 'Pour me a glass of that, Leo, would you? And tell me what the kid said to you; what you know.'

Magozzi pulled his eyes away from Grace. She hadn't said a word to him since it happened. The last time he'd heard her voice was when she was giving her statement to McLaren. 'He didn't say anything, just came up the walk and told me to get in the house.' He went to the cupboard for a glass and set it in front of Gino.

'But you sent Grace into the house before that. Why did you do that?'

Magozzi shrugged. 'I saw him coming, and it just felt wrong.'

'He was saving my life,' Grace said quietly, but Magozzi shook his head.

'She saved mine.'

Gino rolled his eyes and reached for the bottle. 'Oh, please. I talked to McLaren outside. I heard all about the mutual-admiration society you've got going here. A dynamic duo is what you are, and I think that's real cute, but let's not beat it to death. So you have no clue why he came here to dust you?'

'I guess because I killed his friend.'

'Not exactly, buddy. You killed his brother.'

Magozzi's brows shot up. 'Tim Matson was Jeff Montgomery's brother? The dead one?'

'None other. I got him to tell me a few things out there in the squad.'

Grace looked directly at Gino for the first time. 'What'd you do to him?'

'Nothing.' Gino held up a hand. 'I swear to God. Pulled the tape off his mouth pretty fast – hope the kid has no dreams for a mustache – but that was just for his own comfort. And so he could talk, of course. Seems the two brothers have been planning this for over a year – had their asses covered seven ways to Sunday – and faking his death was part of it. They figured if Montgomery got busted before he offed all the people who killed their dad, there'd be another brother nobody would think to look for to finish the job. Man, I'm telling you, talking to that kid is gonna give me nightmares for years. Cold as ice. Dear old dad did a real job on indoctrinating those two, but I'm thinking this one had to be born a natural. Turns out he did Ben Schuler, got a real kick out of playing with the old guy before he killed him. When he heard you killed Jeff, you went right to the top of the hit list, but he was headed over to the nursery after he finished up here to take out Jack Gilbert.'

'He just blurted all this out?' Magozzi asked. 'He didn't ask for a lawyer?'

Gino frowned and scratched the side of his head. 'That's the kicker. He's just so friggin' proud of himself it made me want to puke. Has it in his head that he's some kind of a martyr. What do you bet we're gonna see him on *Dateline* in about a week, then he'll start writing books, they'll give him a computer in his cell and a Web site. Shit, Leo, this is why I hate that Minnesota doesn't have the death penalty. All we do with these guys is make them celebrities.'

He glanced over at Grace. 'You didn't shoot the guy, Grace. I was really impressed.'

'I didn't have a gun.'

Gino started to say 'yeah, right,' then noticed that she wasn't wearing her shoulder holster, and wondered how he'd missed it. 'Holy shit. You came over here without a gun?'

She looked right at him, and for the first time Gino Rolseth saw Grace MacBride really smile. She even showed her teeth a little, and boy, did she have great teeth.

His own face broke into a broad grin, and he gave her a thumbs-up. 'Way to go, Gracie. Really.'

After Gino left, Grace tried to throw away the Beef Wellington. Magozzi knew she was cleaning up, trying to erase herself from this house before she left.

He took the pan from her hands, grabbed a fork, and started eating, clinging to the perfectly ridiculous notion that if he just held on to that pan, she wouldn't leave. She'd have to wait until he finished, and he needed the time.

'For God's sake, Magozzi, don't eat that. It's been sitting in a warm oven for two hours. The pastry's soggy. The meat's ruined. You'll probably die.'

'It's delicious.' He wouldn't look at her. He just sat down at the table and wrapped his arms around the pan and kept eating.

'At least put it on a plate . . .'

'No!'

Grace sat down next to him, watched him eat, and waited.

Magozzi kept looking down at the pan. 'I was going to light a fire. We were going to sit it front of it and drink wine, and then later I was going to kiss you and blow your boots off.'

'No kidding.'

'That was the plan.'

Grace reached over and lifted his hands from the ugly, dented aluminum pan and pulled it away. 'I'm sorry, Magozzi. I think it's a little too late for that.'

He looked down at the stupid table for about two seconds, thinking, no, by God, it wasn't too late for that – at least not the kissing part – and it was high time he stopped tiptoeing around and took control of the situation. He jumped out of his chair and turned to grab her, but she wasn't there. Goddamnit, she was fast.

He found her in the living room, one foot poised

on the staircase that led up to the bedroom, and she was smiling at him. 'Gee, Magozzi, what took you so long?'

He stood there looking at her, feeling like he was trying to fly, but couldn't quite catch the updraft. 'Are you still going to Arizona tomorrow?'

Grace sighed impatiently at him, the way she always did whenever he got hung up on rules or procedures or tried to look too far ahead.

'Magozzi, that's hours and hours from now.'

An exclusive extract from

Dead Run

The new thriller by

P. J. Tracy

Published June 2005

I

Four corners hadn't been much of a town since October 17, 1946. That was the day Hazel Krueger's father set the Whitestone Lodge on fire and danced naked through the flames in some sort of sorry recompense for all he'd seen and all he'd done in a place called Normandy.

Not that the town had been such a thriving metropolis before that – more like a tiny open spot in Wisconsin's north woods where someone had dropped a lake by mistake – but without the lodge and the trickle of fishermen that made the long drive up from Milwaukee and Madison every summer, the town sort of sat down on itself and started to dry up, corner by corner.

By the time Tommy Wittig was born, the lodge road that crossed the county tar had faded back into the forest, and it was only last week that Tommy, approaching his eighth birthday and given to the solitary contemplation of a lonely child, had even wondered aloud why the town had been named Four Corners when it had only two.

Grandpa Dale had told him, walking him out to Whitestone Lake and showing him the crumbled remains of a brick wall that had once framed the base of the old lodge.

'You peel your eyes when you walk through these woods,' he'd said, waving the gnawed end of a briar pipe he hadn't lit in thirty years because he always had his head stuck inside some engine or other and feared blowing his own head off. 'You can still mark the hole that fire burned in the forest when it jumped from the lodge to the trees. Probably would have burnt down the whole damn state if it hadn't started to rain.'

Tommy had marveled at that, wondering where he would have been born if Wisconsin had burned right to the ground that day, and if the flag would have looked funny with forty-nine stars on it instead of fifty.

'Now, if you was a hawk flying overhead, you'd see a fifty-acre circle of second-growth, all strangly with those prickery briars that get stuck in your sneaker laces. That was the fire, and I remember it like it was yesterday. Killed this old town, is what it did. Prime white pines was going up like sixty-foot candles on a birthday cake.'

'Was he really naked?' Tommy had asked, focusing on the single part of the story he found most remarkable. Grandpa Dale had laughed and said that yes, indeed, Mr. Everett Krueger had been naked as the day he was born.

'Did old Hazel see him?' Hazel ran the café that sat on the corner next to Grandpa Dale's gas station – the only other business left in Four Corners – and she was about a hundred years old, as far as Tommy could tell.

That's when Grandpa Dale had squatted down and looked Tommy right in the eye the way he did when something was really serious and he wanted him to pay attention.

'We don't make no mention of that fire in front of Hazel, you understand, Tommy? She was barely older than you when her daddy up and did this thing, and she was right there, watching, just a little girl peekin' through a porthole into Hell, watching her own daddy sizzle away into a blackened stick, can you imagine such a thing?'

Tommy had been trying to imagine it for almost a whole week, and still he couldn't put a picture in his mind of Hazel Krueger as a little girl, let alone one touched by tragedy.

He was straddling his old bike across the street from the café, staring through the plate glass window, watching Hazel's broad back hunch and move over the grill plate behind the counter. Even through the dust-streaked window he could see that great pile of too-black hair wobbling on top of her head, and when she turned around to plop a plate down on the counter in front of a customer, he saw the loose skin of remembered chins cascading down over the place where her neck was supposed to be.

Tommy squinted until Hazel's bright red lips were a blur and her wrinkles disappeared, and still couldn't see the little girl under all those years.

On the other side of the plate glass, Hazel looked up and caught sight of him and wiggled her fingers, and Tommy waved back, suddenly shy. For all the years of his life she'd just been old Hazel with the arms so big they could squeeze the squeaks out of you and the crazy hair and the free French fries anytime he set foot inside the café.

But ever since Grandpa Dale had told him the story of how Four Corners became two, Hazel had seemed like a different person – an exotic and interesting stranger who'd watched her own daddy burn to a cinder.

He heard the old Ford pickup when it was still a good quarter mile behind him, and trotted his bike onto the shoulder close to the trees and looked around frantically. 'C'mon, boy! C'mon, where are you?'

The pup was an early birthday present, little more than a black and tan fluffball with too-long ears and too-big feet and a penchant for wandering. He had absolutely no sense when it came to cars.

'Hey pup!' Tommy laid down his bike and squatted, peering into the trees that marched nearly up to the tar across the road from the café and the gas station. There were ghostly tendrils of morning ground fog still hugging the trunks, and he dearly hoped the pup would come out on his own, because Tommy didn't want to go in there after him. It looked like a scene from one of Saturday night's Creature Features, when mist started floating around crooked graveyard tombstones and you just knew something bad was coming any minute.

It startled him when the pup came bounding out of a dew-speckled fern bank and jumped into his arms, grinning. A wet, busy tongue found his ear and made him giggle just as the battered white pickup topped the rise that dipped down into the town. 'Hold still, you squirmy worm,' he said as he hugged the pup close to his chest as the truck passed slowly, then turned left into Grandpa Dale's station. His mom leaned out the passenger window and crooked her finger at him.

The pup galumphed after him as Tommy pedaled across the road to the station. Halfway there, the oversized feet tangled and set the pup tumbling like a fuzzy roll of black and tan yarn. He scrambled upright, shook his head, then sat down abruptly on short, crooked haunches and let out a plaintive yip.

Jean Wittig watched out the truck window, shaking her head. She was a pretty blond woman with fair skin just beginning to show the cruelties the sun inflicts on a farmer's wife. 'You need to watch that pup on the road, remember.'

Tommy screeched the old bike to a halt next to the truck and looked up at his mother. 'I will,' he said, solemn with the weight of this responsibility.

'We might be late, so remember to help with the milking, and anything else Grandpa Dale asks you to do. What are you grinning at?'

'Nothin'.' Tommy kept grinning.

'Think we're going birthday shopping, don't you?'

'Uh-huh.'

Harold Witting leaned forward and peered past his wife out the window at his son, affecting surprise. 'Somebody's havin' a birthday?'

Tommy's grin widened.

'Hell, we're just goin' to Fleet Farm to pick up some new parts for that old milker.'

'Don't say "hell" in front of the boy, Harold.'

Harold rolled his eyes and got out of the truck to pump gas.

'Here, Tommy,' his mother handed him a dollar bill. 'Run over to Hazel's and get us two donuts for the road. Those ones with the jelly filling.'

'Hey, Mom, did you know that Hazel watched her daddy burn in a big fire a long time ago?'

'Oh, Lord. Harold . . .?'

'Wasn't me. Talk to your dad.'

Grandpa Dale chose that moment to walk out of the station, and Jean fixed him with a look that made Tommy decide it was a good time to go get those donuts.

The café was bustling this morning, with all three of the booths and half of the counter stools filled. Hazel was manic, propelling her bulk from grill to booth to refrigerator to counter with a speed that was absolutely amazing for a woman of her size.

Tommy suffered a pat on the head and a cheek tweak from Pastor Swenson and his wife, respectively, nodded like he'd seen his dad do at the two hired hands who were helping put up hay at the farm, and eyed with some interest the two families in the other booths and a lone woman at the counter. Not many strangers found themselves on the mile-long strip of tar that passed through Four Corners as it connected to County Road Double-P to County Road Double-O, and this many at one time was downright unheard of.

'Here you go,' Hazel distributed five plates at one booth, all expertly balanced on her slab-like arms, then pulled a map out of her pocket and slapped it down on the table. 'But like I said, all you gotta do is head up to Double-P, hang a left, then keep going. You'll hit Beaver Lake in under an hour if you don't get the itch to wander off the county roads again.'

A frazzled looking woman in sunglasses with tiger stripes on them took the map and tucked it in her purse. 'We'll take the map, just in case.'

'Suit yourself.' Hazel poked her fists into hips like bread dough and looked down at Tommy. 'Well, Tommy Wittig as I live and breathe I swear you've grown a foot since I saw you last!'

Tommy blushed because Hazel saw him almost every day of his life, and he was sure everyone in the café, stranger or not, knew that.

'Must be because your birthday is tomorrow and you're growin' so fast.' She tipped her head sideways and for one terrible minute, Tommy thought that pile of black hair was going to fall right off and land at his feet like some dead animal.

'I need two donuts really quick!'

Hazel laughed a big laugh, like a man, then went behind the counter and opened the glass case where her homemade donuts were laid out like jewelry. 'What kind today, honey?'

Tommy looked up at that broad, sagging face with its familiar smear of red lipstick and the dark eyes that always twinkled, and thought how silly he was to have been so leery of old Hazel this past week; to have thought of her like a stranger.

'Hazel?'

'What, hon?'

'Um . . . I'm sorry . . . well . . . I'm sorry your dad died.'

Hazel's face went quiet then, and she looked at him a long time. It was sort of a grownup look, and in a funny-nice kind of way, it made Tommy feel old. 'Why, thank you Tommy. I appreciate that,' she finally said, and then she took one of the little white bakery bags she put donuts in off a stack on the case and shook it open.

By the time he got back outside the mist was gone from the woods across the road, and Grandpa Dale was standing next to Dad at the pickup truck, hands shoved deep in his coverall pockets. If Mom had scolded him for telling the story about the lodge fire and Hazel's dad, it was over now, because all three of them were smiling around a secret. They stopped talking abruptly when they saw him coming, and Tommy knew they'd been whispering about his birthday present.

He walked toward the truck slowly, his eyes on his dad in absolute adoration, pushing back the nagging thought that if Hazel's daddy could die, then maybe other daddies could die. But not his. His was the tallest, broadest, strongest dad in the world, and even fire couldn't hurt him. Sometimes he'd catch a head-butt from one of the cows clattering out of the barn after milking, and he'd holler after her that she was a goddamn milkin' whore, and Mom's face would get all stiff and she'd tell him he'd burn for taking the Lord's name in vain, and that's when he always said he was too full of vinegar to ever catch fire.

His father laid a big, work-roughened hand on his shoulder as he passed and squeezed a little. 'Be good, son.'

'Yes, sir.' His shoulder felt cold and light when his father took his hand away and climbed into the truck.

'Thanks, honey.' His mom took the donut bag and leaned out the window and planted a kiss on his head. 'You be good, now. See you at suppertime.'

Grandpa Dale walked him out to the center of the road and they stood there waving after the pickup as it roared away around the curve toward County Road Double O. The pup sat crookedly at Tommy's side, leaning against his leg, pink tongue lolling.

Grandpa Dale put his hand Tommy's shoulder. It wasn't nearly as big as Dad's hand, nor as warm.

'Unusual number of strangers in town this morning,' he nodded toward the two unfamiliar cars parked on the side street between the station and the café.

'They got lost,' Tommy said.

'I figured. Pumped nearly thirty gallons of gas already just on those two.'

'That's a lot.'

Grandpa Dale nodded. 'Your Grandma's in there working on the books today. Guess she could pump gas with the best of them if the need arises, which means maybe you and me could go fishing in a bit, if we had a mind to.'

Tommy grinned up at him, and Grandpa Dale ruffled his hair.

A quarter mile north of town, Pastor Swenson's twin sixteen-year-old sons, Mark and Matthew, were working in the Wittig's roadside pasture. The house and hundred-year-old barn were behind them, etched against a cornflower sky at the end of a drive as straight and true as the rows in Harold Wittig's cornfield. Behind the barn, Whitestone Lake lay like a giant blue plate in a necklace of cattails.

A prime herd of Holstein grazed close to where the boys were repairing the white board fence, near a sign that read 'Pleasant Hills Dairy Farm.' Jean Wittig had painted the sign herself with green enamel left over after Harold touched up the old John Deere, and everyone agreed that on the whole, the sign looked mighty professional. The 'P' in 'Pleasant' was canted slightly to the right, as if it were in a hurry to catch up to the other letters, but Harold thought that gave the sign zip, and wouldn't let Jean repaint it.

Mark and Matthew had their headphones on full-blast, listening to their favorite heavy metal bands, so they didn't hear the truck making the turn off Double 'P', and wouldn't have thought much of it, even if they'd looked up and seen it coming. It was a sight they were used to – just a truck that looked like all the other dairy tankers traveling from farm to farm on Wisconsin's secondary roads, taking on raw milk from the state's productive herds. It had a dusty white cab and a shiny stainless steel tank that looked like a giant's thermos bottle. *Good Health Dairies* was spelled out in royal blue lettering along its length.

The truck was going forty miles per hour when it hit the place the tar had buckled in yesterday's afternoon heat, right at the end of the long driveway leading back to the Wittig farm. The cab's right front tire bounced violently over the worst of the break, then veered into the soft pea gravel of the shoulder. There was a long, high-pitched squeal as the driver slammed on the brakes, and then, its forward momentum diverted, the truck began a sickening lurch to one side. It balanced on its left wheels for an endless moment as if giving the driver time to think about what was to come, then jackknifed and crashed to its side and slid across the asphalt with a deafening, metallic screech.

Wide-eyed and terrified, the driver lay pressed against his door, the metal handle poking into his ribs, his hands still frozen in a white-knuckled grip around the steering wheel. The cab was pointed toward a distant cluster of farm buildings, and through the stone-pocked windshield, he saw two boys running toward him down the dusty drive. In an adjacent pasture, a tight cluster of panicked Holsteins was running the other way.

'Shit,' he finally managed in a shuddered exhale that broke the word into half a dozen syllables. He flexed his fingers on the wheel, wiggled his toes, then released a shaky, breathy laugh, giddy to find all his body parts intact. His smile froze when he heard the compressor behind the cab kick in, and vanished altogether when he glanced at the dashboard and saw the needle on the bulk tank gauge dropping slowly.

'Sweet Jesus,' he whispered, groping frantically for the small computer unit built into the console. He depressed the large red button in the middle, then hit the 'send' key. A message appeared on the tiny screen, blinking innocently in large baby blue letters.

SPILLED MILK
SPILLED MILK
SPILLED MILK

Mark and Matthew were almost to the truck, running flat out, legs and arms and hearts pumping hard. They dropped like stones a few yards shy of the truck, and for one terrifying instant, saw horror in each other's eyes.

On the other side of the pasture the cows in Harold Wittig's prime herd of Holstein began to sink to their knees.

A half a mile downwind in Four Corners, the screeching noise had split the quiet morning like a thousand fingernails scraping down a blackboard. The puppy wailed and batted at his ears, Grandpa Dale and Tommy both covered theirs with their hands. For a second Dale wondered if those Swenson boys had taken out Harold's old John Deere and tipped it over in the road again, but dismissed the possibility almost as soon as he thought of it. The horrible noise was going on much too long for that, spearing into his brain, making his eyes hurt.

The curious and the worried had already started to come out of Hazel's by the time the awful noise had stopped, all of them looking up the road toward the Wittig farm, shading their eyes in the bright light of morning. The Pastor and his wife were the worried ones, thinking of their sons working up there. The sudden silence was almost more upsetting than the sounds of the crash had been, and they both moved quickly toward where they had parked the big Chevy in front of the café. The others were wandering right into the middle of the road as if that would help them figure out what had happened over a hill and out of sight.

Inside the café, Hazel was waiting impatiently for the donuts she'd just put in the fryer to finish so she could follow her customers outside and investigate for herself. Excitement of any kind was a rare thing in Four Corners, and not to be missed. When she finally lifted the basket and hooked it on the edge of the fryer – another perfect batch – she had only enough time to glance out the window and marvel at the sight of her customers prayerfully sinking to their knees, some of them right in the middle of the road, before her candy-red mouth sagged open and her throat started to close.

When Dale saw the first person go down just a few yards away, he scooped up Tommy in one arm and the pup in the other and tried to race away, but already his heart was pounding too slow for that. He never felt the pup slip from his grasp and tumble to the asphalt, but he never let go of Tommy, not even when he finally fell.

2

Ricky Schwann was freezing his ass off. Damned water in this quarry never warmed up, no matter how hot the summer. It was great when you needed to quick-chill a case of brews, but it really sucked when you were two hundred pounds of muscle in a pair of swimming trunks and had to dive in after it.

Ricky had worked hard his senior year at Paper Valley High to get down to five percent body fat, but now he was wishing he'd porked down a few more Big Macs, just for the insulation.

Ten feet down into the black water his lungs were already starting to burn and his eyes hurt from the cold. He squeezed them shut. The water was so black you couldn't see more than a few inches anyway. He yanked hard again on the rope that tethered the case of beer he was after, but it wouldn't budge. He was going to have to go all the way down. Five, ten more feet, he figured.

He went hand-over-hand down the rope until he felt it veer sideways, snagged on whatever it was that was holding it down. He jerked on the rope and felt it loosen, then opened his eyes in time to see another pair of eyes floating toward him. They were blue, just like his, wide and empty.

'What'd I tell you?' Deputy Bonar Carlson was leaning forward in the passenger seat of the patrol car, jabbing a chubby finger at the windshield. 'Look at the top of those Norways. Yellowing already, and August is still a youngster.'

Sheriff Michael Halloran kept his eyes on the twisting strip of tar so he wouldn't run into one of the Norway pines Bonar wanted him to look at. The forest moved in on everything man-made when you got this far north in Wisconsin, and roads were no exception. He felt like he was driving through a tunnel. 'We are not having a drought,' he said. 'You're doing that Chicken Little thing again.'

'It's going to be a bad one. Maybe as bad as '87.'

'That's such a load of crap. We nearly drowned in June. Broke every record in the book for rainfall.'

Bonar snorted and flopped back, sticking a thumb under the seatbelt to ease the pressure on his considerable, cherished stomach. 'That was then, this is now. Just wait until we get to the lime quarry. I'll bet the water is at least a foot low, maybe two.'

'No way.' Halloran eased the car around an unbanked turn, watching sunlight dapple the road ahead like a strobe. He'd known since the fifth grade that only a fool questioned anything Bonar stated as fact, but he just couldn't help himself. One of these days he was going to prove him wrong about something. The law of averages was on his side. 'Did I miss the turn? Feels like we've been driving for hours.'

'Fifty-seven minutes from the office to the lime quarry, and that's if you don't run into a deer or a bear. How long since you've been up there?'

Halloran thought about it for a minute, and then got sad. 'Senior class party.'

Bonar sighed. 'Yeah. Gives me the creeps every time I pass the place. Haven't dipped a toe in that water since.'

The old lime quarry they were heading for hugged the northern county line, about as far from human habitation as you could get in this part of the state, making it an ideal party site for every teenage bash since the quarry and kiln had closed in the '40's. Fifty feet down from ground level the lime had petered out and buried springs had bubbled up, filling the ugly machine-made hole with icy water. Halloran had always liked thinking about that – man working decades to make a piece of earth ugly, nature covering the scars in a blink, if you just left her alone to do her job.

But the water and the isolation made the place a magnet for kids and kegs, and every now and then something bad would happen. Like at the senior class party nearly twenty years ago, when Howie Dexheimer dove into that cold black water and disappeared, like the quarry had swallowed him whole. Every diver in the county had worked the deep water for weeks, but never found the body. As far as anyone knew, Howie Dexheimer was still down there.

'You think it's him?' Bonar interrupted his thoughts as if he'd been following them.

'Lord, I hope not. I sure don't want to see Howie after twenty years in the water.'

When Bonar was thinking hard, his whole face screwed up. 'Might not be so bad. Water's too damn cold for anything to live in, including most bacteria. The body could be almost perfectly preserved if the alkaline content isn't too high.'

Halloran winced. The idea of a perfectly preserved Howie was almost worse.

Fifteen minutes later he found the two-lane dirt track that made a hole in the woods. Deputy Walter Simons was blocking the access with his legs spread and his arms crossed over his chest, a banty rooster with an Elvis haircut trying to look like Colossus.

Halloran pulled up alongside of him and opened his window. 'Tell me something I don't know, Simons.'

Simons swatted ineffectually at a congregation of deer flies buzzing around his head. 'Goddamn deer flies bite like a son of a bitch, did you know that?'

'I did.'

'Well, it isn't poor old Howie Dexheimer, anyway. I caught a glimpse just when they were pulling him out, and Howie never had hair that long.'

'Hair grows after death,' Bonar told him.

'Go on.'

'So some people say.'

'Does it tie itself up in a ponytail with a rubber band?'

'Hardly ever.'

'Well there you go. Besides, Doc Hanson says this was an older guy, mid-twenties at least, and not in the water that long. No ID, no nothin'. Naked as a jaybird. You want to send Cleaton back out here with the squad? Another ten minutes out in these bugs and I'm going to be a pint low.'

About a tenth of a mile in, the two-lane track broadened onto an open grassy area clogged by cars. Doc Hanson's old blue station wagon, three county cars that had responded to the call, and a brand new Ford pickup that would have eaten up a year of Halloran's salary. Had to belong to the kid who had called it in, he decided. These days half the kids in the district got new trucks, just for graduating.

Just beyond the makeshift parking lot, an earthen ramp that had once been access for heavy machinery led down to the water. They'd called it the 'girlie road' in the old days, and no self-respecting, testosterone-crazed teenage boy would ever set foot on it. There was only one acceptable entrance into the water for them.

Halloran's eyes shifted to either side of the ramp, where the quarry walls rose a good fifteen feet from the black water. Mature trees leaned over the rim as if to peer downward, and frayed ropes hung from some of the bigger branches. He and Bonar had hung ropes just like them when they were young and immortal, swung on them like foolish apes until they arced over the water and let go. Timing had been everything. You let go too soon, you landed on the jagged rocks that climbed the ridge wall. That had been the thrill of it, and with the sharp and fearful eye of maturity, Halloran thought it was pretty much a miracle that they had survived their own stupidity.

He glanced over at five teenagers tangled together in a distressed knot near one of the county cars. Their expressions cycled through the spectrum of human emotion – shock, horror, fear, fascination, and back again as they tried to make sense of their gruesome discovery. He recognized Ricky Schwann, a full head taller and a few shades grayer than the rest of them.

Halloran and Bonar ignored the kids for the moment, got out of the car and headed down the rock-strewn slope to the little beach below, where Doc Hanson's crouched form was partially blocking the view of what Halloran dearly hoped was an intact body. Initially, all he could see of it was a head and a pair of legs so white they looked like they belonged on a plaster statue. As they drew closer, the doc got up and took a step back, giving them their first look at the torso.

'Oh, man,' Halloran's cheeks went up and his mouth turned down when he saw the band of neat, pencil-sized black holes that stitched a perforated line across the white flesh of the dead man's chest. 'We just figured it for a drowning.'

Doc Hanson was holding his gloved hands away from his sides, so he wouldn't forget and shove them in his pockets. 'So did I, until they pulled him out.' He stooped and moved a tangled clump of wet hair away from the open, filmy eyes. 'You know him?'

Halloran and Bonar both took a long look at the frozen face, then shook their heads.

'Me either. And I figure I know just about everybody in this county. Hell, I delivered half of them. But I've never laid eyes on this boy.'

'Identifying marks?' Halloran asked.

Doc Hanson shook his head. 'No freckles, no moles, no scars, no tattoos. He might have had something on his back, but there isn't much left of it anymore. You want me to roll him?'

'Lord, no,' Bonar said, already picturing what that many exit wounds might have done to the body. 'It looks like somebody tried to cut the poor guy in half.'

Doc nodded. 'Eight full penetrations, head-on, another one that scraped his left side, see?' He pointed to a raw strip where tissue had been burned instead of blown away. 'Mowed him down, is what they did. Looks like NATO rounds some fool fired on full automatic, which is flat-out overkill. That stuff fragments like crazy. One good chest hit like any one of these,' he gestured at the body; 'and the job's done.'

Halloran looked curiously at the kindly, time-worn face of the doctor who'd delivered him, who'd given him lollipops with every childhood vaccination and mixed India ink with the plaster so he could have a 'manly-colored' cast when he'd broken his wrist in second grade. Not the kind of man you'd think would know a whole lot about the end results of automatic rifle fire. 'NATO rounds, Doc?' he asked softly. 'You learn about those in med school?'

The softening jowls under the old doctor's jaw tightened a little. ' 'Nam,' he said in a way that made the single syllable sound heavy and dark and final.

Halloran and Bonar shot each other a look. You could know a man for all of your life, it seemed, and still know so little.

The sound of spilling water made them all look toward the shore, where a diver was emerging, looking strange and shiny and alien in his scuba gear. Halloran thought of old monster matinees and wished he were at home watching one now.

The diver pulled off his mask as he waded toward them. 'You're going need a couple more body bags down here.'

Within the hour there were two more bodies lying on the tiny beach – one younger, one older, but both as nude as the first with similar chest wounds. Doc Hanson had two unhappy deputies move the corpses until they were in the order he wanted.

'There,' he said, finally satisfied, gesturing Halloran and Bonar over to where he stood at the feet of the body in the center of the ghastly trio. 'Now look at the wounds, left to right. Looks like the bullet holes almost sew them together, doesn't it?'

Halloran squinted, narrowing his eyes to tighten his line of vision so he saw only the wounds, not the human bodies they had punctured. 'This is the way they were standing when they were shot,' he said quietly, and Doc nodded.

'Just so. Right-handed shooter, sweeping left to right.'

Bonar's lips were pushed out, as if he'd just tasted something very bad. 'Why not a left-handed shooter, sweeping right to left?'

Doc Hanson hesitated before he responded, as if he were reluctant to confess knowing the answer. 'There's a burst when you fire an automatic rifle, Bonar – the bullets come so fast when you pull the trigger, that if you're not used to it, you get a heavy cluster before you start your sweep. See the man on the left, the one we pulled out first? Nine shots. He was the first in line. The one in the middle was hit five times, the one on the right, only three. So this is what happened. Someone lined these men up and executed them all at once.'

There was a hollow sound to Doc's voice that kept Halloran from looking at him. He looked at the bodies instead. 'You've seen this kind of thing before?'

Doc Hanson shoved his hands in his pockets, then pulled them out and looked irritably at the latex gloves he'd just ruined. 'Not in this country.'

ALSO AVAILABLE FROM P.J. TRACY